Christopher Fowler is the director of a film promotion company and lives in London. He is the author of the novels *Roofworld*, *Rune*, *Red Bride*, *Darkest Day* and *Spanky* and of the short story collections *City Jitters*, *The Bureau of Lost Souls*, *Sharper Knives* and *Flesh Wounds*.

PSYCHOVILLE

'Murderous pranks a-plenty in the cul-de-sacs with sex and swearing too' *Loaded*

'Fowler's writing is technicolour, odourvision, widescreen, and the pace of the action makes this a hard book to put down' *Don't Tell It*

'With a superb twist, this hilarious and chilling novel is a masterpiece of baroque brilliance' *The List*

'A dark, tragic story, but the sting in the tale here is not the physical horror, but a startling display of home truths' *Midweek*

'An incredibly talented writer with a keen eye for detail. A timely novel of retribution against Thatcher's children' *Shivers*

'Clive Barker always used to be written up as the English answer to Stephen King, but in fact it's the London-based Fowler who deserves that accolade' *i-D*

'A superb novel about how and where we live, ingeniously constructed, thoroughly recommended' *Samhain*

'Fowler's *Spanky* went a long way towards lifting the horror genre out of its B-movie status. *Psychoville* continues this trend with writing that wouldn't be out of place in a literary novel' *Maxim*

CHRISTOPHER FOWLER

PSYCHOVILLE

WARNER BOOKS

A *Little, Brown* Book

First published in Great Britain by Warner Books 1995
This edition published by Warner Books 1996

Copyright © Christopher Fowler 1995

The moral right of the author has been asserted.

*All characters in this publication are fictitious
and any resemblance to real persons, living or dead,
is purely coincidental.*

All rights reserved.
No part of this publication may be reproduced,
stored in a retrieval system, or transmitted,
in any form or by any means, without the prior
permission in writing of the publisher, nor be
otherwise circulated in any form of binding or cover
other than that in which it is published and without
a similar condition including this condition being
imposed on the subsequent purchaser.

'First day at school' reproduced by permission of
Michael Ivens, first published in *Private and Public*,
Villiers Publications, 1968. Every effort has been made to trace
copyright holders of material used in this book.

A CIP catalogue record for this book
is available from the British Library.

ISBN 0 7515 1432 2

Typeset by Solidus (Bristol) Limited
Printed and bound in Great Britain by
Clays Ltd, St Ives plc

Little, Brown and Company (UK)
Brettenham House
Lancaster Place
London WC2E 7EN

Dedication

For my father, Bill, with love

Acknowledgements

Much more than mere thanks to Richard Woolf and Jim Sturgeon, my family, Serafina Clarke, Nann du Sautoy, Andrew Wille, Nick Ross and Peter Cotton, Mark Hutchinson, Jennifer Luithlen, Pippa Dyson, and to everyone stirred into the good/bad times mix this year; Maggie, Poppy and Amber, Richard Parker, Pam Griffiths, Sally and Gary Chapman, Martin Butterworth, Graham Humphries, Mike and Sarah, Jo Green, Rebekah Wood, Bal and Stephanie Croce, Di Carter, Guillermo Del Toro, Rob Newman, Steve Gallagher, Peter James, Kim Newman, Graham Joyce, Gordon Arnell, Amanda Scofield, Martin Campbell, Pierce and the 007 crew, and the movie-mad staff of The Creative Partnership. Nik and Steve, please make the movie!

First day at school
the large boy
kindly
hurled my ball
with amazing skill
high over the roof

soaring out of sight
out of my prosaic life

Unstintingly
I gave him
my admiration

As others have done
when their respect
money
virginity
honour hope and lives
have been hurled
triumphantly out of sight

– Michael Ivens

Contents

Increasing the Validity of Your Opinions with Explosives

THIS IS *how you make an incendiary bomb.*

You need a container, ideally a magnesium-aluminium alloy can. You need a form of Thermite for the filling, like ferric oxide and aluminium powder. You need a striker, something that provides the initial spark, and you need substances that will set off an intermediate chemical reaction, say barium peroxide and magnesium powder, because you have to amplify the spark to reach the temperature required to ignite the Thermite.

Flash heat is created by the combination of aluminium and magnesium with oxygen. The incendiary effect is caused by the resulting molten iron and the burning container. I fitted all my bombs with decent fuses, which I made by sewing lines of gunpowder into material spills. I could have used firework fuses but it's harder to gauge accurately how much time you have after ignition. Delayed-action bombs can be made with the insertion of a simple clockwork mechanism, the kind you find inside a child's toy, or by the movement of a sensitive needle under the influence of a magnetic field. I chose these over radio-controlled devices, which are trickier to handle with so many microwaves, computers and mobile phones around these days.

The word 'grenade' is from the French for pomegranate, that being its shape. The average grenade holds about three ounces of amatol or ammonal. The ones I have look very old, and I've a suspicion they may be faulty. The problem, again, is in the fuses. After a long period of time the spring above the detonator cap can lose its resilience, in which case the thing won't explode, or the five-second fuse becomes squashed, reducing detonation time to a single second, and you lose your fingers, your arm, your eyes and perhaps your life.

As I was trying to dislodge my first victim's body from its position stuck headfirst halfway down the storm drain, I recalled a little history. The best way to handle unpleasant chores is to concentrate the mind on factual information, don't you think?

On 11 November 1663, Samuel Pepys wrote in his diary about a substance made of gold, aurum fulminans, a grain of which, put in a silver spoon and fired, could give a blow like a musket and strike a hole downward through the spoon without the least force upwards.

My victim was sealed inside a tube of clear plastic sheeting, the ends of which I now had to cut open in order to allow her body to sink. The filthy water entered the tube and flooded over her head, and the rising tide within the drain swilled a nimbus of hair around her face. Wedged down toward the black liquid at a forty-five degree angle, she looked like a torpedo about to be launched, or an off-duty mermaid attempting to take a quick breather. I placed my right boot across her plastic-clad buttocks and gently pushed, my thoughts resolutely elsewhere ...

The first friction match was accidentally invented by John Walker, an English chemist, in 1827. He stuck a stick coated with potash and antimony on the floor and it burst into flame. He never patented the idea. I experimented with my own home-made matches at first. It seemed an appropriate place to start. After all, our lives are all about ignition and extinction. I stopped after I accidentally melted a foot-wide hole through a Formica kitchen counter. I was fourteen years old, and after my father saw what I had done I very nearly didn't make fifteen.

Her body seemed to be well and truly stuck in the drainage shaft. Gritting my teeth, I stamped my boot down harder and she shifted several inches ...

The first chemical explosive was black powder, a mixture of saltpetre, charcoal and sulphur. It was concocted by the Chinese for military purposes over a thousand years ago. 'For military purposes' means blowing people up. Crude, but effective. This was succeeded by nitroglycerin and dynamite, the latter being invented by the Swedish scientist Alfred Nobel, who established the Nobel Peace Prize. However, the favourite explosive of the twentieth century has been TNT, which proved popular in really big wars.

I peered into the square hole and tried to discover what was causing the blockage. What was preventing her from slipping away into the system? Then I saw the source of the problem. A section of plastic sheet was caught on the brickwork, dragging her left elbow out at an unnatural angle and wedging her in place. I kneeled down beside the *hole and gently worked the sheeting loose, then pushed her elbow back to her side. The chemicals I had poured over her body to delay identification gave off fumes that stung my eyes. The grey muck of the drain bubbled into the plastic sheeting, filling it completely. With macabre lentitude her body sank slowly into the torrent.*

In Arabian mythology, the greatest djinn of all was Eblis, who was born from a single pure explosion in the air, totally smokeless. When God demanded that all angels should worship Adam, Eblis refused because Adam was made of dust and therefore not as pure as someone like himself, who had spontaneously combusted into being. God in his fury turned Eblis into a sheytan, or devil, and he became the ruler of the fallen angels, the father of all devils.

I thought of Eblis as I returned the heavy iron lid of the drain to its rightful position. One down, many more to go. This was just the start of my great plan. Soon, dazzled by the searing luteous light, deafened by the force of each fresh explosion, I will look out across an incandescent wall of rippling flame and know that, whatever happens, only the father of all devils can save me.

I am twenty-five years old, and I am not a madman but a man driven to madness. I was just fourteen when my life began to end. Since then, every passing day has been leading to the terrible, glorious moment when I could take my revenge. From that poor woman in the drain to the fire-ravaged horizon, no one will be spared.

I wish for no special pleading on my behalf. My one dear, true companion, that secret other half of me, could explain why I acted this way, but hopefully will never be persuaded to do so. Like the man who walked into

McDonald's with a machine gun, I make no apologies for my behaviour. As the destruction of so many people fast approaches, I find myself wanting you to understand my motives. That is why I have kept up the entries in the red leather diary, in the hope that it will be found and read. These pages explain much of what has happened here. But, like the appearance of a devil-god in a perfect jet of flame, there are moments that remain beyond the reach of mortals . . .

PART ONE

1985

'And perhaps I may come to the country
again, when London is all burnt down'
– Thomas Hood

The Tide Change

'One third of all home-based violence is caused by neighbours.'

1993 British Crime Survey

THE GIRL was dashing along an endless crimson corridor, trying to put as much distance as possible between herself and her pursuer, screaming like a banshee all the way. But the top right-hand corner was out of focus, making it hard to tell exactly what was after her.

The creature wore standard-issue black satanic robes and moved like a tall man running in callipers. Its grasping hands had the talons of a beast, although the only real beasts he had seen were in the London Zoo, and drowsed on artificial rocks, their stubby claws tucked away.

When Billy next looked up, the heroine had somehow managed to shove the stalking hell-spawn into a cellar. She threw her weight against the door and held it shut until the creature stopped hammering. Then she barred it with a convenient plank.

He removed his fingers from his eyes and looked back at the immense screen. Suddenly a screaming latex head burst through the cellar door, drooling and spitting blood, its eyes turned over in its sockets like those of a boiled fish. The girl wailed and fell as the devil-thing grabbed her by the hair. Boy, she was really for it now. She knew too much and would be torn to shreds for daring to venture into the satanists' lair. He had seen the film before and knew what was about to happen. A cut, that was what, a glitch in the soundtrack and a jump to something less disturbing, courtesy of the censors.

Billy kicked his popcorn box onto the floor and looked up at the vast peeling roof of the Woolwich Granada, once voted 'the most romantic cinema in England', now smelling of piss and pine disinfectant and reduced to running dumber-than-crap horror double bills to make ends meet.

There were only a dozen people in the auditorium, mostly pensioners on cheap tickets. One of them, an elderly man in a smart navy-blue raincoat, kept shifting seats furtively every few minutes, looking for someone to wank off. There were no proper usherettes any more, just a little Korean woman who sat with her head in her hands and her unlit torch in her lap, easing the tedium of her job by remaining lightly asleep at the top of the balcony steps.

A muffled drumroll of thunder sounded beyond the exit doors, mingling perfectly with the soundtrack of the film, like part of a new audio gimmick dreamed up by the management. He loved the sound that filled the auditorium. Cineramic sound. Everything was magnified, all drama heightened. Ominous atonal chords accompanied footsteps and the most casual conversations gained dimensional depth, so that shouts of laughter or screams of terror resonated through the building, echoing on long after the film had ended. Cinema was larger than life, and therefore more real. Celluloid fantasies conformed to their own strange sets of rules. Monsters lived, crimes were solved, vengeance was exacted. Inside such tales were changeless truths; it was the world outside that required constant reassessment.

Reluctantly, Billy rose to leave. He thumped up the balcony steps and down the curving gilt staircase to the empty foyer, past the poster advertising next week's attraction, *Back to the Future*, past another warning that the building was to become a bingo hall – refurbishment commencing next month, then slid to a stop beneath the unlit marquee, beyond which the rain fell in a dense grey curtain. Billy had no jacket and knew that his mother would kill him if he got soaked in his school sweater. The bus stop was a fair walk and had no shelter; he'd get drowned. All he could do was wait it out. Being late for tea would make no difference to his mother's mood; he was already in enough trouble, slipping out of school and spending his textbook money at the cinema. He was sure that even his father, who loved the movies, would lose his temper this time. 'We pay out for your books so you'll study and make something decent of yourself,' Billy could hear him say, 'and this is how you bloody repay us.'

He pushed open one of the doors and peered out. Water was spattering noisily onto the steps from the canopy's overflowing gutters. He retreated into the foyer and pulled a dog-eared leaflet from his back pocket, studying it carefully. 'Become an Odeon Cinema Manager' it said. He'd pocketed it last week after visiting another of the area's rundown cinemas. Maybe that was what he would do, become a cinema manager. It sounded like a pretty full life:

As an Odeon Cinema Manager you will be expected to escort film stars and celebrities visiting your town, to approve the siting of publicity posters and standees, and to supervise regular quality checks on your refreshment areas and toilet facilities.

Billy couldn't imagine many celebrities venturing out here. He couldn't see Harrison Ford hanging around for very long in Woolwich, not unless he wanted his car radio nicked. As an Odeon Cinema Manager the wages probably weren't great but at least he would be able to pay his way at home, and he'd get to see all the new films for nothing. There were a couple of foreseeable problems, one being that they were closing down all the cinemas, what with video catching on in such a big way, the other being that Billy March was only fourteen years old.

And there he stood, contemplating the future possibilities, one gangly boy framed in the glass and chrome double doors of the near-derelict Granada, waiting for the rain to ease up at six o'clock on a miserable Wednesday evening in September 1985. It had been a bad year. Inner-city chaos was headline news, violence flaring in Brixton and Handsworth. There were arson attacks on Asians in Ilford, football riots and fires, airline tragedies, the continuing miners' strike. *My Beautiful Launderette* and *Letter to Brezhnev* were double-billing the London arthouses, little gestures of defiance. None of it touched Billy, of course. Enormous changes only occurred to fully formed people. He waited on.

Billy did not know it then, but he was framed in a pose almost exactly same as the one adopted by his father in 1966, when Ray March, then in his late twenties, stood beneath the illuminated awning of the Roxy cinema at the top of Westcombe Hill waiting for the rain to end, with no jacket and just his dreams for company, the memory of the films he had just seen (*The Plague of the Zombies* and *Dracula – Prince of Darkness*) dispersing into the wet night.

It turned out they had much in common, son and father, although Billy did not know it then. He did know that when you left the cinema the spell of the screen stayed with you for a few more minutes, so that everything you saw and did was coloured by the emotions you had just felt. In that brief precious time, fantasy and reality combined to make anything achievable, anything at all. But reality quickly crowded out the magic, and the feeling was soon lost. Billy knew that one day it would be lost forever. And then he would be an adult.

The minute he arrived back at number 35 Westerdale Road, Greenwich SE10, he knew that there was something wrong because he was not in trouble. Normally his mother would be raising her voice by now, saying she was sick of his lateness and his lies, but she wasn't; she was just sitting in the kitchen looking confused, as if someone had re-arranged the furniture without telling her. She hardly even noticed when he entered with theatrical breathlessness, all prepared with his excuse. His father was standing with his hands thrust into his pockets, staring down at something on the kitchen table, speaking rapidly and quietly.

'. . . before Christmas, I mean, how long must this sort of thing take to organise? I'm going to tell them we can't do it. I can just imagine what they mean by rented accommodation. It's unreasonable for them to expect people who've lived all their lives—' He stopped suddenly, aware that someone had entered the room. Angela looked up and caught her husband's eye. She did not want his anger to show in front of the boy.

Billy took advantage of the break to launch into his prepared speech. 'Sorry about being late but there was a terrible accident; a bus nearly hit an old lady, she fell over and I had to stop and—'

'William.'

His father never called him that. Not unless he had done something terrible, and then he used a very different tone.

In the dry warmth of the little red and white tiled kitchen he was able to start pulling off his wet sweater. 'What's for tea?' he asked. After they ate he usually spent part of the evening with his homework spread across the table. But tonight the table was not even laid.

'Your father and I have been talking,' said his mother, as if that in itself was an unusual event. 'Look at you, you're drenched. Get a towel. And hang that jumper up somewhere.' He had noticed that the crosshatch of fine lines around her eyes was starting to deepen. She was forty-two but looked older. She had worked too hard, worried too much, not laughed enough.

Billy returned from the bathroom as fast as he could. He was anxious not to miss any more of the curious conversation he had interrupted. A wave of heat from the ancient wall-mounted boiler swept over him as he re-entered the kitchen.

'How would you feel about moving to a nice new home, Billy?'

'What do you mean?'

His father unfolded the page on the table before him to reveal dense small print and an official-looking letterhead.

'The government says we have to move from here.'

He stared at his father stupidly. He could not see what the government had to do with his parents. 'Leave this house? This is where we live.'

'I know, but it doesn't have to be,' said his mother. 'There are lots of other places that are just as nice,' then, unconvincingly, 'nicer.'

'How far away?' Now they both avoided his gaze. 'Why should we move anywhere else? I like it here.'

'We know you do, Billy, but we don't have any choice in the matter. Remember that song I used to sing when you were little, "The Railway Runs through the Middle of the House"? Well, they want to put a road through ours.'

'They can't do that.'

'They can. The plans have already been approved.'

It seemed an absurd conversation, and not at all the one his parents should have been engaged in. They were supposed to be telling him off for being late, and he was meant to be lying through his teeth about where he had been.

His father had begun pacing about, a clear sign that he was growing impatient. When he turned, the greasy black tip of his quiff bounced just like Elvis's. Ray was a big fan of the King. Two years older than his wife, and two years older than Elvis when he died, Ray boasted that he had seen all thirty-three of the King's movies, and made his family shake with laughter when he sang 'Love Me Tender' in the bath.

'They're going to build a slip road to join the motorway at Blackheath, and the top end of our road stands in their way. This is a compulsory purchase order, a Notice to Treat.' He flicked a hand at the official letter. 'We've been arguing with them for months, and it looks like we've lost.'

Billy tried to read the page from an angle, but it seemed designed to appear deliberately cryptic, full of *henceforth*s and *aforementioned*s. 'So we can choose where we want to live?' he asked.

'We allowed the time to lapse—'

'The time to find another property—'

They both spoke at once until his father glared at his mother and continued alone. 'They allocated a fixed period for us to find a new place, but it lapsed because we were still trying to prevent the plan from being passed. Now it's gone through, and we have to accept wherever they choose to relocate us.'

'But that's not fair.'

'Yeah, well life isn't fair, Billy. We don't have the finances to take any other course.' His father had had enough. Ray opened the back door to the yard and stood on the step, facing out into the rain as he lit a Marlboro.

'The rent will be subsidised and we'll have an option to buy the property if we're happy there,' explained Angela. 'Think of it as an adventure. Think of all the new friends you'll make.'

But he didn't want new friends. There was nothing wrong with the ones he already had. He could not believe that his parents had agreed to be pushed around so easily. He did not understand what had been happening for the past few months, had not attended the public meetings or heard the endless heated arguments that had raged nightly in his parents' bedroom. The fights invariably began with a discussion about moving house, but always arrived at the same points: lack of money, lack of work and Ray March's inability to stand up for himself. His father was a quiet, orderly man who never questioned authority, and did not relish the thought of a confrontation now.

'Where will we go?'

'Why do you have to ask so many bloody questions?' Ray snapped from the doorway.

'It's only natural. The boy has every right to ask.' Angela was slightly built and pleasant faced, sensible in a flustered way, as kind as candlelight. Her hair was prematurely greying to match her eyes, and she wore no make-up. She turned to her son and held out her hands, drawing him to her side. 'There are other things to consider,' she said gently. 'It's not just a question of moving house. Your father and I are trying to sort out the problems.'

'What do you mean?'

'I won't be able to keep my job, so I have to find something else to do.'

'That could take ages. Where's the money going to come from?'

Angela had been working part-time shifts for London Transport and had an evening job behind the tote window at Catford Greyhound Stadium, but she'd been thinking of giving up the dog track because punters were always failing to complete their jackpot combinations before the race bell, and that made the tote operator responsible for the money rung up before the off of the leg. Some nights she came home with an empty purse, her docked pay amounting to more than her wages.

Ray had been made redundant by British Glassware nearly four months ago and knew that there would be little chance of finding suitable employment outside London. Angela kept referring to 'upward mobility' and assuring him that it was all for the best. New jobs for both of them, a clean new house – it would be a fresh start. She seemed genuinely keen to move.

Billy thought of his parents stranded in a strange town without money and began to panic. He was a natural pessimist, diagnosed by his mother as 'highly strung', the kind of nervous boy who could not stroll along a beach without worrying about the incoming tide. 'What are we going to do?' he asked, watching her face.

Angela rubbed at some imaginary mark on the back of her wrist, an unconscious gesture that indicated the end of her willingness to discuss the matter. 'Something will come along,' she said finally. 'Let's worry about one day at a time.'

But it was clear to Billy that a little long-term perturbation might have prevented the situation arising in the first place. It would certainly have avoided the atrocities to come.

The Runaway

'When Ken Kennet accosted Colin Bourne over a defaced garden fence, his neighbour shot him point blank in the chest with a crossbow.' – *The Big Issue*

THAT EVENING he braved the bad weather in order to return his books to the library. This time he was made to wear his school overcoat, a hated object of shapeless black gabardine that was too short in the arms. He closed the front gate and turned up the street, stamping on the flooded paving stones as he went. It was just a short distance to the battered Victorian building wedged beneath the flyover, part of the same stained concrete motorway that would soon cause his family to be uprooted. He tried to imagine what would happen but recognised nothing ahead, just the blank dark hole of an impossible future.

'Bloody idiot!' bellowed someone from a passing car. He had stepped off the kerb without thinking, and the vehicle's tyres had ploughed through a puddle, spraying his trouser legs. 'Dreamers own the future,' his English teacher always said. 'Our dreams die a moment before we do.' He hadn't said anything about dreamers getting wet legs or being thrown out of their homes.

At fourteen Billy was an unprepossessing sight: skinny and bookish, with a pale domed forehead, a narrow chin and large blue eyes that easily reflected fright and surprise. His weight was outstripped by his height, so that it appeared awkward for him to remain perpendicular, and he stooped, unsure how to place himself, where to tuck his chicken-wing elbows. Much of his time was spent walking the deserted suburban streets with an armful of books, rain streaming through his hair and steaming up his spectacles. Later, he came to recognise such moments as among his happiest memories.

He looked back at the street through rain needles slanting in yellow lamplight, at the row of red terraced homes with bedraggled little gardens, the house next door with pearlised seashells embedded in its front wall, the navy-blue builder's yard filled with ladders and buckets, and loved what he saw. All his friends and relatives lived in the surrounding neighbourhood. Rumour had it (the story never having been told to him directly) that Ray and Angela had first met in the Angerstein Arms, a public house at the bottom of the next road. His father's family were from the East End, Bermondsey, generations of tailors, pattern-cutters and seamstresses, people used to patching something from nothing. Now the trade had vanished into mass marketing, the old patterns no longer held, and Ray was the first son forced from the tradition.

Angela's family were from North London, occupying several cramped houses near the Arsenal football ground, and plied a multitude of trades connected with travel. Any cross section of their number would include coach drivers, river pilots, bus conductresses, flight attendants and ferry-men. For a group of people so involved in the business of getting from A to B, it seemed odd that they never went anywhere. None of the Uptons (his mother's maiden name) had ever dreamed of moving out of London. Until now.

The books were overdue and Billy had spent the money he needed to pay the fine, but a few contrite words with the white Rastafarian boy behind the counter deferred the problem until the following week. The library had a polished parquet floor with scores of blocks loose or missing, and buzzing strip lights; it smelled damp even in the height of summer. There was never anybody in the place. There weren't too many recent popular novels on show, but its collection of arcane reference works was truly awesome. Billy loved the top shelves that no one ever sorted through, the ones he had to use a ladder to reach.

As he ran his index finger along the dilapidated spines in the True Crime section, a terrible thought struck him. What would he do if the town they moved to didn't have a library? Even worse, what if it had no cinema? What if it was in the countryside, in the kind of place that got completely dark at night and always smelled of cows, where people spoke with weird accents and you never heard the friendly sound of police cars going past? The scenario filled him with horror.

He had been to the countryside a few times to visit the odoriferous house of Ashley, his mercifully distant cousin, but he had never seen the surrounding fields at night because the family had only ever made day trips. Billy always knew when they had reached a beauty spot because Angela would have to stop Ray from emptying the car ashtrays.

His father always turned back at dusk in order to 'miss the traffic', something he never, ever managed to do. The three of them would spend the day behind a windbreak at a gale-battered, rundown resort on the coast, some heyday-past destination like Hastings or Herne Bay that offered little more than a stub of a pier, a plate of cockles and a spin on a waltzer. After peering suspiciously into his wife's boiled-egg sandwiches and losing a few bob at bingo, Ray would stop on the return journey for a glass of beer and a packet of crisps in one of the Kentish pubs that had a children's room. Then they would get back in the car and head for the glowing patch of sky that marked the city. London never really got dark. Billy never saw true darkness until he moved.

He hated the idea of deserting his friends – not that he had many. He was alone without being lonely, too gawky and awkward to be chosen for teams, too sensitive to be one of the gang, too smart to be popular, too shy to have much confidence in his abilities. He lived in his prodigious imagination and was very happy there. That last term, his form teacher wrote on his report that 'young William's determination to be independent suggests that he will eventually achieve his aims, even if he takes the longer route to arrive.'

Unfortunately it looked as if the whole family was heading for a major detour.

The house in Westerdale Road was very small, but somehow they never got under each other's feet. A narrow, gloomy hallway down to the kitchen, a smart front room that smelled of furniture polish and was only used for guests and television, a kitchen that had once been called a scullery, with steamed-up windows and a deep square sink that doubled as a worktop when you placed a board over it. Everything about the place was old-fashioned, as if the postwar years had brought an end to change. Ray and Angela had made a few concessions to the present, a front-loading washing machine in the kitchen, a second telephone on the upstairs landing, but they regarded most new inventions as untrustworthy, unnecessary and unaffordable. Patterned brown linoleum still covered the stairs. The doorstep was regularly glossed with red lead paint. The best room boasted a brown hide suite and a walnut sideboard full of unused china, fine and floral.

That was where the man stood. Billy remembered watching him through the crack in the door. Tall and bony faced, his hair fashioned in a trendy sort of cut, he seemed too young to be a council official. Billy and his mother were in by themselves, Ray having gone to sort out more mysterious official paperwork, and the council man had turned up unannounced. Billy was in the hall fixing his bicycle and listening carefully. In the last few minutes the conversation had grown more threatening.

'. . . without him. I can't make the decision . . .'

'There's no decision to be made, Mrs March. Either the accommodation is accepted here and now, or the offer will be rescinded . . .'

Rescinded. Billy made a note to look that one up. As he listened, he grew angrier and angrier. It didn't seem right to spend years watching your parents hunched over the kitchen table, reworking the bills with endless patience, for it all to come to this.

'. . . so that your family may be evicted from the property within seven calendar days.'

23

'But my husband was told ... there must be some kind of extension we can—'

'You've already had ample time, love, and you've singularly failed to—'

Billy was kneeling on the floor, trying to find a way to make his bicycle pump stay in its bracket. A moment later he found himself on his feet with blood in his cheeks, fury in his heart and the bicycle pump wielded like a baton in his hand. The flexible tube at the end was still attached, and it was this that raised such a painful welt on the council worker's face.

Billy remembered flailing at him and roaring, the man's hands raised to protect his eyes, a high scream of fear. He remembered his mother pulling him away as he shouted that they wouldn't take the house, not after his parents had worked so hard for it. In the scuffle his mother's favourite china statue, a platinum-haired dancing girl in a flowing green dress, was knocked from the mantelpiece and shattered in the hearth, where it lay like some awful omen. Worse than this, Billy was aware that the satisfaction of landing a blow on the bureaucrat was lost beneath the shame of disgracing his mother.

When Ray came home there was a terrible shouting match that continued until his parents had burned away their frustration. Billy was not punished, and the incident was never mentioned again. He attempted to glue the statue back together, hoping that this would make amends, but it look deformed, its beauty lost, and had to be thrown away.

Three days later, Ray and Angela March went to see the residence they had been allocated. Billy flatly refused to accompany them and stayed home by himself, working on his blueprints for a space station and a series of grotesque comic strips. That night, his mother sat on the end of his bed and tried to tell him how smart everything was at the new home, how they would now have a garden instead of a yard, how they'd be living in a much nicer neighbourhood, but the boy refused to listen.

On the day the March family moved, Billy ran away.

He did not go very far, just to the nearest cinema. He slipped out into the yard as the removal van arrived, and climbed over the fence into the street. The Odeon was showing another pair of forgotten low-budget horrors, *Death Line*, starring Donald Pleasance, and Peter Walker's *House of Whipcord*. Luckily, the woman on the ticket counter was disinterested in her job and could always be relied upon to admit underage kids if they were tall enough.

As Billy watched the films, it was hard to shake the feeling that he would never be here again. There were no trailers for forthcoming attractions because no more movies were to be shown in the building. In a few weeks' time the cinema's twinkling starlight ceiling would be lowered to incorporate strip lights, the seats torn out and replaced with red plastic bingo tables. Who needed a palace of the imagination when there were cash prizes to be won?

By 5.30 he had seen both films, and one of them twice. He stepped out into another wet night and knew that he had been beaten. He was low on money, and a visit with friends or neighbours would be certain to prompt a phone call to his parents.

He sat at a yellow plastic counter in the sauna-steamy coffee bar opposite the cinema while the Jesus and Mary Chain blared out from the radio, and watched the passing buses, knowing that he could only delay the inevitable. Maybe it would all turn out for the best; the area was changing, and his favourite shops were being bulldozed to make way for malls and professional flats. The decade's new policies were taking wing and, if the billboards were to be believed, the good times were here to stay. Britons were buying shares in a bright, golden future. But when he heard the crackle of the police radio and looked up at the constable removing his gloves as he crossed the café floor, Billy knew that the gaudy excesses of the city were no longer meant for the likes of him.

CHAPTER THREE

The Dream Territory

'In planning policies, the "community" has been elevated to the point of a fetish … The idyll of the community fostered for commercial and political ends does not accord with the increasingly private world sought by an ever-increasing proportion of the population.' – Deyan Sudjic, *The 100 Mile City*

BILLY MARCH arrived for his first night in Invicta Cross in a police vehicle. Although the driver didn't have his flashing blue light revolving when the car pulled up, several sets of curtains drifted apart to reveal half-hidden impassive faces, and Billy could feel disapproving stares on his back as he walked up the path to the house.

The officers lectured him for wasting their time, but his parents were strangely understanding about the whole affair and had even kept a meal in the microwave for him. His mother was visibly shaken by the vanishing act but hid her hysteria by vigorously wiping down surfaces with a damp J-Cloth.

'You should have thought of her feelings,' said his father.

Billy tried to make light of it. 'The army wouldn't take

me,' he explained, 'so I've decided to stay on here until I'm old enough for service.' The flippancy earned him a clip around the ear.

Ray gave his son a perfunctory tour around the house, which seemed plain and modern and characterless, but Billy was disinterested and tired and fell asleep as soon as he'd eaten.

The next day was Sunday, and the sun shone down on a changed world. Billy reluctantly climbed from his warm bed and began a survey of his own.

Their house was the same size as the one they had just left, but instead of damp patches and linoleum it had thin white walls, low ceilings, a waste disposal unit and a breakfast nook with a sliding hatch, a pointlessly L-shaped lounge with crisp clean corners, and fitted grey carpets everywhere. Instead of a cramped yard with unruly honeysuckle, dead topsoil and a lollystick gravestone where Joey the tortoise was buried, there was a perfect emerald oblong of grass at the rear and a smaller oblong at the front. The house was not in a terrace but detached, and compared to the others in Balmoral Close looked narrower, as though it had been squeezed into the rear of the street as an afterthought. A deal of sorts had been struck with Greenwich council: the Marches were to rent the property from a building consortium and would have an option to purchase after three years. They would need at least that long to raise the deposit.

Instead of helping his parents to unpack the tea chests that lined the hall, Billy hopped on his bicycle and set out to explore the surrounding area.

All of the roads in Invicta Cross had been given royal names, as if to suggest that the brand new thoroughfares were imbued with historical significance. The bicycle sped through Windsor Terrace, Warwick Avenue, Bedford Gardens, Braganza Lane, Brunswick Road, Spencer Close, Boadicea Parade. Row upon row of pristine homes, neat little orange brick boxes with white porches and peristyles that looked like optional extras glued onto basic dwelling units.

At the northern end of the town was a giant new supermarket, one of the first of its kind, with an area of herringbone tarmac laid out to receive over two hundred cars. To the south was an old electricity generating plant with rusting stumps of pylons, transformers, ceramic insulators and a daunting Gothic brick tower that seemed left over from an earlier era. The station had been rendered inactive in the sixties and now awaited the wrecker's ball.

On the tarmac arteries between these two landmarks stood more new houses, a glass-faced nursery school, a large concrete box marked The Invicta Cross Community Centre, a brand-new pub called The Helicopter, and nothing much else. No corner shops, no cinema, no library, no playgrounds, no parklands; nowhere to walk to or from, nowhere even to sit and watch the world go by. Here in Invicta Cross it was clear that the world did not go by. The world came up to the edge, halted in surprise and carefully made its way around. *My new home*, thought Billy. *The place where I'll be living out the rest of my formative years*.

No wonder so many terrible things happened after that.

For the last twelve years Billy's father had been a foreman in a large glassware company based in Bethnal Green, but when the factory had decided to automate its line and relocate to Toronto, he had declined the offer to emigrate and had taken voluntary redundancy. Since then, he had not been able to find a remotely similar position in the same field.

It wasn't so much that he had disliked the idea of Canada. It was more to do with Ray's attitude to authority. He hated being presented with an ultimatum. He was determined not to uproot his sensitive son and damage his school career. Billy was the one who would get a decent education and make something of himself, the one who would finally put the family name on the map. When the doctor told Angela that she would not be able to have any more children, Ray's resolution increased; he knew that the boy would make good eventually. All he needed was a little confidence.

Billy's father loved London, but the city he had chosen to remain behind for was no longer his to inhabit. Another ultimatum, this time delivered by the government, had uprooted the family after all. This was supposed to be the start of something fresh, but to Billy it felt like the end of the line. If London was the nation's heart, what had they moved to, its spleen?

Invicta Cross was located in Sussex, equidistant from Crawley and East Grinstead, near the last remaining tracts of the Weald forest of Anderida. The oaks of these ancient woodlands had been felled three hundred and sixty years before to fuel the iron foundries, the lakes dammed to drive the forge hammers, and the remaining pockets of wild heath were fast vanishing beneath the cables and concrete of new suburban towns that caused more damage than any industrial revolution.

The area was accessible by rail from East Grinstead,

which was several miles away, and suffered a sporadic and capricious bus service. Invicta Cross had been designed with a specific spectrum of residents in mind; it welcomed couples who drove, commuters, city men who left their wives at home to keep house. During the week the streets were as deserted as the surface of the moon, and the few brave souls who ventured out to walk their dogs quickly vanished back inside with their pets and poop-scoops.

Billy stared at the windows as he passed, searching the blind eyes of each house for indices of life, but he caught only fleeting glimpses: a closing door, an extinguished light, the mumbled fanfare of the distant television.

The development had been built at the site of a long-vanished crossroads, at the end of a newly constructed dual carriageway that extended into what had until three years ago been lush green fields. It was not the product of natural growth but a profitable chunk of instant suburbia, a commuter satellite of luxurious oubliettes capitalising on the great move out.

Billy's ride revealed a strange dreamlike dimension to the neighbourhood. A wonderland of clipped jade lawns and brand-new three-bedroom, twin-garage mock-Tudor homes, where husbands carefully waxed their cars (in the garage, not at the kerb) while their wives overcooked the Sunday roast and the children stared morosely at tele-visions. A temporal lassitude existed in the bare streets, where the air seemed thick and slow, as though the town had been flooded and its residents moved underwater. Single people were unwelcome here. Young families proved to be bigger spenders and were encouraged to settle in up-market bungalows behind tall hedgerows and trimmed herbaceous borders. The richer people were, the more invisible they became, until they vanished altogether.

He had reached Balmoral Close once more. A curtain twitched. Dead leaves lifted in the breeze. As Billy wheeled his bicycle along the path he had the distinct impression that someone was watching him but, like trying to see the back of one's head in a mirror, he was always too late to catch a glimpse. He felt himself slowing down, as if the soporific effect of this dream territory was already seeping into his bones. He wanted to describe the feeling to someone, but there was no one here who would understand.

As his father could not get the gas cooker to work on that first Sunday, Billy suggested ordering a takeaway while they unpacked. A stack of junk mail in the hall allowed an appraisal of the options; pizza seemed the best bet. Having such delicacies delivered free of charge was still a novelty.

The telephone line was unconnected, so Billy volunteered to call from a public box at the end of the road.

The pizzas; they were the start of the whole damned thing.

CHAPTER FOUR

The Alien Pods

'Geraldine King and Amanda Lofting, both 22, complained to a drunken neighbour about late-night noise from his TV set. He set fire to their house, burning them both to death.'
– *Daily Mail*

HE COULD see what was about to happen.

The astronaut was going up to the wrong house. Billy ran down the stairs and pulled open the front door, but was forced to stop and put on his shoes. Then he wrongly knotted a lace and had to hop over in his socks to prevent their pizzas from being eaten by perfect strangers. By the time he had bounced across the sopping lawn, the delivery man had already rung the doorbell of number twelve. Billy could see – and hear – the reaction of the neighbours through the half-open stained-glass window at the side of their hall.

'Who on earth could that be at this time of night?' He saw a middle-aged man with a big nose and odd hair – later identified as Ken Prout – put down his screwdriver and check the hall clock. 'Eight-fifteen. What an unearthly time to come calling.'

Ahead of him, the pizza man rang the doorbell again. It

was electronic and had once played the first six notes of the Carpenters' 'We've Only Just Begun' until Ken tried to fix it. Now it played 'Only Just'.

'Barbara, see who that is.'

'You're nearer,' Ken's wife called back. 'I'm up to my ears in the dishwasher.'

Tutting and shaking his head Ken descended the ladder, at the top of which he had been attempting to install a smoke alarm, and answered the front door. In front of him stood what appeared to be an astronaut in a black crash helmet and a striped leather suit, holding a large box made of padded red plastic.

'That's ssmmffmm pounds thirty-six pee,' the astronaut boomed, thrusting his head repeatedly at the package.

Ken pulled a face and sniffed at the box. 'Get your filthy boots off my step,' he said.

'Daddy, spaceman.' His three-year-old son, Simon, was traversing the hall on his bottom, and pointed a pudgy finger.

'I think that's for us,' said Billy meekly. Ken Prout couldn't see him properly through the hedge, and the delivery man didn't hear, because he tore open the velcro flap of his pizza bag and began to unload the contents. The Prouts' hallway filled with the aroma of spicy sausage.

'Fart,' said Simon Prout gleefully, 'bum fart.'

'You can put those back in your bag right now,' shouted Ken.

'You didn't order them?' boomed the delivery man. 'This number thirteen?'

'This is twelve, you imbecile. Do I look like the sort of person who would order pizza on a Sunday evening?'

'Excuse me, that's for us,' called Billy, trying to make an

appearance through the ornate arrangement of shrubbery.

'We always have a Sunday roast,' said Barbara, smiling inanely as she appeared at the door, unsnapping her Marigolds and beating them dry on her apron. She had lips like a stencilled strawberry and even odder hair. 'What's going on?'

'This halfwit has come to the wrong house. You want next door.'

'There's no one living next door,' said Barbara Prout loudly. Billy assumed they would notice someone peering wanly through the hedge at them, but Barbara wasn't wearing her spectacles. She waited for the delivery man to reseal his bag and lumber away, then checked the state of the porch mat with distaste. 'Mud everywhere. And what a smell. I thought they'd given up trying to find a buyer.'

'Well, someone's living there. They moved in yesterday, while we were at Grandma Prout's.'

'How do you know? Have you actually seen anyone? You must have seen someone.' Behind her, Simon was removing his pants and pointing to his anus.

'Not a hair. But we already know something about them.' Ken Prout narrowed his eyes. 'They're the sort of people who order takeaways. You know, rubbish.'

'Well, at least it was Italian.' Barbara pulled her son's pants back up and sent him on his way, watching vaguely as Simon Prout toddled off into a nearby wall.

'What the hell difference does that make?' asked Ken.

'It could have been worse,' said his wife, reluctantly spelling it out. 'It could have been *Indian*.'

Billy decided that now was not the right time to introduce himself and returned the hedge branch to its rightful place before creeping back to number thirteen. He didn't tell his parents about the Prouts. He figured they would run into them soon enough.

The Marches sat on the floor and tore great chunks of sausage and onion pizza from the box, washing it down with gulps of cola. It seemed common to Angela, eating with your fingers, and not at all the way they should be starting off in their new home, but she wasn't entirely sure where the knives and forks were. They ate in silence, surrounded by a fortification of tea chests. The knowledge that the Prouts considered takeaway pizza to be uncivilised on a Sunday spoiled Billy's enjoyment of the meal. They had only been here a few hours and were already doing the wrong thing.

The ground floor of the new house was almost devoid of furniture. Ray had left the old lounge suite behind, knowing that its shabby state would be accentuated by so many fresh, white surfaces.

'I've been thinking,' said Billy's mother, delicately dabbing her chin with an inabsorbent paper napkin, 'if I can't find any work in an office, I could take a job in East Grinstead as a shop assistant.'

'You were a transport manager,' complained Ray. 'You had responsibilities. Shops only employ kids these days. Cheap labour.'

'You have to take the work where you can get it,' she replied quietly. Billy couldn't decide if she was admonishing his father; ambiguous criticism was an old trick of hers. Ray took the point, chewing thoughtfully.

'I'll come into town with you tomorrow. We'll look together. We can get the lad properly kitted out.'

Billy had been registered at the local school, a low concrete building on the far side of town called Sherington

Mixed Seniors that looked like the bunker in which Hitler had shot himself. He was due to begin on Wednesday, a special concessionary half-week designed to ease him in to new scholastic surroundings. Billy hated the idea of having to create fresh alliances and enemies but promised himself that he wouldn't complain because it was just as painful for his parents to leave their pasts behind. It was the most grown-up decision he had made to date.

'How was your bike ride?' asked Ray, peeling an anchovy from his pizza slice.

'I didn't see another living human being.'

'Well.' His father searched around for something positive to say. 'It always takes a while to get to know people. Sunday afternoons are quiet everywhere.'

Not this quiet, thought Billy. *Even graveyards have songbirds.*

'You'll end up loving it here,' said Angela, 'once you make new friends.'

Billy recognised the desperate hopefulness in his mother's voice. 'I'd rather have a dog than make new friends,' he said. 'A dog or a gun.'

The next morning, he was woken by the angry revving of car engines. He checked the alarm clock Angela had placed beside his new bed. Seven-fifteen. Running to the bare window in his pyjamas, he watched cars pulling out of garages as the wives of Invicta Cross dutifully drove their husbands to the station. By the time he was washed and dressed, the vehicles had returned passengerless. Half an hour later part of the fleet drove off again, this time to take the children to school. Surveying the deserted streets, Billy elected to stay in his room for the rest of the day, and possibly the rest of his adolescence.

*

Georgina Bovis was under the weather when she needed to be under the weatherman. Graham had been promising to take another afternoon off from his job at Croydon Meteorological Centre for weeks now but kept finding reasons to stay at work. He had gone off her, that much was obvious. The *frisson* provided by their afternoons of steaming hot sex had blown over; a cold front had moved in, and no change in the outlook could be expected.

Graham Birdsmith had been screwing her under her husband's nose for four months. He lived two streets away, in Gaveston Crescent, where they had met at his house-warming party. Entranced less by the fact that Graham was in charge of rainfall for the whole southeastern area and more by the clear outline of his erection as he lounged in the lawn chair opposite her, Georgina had allowed him to come calling while her husband was at work and his wife was at therapy sessions.

Those golden afternoons had brought colour to her cheeks, but now the gilt had worn through to guilt; Graham had obviously decided to be a good boy and work at his marriage.

Georgina needed to find a replacement. She lounged at the bedroom window with the net curtain raised around her body like an arctic aurora. It was almost midday and she was still in her nightgown, but it seemed she had nothing worth getting up for. Alan had gone to work hours ago, and one of the neighbours had taken her daughter, Sherry, to nursery school.

Bored, she looked down at the new people, two doors along, and watched as the father came out of the house carrying an emptied tea chest. He bent down to pick up some litter from the front lawn, then rose and looked around, as though he knew he was being watched. Georgina missed no detail of him; the genial features, the rock 'n' roll quiff, the firm chest, the snug-fitting jeans. She decided that she should get to know her new neighbours better.

She moved closer to the window and absently ticked long coral nails against the glass. What a life, what a choice; inattentive Alan covering the dressing table with bar charts and fussily conspiring with his beloved daughter against Mummy, half-hearted Graham making excuses even he did not pretend to believe. Why bother with either of them when there was a fresh challenge close at hand? Too many people were becoming suspicious about the meteorologist's daytime visits. They knew he wasn't nipping into the house of a married woman just to check a raingauge. Perhaps it was time to phase Graham out.

Just then a gormless-looking boy and a tiny, hunched woman came out on the pathway to lend the man a hand, and Georgina allowed the curtain to fall partly back in place. She carefully arranged the netting so that it obscured the woman and her child, framing Ray alone.

At noon the telephone men arrived at Billy March's new home, and shortly after that his parents' bed was delivered; they'd spent the first two nights lying under a duvet on the floor of their bedroom. As Billy unpacked assorted books, model kits and magazines he kept one eye on the windows of the house two doors away. Several times he saw the curtains twitch. It was as if the house flinched when it caught him staring. He could tell that the affable nosiness of his old neighbourhood had no equivalent here. It would be harder to make friends. He knew why, too.

One look at the pristine streets told him that the Marches didn't belong here. They were the wrong class.

There had clearly been some kind of administrative error. Billy didn't know much about middle-class people, but he knew what they looked like and how they behaved. They had wine with their meals and read the broadsheets. They had pride and confidence; above all, confidence. They betrayed themselves by what they didn't do; they did not allow their curiosity to get the better of them and come visiting on the spurious pretext of welcoming the family to the neighbourhood. The women did not stand in the street chatting while they tried to peer through the front windows, and the men did not climb out from beneath their cars to compare engine capacities. Their children did not play outside. Everyone and everything was locked away from prying eyes. These were people who collected things, who kept themselves to themselves, who argued in low voices, who never interfered, who did not get involved. People with burglar alarms.

Billy pulled a stool to the window and sat watching the silent street. In the distance was a strip of green, the fields beyond the town. Everything below was rooftop red, concrete cream and tarmac black.

As he watched, he knew that their presence here was an affront to the other residents and all wrong; only harm could come of it. He wanted to go home, to his real home, and stop pretending that they lived here in this pastel-shaded paradise, where his mother would put on airs and be found out, where his father would amiably suggest a trip to the boozer and be shunned by the young professionals. The game would be up for Billy the moment he opened his mouth. He tried not to speak badly but knew that he sounded common. It was a fact his parents refused to acknowledge. Hadn't his own grandmother once called him a guttersnipe? It wasn't his fault; it was how the other kids at school had sounded. His voice was an implicit criticism of the neighbourhood, a reminder of family roots that no amount of further education would shake off.

His mother's side of the family had always considered themselves to be a social cut above his father's. Consequently, hardly any of them were on speaking terms with each other. Wasn't that the typical behaviour of a working-class family? He looked out at the glinting vehicles in their shadowy carports and thought it unlikely that the new neighbours ever bought their Christmas presents down the market. His father believed that it didn't matter what people thought, but it did. He said that the Marches didn't need anyone else, but they did. His mother wanted them to be like something out of an American sitcom, supernaturally clean and forever checking on each other's feelings ...

A call on the stairs. 'Billy, get ready, we're going into town.'

Croydon.

The very word sent shivers down his spine. Britain's tenth biggest urban development, the link between the inner city atmosphere of Brixton and the prim commuter land of Kent. As Billy walked between the windswept mirrored office blocks, it seemed to him that the town was even more stubbornly devoid of character than Invicta Cross. Litter roared in whirling dust devils at the junctions of vast new buildings. Nothing seemed designed for human comfort, but then comfort was out of fashion while there was money to be made. Among the litter, he passed a local newspaper headline quoting Chief Superintendent Bernie Davis: 'Croydon police are currently dealing with more serious crimes than New York's busiest precinct'.

It seemed unbelievable that anyone could draw a comparison between New York and Croydon. At least there was a decent bookshop here, though, and after twenty minutes he had to be pulled from it.

Later he sat in his room and read Jack Finney's *Invasion of the Body Snatchers* and, as the rain once more began to fall, returned to his place at the window to stare down at the slick black streets, searching for alien pods. They had to be out there somewhere, nestling unnoticed in greenhouses, waiting to germinate into seed people. There had to be *some* explanation for a place like this.

CHAPTER FIVE

The Boundary Marker

'Complaints to local authorities about neighbours are rising by 20% a year.' – *The Big Issue*

OVER THE next few days the Marches settled in, but could not settle down. Billy's mother patrolled with a damp cloth, forever searching for something to clean or re-arrange. She would study a lamp or a chair and move it from one side of the room to the other. 'This hasn't really found its place yet,' she would say, pursing her lips. They bought some cheap new furniture, opting for twenty-four monthly payments. The house took on an inner shape.

During the day, the neighbourhood was a vacuum of silence and stillness. The streets were always clear of pedestrians and, between the morning evacuation and nightly return of the suited troops, cleared of cars as well. Ray was unused to such a quiet existence. His family had always lived near railway lines; shunting and clattering had formed an aural backdrop to half of their conversations. During the endless postwar summers, London's neighbours had kept chickens in their gardens and conducted most of their discussions in the street. Now Ray mooned about at the back door, watching the crows at dusk, sniffing the October bonfire smoke that drifted hazily across distant blue hedgerows, gazing out at the half-hidden neighbourhood, unable to draw comfort from the calm.

Angela kept herself busy. She studied back issues of *Home & Garden*, marking off items they would never be able to afford, helped to paint the master bedroom a sickly pale pink, then set about filling it with springtime prints and photo frames. By Friday the room looked no different from any other parents' bedroom in the town. His mother knew that fitting in began with the appearance of doing so.

Billy started school, and kept a suspicious look in his eye that successfully prevented him from bonding with any of his classmates. He had been placed among aliens who looked and sounded like human beings without actually being so. The playground of his old school in Greenwich had been a deafeningly raucous sprawl-and-brawl danger zone that health-conscious teachers avoided. The Sherington Seniors playground was orderly, quiet, civilised. Computer games were the year's big craze; never had a teenage fad had such a soporific effect. The teachers were distant and disinterested. It was as if they had failed to attain positions at good schools, and had resignedly settled for less than best, barely bothering to give the pupils their attention.

None of the kids spoke to Billy, but then they barely spoke to each other, and when he tried to beak into their cliques he was gently but firmly excluded. If he had been black he could at least have accused them of racism. But there were few non-Caucasians living in Invicta Cross.

Many of the boys in his class had already started accumulating their own credit cards. They discussed television programmes, clothes, sport and music, and how boring their parents were, but none of them seemed much bothered by the fact that they were already behaving with the humourless maturity of their elders. Heartfelt opinions were never voiced. Nobody particularly liked or disliked Billy; it seemed not to occur to anyone that they had a choice. Perhaps, he thought, they were confused by the fact that he sounded common and yet always carried a book in his back pocket.

There was one other boy who ate alone and read through his lunch break while the sportier types organised cricket teams and human pyramids. His name was Oliver Price, and there was an air of wasted disreputability about him that instantly appealed. When first approached by Billy, Oliver had just been kicked in the back and could not speak. His lack of concern over being physically assaulted by his classmates suggested that such attacks were a frequent occurrence. He was so surprised to be addressed by a classmate in civil terms that he looked behind him with a 'Who, me?' gesture when Billy spoke. Billy helped Oliver to his feet and waited while he dusted himself down.

'Do they often do that?' he asked.

'People don't like me because of my father,' the boy explained, wincing. 'He's a funeral director. He's buried some kids' dads. It freaks people out.'

'Doesn't bother me,' Billy shrugged. 'Where do you live?'

'Windsor Terrace. *Ow.* You must be new.'

'Blimey, is it that obvious?'

Oliver pointed to Billy's school tie, the first he had ever been forced to wear. 'You haven't been detagged,' he explained. 'If you don't remove the label before the sixth

45

form catch you, they'll stick your head down the toilet. Here.' He reached over, tore off the tag and pocketed it.

Oliver was the butt of everyone's jokes because of the air of unwholesomeness that hung about him. His nails were dirty, his cheeks were the colour of greaseproof paper, his hair seemed filled with static and his clothes were always covered with food. He spoke of his father with pride, took an unflinching interest in bodily functions and drew enormous pleasure from shocking people. He had a laugh like an automated seaside sailor. There was something patched together about him that ill suited a perfect life in Invicta Cross.

It was hardly surprising that the two boys should become friends. Billy's parents were pleased that their son had found an ally, although their approval became more conditional after Oliver spent an hour describing how he had helped his father embalm the family cat. There was a desperate gratitude about Oliver's alliance with Billy, as if he had always been waiting for such a companion to appear. The funeral director's son looked up to his new, and apparently only, friend, while Billy benefited from Oliver's worldly knowledge. In the weeks ahead, their relationship developed an easy symbiosis.

As the willing outcasts of class 5A, it seemed natural that Oliver and Billy should join forces against the playground's more troublesome elements. Not that there was supposed to be any bullying at the school. Mr Primrose, the science teacher, explained that he would not tolerate aggression in any form. As he said this, one of the senior boys was trying to hold Oliver's hand over a lit Bunsen burner.

It soon became obvious that there was some kind of social

pecking order in existence in Balmoral Close and that the March family was at the bottom of it. Their house had been wedged onto a narrow patch of land between two larger dwellings as an architectural afterthought; their rooms were the narrowest, their drive the shortest, their front garden the smallest. It hardly mattered to Ray, who was eager to make a go of things and wanted his son to recognise the marvellous opportunities that such a new town afforded. But Invicta Cross kept its charms – if there were any – well hidden. Two weeks after they moved in, they still had not spoken to anyone else in the street.

Determined that someone should break the ice, Angela steadied her nerves and went next door to number twelve. It was a wet Saturday morning and, apart from a sour-faced milkman working his way along the road in a whining electric van, the street was cemetery-still. Billy watched from his usual position at the bedroom window and tried to lip-read, but when this talent failed him he ran downstairs and peered discreetly from the lounge, telling himself that he was witness to an important social experiment.

The door to number twelve was opened by the lovely but startled Barbara Prout. She was lovely because she had spent the last hour applying new make-up with hypnotic intensity. She was startled because this was not the sort of neighbourhood where you visited without telephoning first. Angela had no knowledge of such a custom; in Greenwich the neighbours called at each other's houses whether one wanted them to or not. The apprehensive look on Barbara's face suggested that she was expecting to be informed of a death in the family.

'Can I help you?' Her voice was a thin scream with the volume lowered.

'I just thought I'd say hello,' said Angela, suddenly awkward. 'We're the new – um,' she pointed back at the little house, 'just moved in to that place there. I'm Angela.'

Barbara Prout cut an unnerving figure. With her unnaturally wide eyes and coiffure like a helmet of lacquered copper wire, she looked like a cross between a shop-window dummy and an electrocuted squirrel. Billy was fascinated. Her hair was so perfect that it had to be a wig. She wore a flared purple skirt over a pair of black leggings, so that it looked like she'd got dressed twice.

'Angela,' said Barbara, rolling the name around her mouth and holding out her hand. 'I'm Mrs Prout.' She sounded like an old BBC recording; 'Prout' was pronounced 'Prite'. She offered a huge dead smile and stood there grinning, as if no further social etiquette existed to cover the situation. In the background Angela could hear Doris Day singing 'Please Don't Eat the Daisies'. It occurred to her that Mrs Prout might be on medication.

'I've been meaning to come over and say hello all week, but what with settling in and all—' Angela shifted, her breath freezing in front of her. It was cold on the step. Barbara remained motionless. 'My son, Billy, he's indoors,' Angela continued, pointing inanely back at the house. 'My husband, he's—'

Barbara Prout's attention was elsewhere. She stared down at her visitor's trainers. Angela followed her gaze and realised that she had trodden in dog shit on the way over. Half an enormous orange turd lay on the Prouts' clean step. The other half was divorcing itself from Angela's shoe.

Barbara stared at the smear of excrement as though it had been placed at the threshold of her home as a primitive boundary marker, something to repulse household demons. She looked up woozily. 'You must forgive me,' she began, 'I'm not . . . I really haven't . . . I've got something on the . . .' and shut the door.

'I was so *embarrassed*,' Billy's mother told him when she returned. 'What an odd way to behave. She probably meant she had something on the boil.'

What Angela failed to see was that Barbara Prout never intended to acknowledge her new neighbours, and that she had been forced into a situation for which she was quite unprepared. Perhaps she really had no idea how they looked and sounded to the residents of Balmoral Close, or why their family was a threat to the area's aspiring status quo. Later Billy learned to recognise the pinched little glances and button mouths, the conversations that halted as they approached – but there was much he did not see until it was too late. Meanwhile, he spent increasing amounts of time hanging out with Oliver Price who, like many lonely teenagers, was a mine of arcane, disgusting and redundant information.

The pair looked after each other's interests and passed their school lunch breaks discussing all manner of peripheral knowledge, including the ability of Danish peat bogs to mummify bodies, the true meaning of Vlad the Impaler's signature, how James I and Henry III both managed to be assassinated in the toilet, who was the cooler superhero – Perseus or Batman, how touching a dead body stopped you dreaming of it, and why *The Exorcist* was banned as a film but not as a book. In this way they gained more information about the world than their lessons could ever provide for them. They developed an idioglossia that allowed them to communicate without others understanding, and began to explore a weekend mania for rescuing terrible horror films from the bargain bins of Croydon's expanding video stores.

Billy felt that he owed a special debt to his new friend; Oliver would slowly help to lift the dreaded curse of Invicta Cross.

CHAPTER SIX

The Cooling Grave

'A fistfight between two roommates, one 84 and the other 96, ended with the latter's hospitalisation. Said the investigating officer: "We don't know what caused the fight, but at that age they often don't know, either."' – *Midweek*

BOB METCALF angrily watched his stepson from the window. The boy was standing out in the rain behaving like an idiot. Bob hoped the Garibaldis couldn't see. Adolpho Garibaldi was big in the restaurant trade. He had no taste and no style but an awful lot of money, and had placed gold-plated carriage lamps and lemon-yellow stone cladding around the garage in which he housed his Ferrari, but Bob didn't want Adolpho to think he had an idiot son, because Bob liked respect from people with money, even when they were vulgarian crooks.

'What on earth does he think he's doing?' asked Bob.

He was answered by a series of electronic beeps. His wife, Daphne, was seated at her home computer, printing something out. Bob and Daphne brought so much work home with them that they had two computers, one used exclusively for writing, and one Bob shared with their two children, although Brad and Emma only played shoot-'em-ups and platformers.

'If you interrupt my thought processes once more,' said Daphne, her voice strangled with tension, 'I will pull this machine out of the wall and throw it through the window before setting fire to the house.'

The worst thing was, Bob knew that she was only half joking. Daphne considered the time she spent at her desk to be sacred. She would tolerate no interruption, whether it came from her husband, the children or from Jesus Christ himself. Bob knew this and, on days when he was particularly annoyed with her, would interrupt his wife just to watch the wrenching effect it had on her nervous system.

'What you don't understand,' she would cry, her voice quivering with emotion, 'is that I am trying to *write*, an alien process which I know means nothing to you, but means a *hell* of a lot to the reading public.'

For the past four years Daphne had written a mildly bitchy newspaper column for the *East Grinstead Advertiser* and a series of gushing historical romances, the kind of books that had women in diaphanous nightgowns running about beneath raised gold lettering. At some point in the eleven years of their marriage she had fooled herself into believing that she was a female Dostoevsky and constantly stressed the vast gap that existed between creative and noncreative people, making it clear that she placed Bob in the latter category. She was, he noted, quite happy to have him work a sixty-hour week in order to keep her in the manner to which she was accustomed.

He sighed and watched her, drapes of straight dark hair falling forward across her face as she furiously punched at the keyboard. She possessed none of the ladylike qualities that she was so fond of stressing in her prose. Where was her heroine's wasp-like waist, her pale swan's neck, her heaving bosom? Daphne's chest was as big and square and flat as a jumbo box of soap powder.

He returned his gaze to the street once more. This time he could see what Brad was doing. He was carving an ejaculating phallus into the paintwork of the new neighbours' Vauxhall. Bob slipped out of the room and ran downstairs, darting out into the porch and hissing at his son.

'Get in here this minute, you little bastard.' He glanced at number thirteen, but no one was at the windows.

'Fuck off and die in a pit of shit,' replied Brad, folding his penknife shut and sauntering nonchalantly around the car.

'I've a good mind to report you to the police, you foul-mouthed little—'

'If you do, Daphne will divorce you. I'm her son, not yours.'

If only she would, thought Bob, *if only both of you would simply vanish*. But he couldn't afford to have that happen. Brad's father was an incredibly unpleasant New York lawyer and was still very friendly with his ex-wife. He'd make sure Daphne took him for every penny he had.

Brad held his stepfather's gaze, then broke it and turned off down the street, pulling a packet of cigarettes from his pocket.

'Where is your sister?' Bob shouted at him. 'You were supposed to be looking after her.'

'Fuck knows,' came the reply. 'She's probably out getting shagged senseless somewhere.'

'Emma is ten years old, Bradley!' he screamed, but his stepson had already turned the corner. Bob could feel heat suffusing his face. He drew a deep breath and tried to calm himself. The company doctor had warned him about getting upset. It wasn't that he had been a bad father – he'd given the kids everything they'd ever asked for – it was just that he hadn't been able to spend as much time with Brad as he had with Emma. It was nothing to do with Emma being his natural daughter. Things were very tricky at work. The company was expanding. Time was the most expensive commodity of all and had to be rationed carefully. He looked back at number thirteen and was mortified to see the new neighbour opening his front door. Hastily, Bob retreated inside his own house and peered around the lounge curtain, praying that the vandalised section of paintwork on the family's car would not be noticed.

He was in luck. Just then the light drizzle became heavy rain, and Ray March had to dash blindly to his vehicle. Another potentially embarrassing encounter had been avoided. Chastened by his cowardice, he followed the sound of typing and returned to the relative solace of the study.

Billy March noticed the damage to the car, of course, and was pretty sure that he could identify the culprit. Being at that inbetween age, a powerless time of watching and waiting, he noticed a lot more than he was ever supposed to. His father purchased a spray can of touch-up paint and carefully blended in the not-quite-matching colour, rather than face an argument with the neighbours.

'There was all this banging coming from number eleven,' said Angela. 'I wonder what he's building in there. An ark, by the sound of it.'

Billy looked up at his parents, then uncapped his

fountain pen. 'I have now been trapped in Invicta Cross for twelve days,' he wrote in his diary, 'and my mother keeps serving dinner as if everything is normal. Each night our conversation reaches surreal new depths. I feel alienated, like Franz Kafka. Or Morrissey.'

'We should go over and ask him,' said Ray. 'See if he has the nerve to shut the door in our faces as well.'

'I don't think that was her fault,' offered Angela, always erring on the side of generosity. 'She's probably just shy about meeting new people. We should have them over for tea.' Billy knew that she meant for dinner, but to his parents lunch was dinner and dinner was tea.

'What about the other side?' asked Ray. 'Seen any sign of them?'

'There was someone in the garden hanging out washing yesterday, looked like an au pair.' She ladled gravy onto her husband's lamb chops. 'A foreign girl, tiny little thing, Chinesey-looking.'

'Au pair, eh, very smart.' Ray winked at his son and started tucking into his mashed potatoes. Billy toyed with his food and ate half-heartedly, watching them both. He could not understand how they managed to just sit there eating when everything was so wrong. Meals held little appeal for him, especially the way his mother prepared them. She cooked like Billy's grandmother, who now lived in Sheffield; Ray's traditional phone call to announce that they were just leaving the house to visit her was the old lady's signal to put the sprouts on. She made the kind of English meals that slowly set as you ate them.

'What's the matter, love?' asked Angela. 'You look a bit peaky.'

Billy wanted to tell her but had made a solemn vow to

himself that he would not worry either of them, no matter what happened. At four o'clock this very afternoon, Brad Metcalf, their next-door neighbour's son, had slammed against him in the street and had threatened to hack up his face with a penknife blade. That morning the hulking blue-chinned classmate whose eyebrows met at the top of his nose had tried to get Billy to change seats with him in assembly so that he could sit next to his personality-impaired friends, but Billy had refused. Brad had explained that if he didn't change places with him tomorrow, he'd cut the corners of Billy's mouth so wide open that the top half of his head would fall off if he smiled.

Billy told himself he hadn't been unduly frightened, but when he arrived home he was sick in the bathroom sink. Later, when his courage made a partial return, he had gone out looking for his tormentor, only to find the streets as dead and deserted as ever.

The meal passed in uncomfortable silence. Behind them, Margaret Thatcher's face filled the television screen, promising golden opportunities in the years ahead. Her image was replaced by the head of a praying mantis, a trailer for a wildlife programme. Then a map of the Thames and a catchy tune; a new soap called *EastEnders* was just beginning.

Ray had not been able to find a job in Croydon or East Grinstead, and there was no employment for him in Invicta Cross. The Marches were not the kind of people who bought shares; they would miss out on the bonanza of privatisation. Billy had some moneymaking ideas of his own, but something prevented him from confronting his father with them. Respect was all that Ray had left.

Angela had been offered a couple of part-time jobs in

Croydon, but the wages were terrible, and the labour menial. She was a middle-aged housewife, unafraid of hard work but lacking in qualifications; decent jobs were not easy to come by.

Ray checked the saffron lump on the end of his fork with a look of bemusement. For years he had striven to understand the motivation behind his wife's cooking, but he never complained, even when she experimented with cauliflower. 'How was school?' he asked his son.

'Same as usual. Crap,' said Billy, smashing his peas flat with his fork.

'Haven't you made any friends apart from Oliver?'

'Nobody else wants to talk.'

'I don't believe that,' said Angela. 'You're a very good conversationalist. You have lots of interests. There must be some nice people. What about the neighbours' children?'

That was one of the exasperating things he loved about his mother; her naivety was such that she considered conversational ability an asset to a teenager. Billy felt like describing his first meeting with Emma Metcalf, Bob and Daphne's daughter, half-sister to the Neanderthal devil-spawn Brad: 'Hello, you're one of the new poor kids, aren't you? Poor, poor you.' This from a pug-nosed little girl with pierced ears and dyed red hair, dressed in an expensive pink sweatsuit, a ten-year-old Billy felt might not live to see eleven.

He told himself that he genuinely wanted to find something he liked about the place, to be able to tell his parents that he was slowly adjusting to his new life, but as he was not prepared to lie to them silence seemed a safer option. Silence was the one thing the town had in abundance. The silence of a coffin cooling in a grave.

Oliver had told him all about corpses. How rigor mortis went away after twenty-four hours, how the blood sank to the body's extremities, how facial muscles would still contract an hour after death if you put an electric current through them, how bodies bloated in the grave, and what happened to them during cremation . . .

'Can I be excused?' he asked suddenly. He felt sick and wanted to be alone.

'Of course,' said Ray, who sensed that something had upset his son. The boy always bottled up his emotions, just like his old man.

Billy went to his room and lay across the bed, absorbed in a crack-backed copy of Richard Matheson's *I Am Legend*. He had managed to find a library nearby, not well stocked, but they had promised to order books for him. There was no cinema in or anywhere near Invicta Cross. You had to go into Croydon to catch a movie, and it was difficult to get connecting buses back at night. There was one over-chlorinated swimming pool, filled with kids and rules; no running, jumping, diving or having fun. There was a billiard hall, outside which weaselly probation types hung around smoking roll-ups, but you had to be eighteen to join. There was a community centre that dispensed macramé lessons, herbal tea and ping pong to the desperate, and there was something called the Invicta Cross Social Resources Unit, a large glass-fronted building that had posters about battered wives and dirty syringes in the window and was never open.

Billy's eyes drifted across the same sentence for the third time. Fed up, he left the book and went to his usual position at the window, a slim figure framed against an endless grey sky. He could see nothing of interest from here; no neon signs, no takeaway chippies, no sports grounds, no barmy drunks, no chatty tramps, no police cars, no comic shops, no screaming, no laughter, no homelessness, no poverty, no river, no tarts, no junk stores, no rock venues, no danger, no passing buses to jump on, no tube tunnels to thunder through, no litter, no chaos, nothing to show that human beings lived here.

There was nothing at all. It was like being dead.

CHAPTER SEVEN

The Perils of Cork
Flooring

'John and Phyllis Holt sued their neighbours for trimming their shrubbery into sexually suggestive shapes. The Holts demanded the removal of trees and hedges trimmed to resemble phallic symbols.' – *San Diego Union*

BILLY DECIDED that he should stay as far away from Emma Metcalf as possible. She clearly had a crush on him, and as the half-sister of the chimp who spent his days hanging around outside their house, slack jawed and half asleep, looking like he'd forgotten where he lived, this was not a situation to be encouraged. Brad Metcalf was dangerous in an unpredictable way, and Billy was determined not to invoke his enmity, or friendship for that matter.

Oliver Price started spending a lot of time at number 13 Balmoral Close. He was an inexhaustible fund of vile stories and theories, and seemed at his happiest making Billy laugh.

There was a girl Billy liked, but he didn't know why. He had only seen her from a distance, across the school quadrangle going into French, peering back around a corner, but there was something about her that instantly intrigued him. She had wild frizzy brown hair, thin black-stockinged legs, high cheekbones and dark, sad eyes, and according to Oliver was hated by everyone. Her name was April Barrow. She and her mother lived on the outskirts of town and never received visitors.

'Why does everybody hate her?' Billy asked as they assembled chunks of wood and polystyrene in his bedroom.

'Her mother's a witch,' replied Oliver.

'A witch? How much of a witch?'

'Somewhere between *The Wizard of Oz* and *Carrie*.'

Billy considered this. 'That would do it,' he said. 'I wouldn't mind meeting her.'

'Some kid jumped off a building in East Grinstead yesterday. Seventh floor. Forced his leg bones right up through his rib cage. My dad says it'll have to be a closed-lid service.'

'I wonder why he jumped.'

'Drugs. According to my dad, he told the police he could fly.'

'Why didn't he take off from the ground floor, just to be sure?'

'Dunno,' replied Oliver. 'He must have been sure.'

On his way home from school one evening, Billy made a list of things he hated about Invicta Cross: the neighbours who, in the manner of flea circuses, were only rendered visible by the curtains they twitched; the streets as deserted as Laredo before a gunfight; Val-U-Rite, the maze-like thirty-six-till supermarket that put popping out for a packet of Licorice Allsorts on a par with the quest for the

Holy Grail; the eerie silence of the town after 8pm, presumably because everyone climbed into their coffins after *EastEnders* finished; and the effect all this was having on his parents: Ray had taken to wandering about, jangling the change in his pockets and whistling as if trying to ward off evil spirits. Angela was forever standing in the middle of the kitchen clutching herself as if in pain. Neither of them realised how much they were changing. If they did they would have taken trips back to town, like asthmatics visiting the seaside.

A few days later, Billy's father was unexpectedly offered employment as the manager of a self-service store attached to the Esso garage at the far end of Invicta Cross, and accepted, taking his place inside a red plastic box on a slip road to the motorway. The work was dull and poorly paid, but the hours were flexible and Ray figured it would suffice until a more satisfactory managerial position could be found.

His employment was Angela's excuse to announce that she was inviting the neighbours over for 'nibbles'. Billy was sure she had only ever cooked for guests outside of the immediate family once before, when Uncle Ernie's wife died and he didn't know how to work the cooker to heat sausage rolls for the wake.

The evening his mother proposed was fraught with potential disaster, but her mind was made up. In order to become a brochure-perfect wife she would embark on a programme of friend-making and, despite Ray's disapproval and her own impecunity, she set aside the following Friday evening for the event.

'We're short of money,' complained Ray. 'We can't keep

pace with that lot, and I don't like you trying. Company cars. Holidays abroad. Au pairs. Just one-upmanship. It's not what matters.'

'I'm merely trying to be sociable,' Angela replied. 'The boy needs to make friends. I need—' She cut herself short. 'I just don't want people to think we can't look after ourselves.'

Ray took her hand and led her from the kitchen. He sat her down in the sparsely furnished lounge and moved close beside her. 'It's not important what people think,' he said quietly. 'We've got each other, and we're all we need.'

Billy knew he was lying, because it was the opposite of what his father used to say when they had lived in town.

Too embarrassed to phone or call on her neighbours in person, Angela purchased some little invitation cards, filled them out in her best handwriting and slipped them through the letterboxes of the Prouts at number twelve, the Metcalfs at number fourteen and the Bovises at number fifteen.

As Billy's mother had no previous experience of home entertainment, she enlisted the help of her sister, Carol-Lynn, a good-natured bottle blonde whose husband was currently on remand for selling dodgy video recorders and who arrived weighed down with vegetables and fresh-cut flowers from the Caledonian Road market. She had a quick nose around the house, noted the waste disposal, the breakfast nook and the extra cupboard space, and made all the appropriate noises of approval, but it was clear that she didn't think much of the area. Nevertheless, she spent all day chopping and baking and boiling as she filled Angela in on the latest news from London, and then happily went home at six to feed her own three children, which was perfect timing because she didn't get on with Ray and he came in just as she was leaving.

For Billy, having drinks with the neighbours was as desirable as having to watch *Oklahoma!* on TV at Christmas, so he dropped hints with such clodhopping unsubtlety that Ray eventually allowed him to visit Oliver's house for the evening. At the last minute, though, Oliver's father changed his mind and made his son catch up on some overdue homework, so Billy found himself sitting on the couch beside Ray, waiting for the smiles and small talk to arrive.

Ken and Barbara Prout appeared promptly at eight with their son, Simon. All three of them were wearing the same clothes: pale blue jeans, white tennis shoes and matching cream sweaters. When they sat in a row on the couch it looked like faulty TV reception.

Simon proved too small and unruly to sit by the buffet table, so Angela arranged a special side seat for him. Barbara slowly circled the room, carefully studying everything with her wide eyes as if pricing the ornaments for an auction. Angela chatted to her awkwardly through the kitchen hatch as she removed trays of sausage rolls from the oven, then gave up after receiving no reply. Ray poured oversized drinks into the best glasses and tried to look at ease, as if this was how he spent every evening of his life. Billy was uncomfortable in the tight purple shirt his aunt Carol-Lynn had bought him, a market knock-off with an itchy collar, and watched the native rituals in silence.

As soon as Ken Prout revealed that DIY was his secret passion, Billy knew they were doomed. His father, who could barely bang a nail in straight and was relatively disinterested in hardware stores' discount systems, was struggling to maintain his attention even before the hot 'nibbles' had been set out.

'That's the marvellous thing about veneer,' said Ken, running his fingers over the serving hatch lintel, 'you'll never find a finish like that in nature. Not that Barbara notices my handiwork. She prefers bought things. You know,' he finished lamely, 'ready-made things you buy.'

Mercifully, the doorbell rang.

Ray and his son both attempted to answer the door.

Billy thought Georgina Bovis looked as if she had been wedged into clothes several sizes too small for her. Perhaps she wore outfits that belonged to a younger sister. Her pale breasts were thrust out, her stomach was pinched in and her dress was hitched up so much that she appeared to be imploding from the navel. Her hair, a shade of hesperidian red as yet undiscovered in the natural spectrum, was knotted in elaborate Grecian loops and curls. She was caked in heavy orange make-up that ended at her throat, so that it looked like she was wearing someone else's head. *Dynasty* was nearing the end of its television run, and she had copied the Joan Collins look, wearing shoulder pads that gave her the upper torso of a quarterback.

Her husband, Alan, was a broad collection of curves, in his late thirties but already jowled, his bulk contained by a tight grey office suit, a Marks & Spencer's tie and elastic-sided shoes. He sold advertising space for the *News of the World*. Georgina didn't appear to be built for work, or any kind of rapid movement. Someone had obviously told her that elegant people moved slowly, because she was creeping about the lounge like an action replay. The Bovises had an eleven-year-old daughter, Sherry, but tonight she had gone to football practice, much to the disgust of Georgina, who considered the sport and her tomboy daughter 'unlady-like'.

Bob and Daphne Metcalf arrived carrying a reasonable Chardonnay and an economical bunch of garage flowers. Their delinquent children were mercifully absent.

'Bob is a financial consultant for a well-known international soft drinks company,' Angela told her husband, inadvertently sounding like a game show hostess.

Daphne Metcalf wore an appliquéd fountain pen on her blouse as a display of her credentials and glared across at Alan, who was already on his second gin and tonic. Alan Bovis had never liked his condescending writer neighbour. She made tiny cat-coughs when anyone smoked within ten feet of her and peered distractedly over people's shoulders as she talked to them. Worse still, her books were pornographic trash, featuring sex scenes that, judging from the listless demeanour of her husband, were not rooted in experience.

Barbara Prout stood at the unlit fireplace and watched in silence as Angela carried in a tray of quiche Lorraine. From time to time her attention wandered vaguely to Simon, who was trying to remove his trousers, but she seemed to have no real interest in the child or anything else, and remained at the fireside in her Prout-clone outfit, distractedly watching the activity in the room like an underpaid spy.

Angela had settled on a stand-up buffet because their dining-room table was not large enough to accommodate everyone. She decided to follow some nicely arranged Sainsbury's paté with a beef stroganoff because it was inexpensive and sounded posh and there were so many people to feed. She studied the group through her serving hatch as butterflies settled in her stomach.

Unused to such gatherings, Billy felt surrounded by people who were exotic without being beautiful, like Venus flytraps. He could almost hear the cicadas in this jungle of neuroses and longed to be upstairs reading his book in cool, comfortable solitude. He imagined the assembled group as characters in an Agatha Christie novel, serially despatched in novel ways. A steel piton through Georgina's neck, pinning her to the wall; a wire garotte lifting Ken kicking from the table; a ground-glass martini slipping from Alan's hand as blood frothed over his teeth; razor blades tucked into Daphne's computer keyboard . . .

'. . . imaginative child, more sensitive. He doesn't really enjoy team games, do you, Billy? Always has his nose in a book, and if he isn't reading, he's making up stories.'

His mother was trying to make him sound special, and it wasn't working. They were looking at him as if he was an unpopular museum exhibit. He didn't want to be the centre of attention.

Ray stayed out of the conversation; he chased the group around the room, incrementally topping up drinks, and followed his son's example by keeping his mouth shut.

Georgina pulled the front of her décolletage even lower. At this rate only divine intervention could prevent her nipples from popping out like unwrapped fruit pastilles.

As they perched in various corners to eat from perilously flimsy cardboard plates (a market job lot supplied by Carol-Lynne, who said, 'They'll be fine so long as you don't put anything wet on them'), Billy eyed the assembled guests with poorly concealed horror. Ken Prout was going bald and had unwisely decided to groom the sides of his hair across his sparse top, like Desmond Morris. He appeared to have either too many teeth or too small a mouth, so that his face worked in a strange Muppet-like manner when he spoke, and he tended to lisp. His nose was enormous and covered in large open pores; it looked like part of his face had been deliberately magnified for examination purposes. He was an accountant for a large Croydon-based insurance firm and possessed a seemingly inexhaustible fund of stories about the insurance life, most of which involved sums of money he'd saved the company by finding ways of avoiding the payment of claims. But at least he had something to say, whereas Barbara Prout seemed to have been vacuumed clean of any conversation whatsoever. Billy could only assume that she was drugged. She stared at her son as if she hated him.

'I spoke to you once at the shops,' said Georgina Bovis, waggling a glitter-nailed finger at Daphne Metcalf. 'You're a writer. What have you written that I've read?'

'How do I know what you read?' replied Daphne rudely.

Georgina ignored the remark, choosing to reply to a question that hadn't been asked. 'My husband, Alan, works for a newspaper.'

'I thought you said he worked for the *News of the World*.'

Barbara meanwhile sectioned her paté meticulously and studied a small square. 'Do you have trouble blending this to the right texture?' she asked. 'I always add too much garlic.'

'Er ...' Angela looked nervously across at Ray for support.

'Are we going to be having a lot of meat?' asked Daphne in a polite-little-girl voice designed to make her hostess feel bad. 'Because I'm actually a vegetarian.' She had been a vegetarian for less than three months, but did not volunteer the fact.

'I'm so sorry,' flustered Angela. 'I didn't know. Can I just serve you some of the salad?'

'Don't worry yourself. Really, I'm fine. What's the main course?'

Everyone stared at the large earthenware pot that Billy's mother had just set in the centre of the table. There was a picture of a cow on the side of it.

'There are plenty of vegetables,' said Angela desperately.

Daphne gingerly raised the lid and winced. 'They've been sitting in the gravy. They're probably bloated with animal blood.'

'I haven't had this in ages,' said Georgina, joining Daphne at the pot. 'Beef stroganoff, isn't it? We used to make buckets of the stuff when we were art students. Very economical. You could stretch it for miles when you were on a tight budget.'

The men helped themselves and began chewing thoughtfully. Then after a while they just chewed. Their plates began to sag and leak.

Billy watched his mother pantomiming an interest in Ken's stories but saw how carefully she studied the others, making sure that at all times her family was doing the right thing. Angela's voice grew more refined during the course of the evening as she tried to remove the social barriers that she felt existed between them.

'How long have you lived here, Ken?' she asked, pointing out the wine bottle to her husband so that he could fill their neighbours' glasses.

'A little over two years,' said Ken. 'We were among the first to move in. Bought into the place at just the right time. Property's going to soar around here soon. Maggie's policies are really starting to pay off. This is prime commuter belt. Of course, when we arrived there were just fields beyond the next street, so you can imagine it was a nightmare with the boy.'

Ray must have looked puzzled, because Barbara added, 'Tracking in mud,' before lapsing back into silence. She toyed with her fork, pushing chunks of beef around her wilting plate, but ate virtually nothing. On several occasions when the conversation dried up, she checked her watch.

'Ray, didn't I see you at the garage this morning?' Georgina suddenly remembered. 'He's the man in the little glass box at Esso. Aren't you? You're in that funny little isolation booth behind the pumps.'

In a room full of professionals, the weight of this remark was quick to settle. Georgina failed to notice. As her husband ostentatiously drained his glass, she stabbed him with an angry glance. 'You won't get any more out of that bottle, you know, not without boiling the cork.'

'Have you had the pleasure of my wife?' asked Alan, accepting a refill from Ray as Georgina shot him another poisoned look. His slurred speech suggested that he may have had a drink or three before dinner. In fact, he'd been out with his Farringdon printers and on the piss since noon. 'She thinks monogamy is a type of wood. Don't get too near her or you'll fall in. No, she's a lovely woman really.'

'Bob tells me you were relocated here by Our Lady of Downing Street,' said Alan.

'I think we were in the way of progress,' admitted Ray. 'It was a bit of a shock, but we're settling in now.'

'This place must be a strain for you,' said Ken.

'They're subsidised.' Barbara pushed aside her untouched plate. 'Aren't you? Some sort of rent now, buy later scheme, isn't it? Another bright idea from the GLC loony lefties. Maggie can't seem to weed them out of local government.' Throughout the meal, she and her husband had constantly referred to the prime minister in a manner that implied they were old school friends.

Ray threw her a furious look. 'We had no choice in the matter,' he explained. 'We lived in my uncle's old house in Greenwich. They wanted to build a road through it. There was nothing we could do.'

'Unlikely,' said Ken. 'The plans for long-term road schemes are available upon request at your local council office and can be successfully petitioned against. Still, all's well that ends well, eh? I imagine this place is quite a step up for you. Nice to be given the chance to get out of the smoke and put down roots in the country's heartland.'

Billy tried to catch his mother's eye, but she was busy delivering a choice of desserts. She was very proud of her puddings, but everyone opted for the shop-bought chocolate mousse. Ken Prout had clearly remembered to take his conversation pills; he propelled the discourse through his staunch belief in his party's traditional family values ('You'll never see another call-girl scandal in parliament, not with Jeffrey Archer as deputy chairman'), past the problem of 'our tinted brethren' and their natural propensity for rioting ('You only have to watch black South Africans on the news, they can't stand still for a minute'), and on to the perils of cork flooring ('The good lady wife would never have twisted her ankle if she'd been wearing sensible shoes').

Billy could tell that his father wished everyone would just piss off home. Bob kept asking embarrassing questions about how much rent they were paying for the house, Daphne related every conversation topic back to her writing, Alan was drunk and appeared suddenly tired, as if he'd become unplugged, and Georgina started casting flirtatious glances at Ray.

His parents lacked the easy grace required to make this kind of occasion a success. What was the point of playing social one-upmanship if you had nothing to bid with? If they weren't good enough for their neighbours, then surely the reverse was also true. Nobody seemed to be having a very pleasant time. They looked as if they'd been stuck in a lifeboat together and were being forced to make the best of the situation. He was sure that any minute now someone would suggest a singsong to keep their spirits up. Billy didn't understand why they had bothered to accept the invitations at all.

Georgina started to tell a joke, but her husband tried to stop her. 'Christ, not this one again,' he complained. 'I hope you're not a Catholic, Daphne, you won't like the bit about the bishop and the blow job.'

'Examples of oral humour are always worth collecting,' said Daphne, smiling so brightly that the room temperature dropped. 'My historical novels require a wealth of background material. I research my facts mercilessly.'

'You do surprise me. I thought it was just a lot of fucking in hoop skirts.' Alan smirked and thrust his nose back in his glass. 'Research, eh? You must be knackered after a really long book.'

'Alan told me this joke,' said Georgina hastily, 'at a party we went to the night the Argies surrendered at Port Stanley. I remember distinctly, because it was the last time we made love.' She released a coarse, sarcastic laugh.

'Take no notice of her,' Alan instructed. 'My wife's clitoris is situated on the ground floor of Harvey Nichols.'

'I think you're being very rude,' said Daphne.

'Why do women always take offence?'

'We bruise easily.'

Alan snorted. 'So does old fruit.'

In Billy's eyes the Metcalfs, the Bovises and the Prouts were far less interesting than any of the March relatives back in the city. These people were suburban caricatures made flesh, a modern-day McGill postcard of insult and innuendo. He watched Simon Prout for a while. The child was putting chocolate mousse inside his pants, then picking his nose and burying the mined ore in his dessert.

Georgina stubbed a cigarette out in her mousse and asked Ray if he thought she needed breast reduction.

Daphne told Angela that she would have to read more if she ever hoped to improve herself.

Bob described the day-to-day office politics of an international soft drinks company to Billy, who feigned polite interest but was actually wondering what it would be like to ride into the Carpathian Mountains in the late nineteenth century like Dr Van Helsing, pursued by wolves.

Georgina told Angela that she was a freelance cosmetics representative for Estée Lauder and could probably do something with her droopy facial muscles.

Bob asked Ray if Ken Prout had managed to sell him insurance yet.

Angela asked if anyone wanted more coffee, then headed for the kitchen to start soaking the cutlery and calming her nerves.

Alan asked for a brandy and Ray was forced to admit that there weren't any after-dinner drinks in the house.

Billy felt himself passing out with boredom.

Mercifully, the evening ended early. When Barbara Prout discovered that her son had smeared his testicles with chocolate she released a horrified squeal and hoisted him from the room. On the doorstep a few minutes later, Ken tried to sell the Marches an insurance policy.

That was the cue for everyone else to leave.

Alan was so drunk that he slipped off the front step, released a shotgun fart and fell sideways into the hedge. Georgina kissed Billy's father goodnight and allowed her thigh to brush against his groin as she did so. Daphne waited impatiently by the gate for her husband with her arms folded, her shoulders hunched and a sour, flattened look on her face. Bob recognised the look and edited his small talk down to a fast 'Night all.'

Ray and Angela said goodnight to everyone, closed the front door thankfully and had an argument. The evening, they concluded, had not been an unqualified success.

Billy went up to bed with two books, Robert Graves' *Greek Myths, Volume I* and Ira Levin's *The Stepford Wives*.

'I could tell they didn't like us,' he heard his mother say.

'Fine by me,' replied Ray. 'I didn't like them.'

'That's not the point. We should at least try to fit in.'

'What, and have Billy end up like their kids? No bloody thank you.'

The matter was closed. They never tried again, and the dinner offer was not reciprocated by any of the three families the Marches invited over during their first month in Invicta Cross.

CHAPTER EIGHT

The Goddess of the Hearth

'Placed and built anonymously, [suburban houses] express isolation, lack of relationship, and fail to create human bonds in which people feel themselves part of the fabric which connects them to their fellow men.' – Christopher Alexander

'I AM *waiting for something terrible to occur,*' Billy wrote in his diary. '*The worst situations creep up on you like incoming tides, and you don't see what's happening until it's too late and you are completely cut off.*'

Autumn gave way to an early, bitter winter. Clotheslines froze, street lights glittered with frost, and the hardy dog-walkers of Invicta Cross abbreviated their routes.

One evening, Billy's mother announced that she had found a way of earning money, although she did not sound very pleased about it. She had taken a position as a cashier, she said, over at Val-U-Rite, just until something more permanent could be worked out. Billy knew that the job would be humiliating for her; she would have to serve the ladies of the neighbourhood. In Invicta Cross, the women were wives first and foremost. If they worked, they took professional positions and commuted or held local jobs of discreet gentility, helping out at the Oxfam shop or organising fundraisers for needy children. They worked in order to have something to do.

An imperceptible wall rose between the March family and everyone else. The older residents were relieved, as if a natural order had been restored. These cuckoos who had appeared among the nicely feathered nests of Balmoral Close had found their natural level in service, and those who had felt uncomfortable socialising with a working-class family could rest easy once more.

After school Billy sometimes visited Ray at the garage, where an endless stream of Land Rovers, Volvos, BMWs and Mercedes required attention. His father sat on a high stool in his glass box next to the pumps, selling air fresheners, de-icer, microwaved enchiladas, music cassettes, oddly coloured flowers and sacks of Bar-B-Q charcoal. The shop smelled of petrol, woodland pine and cooked meat in various degrees and looked out onto a concrete square with two tall white poles supporting a gigantic illuminated flat roof. On the other side of the road was a Texaco garage, and this had a glass supermarket box constructed in distorted mirror image to its rival, so that the two managers could sit and stare at each other all day.

When it became clear that Ray was bothered by him hanging around the garage witnessing how little he had to do, Billy began visiting his mother instead, but the Val-U-Rite supervisor argued, no doubt correctly, that he was affecting her concentration and banned him from the store while she was on the checkout. Angela was the oldest woman on the tills, surrounded by teenaged foreign students from Crawley. A few were friendly but most kept to themselves, and besides, there was little opportunity to talk. She passed the jars and packets before the new computerised barcode reader with mechanical precision, its red X illuminating her face from below, and thought of other times and places in an effort to stem the numbness she felt creeping over her. When she looked up she saw women curving insignificantly away from her in rows, fifteen on one side, seventeen on the other, all making the same rhythmic motion. It was like being trapped between a pair of endlessly refracting mirrors.

Angela saw less of her husband now because their schedules clashed. On the occasions when she served one of the wives from the close, she nodded politely and said nothing. Convinced as a child that she was beneath notice, she had always lacked self-confidence, and now those seedling fears planted by her parents had found reason to take root.

At night a row of storm-damaged elms clattered angrily in the wind at the other end of the close. The road bothered Billy. He had discovered on his first bicycle trip through the town that Balmoral Close crossed Windsor Terrace and continued in a broad curve toward a barren field, where it should have ended in another close of houses, but for some reason the road was not finished. It came to a dead end, the tarmac and paving stones petering out into mud pools and spiny clumps of grass. He showed it to Oliver. Billy felt uncomfortable standing there at the edge of their little world, beneath the last buzzing streetlight, listening to the wind sighing in the trees. The broken road bothered him because it had been built with great purpose, and yet led nowhere. It was the point at which civilisation came to an end, and beyond was just darkness, as if the Promethean trick of creating a civilisation from serpent's teeth had failed on such barren land. Here Hestia, goddess of the hearth, had built a town, her houses protected by sacred fire, but without human warmth even they had grown cold and died, and no earthly flame could rekindle them.

'It's weird,' he whispered, 'the town's just a few feet away from nothing.'

'We're just a few feet from nothing wherever we go,' said Oliver. 'They stick bricks and tar on top of the fields and tell us it's civilisation, but the streets can be taken away again. The past is just – under – here.' He stamped a boot on the cracked concrete and looked out at the night. 'A really big storm could peel this town up and suck it away into the clouds.'

'I'd like to see that.'

'You may not have to wait too long,' said Oliver darkly.

The two boys fell silent and stared off into the unforgiving susurrant woodlands.

The Lookout Tower

'In 1980, the New York City Health Department reported a city total of 1,207 human bites requiring emergency medical treatment, up 24% from the previous year's figures.' – United Press International

IT WAS much higher than he had realised. The square brick tower was older than the rest of the building, but the whole place was now derelict. Although it had most recently functioned as an electricity generating station, the property had once belonged to the water board. The rusting metal doors were still assigned with lightning-bolt warnings, and bulbous steel shafts rose like the components of an old valve-operated radio, but the tower was another matter altogether, its elaborate structure with absurd little turrets and decorative brick balconies encrusted with the corbels and brattices of a medieval keep. The Victorians had managed to romanticise as lowly a structure as a water tower, and it had survived the changing utility of the surrounding building. Now, being the only structure of interest for miles around, it was closed to the public. But not for much longer.

From where he stood astride his bicycle, Billy could

make out a metal ladder running up one side of a turret. If the entrance to the stairwell was blocked, it should be possible to scale the steel rungs all the way up to the roof and look out across the town. But the area around the plant was sealed off; razor wire adorned the walls, and the main gates were padlocked, although there didn't seem to be any kind of security system in operation.

At school the following Monday, he asked Oliver about it.

'Too dangerous.' Oliver hitched his glasses back up his nose gloomily. 'You're not thinking of breaking in there, are you? Two years ago some kid climbed inside and got electrocuted. Fried to a blackened crisp. They swept him up into a dustpan.'

'But the power must be shut off now.'

'Who knows? Perhaps they left something on by mistake.'

Billy studied his friend. Oliver was the palest boy in school. This was because he sometimes helped his father at the weekends ('Only in the front office,' he was quick to stress, 'I'm not allowed back with the coffins') and Mr Price felt that a suntan was disrespectful on a mourner.

'How many dead people have you seen, do you reckon?' asked Billy. They were sitting in the cafeteria watching the rest of the class hammering up and down a wintry football field. He and Oliver were two of the four boys in class who were never chosen to play for the teams. The other two were Raymond, who had one leg shorter than the other and wore a steel brace, and Leslie, who had once told his teacher that he was a woman trapped in the body of a man.

'Phew, tons,' said Oliver casually. 'It's no big deal.

They're all pretty much the same. Sort of blotched and saggy. I can take you to see one if you want.'

'Your dad would never let you,' said Billy.

'You're right; he says I don't have enough respect for the dead. He says I'd make a good serial killer because I lack a moral dimension and have no sense of remorse. Cool, eh?'

'Yeah, neat. I feel like I see dead people all the time around here.'

'Maybe the whole town died and nobody noticed yet.'

'Maybe your dad decided to save on coffins and has been propping up his customers in bus shelters.'

'Maybe they're all cursed, like the Flying Dutchman, only they're doomed to roam Val-U-Rite with their trolleys for all eternity.'

They had a good laugh at that. Billy felt that he and his new friend shared the same end-of-the-dial wavelength. Oliver had shunned the technological revolution in order to read more books, so he usually understood what Billy was rattling on about. Most of the other kids were gradually becoming sealed inside the wonderful world of video.

'Can I ask you something?' said Oliver.

'Fire away.'

Oliver took a bite of his cheese and mustard pickle sandwich and watched the distant flurries of mud that indicated battling football players. 'Why do you hate it here so much?'

'It's the most boring place I've been to apart from my cousin Ashley's house, and he spends his weekends re-running old episodes of *Star Trek* trying to spot continuity errors and writing to Gene Roddenberry about them.'

'I've never lived anywhere else, so I've got nothing to compare it to. We were here long before the new town was built, back when there were only five houses.'

'What was it like then?'

'You could hear a cow fart half a mile away. We nearly moved when my dad got divorced, but we won't now that he gets the Crawley overspill. There are a lot of old people in Crawley. He was so busy in last winter's sudden cold snap, he nearly expanded.'

'How often do you visit London?'

'We never travel. My dad has a prostate problem that won't allow him to sit down for anything longer than the news headlines.'

'You mean you've never been there?' Billy was amazed. 'Not even once?'

'Not once. Dad talks about the place as if it's hell on earth. My mother moved there to be with her fancy man. An asthmatic shoe salesman called Dirk. How low can you get?'

Two days later, Billy convinced Oliver that they should skip school and go up to London for the day. Oliver always had money on him and agreed to pay their way in return for being shown the sights. The funeral director's son had never visited a city larger than Croydon. His father's hatred of London was inextricably linked to his wife's infidelity. He regularly escaped the smell of formaldehyde by heading onto the windswept Sussex Downs and rejoicing in the pungent reek of cow dung.

Billy was sure that if he went to London with Oliver something mystical would happen and he would receive a sign to show that the goddess of the city regretted losing him.

On the appointed morning, the two boys left early and

met at East Grinstead's railway station, dumped their school ties in their backpacks and caught a train to Charing Cross. From the carriage window endless rows of suburban houses passed like ridges of discoloured teeth, slowly giving way to blank rectangles of tarmac and concrete, then the fuliginous stone walls of factories and warehouses. Finally garish 96-sheet billboards replaced any visible humanity, and they crossed the burnished brown river to Charing Cross station.

They alighted before the train had barely stopped.

At the bottom of the steps leading down from Villiers Street to the river, they paused to look at a bearded homeless man who was prostrate on the pavement, wrapped in a voluminous white blanket, his head resting against a concrete fresco. A friend bent beside him, clutching his hand. They looked like figures from a forgotten biblical painting.

In the space of a few hours they circled Cleopatra's Needle on the bulb-beribboned Embankment, walked over the poems etched into the worn paving stones opposite the Houses of Parliament, passed the grey gryphons guarding the Holborn viaduct and the hobbled ravens of the Bloody Tower, drank coffee beside the booksellers setting up their tables beneath Waterloo bridge, pushed through the tourists clustered expectantly around Eros to reach the theatre lights of Shaftesbury Avenue, played video games in the Old Compton Street arcade, and ogled the dull-eyed girls in the windows of the Brewer Street strip joints. They turned north by the curved park railings and the creamy pediments of the Regents Park houses, past wide gravel drives and Grecian friezes picked out in white like carefully iced cake decorations.

In the afternoon they returned to the city's heart, and in a nearly deserted Trafalgar Square the air suddenly stilled, so that they raised their heads and listened, searching the canescent skies. For a moment it seemed that even the traffic was silent, and the only sound was the wind shifting the fountain plumes as it crossed the square.

Billy stared at the great dark Landseer lions, and suddenly his vision was obscured by the diagonal static of drifting snow. He looked around at Oliver and laughed. Snow! In moments the lions were all but obliterated in the swirling flurries. Even the pigeons had settled on the ground, subdued by the spectacle. Billy capered around his bemused friend like a mad creature, delighted in the way that such a simple, natural phenomenon could transform a city. He looked across the square to Whitehall, where the snowflakes were no doubt settling in the bristles of the guards' busbies, and to the entrance of the Mall, where he felt sure that the Queen had risen from her bureau and gone to the window, momentarily lost in thought. To achieve such a transformation so effortlessly, and then as the snowfall ended to return to normal so quickly was one of the city's secrets. There were others, many others, but Billy knew that they would remain concealed until an appropriate occasion.

They headed home, their heads tipsily buzzing with the sights they had seen. Oliver was sworn to secrecy on receipt of a promise that they would plan another trip for the following month.

It was dark by the time the train drew into Invicta Cross. Street lamps dotted the silent town, as precisely spaced as the lights of landing strips.

Billy just managed to make it back in time for tea, but

there was a strained atmosphere in the little house, and his mother looked as if she had been crying. The meal was perfunctory, and afterwards, when they usually gathered around the television, his parents remained in the kitchen talking.

He gleaned a garbled version of events, something to do with Angela being insulted at the supermarket. He listened carefully. A heated argument. A cruel insult. Hurt feelings. Talk of resignation. His mother had a gentility ill suited to name-calling. He screened out his parents' anxious voices and concentrated on the television, where a young actress was explaining that her life had become much more fulfilling now that she had found a way to control her dandruff. Bored, he rose and headed upstairs.

Quietly unlocking his bedroom door Billy slipped inside, turned on the light and surveyed his handiwork. He wished he had a brother to help him. Perhaps he would recruit Oliver for the task. He would need help with the electrics. He dug out a cassette by the Smiths, 'Meat is Murder', and inserted it into his player.

Billy had begun to build an elaborate model of the town, constructing it in balsawood, cardboard and plastic. He was in the process of tracing the road layouts and scaling them up from an Ordnance Survey map. Only a couple of buildings were in place on the four-foot-square piece of hardboard the builders had left behind, but they were already threatening to push beyond their allotted ground-space. In order to include the school and the supermarket he would have to attach another section of board. The map accurately provided him with the town's scale and co-ordinates but failed to breathe life into the model. He had no way of depicting the backs of buildings, the gardens, the areas invisible from the streets. The only existing photographs of Invicta Cross were in the community centre and could not be removed. To capture the essence of the place would take something more.

He was not sure why he had started the model, except that it seemed a necessary thing to do if he was ever to feel comfortable living here. At least it was a more constructive pastime than taking the kitchen clock to bits, something his grandfather – and now his father – always did when bored.

Half an hour later his parents began rowing again, so Billy increased the volume of the Smiths cassette and switched his attention from the miniaturised town to a battered library copy of Angus Wilson's *Encyclopedia of Murder*. He was shocked by the strange reasons people had for wanting to kill one another. Infidelity figured highly, of course, but so did boredom, intolerance and bravado. Sometimes murderers appeared normal all their lives, then in a single brief dilation of horror committed violence so dreadful that it scarred their every waking moment until death.

While his parents argued on in the room below, he fell asleep with the book nestled in the crook of his arm.

On Friday evening Billy left school early and headed for the water tower. It was already growing dark when he arrived, but he had brought a torch as well as a sketchbook, pens and various tools borrowed from the makeshift workshop his father had set up in the spare room. Ray's wirecutters weren't strong enough to break through the rusty chains binding the side gates, but he was able to scale the weed-covered wall and lower himself down the other side with a length of nylon clothesline.

The door to the tower presented more of a problem, as a modern Yale lock had been fitted to keep it tightly sealed. Luckily, the Pre-Raphaelite pretensions of the architecture had demanded a pair of fake arrow slits on either side of the wall above the doorway, and these had become damaged over the years, so much so that he was able to crumble the soft red brick and allow himself entry.

Inside was a freezing stone chamber that contained a dozen flights of stairs. He ascended amid the rattle and burble of acrid-smelling pigeons, and at the top, after forcing the small door, found an arched room that overlooked the entire town.

He realised at once that from here he would be able to study the area and provide his model with the form and colour it would otherwise lack. He cleared a patch by the north parapet, which overlooked the streets around the little house in Balmoral Close, and began to sketch.

CHAPTER TEN

The Witch's Daughter

'David Demers of Clearwater, Florida, has been receiving death threats from all over America because he decided to get rid of his three-legged dog by leaving it in the middle of the freeway tied to a bowling ball.' – *West Palm Beach Post*

RAY CARED about his wife's happiness; he just could not do anything to help her. What had happened was something that would not bother a man. Indeed, he had a hard time seeing what the fuss was about.

Women were and would always remain a mystery to Billy's father. While talk-show husbands discussed the empathy they felt for their wives, Ray remained on the outside of their world looking in. His mother, a cantankerous, hardworking woman who had ruled their household like the foreman of a road gang, allowed no male to know her thoughts. In those days, revealing feelings was a sign of weakness. His bemused father had quietly acquiesced. Now Ray struggled to understand his own wife.

Angela was being deliberately ignored by the other women at the supermarket; not the cashiers, but the customers. Barbara Prout, Daphne Metcalf, Georgina

Bovis and the others were giving her the cold shoulder, and when they weren't doing that they were insulting her in stage whispers and purposely making her job harder, switching foodstuffs after she had already rung them up, blocking the aisle with shopping carts and complaining loudly about the service.

Ray figured that being cut dead in the local supermarket wasn't exactly the worst thing in the world and that Invicta Cross was still a good place to live. He suggested to his wife that she should go to the community centre on Brunswick Parade and join a few local societies.

Angela had no skill in social integration but was determined not to be excluded from everyday life in the town. She appreciated that the women formed cliques and found it difficult to accept new faces, but she could not understand the vehemence of their rejection. Whether she was working at the supermarket or doing her own shopping, she never failed to register each sly glance and mocking tone until she became hypersensitive, checking every look and remark to see if it included a personal slight. If it did, she told her husband that evening and watched as his frustration grew.

She visited the Invicta Cross Community Centre and spoke to a raw-faced young woman named Sandra Brickett whom she had sometimes seen entering a house at the other end of Balmoral Close. Sandra informed her that, sadly, most of the clubs that admitted women – bowls, social, handicrafts and rotary – had closed membership at the present time. She intimated that the women's golf society might eventually have a vacancy but stressed the steep membership fee with a relish that suggested it was beyond Angela's ability to pay.

Instead, Billy's mother joined the Invicta Cross Knitting Circle and was introduced to half a dozen elderly ladies, none a day under seventy, who clacked their needles in silence and occasionally cast their shapeless woollens aside to confer on bladder problems. That was her first and only visit.

Although shiftwork left Angela with little time on her hands, she tried to join the art club, the cycling club and the library club, and in every instance was smugly informed by Sandra Brickett that membership was presently unavailable. When Ray would no longer listen to his wife's tales, she turned to her son for comfort, and Billy dutifully recorded each new transgression in his red notebook, promising not to let these perceived grievances go unpunished.

Ray had his own problems; the Marches were consuming capital, not that they had much in the way of savings to begin with. Unless a way could be found to earn more money they would be forced to give up the house, even with its subsidised rent. When Ray visited his bank in Croydon, the only practical measure suggested by the junior clerk who saw him was that he should get a better paid job, or find something to sell.

Oddly enough, when the opportunity to sell something came along, he did not take it.

It was a Sunday morning, warm for the start of November. The street's weekly car-waxing marathon had commenced; buckets of soapy water were being sluiced across bonnets, tins of Simonize and T-Cut were being prised open with screwdriver blades, interiors were being transformed into olfactory pine forests with dashboard sprays, and somebody came to call on Ray March.

The proffered hand belonged to a tall, good-looking

man in his early thirties with immaculately waved blond hair and a sharp white smile. His name was Justin Brickett, and he said, 'I do believe your wife knows my wife.'

Unaccustomed to such a display of friendliness, Ray stepped back and silently ushered the neighbour in. Angela emerged from the kitchen and matched the look of surprise on her husband's face. It was hard to believe that this elegantly dressed man was married to a woman as plain and pompous as Sandra Brickett.

'Mrs March,' he cried, shaking her hand, 'this is a pleasure. I've heard so much about you.'

As she cautiously accepted his grip, Angela could imagine what he'd heard. Justin was wearing a red cashmere polo sweater, checked blue trousers and tasselled brown loafers. He looked like an American golfer.

'I hope you're settling in nicely.' He exuded the geniality of a game show host as he wandered into the lounge.

'Well, it hasn't been quite—'

'Got to know a few friendly faces,' he said, cutting across her, 'which is good, it really is, because that's what it's all about really, isn't it, families getting together and making friends, sharing good times together, and that's where Christian charity really does begin.'

He wants a donation, thought Ray instantly. He's god squad and it's Sunday. Shit.

'My wife has probably told you about the work I do at the centre, my efforts for the Young Christian Brotherhood at St Peters.'

'Would you like a cup of tea?' asked Angela, always her first line of defence.

'Thank you, Angela, hope you don't think I'm being too familiar.'

Justin produced a pipe and proceeded to light it. This was the item required to complete his image, making him look like a 1970 Littlewoods' catalogue model, the sort of person you turned over a page to find standing in a pair of Y-fronts checking his watch. Ray followed him to the French windows.

'Nice garden you have there,' said Justin, sucking wetly at his pipe. 'Funny to think that this was just waste ground a couple of years ago. They couldn't do much with the land left between the two end houses, so they built this place, did you know that? Nobody wanted to buy it, so it was eventually offered to the government at a knockdown price.'

'You know a lot about this road, then.'

'I dabble in real estate. Give them a hand at the local branch, offer advice, sort out conveyancing problems, that sort of thing,' he said airily. 'Being one of the oldest residents, I know the area pretty well, I can tell you. I was just thinking, you could have a bit of a problem here.' He tapped the glass with his pipe stem.

'What sort of problem?' asked Ray defensively.

'Subsidence.' The smoke chugging from his pipe burst in a hazy halo against the window. 'This ground behind you is marshland, always has been. Pretty soon more houses will be built to the rear of the close, and the area's water table will change for the worse. We advised them not to add another property here. Marshes never really go away, they're just held at bay. You could find yourself with a sunken garden that no insurance company would agree to pay out for. Not to mention having to spend a fortune in drainage and damp courses.'

Angela sent her husband a look of concern. Justin gazed

back at the lawn, but this time his eyes had fastened greedily on something in the distance. 'Still, you could actually make a bit of money for yourself.'

'Oh, how?'

'See your side path, here. If you got rid of your garage and the path and resited the fence over this way, it would leave a perfect square.'

'What do I want a perfect square for?'

'To sell, of course. A nice little plot of land.'

'But you said it was sinking.'

'If you sold to a commercial concern, anyone building on the ground would drain the land first. It wouldn't be your responsibility.'

Ordinarily Ray would not have listened, but he remembered the mountain of bills that were still to be paid. 'I'd have to keep my car in the street.'

'That wouldn't be a problem, surely.' Justin had obviously seen the mismatched paintwork on the March family car.

'And the garden we'd be left with would be tiny,' added Ray, puzzled. 'We've never had a garden before.'

'I mean to say,' Justin leaned forward through a wreath of pipe smoke and smiled, 'if you're short of a few bob, it seems like the perfect way to make some money.'

'Who said we were short? We're fine.'

'All right, old chap, keep your shirt on, it's just that a little dickie bird told me you could use some folding readies, that's all.'

'Who said that? Who's been saying we need money?'

'Never you mind, it was just an idea.'

'Well, you tell Mr Whoever-it-is to mind his own bloody business in future.'

'I didn't mean to offend you, Ray. I just wanted to help. I know someone who might be interested in such a plot of land, and thought I'd—'

'I don't care what you thought,' Ray snapped indignantly, 'we don't need any help from you or your friends.'

'Have it your own way.' Justin raised his hands. 'I'm only being neighbourly.'

Just then Angela returned to the lounge with a laden tray.

'I won't stay for tea, Mrs March, thanks all the same. Must get on; we're having people over for brunch. Hope to see you at one of our St Peter's coffee mornings some time. I can see myself out.'

Justin Brickett sailed into the hall leaving a wake of Old Briar fumes.

'Did you mention something to his wife about us needing money?' Ray was apoplectic.

'No, of course not,' said Angela. 'What on earth did you say to offend him?'

They were still arguing about the visit when Billy collected his bicycle from the hall and announced that he was off to take a look at a dead body.

The sudden hail of lemons that exploded from behind the wall of leaves caught him so much by surprise that the back wheel of his bicycle skidded around him, and he was flung over the handlebars onto the wet lawn.

She emerged sheepishly from the hedge and helped him back onto his feet. The citrus fruit rolled along the walkways and into the gutter as he wiped himself down.

'The bottom of the bag was wet,' she explained. 'It broke. Are you all right?'

Billy raised the bicycle and examined it. There seemed to be no damage. He looked around his feet, puzzled.

'What do you need so many lemons for?'

'My mother,' she replied, crouching to gather them. 'The juice is good for her skin.' He took a careful look at her now. Frizzy auburn hair pushed back with a tortoiseshell slide, old school raincoat, thick black stockings on stick-thin legs.

'My name's April Barrow,' she said, dropping lemons into her gym bag. 'Who are you?'

'Billy March. We go to the same school.'

'I know,' replied April. 'I've seen you. You don't have any friends, do you? You're always sitting by yourself.' She sounded almost hopeful.

'I have plenty of friends,' he said defensively. 'You just haven't seen me with them.'

'It's okay, I don't have any friends either.' She rose to her feet and looked back at the sky. Heavy black storm clouds filled the far end of Gaveston Crescent. 'It's going to pour with rain any minute. I'd better be going.'

It seemed important not to let April leave just yet. He found another lemon under the hedge and handed it to her. 'You shouldn't tell people you don't have friends. It makes them think there's something wrong with you.'

She accepted the lemon, zipped up her bag and turned to leave. 'There is something wrong with me.'

'I can't see anything abnormal from here.'

'That's because most people look the same on the outside, so you can't see how they really are. People are like wasps' nests. Smooth on the surface, buzzing and angry inside.'

'Are you upset, then?'

She turned to face him. 'Yes, of course I am.'

'What about?'

'You don't really want to know. This is a set-up. You just want me to think you're interested. You'll pretend to be a friend then you'll tip pig's blood all over me. I saw *Carrie*. That's what they call me in class.'

'You've got the wrong picture of me.' He leaned his bicycle against a nearby plane tree and folded his arms.

She was taller than him, around the same age, and although she was as pale as Oliver and wore no make-up, she had extraordinarily rosy cheeks, like a healthy child in a thirties advertisement.

She pursed her lips and thought for a moment. 'My father died when I was seven, and my mother went crazy, so I went to live with my aunt. Then the doctor said my mother was better, and we moved here. But she's not better, she's just learned how to hide her feelings. She'll pass them on to me, and there's nothing I can do about it.'

'Craziness doesn't work like that.'

'It's a hereditary disease, Billy March, and I come from a long line of lunatics. We die young, and we have only ourselves to blame. Tobias Smollett once said, "One half of the nation is mad, and the other not very sound." These days even ordinary people behave strangely. It's a reaction to oppression. Abnormality upsets the status quo. Nature obliterates the outsider. Anyway, it was nice meeting you.'

'Wait! Perhaps we could get together and have a normal conversation some time.' He grabbed the bicycle and began wheeling it after her. The first fat drops of rain had begun to spatter the pavement. 'You can't put me off that easily. The mad act might work with the other people round here, but not with me. I see through you. You want to be friends.'

It was starting to rain hard now. She pulled up a gabardine hood, and her eyes were lost in shadow. 'You think so, do you?'

'Er, yes.'

'And is my desire reciprocated?'

'Absolutely.'

'My mother says I have strange ideas.'

'So do I. I have all sorts of strange ideas.'

'Name one.'

Billy racked his brains. 'I have this theory that Invicta Cross is actually a graveyard. Everyone here has died but they won't stay buried.'

'That's not very strange at all,' April said, moving slowly off into the rain. 'I think it's a perfect place. Except for the fields. Too many clumps of grass and funny-shaped trees. They're all in the wrong places and it's nowhere near flat enough.'

Then she was gone, lost in a descending curtain of drizzle, and Billy was left wondering whether April Barrow was demented or just bored, and what she could possibly have meant by her last remark.

CHAPTER ELEVEN

The Silver Clasp

'In 1989 a wave of food-throwing from speeding cars broke out in the East London suburbs; a 54-year-old jogger suffered stomach injuries from a hurled cabbage, a 58-year-old woman lost the sight of one eye from a thrown egg and a man died after a turnip punctured his lung. Since then there have been a further 23 incidents involving injuries caused by melons, potatoes, cabbages and more eggs. Police fear the attacks are spreading.' – *Daily Telegraph*

JUSTIN BRICKETT moved away from the glass wall that separated him from the empty streets and returned to his cluttered office on the first floor of the Invicta Cross Community Centre. There were dozens of pink and blue cardboard folders requiring his urgent attention, but he was unable to settle this morning. His conversation with Ray March still rankled. He disapproved of having his community littered with dropouts from the city. People like the Marches brought nothing but trouble; their offspring were precocious and dissatisfied, fraternised with undesirables and bred insurrection in the classroom. The pupils of Sherington Senior School, where Justin taught religious education, were easily swayed by tales of urban adventure. One minute they were quietly preparing for their exams, the next they were fans of some troublesome working-class band, wearing their baseball caps backwards and strutting about like the black city boys.

Justin was determined that it wouldn't happen here. He had read about the corruption of communities from within, how a few bad apples spoiled it for everyone. He'd already seen Ray March's temper, the anger of a junkyard dog protecting its litter. A pity, because he had hoped they could come to an amicable settlement, and now there was clearly no chance of that happening.

He ran a hand through his glistening blond locks and exhaled. What to do, what to do? His fingers drummed the desktop. He dug out the housing file and pulled it to the top of the pile.

The March family's house had indeed been an afterthought, the last to be built in the close. Determined to wring every last penny from its investment, Invicta Estates had squeezed number thirteen between the existing properties, ignoring the fact that the land behind would then be access restricted. At the time, it wasn't a problem. To the rear of the close lay a large area of barren waste ground that no one had ever shown the remotest interest in purchasing.

But then the Yuppie had been invented.

The property market had shifted from bust to boom, the town had won a fistful of government grants as it soaked up Greater London's commuter overspill, and suddenly everyone was looking for cheap land.

Sensing that there was money to be made, Justin had traced the ownership of the property to two elderly brothers, retired farmers who were now too frail to work the fields properly. It was only when one of the pair fell ill that the uncomfortable reality of the situation became apparent to them, and the remaining healthy brother succumbed to the generous offer proposed by Justin's property company.

The scheme was simple; through their church connections and their work at the Invicta Cross Community Centre, the Bricketts had been able to form a co-operative with several of their neighbours, and quickly raised the money to purchase the overgrown property. What they neglected to tell the vendor, who had naively hoped that the ground could be preserved in its original form by turning it into a recreation area, was that Justin Brickett's property group had already drawn up plans to transform the site into a golf course. The soil was perfect for landscaping, the catchment area ideal. It was just what the town needed to attract serious money.

There was just one snag.

No one had expected Invicta Estates to complete their quota by building another house at the end of Balmoral Close. The council ruled that the developers were acting within their rights. The two deals passed each other in the pipeline, one accidentally destroying the other. The farmers sold up and retired, the site became the property of Balmoral Close Co-operative Land, but the proposed deal with the company who had been commissioned to create the golf course was placed on indefinite hold, because now the limited access to the property contravened the council's minimum building requirements.

The March family moved into the newly created number thirteen, unaware that they blocked the entrance to a goldmine.

It wasn't as if Justin and his partners needed the whole of the property. Fifteen feet would do it, a miserable alley five yards wide that would create a driveway to the proposed clubhouse and sports shop. They had tried transposing the site, so that the course began at the north end of the grounds instead of the south, but it was impossible; the soil was too soft to support the building's foundations and, due to the land's problematic water table, there was only one possible area to site the proposed lake which was such an integral part of the design.

If only the government had placed a middle-class family in the house, thought Justin, people who wished to better themselves and who understood the values of property and community, they would surely have seen reason and offered to sell or exchange – but no. One visit with the Marches told him all he needed to know about them. They were the descendants of artisans, labourers, machinists, seamstresses and carpenters, workers ants who kept their heads down and brought home the bacon, who got drunk and knocked their wives about, who sponged off the state and bred illegitimate children, who aspired to nothing more than the latest Ford or the biggest television set.

He knew that this was just the thin edge of the wedge; others would soon follow, and what the community had worked so hard to create here would become diluted and destroyed. City kids brought drugs, their parents spread moral lassitude. Perhaps this was a natural development, this fanning out of bad behaviour, a symptom of the times that decent people were powerless to alleviate.

Justin Brickett never stopped to wonder if he was wrong. As far as he was concerned, the meek had no right to inherit the earth.

*

Billy should never have told his parents. His father had a Victorian attitude to death. Happy to search for portents and omens forewarning of sudden demise, Ray still refused to allow any serious discussion of the subject in his presence. Finding out that his son had been taken into a funeral parlour and shown a corpse greatly disturbed him, as though by viewing a dead body the boy had somehow tracked death into their house like mud.

Ray's fears stemmed from seeing an ancient aunt laid out in the front room, an event that presaged his mother's long illness. His childhood had been filled with colourful cautions from superstitious relatives who happily filled his head with rubbish; budgerigars brought doom, cats caused the deaths of unborn children, and you never passed a chair across a table for fear of causing an argument. In their old city setting, these beliefs sat comfortably among the back-to-back houses of communal slums. Here in Invicta Cross the cold light of common sense settled on the sterile streets, and Ray adapted as best he could.

He could not forbid Billy to hang out with Oliver; the boy had no other real friends – but he did decide to keep his son home more often. Since working at the garage on shifts, Ray was concerned that he was not spending enough time with Billy. As events turned out, he needn't have worried, because he was about to start spending much more time at home.

One damp Tuesday morning during the second week in November, a customer paid for a tank of unleaded petrol with money taken from a scuffed silver clip filled with ten-pound notes, which he tapped impatiently on the counter of the garage shop. That evening, the customer, a Dr Ernest

McMann, returned to the garage and insisted that he had left the silver clip on the counter.

The doctor demanded to see the garage supervisor, and an argument arose, fuelled by Ray's indignation at being obliquely accused of dishonesty. McMann was the local GP, considered by everyone to be beyond reproach.

'Are you absolutely sure you didn't pocket it by mistake?' asked his boss, a ginger-haired boy named Dave, sixteen years his junior. Ray knew that a quick-flaring temper was his downfall and tried to control himself.

'Of course I'm sure,' he said. 'The thing had a silver shield with a blue stone in the centre. I remember it distinctly. I would never have picked it up without realising.'

'Then I'm afraid I must ask you to turn out your pockets.'

Determined to receive an apology, Ray did so, triumphantly emptying his wallet, keys and a handful of coins onto the counter. He looked from one uncertain face to the other.

'There. Happy now?'

It was clear from the look in McMann's eyes that the doctor was unconvinced by this display, however, and he insisted on calling the police. The three of them sat in embarrassed silence waiting until a stony-faced officer arrived, but PC Morris Diller was unable to resolve the problem. McMann repeated his accusation and Ray's worn patience broke.

'This is ridiculous,' he shouted. 'I deal with money all the time. Either I'm trusted enough to be believed when I tell you something, or I work elsewhere.'

'Perhaps you should work somewhere else, then,' said

Dave, whose younger brother already had his eye on the job.

Unable to stop himself, Ray released a spectacularly abusive diatribe that shocked them all. After the disgruntled doctor took his leave, it was mutually decided that a termination of employment would be the best solution.

Unable to face his family's questions, Ray headed for the Helicopter and proceeded to get drunk on the little money he had left.

There was another row at home that night. Billy lay in bed with the pillow stuffed over his ears. He tried repeating an incantation, a mantra that would force his parents to lower their voices and embrace in silent reconciliation, but the magic powers he was sure he had once possessed were gone; they no longer worked as they had in Westerdale Road; nothing worked as it used to. The necromantic abilities he had carried with him from the city were fading and would soon be lost forever, leaving his family unprotected and open to infinite harm. 'Something terrible will happen soon,' he had written in the red leather diary, and part of him perversely longed for chaos.

CHAPTER TWELVE

A Map of the Mind

'The suburbs of London cling to one another like onions on a rope. The houses delight in a uniformity of ugliness, staring you out of countenance with three windows in front and a little green door at one side, giving to each house the appearance of having had a paralytic stroke.' – J. F. Murray, 1843

NOVEMBER PASSED in a blast of wet leaves, and the laden skies turned to wintry jaundice. The one bright spot was the awaited reappearance of April Barrow, who had spent two weeks away from school for reasons that nobody seemed to know. Billy didn't care about his unpopularity in class, but he increasingly found himself wishing he could confide in someone. Oliver was too strange to mirror anything but his own state of confusion and often seemed to be staring at him in an unnerving manner, as if studying a laboratory specimen. Billy needed to be able to take a reading from someone normal, someone who could offer advice. He needed the friendship of a female, but he didn't know any, unless you counted April.

April was ... different.

Her encounters with other people of her age were little

more than exercises in mutual unease, so she kept her own company, avoiding the girls who hung around the community centre smoking. When her classmates visited each other's houses to swap make-up, clothes and boy scandal, she looked on without contempt or envy, but listened carefully to their conversations as though attempting to decipher a foreign language.

One evening, Billy secretly followed April home on his bicycle, but she carried on marching through the town until she reached the farthest corner, then sat alone in a vandalised steel shelter that faced the fields beyond Invicta Cross.

She watched as the yellow industrial diggers churned up the clay-rich soil of the fallow land, furling great brown arcs behind them like the wakes of ships.

'Every day they come a little nearer,' she said aloud, making him start. He was surprised that she had realised he was there. 'Soon the next town will be touching this one, and all the greenery will have been paved over. The trees and fields will all be gone, replaced by acres of clean, white concrete.'

Billy stepped from his lurking place behind the shelter. The smell of struggling bonfires filled the air.

'You sound like you're looking forward to it,' he said, leaning his bike against the shelter posts.

'I am.' He noticed now that her voice bore traces of a Newcastle accent. She continued to stare straight ahead. 'Everything will be neat and tidy at last. I like trees when they've been planted in evenly spaced rows. Nature makes too much of a mess. You can't draw an accurate map of the coastline because it's always changing. But a concrete promenade stays the same forever, and can be mapped out perfectly.'

'You really must like living here, then.'

'No,' she said, looking at him for the first time. 'My mother and I know no one.'

'Why not? The other day you said the place was perfect.'

'I mean that it's ready for its transformation.'

'Into what?'

'The future, of course. When everything will be squared away. Kerbs, gardens, shops, people, thoughts. Only the birds will bring chaos with their unruly flight patterns.'

Her thought processes were a mystery to him. She rarely provided any explanations, and even when she did he failed to understand her fully.

'Why were you following me?'

'I wanted to get to know you.'

'And the normal avenues of introduction didn't appeal. Well, now you're here, what do you want to know?'

'Where have you been for the last two weeks?'

'I was unwell.'

'What was wrong with you?'

She considered the question for a minute. 'I have a disorderly constitution,' she decided finally.

'You've got an accent.'

'We came down South to find work for my father, but he left us.'

'You told me he died.'

'I prefer to think of him as dead. It would be easier for my mother if he was. Have *you* ever been ill? Really ill?'

'No.'

'I have. Pneumonia at four and again at nine, pleurisy at twelve. I'm not afraid of dying because I've already had the dress rehearsals. But I'm frightened of losing my mind, because I won't necessarily know it's happening.'

Billy sat down beside her and looked out across the desecrated field. 'You came to the wrong place to live,' he murmured.

She wanted to climb the tower, of course.

He had shown her the scale model in his bedroom and she had immediately offered to help him complete it, but it seemed that she was only interested in certain aspects of the task. April demanded accuracy. She had no interest in building a town of the imagination but was anxious to map out the area within a grid of perfect squares, each one containing its correct quota of concrete and steel, tarmac and brick.

It always looked as if April was preparing to speak and share her thoughts with him. She screwed up her eyes, tipped back her head and parted her lips as if about to sneeze or release some extraordinary idea, but she always caught herself at the last moment and backed down. This strange hesitancy made her all the more mysterious and untouchable.

She and Billy began to spend much of their time together.

Oliver accepted this challenge to his position as Billy's best friend with surprisingly good grace. He recognised another outsider and adapted to April's odd, elliptical conversation as if it was a standard form of communication. For a brief period the three of them went everywhere together.

'I thought I was the only one with a normal personality,' Billy wrote in his red book some time later. 'The other two were strange and needed help. But Oliver said I was worse than they were, that I needed even more looking after because I was a born victim. I couldn't see that at all.'

'My father says the GLC are going to make lesbianism compulsory,' said Oliver as they all worked on the model town. 'Even for men.'

'Alarmist, irresponsible reportage,' said April, attempting to glue a chimney to the community centre. 'Ken Livingstone keeps newts, but it's not an interesting story on its own, so the right-wing press trump up a piece of reactionary scaremongering aimed at the most base human instinct, which is fear of being different. What do you think, Billy?'

'You've got glue all over your sleeve,' said Billy.

Then the three of them became two. Sensing that he could not always enjoy his classmate's undivided attention, Oliver allowed April to take his place. She was more fascinated by Billy's model town than he was, and Billy needed someone to help him construct it with precision. April was the ideal workmate.

The pair of them were like research assistants sharing the enforced intimacy of a laboratory in which the experiment was understanding the nature of Invicta Cross. Billy soon learned that his partner responded more readily if he phrased his questions and requests in quantifiable terms. April would happily discuss all problems that involved weights, heights and distances, and was passionately opinionated on a variety of odd topics including the incidence of light aircraft accidents and the flammability levels of man-made fabrics, but she balked at the mention of her home life and refused to discuss anything that might reveal her true emotions.

Ray and Angela thought she was strange, but were glad

that their son had made another friend. His father could never remember her name, and always referred to her as 'the map girl'.

Angela asked April if her mother would like a visitor, but the offer was politely and firmly refused. Ray, in the meantime, applied to the Invicta Cross Community Centre for a job advertised on their noticeboard as an Area Safety Officer, but was turned down by Justin Brickett, who told him he wasn't qualified despite the fact that the ad had stated 'experience not necessary'. They parted in an air of acrimony and mutual suspicion.

While the neighbourhood women painted and powdered themselves, and cooked and cleaned for their men, Angela wearily increased her overtime hours at the checkout.

And Billy took April to the top of the tower.

'It's incredible,' she cried excitedly, leaning out into the wind. 'You can see the exact shape of the town, like a blueprint for the designers.'

She was right. From here the grand plan was plainly visible. The wealthier houses were on higher ground, and in the lower area where he lived the roads petered away into the surrounding marshes and fields.

'It looks like the money ran out,' said Billy, indicating the dividing line between grass and concrete. 'As though the developers just stopped building one day.'

'That's exactly what happened,' said April. 'A couple of months before you arrived the bulldozers cleared out. Look over there.' She indicated a distant patch of activity. The faint sound of pumping machinery reached their ears. 'The superstores are coming. Everything you'll ever need, all under one roof. The world will be finished then.'

It was impossible to tell if April meant finished as in

doomed or merely completed. Her kinked auburn hair was tied back with a rubber band. Her chin jutted into the thundering gale. Her strong white hands gripped the cold brick of the tower ledge. In that moment, in the evening's ebbing light, she was as magnificent and ageless as a temple deity.

CHAPTER THIRTEEN

The Bottle Message

'Three homes in picturesque Hall Wath, Bassingham are under attack from an unknown tormentor who has poured oil in ponds, poisoned cats, broken windows, contaminated food, damaged cars and dumped sacks of excrement in gardens. "Our tranquil home has become a hellhole," says one neighbour. Police are baffled.' – *Daily Mail*

'I KNOW about boys like you,' said Mrs Davenport, narrowing her eyes. 'You're trouble.'

Billy did his best to look surprised.

'You're the one who's been leaving the notes in the milk bottles, aren't you?'

Billy's eyes widened further. It was true that lately he'd taken to leaving rescue messages in the school's empties, but he was amazed that anyone knew it was him. He regularly displaced his frustration by writing notes and dropping them in letter boxes, milk bottles and National Westminster cheque deposit envelopes. April had first suggested the idea, thinking that it might help him to relax.

Mrs Davenport was not a headmistress to be messed with. Her three hundred pupils were drilled in correct behaviour. Like a sergeant, she expected if not blind then

---

extremely myopic obedience from both teachers and pupils. Sadly, such discipline caused subversion in her classroom. Behind her back there was a brisk trade in cigarettes, flick knives, low-grade drugs and test answers.

Billy had been summoned to her office for an unknown crime. He had no particular affection for his old city school, but he loathed this one. The move, coming at the start of his third senior year, had badly disrupted his studies. Although the syllabus topics corresponded, teaching methods here were blander, dulled by endless corrections demanded by the Invicta Cross PTA. The parents were campaigning for the teaching of more traditional values. A good grounding in British history, English, geography, religion and the sciences would see their children through. Inflammatory material was excised. Religious belief was emphasised. Opinions from the children were neither sought nor desired. Independent thinking was discouraged in favour of sportsmanship and team spirit. The arts were barely tolerated. Liberal studies had not yet been invented.

'I have one such note here.' Mrs Davenport adjusted her spectacles and studied the scrap of paper she had unfolded. '"Help, I am a prisoner of the Sherington Maximum Security Penitentiary." It then goes on to make scurrilous accusations about a member of staff, and there's an unpleasant drawing of what appears to be someone having carnal relations with a goat. Is this supposed to be funny?'

'It's not a goat. It's Beelzebub.' Billy stared at her insolently. From the start, Mrs Davenport had singled him out for special attention. She monitored his timekeeping (a quality she prized above all others), supervised his homework and spied on his playground behaviour. He was the first boy to be dumped on her by the state, and she was determined that he would not be allowed to influence the others.

What bothered Mrs Davenport most about Billy was his lack of discipline. In class he queried everything, raising his hand every five minutes to ask an awkward question or to offer an irresponsible opinion. At break time he hung out with other social misfits: Assan, the only Asian boy in the school, Oliver, the funeral director's son, and the Madison twins, who had been caught covering McDonald's with stickers condemning America's cultural imperialism. The twins had been suspended not because flyposting was illegal but because they had performed this subversive act while attired in school uniform.

Mrs Davenport thought that the March boy could be defused, as it were, by placing him in a different class. When that failed to have any effect she arranged extra homework for him, ostensibly to allow him to catch up after his move. But Billy handled the studies adequately and still found time to stir up trouble. His religious instruction essay, entitled 'God is Dead and Damned in Invicta Cross', gave Mr Brickett apoplexy, and his request to form a film society was denied after he submitted a list of selected features that included *The Exorcist*, *A Clockwork Orange* and *Plague of the Zombies*. Refusing to take no for an answer, the wretched pupil had requested a class referendum, only to be publicly humiliated when his peers voted against him.

Not that he gave up easily. The boy seemed determined to make those around him think for themselves. Not undesirable in certain parts of the private sector, of course, but dangerous in a public institution. He had such *odd* ideas.

Fate, however, was on Mrs Davenport's side. Two days after the business with the milk bottles (the headmistress, unable to pinpoint any actual misdemeanour, let him off with a warning) Billy's lucky streak came to an end.

Oliver was away having an infected root canal drained and, as no one else was around to share his lunch, Billy sat alone beneath the awning of the cycle shed watching a light drizzle settle across the slick red roofs of the estate. He was thinking about his father being fired for an unproven theft. He was annoyed that Ray had not stuck up for his rights and wondered where the silver money clip had really disappeared to. Not that he doubted his father's word for a second. It just seemed that the business remained unfinished. Ray's name had not been cleared, the evidence had not turned up – it was like one of those ongoing court cases you followed in the paper only to miss the final verdict.

He was puzzled to see several of the wealthier kids who hung out together approaching him, and even more surprised when they asked him if he would join them.

'Why?' he asked warily. 'Where are you going?'

'Over to the corner shop,' said Gavin Diller, one of the boys in the class above him, who was usually to be found hanging around Balmoral Close with the highly toxic Brad Metcalf. He was a heavy-set lad with cropped blond hair and a small pouting mouth like an upturned smile. 'We need your help.'

'No, you go ahead without me,' said Billy, who could tell that the gang was on a cigarette run, which involved stealing as much as possible when the local tobacconist's back was turned.

'You're the sharp talker around here,' said Gavin. 'Everyone knows that. You can keep the owner busy. It's not like we're really doing anything wrong. It's a traditional event.'

'No, but thanks for the offer.'

'Billy, you're the only man for the job.'

It was true; no one else in the group could manufacture a sentence that included a verb and a noun. Besides, how could he ever get respect if he didn't do something disreputable? He was cajoled into acceptance, and found himself tagging along behind five booming lads who would never normally grant him the time of day. Gavin was right, of course; shoplifting was a traditional schoolboy activity, but Billy's nervousness increased. As the others moved off into the narrow, cluttered aisles of the store, he walked to the front and distracted the proprietor's attention with questions about last week's delivery of magazines. After a minute or so the rest of the group returned and gathered around him. Billy felt his jacket pockets being pulled open and stuffed with contraband.

The sudden whispering flurry of activity alerted the shop owner, who twirled around with an angry shout. Before Billy could protest, the rest of the merry band had slipped from the shop with shouts of laughter, and the incensed owner was calling his sons up from the stockroom. They clattered upstairs and painfully seized Billy's arms while they rang for the police.

The two constables appeared fierce but clearly understood what was going on; Billy had been used as a late player in a long-running conflict involving the store. This wasn't about shoplifting at all but a series of escalating revenge attacks on the Turkish proprietor's sons by three of the boys in Billy's class. The police, anxious to avert racial problems in the area, recognised that the boy had been duped, but that did not stop them from making an example of him.

Billy was suspended from school for two weeks and required to undergo a further interview with the police. Gavin Diller sent him a note warning him to keep his mouth shut, not that a warning was necessary; he had already decided not to rat on his classmates, knowing that to do so would exacerbate the situation.

His parents believed him when he told them he was innocent. After all, Ray had just faced the same predicament. The worst part was that word had got around about Billy's father, and the synchronicity of his son's misdemeanour lent validity to both crimes. The family from the city were now a family of thieves, the butt of unpleasant jokes, the gypsies of the neighbourhood.

The officer appointed to file the report on Billy was a curt, overweight constable named PC Morris Diller, and it was only while he waited in the freezing interview room that Billy realised the policeman's son, Gavin, had been partially responsible for the theft. He did not know that Diller was the officer who had also dealt with his father.

At the time, these incidents seemed unconnected. Later a pattern began to surface in Billy March's mind. But by then, the situation could no longer be relieved by placing a message in a bottle.

CHAPTER FOURTEEN

The Shattered Fence

'Someone recently stole four concrete lamp-posts from a housing estate in Barnsley. A local councillor said, "We can't imagine the strength of someone who can uproot a lamp-post. Whoever is responsible is either a fool or completely disturbed."' – *Daily Mirror*

'SMALL THINGS that happened,' wrote Billy, 'in a garage, a corner store. Nothing big or really memorable. Who'd have thought they would add up to so much? Then there was the business with the fence, and the letters . . .'

It was a miserably cold Christmas, a time of hard frosts, mean winds and early snows. Billy had never seen such weather. London rarely froze; the combined warmth of so many people, cars, pipes and radiators packed together kept the ice from thickening beyond a millimetre. In London most walls were shared. Here in Invicta Cross it was a different story. Algid winds swept the frost-scalded fields, scything through the streets to hammer at the front doors.

The little house began to show its faults. Pipes split and boards cracked. Tiles blew from the roof. Draughts sprang from every angle, sharp little knives of air that could slither through the tiniest gap. The wind moaned dully under the kitchen door and thudded persistently at the bedroom windows until plaster and wood splintered just enough to allow the damp of a sudden thaw to freeze again and split them further. Ray complained to the local agent in charge of the property, which did no good at all, then set about repairing the damage himself, but his enthusiasm proved greater than his ability.

Angela worked longer hours in the run-up to Christmas, taking on extra duties stacking shelves. The neighbours remained invisible, although Georgina Bovis took to coming around when Angela was at work. She appeared on the most spurious of pretexts, as if wanting to be questioned on her motives. Ray allowed her in for a brief visit, then kept well out of her way, as if frightened of becoming irradiated by her sunny sexuality. If she was to fully realise her caricature image as the neighbourhood vixen, she would have to make a sexual advance, but showed no sign of doing so. Disappointed, Billy realised that she was probably happy to wait for Ray to take the initiative, that the flirtatious dance she performed as she circled him was the part she enjoyed the most.

During her calls, Billy stayed in his room keeping his neighbourhood charts up to date in his red leather-bound diary. Dr McMann, Justin and Sandra Brickett, PC Morris Diller and his son Gavin, Mrs Davenport, Adolpho Garibaldi, the Metcalfs, the Bovises and the Prouts all warranted separate numbered tables.

It had been April's idea to start cataloguing the details of Invicta Cross's residents. In this way she felt that the statistics, once added to the completed model of the town and her own grid map of the area, which she planned to create from Polaroids taken in the tower, would somehow help them to appreciate the true nature of their surroundings and fix the town in perspective.

April's preoccupations remained mysterious to Billy. When she wasn't quantifying her world, she was poring over old movie magazines, studying the clothes of fifties starlets. For her these blandly smiling women were representatives of a time when appearances were constantly maintained and surfaces stayed perfect. Americans in the fifties were true Victorians.

The model town had grown to consume over half of Billy's bedroom and would have to be moved to the spare room while it could still be taken through the door in two halves. Ray was puzzled by the project but suggested to Billy that he might be able to get the finished model exhibited in the community centre. His son refused to consider the idea.

At two in the morning on the first Sunday in December, Alan Bovis drove home drunk from an office party, swerved to avoid an imaginary squirrel and crashed his Audi into the fence bordering the Marches' property. He managed to get the dented vehicle into his garage before anyone saw him.

When Billy and his father had cleared up the debris the next morning, Ray discovered that the exterior of the house and its grounds were not insured for accidental damage. He worked out how much it would cost to have the fence replaced and quickly realised that he would not be able to afford the repairs until after Christmas, and that was with buying the wood secondhand and fixing it himself. Meanwhile, the fence had to stay as it was.

A few days later, an anonymous letter was posted through the front door of 13 Balmoral Close, demanding that the fence be fixed because it was an eyesore. If no action was taken, the Marches would be reported to the neighbourhood action committee. In a rare gesture of defiance, Ray nailed the letter to the shattered posts and left the fence as it was. He failed to recognise the look of mortification on his wife's face.

Billy noticed the difference in his mother almost immediately. There had always been an air of faded gentility about Angela, an attitude of almost unbearable politeness and apology that characterised so many women of her generation. All she had ever wanted to do was to blend in and vanish. Instead she and her family were daily becoming more conspicuous and reviled. She tried not to think about their changing circumstances, pretending that everything was fine when the boy was around, but at night she found herself unable to sleep with the worry of it all. Too embarrassed to visit Dr McMann, she had her sister bring her sleeping pills, and her nights passed a little more easily. She talked to Carol-Lynn. She explained how Ray refused to entertain the idea of moving out, how he equated it with failure, how they couldn't afford to back down now because to do so would be to admit that the family had been defeated.

Carol-Lynn made a show of sympathy, but with her husband still detained at Her Majesty's pleasure she had enough problems of her own and couldn't really see what Angela was complaining about. She stayed until six, then dutifully left to feed her children.

The next day, a bill arrived. It had been prepared by the

Invicta Cross Neighbourhood Committee, a fee to be charged in advance for fixing the damaged fence. The families Bovis, Prout, Metcalf, Brickett and McMann were all listed as committee members. Incensed, Ray headed for the community centre with the letter screwed up in his fist.

'Let me explain something to you,' insisted Justin Brickett, who had agreed to the meeting only after his secretary had failed to prevent Ray from barging into his office. 'We are in the middle of delicate negotiations with the Balmoral Close contractors. We need them to finish that part of the close which runs beyond Windsor Terrace, and then we have to ensure that the development corporation completes the remaining sections of the neighbourhood. We cannot afford to let them lose faith in us at this stage. They have to know that we can attract the right kind of buyers for the area. What are they going to say when they see the mess in your front garden? They'd have every right to think that the neighbourhood was already heading down-market, that the home buyers with spending power have already started looking elsewhere. It doesn't take much to tip the balance out of our favour. The government has just woken up to the fact that the suburban area surrounding London contains prime property. Why should anyone invest in us if we can't play our small part by keeping the neighbourhood neat?'

'There are tyre tracks on our lawn,' said Ray doggedly. 'Somebody did this on purpose. I won't pay blackmail money, and I'll get the fence fixed when I'm good and ready.'

'If the money's a problem, Ray, I'm sure we can come to some sort of arrangement,' offered Justin.

'It all comes down to cash with you people, doesn't it?' Ray finally allowed himself the luxury of losing his temper. The veins stood out on his neck as he shouted. 'That's why my kid gets a rough ride at school, why my wife can't even get a nod from any of the stuck-up bitches around here—'

'There's no need for gutter language, Mr March,' said Justin coldly.

'Why don't you have the committee send me a fucking memo about it?'

'We were rather hoping you'd leave your old habits behind.'

'There's something going on here, Brickett. I'm not an idiot. You're playing some kind of game with us, and I'll see you all damned before my family suffers for it. One rule for you and another for us, is it? Well, we'll bloody see about that.'

He stormed out past the smirking councillor, shoved the secretary aside and slammed the chamber door on his way out.

Instead of returning home, Ray went to the Helicopter and ordered a large whisky. Everyone else around them was getting rich, he complained to the landlord, while his own family just got poorer. A cruel game, that's what it was, and they were all in on it. The government had moved them here against their wishes but took no responsibility for the consequences. Steeped in self-pity, he stayed there drinking until the bar was shut, his money had gone, and the landlord was forced to throw him out.

Angela was in tears as she tried to pull her husband up onto a kitchen chair. Billy sat cross-legged at the top of the stairs, watching through the landing banisters. It frightened him

123

seeing his father like this. While Ray had been out getting drunk, someone had thrown a stone through the hall window. It was just a pebble but it had shattered a pane that was already cracked, so that now they would have to repair it. Billy had dashed into the street, but misty darkness had obscured the retreating culprit.

It seemed to Billy that the entire neighbourhood was making a concerted effort to humiliate his family. He left his mother crying beside his unconscious father and took a walk over to the Metcalfs' garage. He had a half-formed idea that Brad Metcalf had somehow taken the keys to his father's car and had driven it into their fence. He had no proof beyond the fact that he hadn't seen their BMW since the night of the accident, and was trying to find a way into their garage when Bob Metcalf shone a torch into his startled eyes.

'What the hell do you think you're doing?'

Billy stood his ground. 'I was wondering where your car was.'

'I don't think you're in a position to start asking questions while you're trespassing on my property.'

'You knocked our fence down,' he managed breathlessly. 'I could call the police.'

'Don't be such a silly little boy.' Bob Metcalf impatiently thumbed the garage door's remote, and the door slowly rose to reveal the gleaming automobile. 'See, nothing. Now don't you feel stupid, going around accusing innocent people?'

Billy felt his cheeks suffusing with heat. This was all his father's fault, refusing to pay the repair bill for the fence, forcing him to take action on his own. As he turned away and walked back down the Metcalfs' drive, he felt tears of anger and frustration filling his eyes. He passed the fence with the smashed staves of its twisted spine thrusting up like damaged bones and kicked at one of the boards with his boot until the entire length had cracked in two.

Georgina Bovis, more disinterested in her marriage vows than ever and still being denied her nonconjugal rights by Graham the weatherman, came over to number thirteen that night to talk with Ray but was frostily warned away by his wife, who insisted that he had retired to bed unwell.

Georgina patted Billy on his head, spraying him with cigarette smoke as she passed, and could not resist commenting that the boy was going to be every bit as handsome as his father. His mother hastily showed her the door and slammed it hard behind her.

'Good riddance to bad rubbish,' she snapped.

'She's like Cruella De Ville, only she wants to make Dad into a coat instead of a bunch of Dalmatians,' said Billy, wafting away the smell of perfume and returning to his model in the bedroom.

The next morning was Christmas Eve and, while Ray was still in bed nursing his throbbing head, Billy went downstairs to collect the mail. He was shooed off by his mother, who hastily pocketed a small brown envelope. It was the first of many such letters they received at the house, but Billy did not discover their contents until it was too late to act on them.

Later that day, he hung tinsel on the shattered fence and defiantly sprayed 'A Merry Christmas to All Our Fans' across the slats in dripping crimson paint. After all, he reasoned, wasn't that the kind of behaviour they all expected of him?

He looked out across the estate and up into the darkening sky, wishing that snowflakes would once more drift down and obscure his vision, as they had before the Landseer lions in Trafalgar Square, but he knew that such potent wish magic could not be summoned within this sterile realm.

CHAPTER FIFTEEN

The Sepia Envelope

'Bridget Cunningham spent four years harassing her neighbours, complaining to police over 200 times about everything from inconsiderate parking to impersonating her walk. Mrs Cunningham hung a pigskin on her clothesline and gave the Nazi salute to her Jewish neighbour. She and her brother Robert regularly fired up a circular saw beneath the neighbour's window and sprayed their children with insecticide. In court for the ninth time, the couple wore tea cosies on their heads with the eyeholes cut out because they wanted to look like terrorists' – *Night and Day*

'YOU CAN'T call a dog Dracula,' said Ray. 'It stands to reason.'

'What about Crippen?'

'No.'

'Ripper?'

'No. Call it something normal.'

'Squeaky.'

Ray was suspicious. 'Why?'

'Squeaky Frome, Charles Manson's sidekick.'

'No.'

They settled for Victor, as in Frankenstein. Ray had collected the torn-eared piebald puppy from the Croydon RSPCA on Christmas Eve. The last thing they needed was another mouth to feed, but Billy had been nagging him about getting a dog for ages. Ray had refused him a pet in the city but could find no excuse now that they lived near open land. He elicited the usual promises about exercise and feeding, and cited the slogan 'A pet is for life, not just Christmas', but suspected that he would still wind up with the walking chores.

Early on Christmas morning, Billy awoke to find an armchair festooned with Christmas lights at the end of his bed. It was something his father used to do when his son was very small, and made Billy remember Christmases in the little house in Greenwich, when Ray would always bring him a cup of tea with a seasonal sip of Scotch in it, a tradition (disapproved of by his wife) that he swore had been in the family for decades.

On Christmas night several of Angela's relatives made an unannounced arrival. They seemed the worse for wear, and appeared on the front step singing obscene lyrics to 'Once in Royal David's City' before Angela hushed them and dragged them inside. Ray's uncle Stan stopped by and insisted on playing the trumpet, an instrument he always carried around at this time of the year in the mistaken belief that an off-key rendition of 'Moonglow' was somehow a contribution to the yuletide festivities, and Angela's harassed sister even found time to drop off a bottle of Madeira and a batch of incredible, inedible iced fancies.

A good time was had by all until Ken Prout came over to complain about the noise. Ray invited him in but he refused the offer of a drink because Barbara was waiting for him, standing in the doorway of the Prout-house with her arms tightly folded and a sour look on her face.

'She doesn't let Prout out,' said Angela after their neighbour had returned home. 'He's not allowed to go on Proutings.' She was a little drunk, and thoroughly enjoying herself.

'He doesn't get Prout and about much,' said Ray, sniggering. 'I should have given Prout a clout on the snout.' He collapsed on the floor, helpless with laughter.

Billy held the little brown mongrel in his sweater and watched, glad that they could forget their troubles. But later that night the telephone rang and his mother looked upset; something had clearly happened that no one wanted to talk about, at least not in front of teenage boys.

It finally snowed that year, in thin fine sprays that tarnished to slush, then froze again. It gave the residents of Invicta Cross an excuse to carve and grit neat walkways to their cars. Perfect demarcation lines showed that they were careful not to clear any snow from their neighbours' paths.

Up in the water tower the below-zero temperature was aggravated by wind-chill. Billy scraped a crust of snow from the metal sketch box he kept under the parapet and tried to raise the lid, but it was frozen tight. Too cold to work on his drawings today. He needed to map out the northeastern corner of the town so that he could reproduce its contours accurately on the scale model. The newly whitened backstreets, as yet unscarred by tyre tracks, had a clinical cleanliness that April approved of.

She had worked on the model with an angry energy that suggested she was conforming to an undisclosed timetable. She had wanted to improve the map by finishing its roads in a manner that the full-scale town had not yet managed, but Billy, for reasons unknown even to himself, had been adamant about the accuracy of their construction. Perhaps April thought that something magical would happen when the model was completed, that it would somehow change places with the town, healing outwards from its epicentre until everything was absorbed in its pastel perfection.

April's mother had taken her off to Scotland for the Christmas holidays, and Oliver had the flu, so Billy had climbed the tower with Victor inside his jacket for company. The bare arched room atop the brick column had become the only place where he could think clearly. He sat on the freezing stone with the puppy snuffling around beneath his scarf, filling his chest with the warmth of another heartbeat, and tried to understand.

This morning, two letters had been hand delivered to the house. One was from the neighbourhood association, demanding that Ray repair his fence immediately or be taken to court for creating a hazard in the street. The other was a mysterious sepia envelope addressed in ballpoint to 'The Residents of Number 13'. The first had been opened; the second had not. If Billy's parents kept secrets from him, it was only to spare him pain. When he was nine years old, they had told him that his cancer-racked Aunt Vera had gone to live in another country. His inquisitive morbidity had eventually forced them to reveal the true nature of that far-off land. Billy had been satisfied with their awkward explanations and solemnly thanked them for their honesty. After that they promised they would never lie to him again. But they were clearly doing so now.

He looked down at the fresh clouds of snow rolling across the hardened fields and wondered what he could do to restore his family's happiness.

Below him, a mile and a half away, Ray stood in his garden on starched tufts of white grass studying the backs of his neighbours' houses, wondering the very same thing. In his fist he had a crumpled sheet of paper. In the kitchen, his wife sat crying.

Something bad was happening to them; that much seemed sure. The wind had shifted, the skies had changed, the very air had displaced itself. Misfortune had arrived like an undesired lover and was closing their world in the shadow of her wings.

High in his vantage point of crumbling stone, Billy looked up and wiped a freezing droplet from his nose. Tomorrow was New Year's Eve. A chance for everything to begin again. He stared down at the half-finished roads and the dead fields, and the thought filled him with nameless terror.

Invicta Cross celebrated the New Year sedately. A few whistles were heard at midnight, the distant sound of a crowded pub, some rowdiness from the council-flat kids who hung out at the bus station, bored and broke. Ray and Angela stayed in and drank a toast at midnight, while Billy watched television soundbites from revellers around the world. Just after the hour the telephone rang and his father took the call, but instead of wishing the caller a Happy New Year he released a string of obscenities into the mouthpiece that surpassed Billy's own feverish powers of linguistic invention.

Billy had never heard his father swear so violently. It occurred to him that the old man was drunk; he'd been hitting the bottle pretty heavily through Christmas. Why else would he fly off the handle over someone phoning late?

Ray looked about himself as he replaced the receiver, embarrassed by the outburst. Then he told his wife he was going out.

Billy lay in bed staring at the ceiling, listening for the front door latch, willing it to open; he fell asleep before his father returned home.

The next morning, Ray went out to the Vauxhall and found that all four tyres had been slashed with a broad-bladed knife. He reported the vandalism to the police, but all they could suggest was replacing the lock on the garage door. Ray worked out the cost of replacement tyres and, after a long, heated discussion with Angela, went up to London by himself.

When he returned he spoke quietly with his wife, who made a phone call to her sister, then he and Billy set off to buy paint and wood, and four secondhand tyres. That afternoon Billy helped to restore the fence to something of its former shape and watched while his father tore the housing association's request into shreds before tossing it into the wind.

Ray never said where he got the money from, but Billy knew that this was the only time in his life that his father had ever borrowed money. Ray treated the episode like an act of treason on his part and would not be drawn on the subject.

Billy was disappointed. This was his first time inside a police station, and it was nothing like he had imagined it would be.

Instead of police running everywhere, rowdy hookers

being booked and careworn detectives discussing the killer's modus operandi as they dunked doughnuts in cardboard cups of coffee, there was a single row of orange plastic bendy chairs, a small glass partition, a couple of dog-eared crime-stopper posters and the distant sound of a telephone ringing. The placed smelled of disinfectant, and had an aura of melancholy and cheapness, rather like Oliver's father's funeral parlour, where the walls were covered with fawn fake-pine veneer. Another illusion shattered.

There had been two people ahead of them (an elderly man complaining about a car tax problem and a girl who wouldn't stop crying), then Ray had been called into one of the interview rooms. He was gone for forty-five minutes and emerged with a look of frustration on his face.

'Come on, kiddo, let's get out of here.'

He folded the brown envelope back in his pocket and held open the swing-door for his son.

'What happened?' asked Billy. 'Did you do something wrong?'

'Not me, lad, somebody else. I was just trying to find out who.'

'What did the police tell you?'

'They said they'd look into it.'

Ray fished a cigarette stub from his top pocket and lit it, flicking the match into the gutter. Smoking was one of the few pleasures he was determined to be able to afford. He had passed PC Morris Diller on his way to the interview room. It was an unfortunate coincidence that they kept crossing paths with the same constable. He looked back with suspicion as he passed Ray in the corridor, confirming the latter's status as a persistent troublemaker.

Billy wanted to ask all kinds of questions about the police interview, but one glance at his father told him it was a dangerous idea. Instead he suggested a trip to the cinema.

'Mum's working late,' he said hopefully. 'We could be back before her and bring home fish and chips.' When he saw the blank look on Ray's face he added, 'I've got some money.'

His father, a mere mortal who was no match for Billy's cunning master plan, was fooled into trekking to the Croydon Granada to see *Cocoon*. Three hours later they returned to the house laden with cod and chips and cola and pickled wallies, and set the table for a feast.

That was when the hospital called.

CHAPTER SIXTEEN

The Imaginary Oil

'People are so different now. You get into your box, shut it up and just pray that no one's going to start anything.'
– J.J., 44-year-old homeless man

ANOTHER ORANGE bendy chair. Billy bounced back in it, trying to see how far it would go without breaking. Presumably all the area's services were issued with them, just as they were issued with overworked, distracted staff officers who looked through you as they spoke. Billy and his father sat in the crowded corridor waiting for news, but none came. Nurses scurried past, efficiently tick-tacking across the grey linoleum tiles as they checked their notes, old ladies complained as they were wheeled through whumping double doors, indistinct messages bing-bonged in the background.

The place was surprisingly busy for 11.15 pm. Billy wrinkled his nose and blew hard. He was bored. He wanted to see into the rooms beyond the swing doors. There was a strong smell of bleach, and something sweet beneath it, like the scent of a rock shop. *The Stench of Death*, he thought, starring Peter Cushing and Christopher Lee, now playing with *The Reek of Corruption*, starring

Veronica Carlson and Martine Beswick, a Hammer Double Horror Bill. If the Hammer Dracula films were set in Transylvania, why on earth did Michael Ripper, who always played the innkeeper, adopt a heavy Somerset accent? 'Oi wouldn't go up to Carstle Drac'lar if Oi wuz you,' he'd say. Why was that?

An elderly man in a blue towelling robe squeaked over and sat down beside them. He was yellow with age, at least a thousand years old. *Return of the Mummy*, Tigon Films, 1972: Im-ho-tep seeks revenge on the descendants of those who entombed him alive by forcing them to wait in hospital corridors. The old guy had brown teeth and was holding a steel rod with a clear plastic bag dangling from a hook at the top. The other end entered his arm, which was blue with bruises from the constant relocation of the drip. Billy loved horror films, but this was too real and grossed him out.

He thought of his mother lying somewhere in the hospital and wondered why they couldn't see her. Was she still unconscious? Were the doctors doing something so gruesome that they couldn't go and watch for fear of the sight turning their hair white and sending them mad?

'All I know, Billy, is that she slipped over in one of the aisles,' said his father.

'Slipped on what?'

Ray fished for his cigarettes, exasperated. 'How the bloody hell should I know?'

'If it was a loose tile or somebody spilled something that hadn't been cleared up, she can sue the store for negligence.'

'Let's not get ahead of ourselves, lad. Let's make sure she's all right first.'

They sat there for another hour and a quarter, Ray tucking the cigarette in the palm of his hand because there was no smoking on the ward. Finally a nurse found them.

'I'm afraid you can't see Mrs March at the moment,' said the harassed young Asian woman, searching her pockets for notes. 'She was given a pain neutraliser and some nitrazepam to help her sleep. She's torn the medial cruciate ligaments in her right knee.' She indicated her own knee. 'They're the muscles that keep the patella in place. Nothing too serious. But she also took a nasty bang on the head and was unconscious for quite a while, so she's going to be kept in overnight, and then she will probably be released to you after the doctor has seen her tomorrow.'

'She won't be able to walk, will she?'

'No, her leg will be in plaster for a while, and then she can have a wheelchair until her operation is scheduled. After that she'll just need a stick until the muscle heals.'

'How long will it be before she can have an operation?'

The nurse was looking over Ray's shoulder, scanning the corridor, her mind clearly on the problems of her next patient. 'Your wife won't be a high priority case so there could be a bit of a wait, but hopefully something should be done by late spring.'

'You mean she'll have to stay in a wheelchair all that time?'

'It can't be helped,' she said, keen to move on. 'The patient catchment area for this hospital has doubled since the new town was built.' She patted him reassuringly on the arm. 'She can speed the system up by going privately, of course. There's no point in you waiting any more tonight. Your wife will be fine, I promise you. Come back in the morning. Now you must excuse me.'

The nurse slipped between them and moved off to attend to a jaundiced old woman lying on a nearby gurney.

'What do we do now?' asked Billy.

'We do what we're told,' said his father with a shrug.

That's the trouble with the March family, thought Billy. *It always does what it's told. Generations of men and women who pride themselves on never taking time off, on never missing a day's pay, who are cheerfully directed to their tasks by better-educated people who don't have to get their hands dirty.*

Billy wondered if thoughts like these made him a socialist.

He was sitting at the top of the water tower with the mongrel snoring inside his jacket. He rose and stamped his feet on the frosted bricks. April had returned from Scotland and had come to join him in his lonely vigil. Her sallow face was surrounded by a vermillion tartan scarf. She looked like a Victorian print of a man with a toothache.

'Where's Oliver?' she asked.

'Dunno. Not answering the phone. Thought he might be up here.'

'How's your mother today?'

'She still hates the chair. She can't reach any of the kitchen cupboards. We have to lay everything out for her. She won't let us cook.'

'Of course not. It's a woman's lot, is cooking.' April spoke without a trace of irony. 'Cooking and keeping things neat. My mother told me what happened to your mother.'

Billy was surprised but interested. His mother had refused to be drawn on the subject of her accident, much to Ray's annoyance. 'What did you hear?' he asked.

138

'She had an argument with one of the other checkout ladies and left her till. Then she fell over. But all is not what it seems,' she added darkly.

'What do you mean?'

'Your mother says there was a pool of cooking oil on the floor. But was there?' She leaned close, her eyes wide. 'The store manager says not.'

'That's stupid. My mother wouldn't lie. Why would she make up something like that?'

'To get compensation. You need the money.' She turned to him, her face as blank as stone. 'You're the gypsy family, got caught stealing, out for what you can get. Everyone knows about you. You have a reputation that will not be shaken off. There are enemies afoot.'

Billy rose angrily. The dog squirmed sleepily inside his jacket. 'You're supposed to be my friend, April.'

'We have an alliance,' she said simply. 'Isn't it better for you to know what's going on? Forewarned is, after all, forearmed.' She looked back across the fields, her breath condensing. 'I want to work on the model today. We still have much to do.'

'You're a very strange girl,' said Billy disappointedly.

'It's a good job for you that I am,' she replied. 'Normality is our common enemy.'

Although the snow was once more falling and feathery burs were settling on their eyelashes, they stayed at the top of the water tower and sketched until their fingers were numb and the light began to fade.

As the days passed, the temperature continued to fall. The snow settled and hardened at the edge of the roads in gingery rinds of slush. At number 13 Balmoral Close it froze the doors and windows, contracted the pipes and sealed the drains. The outside world thickened with stillness. Only the occasional muffled passing of a car broke the silence.

Angela Marsh was not a good invalid. She hated being imprisoned on the ground floor and was further restricted by the width of her chair, which could not fit through the toilet door or even handle the little step from the lounge to the kitchen. She rang the store and spoke to the manager but was told that her poor attitude to the quite straightforward situation of her accident now made her unsuitable as an employee. She was fired, and the store had no responsibility for her injury.

Angela promptly called a lawyer.

'The problem, Mrs March, is one of proof,' explained the legal woman who, judging by the width of her shoulder-padded suit and the complex braiding of her bleached coiffure, was clearly a fan of *LA Law*. As Angela was still immobilised, the lawyer had reluctantly come to the house. 'You say you slipped on spilled oil, and the company says that you didn't.'

'Surely it's your duty to believe the plaintiff?' asked Angela.

'What I believe is immaterial to your case. It's what I can prove that's at issue here. We cannot just let it come down to your word against the store's.'

'Why not?'

'Because, my dear lady, they will win.'

'How on earth can they?' asked Angela. 'I'm the one who's injured.'

'Not the issue. They will argue that it's not the company's fault.'

'And they'll get away with that?'

'Certainly. All the evidence is on their side.'

'What evidence?'

'Just before the accident occurred, you had an argument with one of the girls and were seen to leave your work station.'

'They wouldn't allow me a break. I told you, the times are staggered through the morning, but nobody came to relieve me. I simply took what was mine.'

'You did so without permission, a verified fact. You broke a company rule. You left your till and headed for the restroom at the rear of the store.'

'That's right. I turned quickly into the aisle and that's when I slipped over on the oil. I've already told you what happened.'

'You didn't get any oil on your clothes.'

'No.'

'What kind of shoes were you wearing?'

'Ones with low heels.'

'You still have the shoes?'

'Of course.'

'Your leg went from under you. Forwards or backwards?'

'Backwards, I think.'

'You must be exact about this.'

'Backwards. Then I fell and hit my head on the floor. I lost consciousness for a while, I don't know how long.'

'Here's the problem area. In a court of law, the store's argument will be that against company rules you stormed away from your station in a temper—'

'I never lose my temper—'

'Please let me finish. That you stormed off after arguing

with one of the girls and slipped in your hurry to leave the building. Now, I have to tell you that one of the shoppers, the woman who found you, says there was no oil to be seen anywhere on the floor, and when the manager was called he saw none either.'

'Who found me?'

There was a rustle as the lawyer checked her notes. 'A Mrs Barbara Prout,' she replied.

Later, after the lawyer had gone, Angela wheeled her chair to the edge of the steps and watched the dog chasing sparrows across the frozen garden. The gelid air bit into her bandaged leg, but she barely noticed as she began to wonder if the cause of the accident had been imagined after all.

CHAPTER SEVENTEEN

The Jigsaw Field

'A Pontiac man astonished doctors by deliberately cutting off his left hand with a power saw twice in one year. The first time, it had been reattached using microsurgery. Michael Downing, a jobless Londoner, sawed his left leg off below the knee, then cut off several fingers "for practice". An ambulanceman said: "He seems to have an obsession about cutting parts off his body."' – *The Sun*

'I AM given to understand,' said Angela March, trying to control the quivering vibrato in her voice, 'that you have testified against me to the management of the store.'

Uncharacteristically, she had summoned up her last reserve of courage and had gone over to the Prout household to complain. Although she had still not been given a date for her operation, she found that the aluminium crutches Billy had collected from the hospital gave her a greater degree of mobility, even though they caused bruises beneath her arms.

'I wouldn't say *testify*,' said her neighbour icily. 'They asked me what I saw, and I told them the truth.'

'You said I was involved in an argument. You said there was no oil on the floor. I didn't even see you in the store.'

'But I was there.' Barbara folded her arms defensively. 'I saw exactly what happened. You had words with someone, shouting in public, then you stormed off. I was just doing some shopping. I saw the floor of the aisle where you say you slipped. It was perfectly clean and dry.'

'You're lying, and you know it.'

Barbara Prout stared back, clear eyed and calm. 'Why on earth would I lie, Mrs March? What *possible* interest could I have in your affairs?'

'That is just what I'm asking myself,' Angela replied.

Billy had been out with Oliver, taking Victor for a walk, when he saw his mother stumping awkwardly through the snow toward her neighbour's house. Now he stood behind a tree and listened. Angela was a naturally timid woman, with little confidence of her own. She was rarely driven to anger. It took a lot to force her into action.

'What I don't understand,' she said, 'is what you have to gain by this. I'm owed some kind of compensation for the injury, but I haven't got a case if you insist on telling this untruth.'

'I can only say what I saw,' explained Barbara in exasperation, 'and I saw no evidence that your unfortunate accident was in any way the responsibility of the store. What do you expect me to do, lie for you?'

'I don't know,' cried Angela. 'Perhaps you weren't looking properly. I'm sure I remember seeing—'

'I have nothing more to say to you, Mrs March. I don't appreciate your accusations.' Barbara started to close her front door, but Angela shifted the leg of her crutch in the way.

'Why are you doing this?' she pleaded. 'You know my husband's out of work. You can see the problems we're having.'

'Then perhaps you should consider your motives for trying to push this claim through,' snapped Barbara. 'Why don't you give some thought to moving? I'm sure you'd be more comfortable in a council flat back in London.' Carefully dislodging the crutch, she slammed the door shut.

Billy ran toward his mother as she toppled backwards from the step. Picking her out of the snow, he slipped her frail arm under his and gently led her back to the house. She tried hard not to let her son see her cry, but by the time they reached their hallway she was sobbing hysterically.

In a small town like Invicta Cross gossip was rife, and most of it began in the supermarket. Angela's reputation was quickly blackened. In the eyes of the neighbourhood she was a liar, trying to claim for an injury she had brought upon herself. Clearly she had no decency or respect, trying to pull such a cheap stunt. How much further was this family prepared to humiliate itself for a cash handout?

Barbara Prout bumped into Georgina Bovis at the hair salon on Boadicea Parade and told her that somebody should do something; the Marches were bringing down the property value of the street. Georgina saw Sandra Brickett in the newsagents and wondered if her husband could do something because without proper guidelines all sorts of families could start turning up in Invicta Cross, and then where would they be?

Sandra Brickett mentioned the matter to her husband over their Marks and Spencer's *Saumon en Croute*, and he replied that something was already being done. When Sandra requested further details he smiled darkly and continued cutting up his fish.

*

Billy took Victor for a walk, and while he was out visited Oliver to announce that he was going to run away from home.

'But what about your parents?' asked Oliver, who was just putting the finishing touches to a matching pair of Plasticine vampires. 'You can't leave them behind.'

'You're right. I'll take them with me.'

'It's not really running away then, is it?'

Oliver wasn't himself. Usually he hung on Billy's every utterance, but today he seemed more interested in his stupid models. Billy began to wonder if he'd been got at along with everyone else. Perhaps his father had said something about staying away from bad influences.

'Do you think I'm a bad influence?'

'No, of course not,' said Oliver. 'You're too passive to be harmful. You let people walk all over you. You know what happens eventually?'

'No, what?'

'You snap. One day everything's fine – the next, you're walking into Woolworth's with a loaded shotgun in each hand.'

'Come on.'

'Happens all the time. My dad had a client who'd cut his own hands off. He'd been angry about something for years and had finally gone over the edge.'

'Wait a minute,' said Billy, 'how did he do the other hand?'

The next day, Billy dashed around to Oliver's house but his usual three-ring signal on the doorbell was not answered. He stood outside watching for a minute and was sure that

146

he saw the upstairs curtains move slightly, but when nobody came to the door he climbed back onto his bike and headed to the water tower. He was sure Oliver had been told to stay away from him.

At the top of the tower he was surprised to see a figure already hunched at the battlement. He was pleased that April had found the way up by herself but annoyed that his privacy had been invaded.

'I thought you wouldn't mind,' she said, reading his thoughts as she turned to face him. 'After all, it belongs to all of us, and I know you believe in equality.' She was wearing a red tam-o'-shanter, her tartan scarf and a long grey military coat. She looked like a girl drawn from one of his mother's childhood comic annuals.

'Of course I believe in equality.'

'Just as much as others don't,' she said, turning back.

'What do you mean?'

'Oh. Well. Have you ever noticed the absence of black people in the neighbourhood?' She pulled an enormous pair of binoculars from her coat pocket, focused them and surveyed the town. 'Have a look. Not a darkie in sight.'

'You shouldn't call them that.'

'That's what my mother calls them when she's being generous,' she said airily. 'Mind you, she formed most of her opinions in the 1950s and they've been atrophying ever since. But you must have noticed. You'd think they had a sign up, "Whites Only".'

'It's illegal to keep people out,' said Billy.

'Oh, there are subtle ways of getting around that. This is what I wanted to talk to you about. There are ways to get around everything if you have a little money and a little power.'

147

'How do you know so much about it?'

'I watch *Dynasty*. I listen to gossip. Only the blindest fool could fail to see what is happening here.'

Billy felt his cheeks reddening. He was sure that the conversation was somehow leading to his family.

'For example,' continued April, 'just suppose I wanted to drive your parents out of Invicta Cross. How would I set about it?'

Billy sat on the wall beside her, his stomach gently sinking. 'I don't know,' he said meekly. 'How?'

'I would spread scandal behind their backs. Get them a bad reputation. Make them feel uneasy about living here. Point out how they can't really afford to stay in the area.' She glanced casually at his darned socks. Billy awkwardly tugged his jeans down to cover them. 'Or perhaps I might go further. Stage a little charade. Make something disappear and apportion the blame wrongly. Something valuable, say a money clip. That would brand the father as a thief. Then I'd discredit the mother. Wait for an opportunity to make it look like she was a liar as well. Tell a little fib about her, perhaps. Say it was her own fault that she slipped. Drop a cloth on the floor, wipe up the oil. The store would be grateful. They'd be spared a messy court case and would save a fortune.'

'No,' said Billy, shaking his head, 'no one would do that. Nobody would be that nasty.'

April advanced on him.

'But why stop there?' she insisted. 'Assume the boy is a bad apple, too. Raised by those parents, what chance could he have? Tell your own children to stay away from him, freeze him out, maybe draw him into trouble, lead him down the garden path and strand him in a sweet shop holding someone else's stolen goods.'

'You can't know that!' he shouted.

'Can't I?' teased April. 'Then why do I know so much more than you? Maybe somebody even knocked your garden fence down on purpose, just to embarrass you in public.'

Billy thought of the Neighbourhood Committee letter, the insistence on repairs, the constant harassment, and suddenly realised why his father had gone to the police station.

'Letters,' he heard himself saying, 'letters and obscene phone calls. Somebody's been calling my mother and sending dirty letters.'

'Old news,' said April lightly. 'Wake up, Billy, and tell me something I don't know.'

Suddenly he found himself at her throat, shoving her shoulders back hard against the edge of the parapet, shouting, 'You're a filthy liar!' in her passive face. She remained motionless until he calmed, then pushed him away and dusted the snow from her sleeves.

'I thought that being a working-class boy you'd be less naive, more cynical. They always are on television. "Street smart", I believe the expression is. But the others are more street smart than you. They have already beaten you down to nothing.'

'You made this up, didn't you?' he said, close to tears. He hated the idea of his life being made to sound so simple and empty.

'No,' she replied, 'it's just what my mother says. Oh, don't worry, she's an outcast here as well. She calls the police to tell them there are people in the garden at night, but nobody believes her, not even me. She shoplifts all the time. We're outcasts, and so are you. I could tell that without even speaking to you. Victims are always able to recognise each other.'

Billy thought it through. Such an absurd conspiracy made no sense. 'Why would anyone go to so much trouble?' he asked.

April kicked at a frozen mound of snow with her shoe. 'Because you're not wanted here.'

Billy walked to the far parapet and looked out across the town. In April's strange make-believe world she wanted everything to be orderly and perfect, and this seemed like the sort of theory she'd concoct to rationalise inexplicable events. But it felt true.

'I bet they'll find a way to keep Jewish people out of the golf course, too,' she said.

'They haven't built a course,' he replied, looking out across the threadbare white fields that had been earmarked for the range.

'Not yet,' she agreed.

And then he saw it. The section of frozen pasture shaped like a missing jigsaw piece, and the only hindrance to its access. He would never have spotted it from the ground, but from up here the intended layout was as plain as day.

'All the residents are shareholders,' he said. 'They can't make a penny until they have planning permission. They need us out before it can be built.'

'And poor little Billy thought there was no conspiracy,' she said, smiling. 'I think I finally deserve to be given a big, wet kiss.'

CHAPTER EIGHTEEN

The Witch House

'Stan Skelton, a boundary-obsessed pensioner dubbed The Neighbour From Hell, was ordered to dismantle a 20-foot-long steel gate he erected overnight across his driveway to block a shared access and imprison his neighbours. He warned the couple next door to estimate their times of arrival and departure, refusing to unlock the gate at unspecified times. Defeated in court; neighbours threw a street party.' – *Daily Mail*

BILLY POUNDED along Gaveston Crescent and into Windsor Terrace, his breath burning in his lungs, desperate to tell someone what he had discovered. None of them was safe. His mother had already been physically injured. This was a war, small-scale perhaps, but a war all the same. Ray wouldn't do anything; it was all down to him now. Somehow he would find a way to save the family.

'Wait a minute, where the fuck do you think you're going?'

A boot shot out and kicked at his legs, sending them out from under him, slamming him to the slush-slick pavement. Gavin Diller raised his boot and placed it on Billy's chest, pinning him down.

'I've got some advice for you,' he breathed. 'Stay away from April Barrow.'

'Why should I?' Billy shoved the boot aside and raised himself on one elbow.

'Because she's my girlfriend,' the policeman's son replied.

'You'd better tell her, then.'

'She'll know about it soon enough. And so will you if you're not careful.'

'Like that really frightens me,' said Billy, attempting to muster some bravado.

'It should do, sonny,' replied Gavin, sounding remarkably like his father, ''cause if I see you anywhere near her again you'll soon be stuck down the nearest drain trying to find the remains of your teeth.'

Billy doubled his speed. The yellow sky threw a strange, terrible light across the town. Nothing was normal now. Even the most familiar sights were imbued with an air of menace. Fences could hide murderers, like Magwitch in *Great Expectations*, trees clattered their bare branches like the bones of the rising dead, the wind scooped fistfuls of fresh-fallen snow and tried to blind him, and always there were houses, rows upon rows like orderly tombstones, concealing their occupiers behind thick shrouds of curtains.

Ray was slumped on the sofa, staring at the television. He'd been drinking and was half asleep. Angela was upstairs in bed, existing on a diet of warm milk and strong pain killers. Even Victor was gently snoring beneath the radiator.

Billy tried to regain his breath, woke his father and

Christopher Fowler

gasped out his story. In his enthusiasm he rendered it incomprehensible and preposterous. Ray waved him away with a 'Not now, son,' and pretended to be studying a game show. The shrill screams of contestants filled the lounge.

'Don't you see?' shouted Billy. 'They're doing it deliberately, trying to force you off the land!'

'Just like a John Wayne movie,' slurred his father. 'Billy, you've seen too many films. This is just—' He turned to face his son, made an effort to concentrate. 'Y'see, it's like *The Beverly Hillbillies*.'

'What?' cried Billy. 'What?'

'*The Beverly Hillbillies*. We're the wrong place – I mean, the wrong people in the wrong place. You wouldn't understand 'cause it's an adult thing, but not everyone can fit in everywhere. It was all a mistake being sent here. Government don't care, just moves people about.'

'Dad, you're not listening to me!'

'Billy, Billy boy.' Ray reached across and ruffled his hair none too gently. 'When you're older you'll see. You got too much imagination, always did have. Too many films. Now keep it down, your mother's trying to sleep.'

Billy rang April.

'You're in danger as well,' he panted. 'Gavin Diller warned me to stay away from you.'

April sounded calm and casual. 'Oh, him. He wants to have sexual intercourse with me. He probably sees you as a rival for my affections.'

'You know about him?'

'To be honest, I had even thought of letting him try.'

'April, how could you?'

'Oh, easily. I'm nearly fifteen and someone will have to do it soon. It would get the whole sordid business out of the way once and for all. I only intend to have sex once, for scientific purposes. Every TV show you ever watch seems to hinge on the act, so there must be something worth investigating. I suppose you've told your father about the conspiracy.' She sounded almost amused.

'He doesn't believe me, April. He thinks I've got an overactive imagination.'

'You do. But you can be changed. Modern science has ways. Electrodes can be planted in your brain to neutralise your desires. In the future there will be no painful crises of conscience because we'll all be doing exactly what we're told.' She sounded as if she was barely paying attention. He gave up on her. That only left Oliver.

'Slow down, I can't understand a word you're saying,' said Oliver.

Billy explained again.

'It's possible,' came the thoughtful reply, 'although I'd hardly credit the people round here with the ability to co-ordinate such an operation. What are you going to do?'

'I don't know. My mother doesn't have proof, nor my dad. I suppose I'll have to find my own.'

'Listen,' said Oliver, 'I can't stay on because my father's expecting a business call. Somebody died. I'll speak to you later.'

Billy went to his room and sat before the model of the town, studying the jigsaw piece of emerald felt, trying to imagine how it would look with the golf course built. In his mind, other parts of the puzzle began to fall into place. It was why the building had stopped. It was why the road tailed off into wasteland. If the council couldn't guarantee the promised leisure amenities, the contractors weren't prepared to invest. The more he thought about it, the more the conspiracy grew.

He looked at the tiny scale models of the neighbouring houses, then went to the window to compare them with the originals, but fresh falling snow obliterated the view, as if nature itself were protecting the interests of the residents.

He decided to visit April. Quietly removing his bicycle from the hall, he let himself out into the freezing night and pedalled off through the fading tyre tracks on the ivory roads.

He rang the doorbell, but it looked as if nobody was home. No porch light, nothing from the front windows; then he heard unsure footsteps from the rear of the house. After that, silence.

'Who is it?' A querulous voice piped up through the door, startling him.

'I'm a friend of April's.'

Silence again, as this reply was carefully considered. Then a lock was undone and the door was slowly opened. Billy stepped back in alarm. The woman who peered around the door looked quite mad.

'My daughter has very few friends,' said Mrs Barrow, half-heartedly brushing a long grey hair from her eye. She wore no make-up and was dressed in a shapeless brown woollen smock with a frayed hem. She wore nothing on her feet, and her toenails were black with grime. She looked like an old hippy. The hall smelled of cats and damp and patchouli oil. 'Come in,' she said. 'April's doing her homework.' Billy stepped inside.

The house was poorly lit and incredibly untidy. Bundles of mildewed newspapers filled the corners, and cats skulked behind pieces of ratty furniture. Mismatched rugs overlapped across bare boards, and in several places the wallpaper was peeling from the walls as if the house was trying to shed its skin. If the March family was short of money, Mrs Barrow and her daughter were a damned sight shorter.

Billy was ushered into a gloomy lounge and offered a seat within the coils of an amorphous sofa covered in cat hairs. In the corner, a small portable television was offering a fuzzy close-up of the cancerous pimple on Ronald Reagan's nose. Mrs Barrow scratched insistently at the backs of her hands until Billy felt like scratching too.

'Perhaps you'd like some camomile tea,' she offered.

'No, really, it's all right.'

'But you must have something. It's freezing outside. April will be down in a moment.' She left the room, and Billy stared about him.

The ancient television had dirty dinner plates on top of it. A brown clay pot filled with tissue-paper flowers and dozens of half-burned joss sticks sat in an empty hearth. Two cats were cleaning each other on a partially unravelled rug. A dangerous-looking bar radiator buzzed in one corner. No wonder April had made a fetish of her neatness, living in such chaos. No wonder nobody talked to her mother.

A sudden thought chilled him. Was this how his own family looked to others? Was the reason for their ostracism justified after all?

'I don't know why you're here,' said April testily. She was standing in the doorway in an old green sweater, glaring angrily at him. It was obvious that he had committed a cardinal sin, crossing into forbidden territory and

156

surprising her at home like this, like an uninvited vampire. One glance at her face revealed how ashamed she was of her surroundings.

'I had to see you, April,' he said. 'I didn't mean—'

'I don't like being spied on,' she replied.

'I didn't complain about you climbing the tower without me. This makes us even.'

The reasoning seemed to mollify her. She came into the room and dropped cross-legged beside the cats.

'My mother's not really mad, you know,' she said. 'She talks to herself. A lot of people do that. She bumps into things. She has an inner ear problem. She thinks people are watching her when she goes out. Other kids call this the Witch House, but then I suppose you know that already.'

'I really didn't, honest,' said Billy, who had heard exactly that.

'She's very kind and loving,' continued April, absently disentangling the cats. 'She just hasn't been the same since Daddy went away.' She pushed one of the whining creatures from her lap. 'He never divorced her properly because he didn't want to have to pay us any maintenance money. We couldn't take him to court because we weren't able to find out where he was living, so we had to go on Social Security.'

Billy felt that he was hearing things he shouldn't, that these were adult problems he was not ready to have explained yet, but he listened.

Mrs Barrow arrived with tea and weird herbal-smelling scones of extreme density and flatness, and chattered desperately on about the snow long after her daughter and guest had ceased to listen.

Billy and April quietly watched each other, and over the

hour a tentative, unspoken agreement was reached. *We are both in the same situation*, Billy was sure their eyes said, *we have nowhere else to turn but to each other*. It was hard to tell exactly, but he wondered if perhaps he hadn't fallen in love.

CHAPTER NINETEEN

The Printed Word

'A man slumped in a van parked in Oklahoma City had been dead for three days and had collected twelve parking tickets before anyone noticed him.' – *Ashbury Park Press*

AT FIRST he thought that the floor had sprouted a carpet of crystals.

Diamonds glittered brilliantly in a rainbow spectrum of light, throwing iridescent prisms of colour onto the walls. Then he saw that it was glass from a broken window at the rear of the room. The shattered shards crunched and squeaked beneath his sneakered feet.

They had been burgled.

The lock on the back door had been forced, the screw that had held it in place now thrusting from a forest of splinters.

Ray had taken his wife to the shops. Billy had come home early from school to find the house empty and emptied. Everything of value had gone: the video recorder, the stereo unit, his mother's jewellery, a set of medals belonging to Ray's grandfather. Worse, the house felt intruded upon, damaged by the random malevolence of strangers.

Responding to Billy's call, the ubiquitous PC Morris Diller turned up and took some notes. An hour later, a gloomy-looking man appeared and disconsolately dusted the furniture for fingerprints. The dog stayed upstairs, whimpering beneath Billy's bed. It took him half an hour to coax the terrified animal out.

Angela cried when she returned and saw the mess. Her mother's cameo brooch had gone, a trifle she prized far beyond its actual worth. Ray waited for the police to leave and cleared away the worst of the damage, filling dustpans with tinkling chunks of broken china. PC Diller had been careful not to raise their hopes. Quite the reverse; only eleven per cent of the district's burglaries were brought to some kind of conclusion, he informed them before castigating them for not installing stronger locks.

To Ray and his wife, the break-in was an unfortunate but common aspect of modern life. To Billy, it was one more piece of evidence in a labyrinthine conspiracy that continued to unfold around him like the petals of a poisonous plant. After this, he allowed Victor to sleep at the end of his bed every night.

The days passed, and Billy's determination to do something positive evaporated along with the snow in the muddy brown streets. He did not know where to begin; making accusations against the neighbours would only cause more trouble. The culprits were all but invisible these days, fleeting ghosts who appeared briefly in the chill air on the way to their cars, visiting one another to arrange dinners and committee meetings.

There was little more sign of life in the shattered house at the end of Balmoral Close. Steadfastly refusing to believe his son, Ray dismissed his accusations as the product of an overactive imagination. He repaired and painted, replaced locks and rebuilt window frames, fitted burglar chains on the front and the back doors. An alarm system was out of the question; the monthly payments were beyond their depleted budget.

One evening, just after he had gone to bed, Billy saw his father standing in the open doorway, staring at the scale-model town with a thoughtful expression. He stepped into his son's bedroom and approached the prototype, running his fingers lightly across the balsawood rooftops, like a blind man trying to memorise their topography. Billy pretended to be asleep but wondered if his father was finally starting to see a pattern in the events of the last few months.

Ray looked for employment, but his efforts were distracted. He disliked being away from his wife, who was marooned in the house until her operation, now scheduled for early June. With her left leg still heavily bandaged, she was unable to drive, and the shops were too far away to reach on foot.

Billy watched his parents change. The burglary affected his mother more than she was prepared to admit. She was increasingly dependent on the painkilling tranquillisers that Dr McMann had so readily supplied her with and, naturally, Billy suspected the doctor's motives. His father's afternoon drinking was starting a little earlier each week. They were out of money, and out of luck.

The house began to grow shabby, and the garden became overgrown. Billy did what he could, but it wasn't enough. The Prouts and the Metcalfs averted their eyes from number thirteen as they passed, shooing their children ahead of them. Only Georgina Bovis peered over occasionally, anxious to discover what had happened to Ray.

Billy remembered this as a time of silences, of recriminatory sulks and stares. He was doing poorly at school in all subjects except chemistry and physics, and he had given up trying to make friends. Assan had been removed from Sherington by his parents, who were tired of hearing about the violent playground scrapes their son faced daily. That left Oliver, who at least could always be relied upon for revolting stories about his father's funeral parlour. Oliver would sit happily next to him throughout the lunch break, surreptitiously studying Billy's body language, as though memorising his friend's movements in case he was ever called upon to duplicate them. After a while his steady, unflinching gaze made Billy nervous. He had noticed that, despite the strength of their comradeship, Oliver was starting to see less of him. He hardly ever came over to Balmoral Close any more, citing his father's insistence on evening studies.

One freezing evening, Billy had a terrible, stupid argument with Oliver. It began over nothing at all and turned into a shouting match. They were at Oliver's house, in the upstairs back bedroom, working on a complex, electrically powered model of a star cruiser which was beginning to look as if it would never be finished. It was the last model they would make together; they were growing out of such toys, but had no other communal activities with which to fill their time.

'It's not as if my dad is beating me up, or we're trapped in a flat in Tower Hamlets with people chucking shit at the door,' said Billy, trying to end the fight. 'There's lots worse off than us.'

'That's the trouble with people like you,' Oliver complained. 'You're so fucking liberal. There's always a more deserving case. It doesn't make you a better person to suffer in silence. Your grades are in the toilet, your hands shake all the time, you jump at the slightest sound – look at you! What will it take for you to do something?'

'Well, it's not your problem, is it?'

'It is my problem. I don't want to see you hurt.'

'Why not, what's it to you?'

'I—'

'Go on, tell me.'

'Skip it.' Oliver scooped up the star cruiser and hurled it against the wall. The freshly glued wings came off as it fell.

Ray was drunk again. It was a Friday evening, and Billy sat on the floor working with modelling clay, finishing a replica of the water tower. Once this was completed the entire scale model would be finished. Billy had finally been allowed to prepare their evening meal. He enjoyed cooking; it reminded him of chemistry class. But tonight, it was his mother's turn.

'Billy,' she called from the kitchen, 'come here a minute, would you?'

She looked smaller and older than when they had first arrived here, four and a half months ago. He had noticed that her back was developing a permanent hunch now that she was forced to carry her body differently when she moved. She pretended to be happy enough, but the dark circles beneath her eyes suggested dream-plagued nights. She was trying to reach the rice jar, but the shelf was too high and the muscles of her leg would not be stretched.

'Here, let me get that.' He passed the jar down.

'You're a kind boy, but you really should get out more,' said his mother, watching him fondly. 'It won't do you any good hanging around the house with us. You should go and visit your girlfriend.'

He hated it when she called April that. 'Her house smells funny,' he explained, dabbing a finger around the top of the pastry bowl. 'And her mother's a pain.'

'What about your friend Oliver?'

'His dad doesn't like him having visitors any more. Oliver says he's fed up with people always asking him about the dead bodies.'

'Well,' she sighed, exasperated. 'What about going to the pictures with someone from school?'

'Are you trying to get rid of me?' he asked suspiciously.

'No, of course not, I just don't think it's healthy for a boy of your age to spend so much time on his own.'

'I'm not on my own,' he said, 'I'm with you.'

'We don't count,' she said, absently stirring at the bowl. 'You need people of your own age.'

'You're not old.'

'I don't know. I think we're getting old rather faster than we'd intended.'

'That's what this place is doing to you.'

'Billy, please don't start again.'

'Well, Jesus Christ—'

'Don't blaspheme.'

'Sometimes I think we all died and went to hell. Milton said it's better to reign in hell than to serve in heaven. What does that mean?'

'I don't know,' she replied, 'ask your father.'

There wasn't much point in doing that. Billy could see

164

him from the kitchen. He was lying across the couch half crocked.

'Probably that it's better to control your own destiny and be the master of your fate,' Billy mused. 'April says we should have done that when we first arrived here, become the masters of our fate I mean, and we wouldn't be in the mess we're in now. She says she knows who sent you those letters—'

There was a smash as the pastry bowl slipped from Angela's hand and shattered on the floor. 'For God's sake!' she shouted. 'Could you go and just – *sit down* – quietly somewhere? I *really* can't take much more of this.'

Billy was shocked by her outburst. Angela never shouted at him, ever. Perhaps he had overstepped the mark, mentioning the letters. Ray had told him he wasn't supposed to know about them, that it would only worry his mother. He stormed out to the hall and grabbed his bike, heading for another lonely ride through the gently curving neighbourhood streets.

His pedalling was hard and furious, and he only slackened his pace once he reached the edge of town, where the lights were swallowed by the inky blackness of the fields beyond. Fine, he thought as the idea came to him, if they wouldn't do something, it was time to take matters into his own hands.

On Saturday morning he went to the offices of the *East Grinstead Advertiser*, and sat outside the deserted staff room until an irritated secretary could find someone to see him. According to her their journalists were all unavailable, but one of the paper's freelancers, who also handled the classified ads, would listen to his story.

Gary Mitchell was new at the writing game. He had churned out a monthly column for an ill-fated horror magazine until it had folded without paying him, and he'd been handling baking contests, swimming pool openings and dog shows for the *Advertiser*, but he longed to be given something meatier. The problem was that the older hacks carved all the best assignments up between them, leaving him stuck with the horoscopes, which were traditionally knocked out by the last person to leave the building on a Friday night.

But Gary lived in hope. He sat and listened to the boy's story, running his hands through his bristling red hair as his eyes widened in disbelief.

'You see,' explained Billy, 'it turns out that the whole thing was masterminded by Mr Brickett—'

Gary was struggling to keep his notes up. 'Wait, you mean Councillor Brickett?'

'Probably,' continued Billy, 'because he's posh and we're not, and he wants to keep the town white—'

'What do you mean, white?'

'I didn't tell you. Assan, my friend at school, he's had to leave because he's black, well, Indian, and they're trying to get us to leave too, which is why they burgled our house and slashed my dad's car tyres.'

'Who slashed your tyres?'

'The neighbours. Because when we go they'll demolish our drive.'

Gary was confused. 'Why would they want to do that?'

'To get to the golf course, obviously. It has to be a certain width, otherwise they won't get planning permission. And they all have shares in it, so they're all in on it.'

'Wait, this is a pretty big conspiracy, and all a little far-fetched, don't you think?' asked Gary. 'If they need the land so badly, why don't they just offer your family money to leave?'

'It costs nothing this way. First they made my dad lose his job by hiding this clip full of money and accusing him of stealing ...'

'They did that, too?' Gary's pencil flew across the page. 'Will your father talk to me?'

'Probably not. He's not very well. They made him ill. They may even be poisoning him, putting something in the alcohol. He drinks a lot of Scotch.'

'What about your mother, can I get an interview with her?'

'She wouldn't want to talk to you.'

'Why not?'

'They already tried to shut her up once.'

'Shut her up? You mean somebody tried to kill her?'

'Not exactly, but she could have died. She can hardly walk now.'

'And she won't talk to me.'

'I don't want to involve her. Besides, she thinks I'm making it all up.'

'Then how do you suggest I verify your story?' asked Gary, with a little smile.

'Talk to the perpetrators, or to my friend April. She knows the truth because Morris Diller's son fancies her, and he's a policeman, or rather his father is, and they're all in on it as well.'

Gary had heard of paranoia, but had never seen evidence of it in one so young. 'So the police are involved, too,' he said, setting aside the notebook.

'Well, obviously,' said Billy, wondering if the reporter

was paying any attention at all. 'I mean, Diller is Brickett's best friend. The squad car is always parked outside his house. They're probably both masons, or satanists or something.'

'I'll have to think about this,' said Gary, rising. 'Let me get back to you.' He needed a story, but this wasn't it. Still, he thought, tapping the end of his pencil against his teeth, it had given him an idea for a saleable feature article.

Angela was mortified when she saw the result a week later.

'How will I ever be able to go outside again?' she cried, aghast. 'Billy, how could you have done this?'

Page five of the *East Grinstead Advertiser* read:

Misery of modern-day East End evacuees

Their story is eerily reminiscent of a wartime scene, when the East End of London sent its children to the country only to find that their back-alley kids failed to adjust to rural ways. The working-class March family are typical of a new wave of well-intentioned paupers created by the ill-conceived plans of loony-left inner-city councils, in which needy citizens are relocated in well-to-do suburbs. The Marches arrived in Invicta Cross expecting a bright new life. Instead, misery followed as they found themselves faced with high prices and low self-esteem. Neighbourhood hostilities have created an 'us and them' mentality that is tearing families like the Marches apart.

It went on in a similar vein for several columns. There was even a photograph of the outside of the house with a close-up of a broken window that Ray had yet to mend.

'I don't know what on earth your father will say when he sees this, Billy.' His mother folded the paper shut and pushed it away. He was surprised to see her so close to tears.

'I was only trying to help.'

'Well, you haven't, don't you see? You've made things worse.'

'I don't understand,' said Billy. 'I explained it all carefully, but he's turned it around so that it looks like everything's our fault.'

It occurred to him that maybe Gary Mitchell had been got at. Perhaps he was part of the conspiracy as well. Looking back at his mother, he wisely decided to keep his mouth shut.

Ray came home from the job centre via the Helicopter, and he was seething. Someone had shown him the article. 'Where is the little bastard?' he shouted. 'I'll fucking kill him.'

'It's not his fault,' said Angela. 'He didn't know what he was doing.'

'He will once I've finished with him,' hissed Ray. But by the time he reached the bedroom, Billy and his bicycle had slipped out of the back door.

CHAPTER TWENTY

The Holly Bush

'Rape Trauma Syndrome is a condition in which victims obliterate details of their ordeals from their minds, sometimes adversely affecting their ability to pick out an attacker in a police line-up.' – *Philip Paul*

'I DIDN'T KNOW you drove a car,' said April, eyeing the Nissan warily. It meant that she wouldn't be able to escape as easily as she had planned. 'I thought we were going by train.'

'I'm not going to freeze my bollocks off on a station platform,' said Gavin Diller. 'My dad bought this for me. Seventeenth birthday present. Get in.'

He barely waited for her to close the passenger door before starting the engine and moving off. Frost had already begun to crystallise on the sparkling pavements, and their breath fogged the windscreen. Gavin turned up the heater and smeared the condensation away with the back of his glove. He was a large, ungainly boy who seemed to overlap in every direction. His cropped hair stuck up in a startled buzz cut, but this appearance of alertness ceased at his eyes, which watched her sleepily as he drove.

April was unable to understand why she had accepted Gavin's offer of a date when common sense told her it was a bad idea, and this rogue element in her personality annoyed her. How would the world ever reach a perfect state if she, the most organised person she knew, could not control her own emotions? She recognised her desperate need to escape the chaotic clutter of the Witch House and the inane, unceasing chatter of her mother, but was this the right solution? Gavin was the first person ever to ask her out; even Billy March had not done that. Billy was precious to her, but still too young, too ill defined. And he was facing far too many problems of his own.

There was something sturdy and sensible about Gavin. His father was a policeman. There was order in his life. Everything was squared off, cleared up and simple; black or white, yes or no. She liked that. He had asked her to the cinema to see a big, loud, stupid Arnold Schwarzenegger film, and she had accepted. She anticipated no intelligent conversation, no dithering indecision. She wanted to see what an evening with an ordinary man was like. And she had to admit that she found Gavin attractive, in a basic, hormonal way. She had slipped quickly from the house, telling her mother she was going to help Billy with his homework, knowing that Rose would believe her enough not to check.

'Why do you dress like that?' asked Gavin, glancing away from the road.

'Like what?' she asked, defensively smoothing out her mother's pleated skirt.

'Like some old lady. My gran's got a jumper exactly the same as yours.'

'I knitted this from a 1939 Boots pattern book that was

extremely popular in its day,' she explained. 'Such clothes are the product of Britain's last civilised era, a representation of that decade's superior morality.'

'You what?'

'The world was on the brink of the abyss. The end of social order.'

'I'm not with you,' said Gavin, cutting up an Austin Metro and clipping the lights.

'It doesn't matter,' said April, sighing. 'Your car is very clean.'

'I take it down the wash every Saturday morning,' said Gavin, cheered that the conversation was back on solid ground. 'You wanna go for a drink before the film?'

'That would be nice.'

They parked in the courtyard of a pub called The King Edward, and April was not heartened by the fact that the sign above the entrance seemed to represent Edward VI, the sickly young monarch who had died of consumption. Watching Gavin as he struggled to set his car alarm, she decided not to choose this as a topic of conversation. The only King Edward he was likely to be familiar with was a potato.

The pub was crowded, smoke-filled, edged with beeping, flashing machines. Everyone seemed to know Gavin. Several girls waved at him.

'My old man drinks in here with his lads,' said Gavin. 'It's a coppers' pub, so it never shuts. I've ordered you a gin an' tonic.'

April smiled uncomfortably as he shouted at one of the girls near the bar. Perhaps this hadn't been such a good idea after all. She had no desire to begin drinking alcohol, and felt entirely unsuited to the noisy joys of modern youth. She wished Billy would turn up and rescue her, but he looked too young to ever be allowed in such a pub. As Gavin released a bellow of laughter, she accepted the gin and drank deep from the glass.

Billy sat between his parents on the sofa watching a quiz show in which contestants were asked questions about their shopping. The only illumination in the room came from the television, the one electrical item that had been spared in the burglary. His mother was barely conscious after taking her post-dinner painkiller. His father was in an alcohol-induced stupor, asleep with his mouth open.

Billy slipped carefully from his position and went to the back door, opening it. Twenty minutes ago he had let Victor into the garden. Normally the dog would be scratching at the paintwork by now. He looked out into the bitter darkness.

'Victor?' he called softly. 'Get in here.'

No sound was forthcoming, so he turned on the rear porch light and walked onto the overgrown lawn. The back gate was wide open. It was always kept locked from the inside. Someone must have reached over to unlock it. He stepped out into the street, pulling the door shut behind him, and looked about. Victor was lying on his side in the middle of the road. A thin black streak of blood extended from his nose all the way to the gutter. Although his thorax had been crushed almost flat he was breathing faintly, and his eyes followed his master as he kneeled down beside him. Victor's expression was one of mute apology, like a botched sacrifice, the warmth of his body dissipating on the frosted tarmac as Billy held his paw and cried.

*

April set her second empty gin glass down a little too hard. She was starting to like the taste of Gordon's and tonic. 'We should be going,' she said. 'We'll miss the film.'

'My mate Derek has just arrived,' said Gavin. 'I've got to buy him a drink 'cause I owe him one.'

'All right, then,' said April, 'but you had better be quick.'

A disco had been set up in the corner of the pub, and the raucous thumping sound of Frankie Goes to Hollywood's 'Relax' had ended any danger of serious conversation. Gavin returned from the bar holding fistfuls of drinks, trailed by a tall, sharp-featured boy in a black leather jacket. Derek pulled a stool between his legs and dropped onto it like a settling insect. Gavin slid another drink in his date's direction.

'Couldn't leave you out of the round, could I?'

'But we barely have enough time to—'

'We're not going anywhere until you drink it,' said Gavin, beaming a chilly smile. Derek's head was so long and thin that April asked him if he'd been a forceps birth. He released an unfortunate peal of laughter and bounced about on his stool. April avoided a spray of cigarette smoke and shifted uncomfortably, feeling for the first time that she was not quite so in control of the situation as she had supposed.

By the time Billy had carried Victor back into the yard, the dog was dead. He could feel the shattered mesh of broken bones beneath the creature's cooling fur, and his anguish was fast replaced by anger. There was no doubt in his mind that this act of cruelty had been perpetrated deliberately. It was pointless attempting to fix the blame; it could have been any of them. The house was circled by a ring of hate. He could feel it rising in waves from the surrounding streets and buildings.

He went to the shed and found a shovel, cracked open the hard black earth at the rear of the garden and admitted the animal's body. Hot tears dropped onto Victor's fur from his cheeks as he laboured over the makeshift grave.

From inside the house came flickers of sickly blue light. There his parents lay, anaesthetised and unperturbed. They could not help him now. There was no point in pretending any longer. Evil gods had taken to the air, their cursed batallions swarming through the night skies. The penants of war had been raised and would remain aloft until the enemy had been routed.

'We're going the wrong way,' said April, clearing a patch on the window and peering out.

'The film started ages ago,' Gavin explained. They were giving Derek a lift, apparently. He sat behind them giggling inanely as the car careened through the back roads. April presumed it was a nervous habit designed to cover his social ineptitude. As they bounced across a junction, she instinctively stamped her foot to the floor.

'We'd better get back, then,' she said.

'Plenty of time yet.' The car slid slightly on the frost-sheened road.

April tightened her grip on the door handle. 'Don't you think you should slow down?'

'What, in case one of my dad's pals stops us?' Gavin grinned in the darkness. Derek let out an adenoidal snort and reached between them to turn the music up.

'Where are we going?' She felt panicked now, by the

speed of the car, by Derek breathing hotly at her ear, by the sour spill of alcohol in her empty stomach.

'Place I know.' He swung the steering wheel and they turned up a steep, narrow lane. She could see nothing outside.

'I think it would be better if I went home,' she said, trying to sound casual. Behind her, Derek snorted again. 'You should try blowing your nose.'

Gavin's left hand shot out and grabbed her cheek hard. 'That's no way to talk to my best pal, April,' he said. 'Tell him you're sorry.'

'Go to hell.' She grabbed at the door handle, but he was faster, sealing the car from the central locking switch. The vehicle swerved, thumping against the grass bank at the roadside. April acted without thinking, swiping out at the nearest face. Gavin yelped in pain and swore.

The Nissan's brakes slammed on, and the car swung around in an arc as its wheels sought purchase on the glazed roadway. They came to a hard halt, tipped at an angle, half buried in a dense clump of holly bushes. April pulled up the locking button and shoved open the door as Gavin snatched at her.

Holly leaves enclosed her, stabbing and scratching, as he grabbed her leg. Seizing hold of the nearest thick branch, she pulled herself forward, then kicked back hard, slamming the door on his hand. He yelled and released her, scrabbling for an exit on his own side. Derek was still trapped in the rear of the two-door vehicle.

April tried to free herself, but the car blocked her exit from the bushes. The leaves pricked and clawed at her flesh as she forced her way deeper in, hooked by her clothes, praying for an opening on the other side of the bush. By the time Gavin and his friend came for her, she was pinned as helplessly as an insect on a needle. A heavy arm encircled her waist and dragged her free, scraping open dozens of hairline wounds as it pulled her backwards through the leaves into the light of the headlamps.

Billy finished tamping down the ice-jewelled earth and sat back on his haunches, wiping his eyes. He wore no jacket, but he was sweating. He threw the shovel aside and looked back at the lopsided mound. It would have to do for now. He wanted to run through the darkened streets shattering all of the windows with bricks, setting the neighbourhood on fire, but his father had taught him to control his temper. Yet how fondly – and how often – had Ray retold a story of his own youth, when he had beaten a bullying workmate in a brawl that had ended with the two young men falling into the Thames.

Billy looked back at the silent house, knowing that what happened next would happen anyway; whether his parents found work and managed to make a go of it would make no difference. They would always be outsiders, excluded and ignored, and there was nothing he could do about it. Invicta Cross held all the cards.

He went into the hall and collected his coat. He needed to ride his bike for a while. Ray and Angela wouldn't even notice that he was missing, and with any luck he would be able to go straight past them to bed when he returned. He was too tired, too heartsick to explain what had happened to Victor. Instead he mounted his bicycle and pedalled off in the direction of the town's centre.

As he cycled, he passed the end of another unfinished road. Where the streetlights, kerbs and smooth black tarmac ended, trees shook in howling darkness, and the real world began. Here, at the petering out of the road, a half-built house stood silted up with snow, and a buffeted builders' sign proclaimed: INVICTA CROSS – A PLACE FOR EVERYONE.

Yes, thought Billy bitterly, *and Everyone In His Place.*

The windows of the Nissan were completely steamed up. The vehicle rocked violently from side to side, like an excerpted scene from a bad comedy sketch. Muffled crying came from within. Occasionally a palm was slapped against the glass. Then a girl's shoe slammed out against the rear window, squeaking and scraping. A sudden scream of pain was cut short.

After she bit his fingers the second time, Gavin found that the best way to keep his date quiet was to give her a quick hard punch against the side of the head. That way, she wouldn't look so bruised. Derek was moaning on in the background about wanting nothing to do with it, but it was too late for that. He was involved now. Gavin gave her one final thrust and withdrew, flicking semen onto the seat beneath him.

'I'm gonna take my hand away now,' he panted, 'and if you shout again I'm going to break your fucking nose, do you understand?'

Beneath his fist, April nodded.

He released her and she scrambled away from him, up against the passenger door. Gavin zipped up his jeans and buckled his belt. His lower lip was starting to sting and swell where she had bitten him.

'Well,' he said, 'that was more fun than going to the pictures, wasn't it? Have to do it again some time.'

'Christ, Gavin,' said Derek nervously. 'I mean – Christ.'

Nobody spoke as Gavin started the car and reversed out of the bush. There was nothing to say. April felt shockingly calm as she assessed the options. In a few minutes the fields disappeared, to be replaced by darkened buildings. They were in East Grinstead now, and the Nissan pulled up sharply against a kerb, denting a hubcap. Gavin climbed out and released Derek from the back seat.

'I'll see you next Friday, Gavin,' said Derek. 'My sister's birthday bash.'

April could scarcely believe her ears; now that his state of panic had subsided, Derek was acting as if everything was perfectly normal. She had imagined going to the police with him to report the assault, but now, as she watched him walk quickly away from the car with his hands in his pockets, she realised that he was either more scared than she was, or more stupid.

'I'll give you a lift home,' said Gavin casually. 'You shouldn't have gone into the bushes like that. Got yourself some nasty scratches.'

She said nothing. She had to think, but was too tired. She had scraped her knee against the car door. Oddly enough, it didn't hurt down there, between her legs; she felt nothing down there, just a sense of disgust at her own foolishness. She could smell her own sweat, her own fear, and wanted desperately to bathe, to scald away the dirt, the turmoil, the muck of him.

As Gavin pulled up at the end of her street, he nearly clipped the tail end of a passing bicycle. She fumbled with the door lock and staggered out onto the pavement, and there was Billy, dropping his bike and running around the vehicle toward her.

'April – what's happened to your face?'

His hands reached out but she knocked them away.

'Fell into a bush,' she tried to say, but found that her tongue was swollen and sore, so she laughed instead.

'You can fuck off, for a start,' said Gavin, slapping his hands against Billy's chest and pushing him away.

'What have you done to her?' shouted Billy. April looked dazed. She had fine slashes across her face, hieroglyphic wounds that spelled a secret language of pain.

'She just told you, she fell into a bush, so piss off home.'

'You did it.' It seemed obvious to Billy. He swung his fist wide but his arm was caught by Gavin, who slapped him loudly across the face and kicked him backwards to the ground.

'I hope you're feeling better in the morning, April,' said Gavin, checking his hand and shaking it out. 'I'll call you soon, okay?'

They were both relieved to see him get back in the car and drive off.

'I have to go indoors now,' said April.

She was slurring her words, as if she was drunk. Now that he thought about it, he could smell alcohol on her. She was only wearing one shoe. How could she have gone out and got drunk with someone like Gavin? And why would she have taken off her shoe?

'I can't believe you went out with him,' he said angrily. 'I thought you hated him.'

'I have to go now,' she said again, looking around half-heartedly for her shoe. 'My mother is expecting me.'

'April?'

She was staring right through him. 'What?'

'Somebody ran over Victor. He's dead.'

'Victor.' She considered the name for a minute, but failed to recognise it.

'My dog, April. Somebody killed my dog.'

But she had already turned away toward the house, moving with the twisting gait of a sleepwalker unable to awaken from a ferocious nightmare.

CHAPTER TWENTY-ONE

The Prince of Denmark

'Between February and June 1992, five of Stockholm's favourite statues including a centaur and a figure of Bacchus were dynamited in the dead of night. Police are baffled.' – *The Guardian*

FOR NEARLY a week she engaged herself in a damage limitation exercise, refusing to leave the house or answer the telephone. What she told her mother was the truth, that she had fallen into a holly bush, but that was where the story ended.

Rose Barrow was quick to believe her daughter; she could always be relied upon to shy away from unpleasantness. She had survived the break-up of her marriage by acting as if nothing was wrong, by conveniently glossing over the facts surrounding her subsequent nervous breakdown, by imagining her husband dead, by pretending that her daughter was not growing up in pain and isolation.

April developed an intensely morbid fascination with her abuse at the hands of Gavin Diller. Her fingertips skittered back and forth across the fine welts on her cheeks as if hoping to discern some hidden meaning among the healing whorls.

Unsurprisingly, only the physical scars healed. She refused to consider the thought of going to the police because she felt sure that Morris Diller would support his son. Derek would do whatever Gavin told him to do; clearly that was his designated function as a friend. She worked at controlling her emotions more tightly than ever and returned to school the following week as if nothing had happened. It did not occur to her that she was starting to behave as her mother had done years before. April told herself that everything was normal, that revenge was pointless, that there was nothing to be gained on any side by making the matter public. The neighbours already considered her and her mother to be peculiar; to accuse a respected policeman's son would only confirm their beliefs.

But the nightmares refused to go.

As the days passed, the intensity of her fever dreams increased. She considered telling Billy the full story of that strange evening, but eventually decided against it. She did, however, tell her mother that she had had 'a problem' with a neighbourhood boy, something she very quickly regretted doing, for, much to her surprise, Rose decided to visit the police and have a private word with PC Diller, who promised to take the matter up with his son.

A day later he visited Rose at home and gently explained that he had spoken with the boy about this delicate matter. Gavin had admitted to his father that he had spent the evening with April, but he denied threatening or attacking her in any way. If anything, his son had told him, April had led him on, even going so far as to ask him to make love to her. Of course, he had not done so. After all, their date had been chaperoned by a third party, and Derek would be only too happy to give his version of events.

Rose was suspicious, but could not see how to take the matter further unless her daughter wished to press charges. Instead, she took this as a further sign, if such were needed, that they should not stay in the neighbourhood, and began making complex, chaotic plans to leave.

Exactly one month after April's assault, Ray was persuaded by Billy to check out the local area building plans in order to prove once and for all that his son's theories were unfounded. Instead he saw the inked-in site of the proposed golf course for himself. At least, that was what it looked like; a separate area of green diagonal lines that bisected the end of Balmoral Close.

Armed with this vague knowledge Ray attended a monthly neighbourhood committee meeting, held in the Bricketts' house. He arrived after the reading of the minutes had commenced and was greeted coolly by the Prouts and the Metcalfs. Ray sat silently through the arguments about litter bins, poop-scoops, traffic bumps, satellite dishes and roadworks. Toward the end of the meeting, when Georgina Bovis asked if there were any further matters to be raised, he stood up.

Fifteen people were seated around the Bricketts' spacious pastel lounge. All eyes turned to him. Ray cleared his throat.

'I just wondered,' he began, 'how I can explain things to my son.'

'What do you mean?' asked Barbara Prout solicitously.

'He seems to think that a number of you have a vested interest in moving us out.'

Sounds of disapproval rippled through the room.

'I know you think we're troublemakers. It's true we've had a run of bad luck since moving here. My son thinks it's because you need our property.'

The murmurs of disapproval became shouts of 'Rubbish'. Justin Brickett silenced the group, then turned to face Ray.

'No, I can see your point, Mr March,' he began, holding up his hands for silence. 'It's common knowledge that the construction of a golf course was once proposed on the site backing your house, but it's an area that also affects almost every other property in the street. I really do think you're unfairly singling this out as an excuse for your misfortunes – misfortunes, I must add, that you have brought upon yourself.'

Cries of 'Fair' and 'Quite right' filled the room. Even Georgina Bovis, who usually championed him, had joined the opposing side.

'I just can't help thinking it strange,' Ray added doggedly, 'that so many bad things should happen to us.'

'Bad things happen to everyone, March,' said Ken Prout. 'Welcome to the real world.'

'My son says—'

'Your son!' Daphne Metcalf was on her feet. 'Your son knows nothing! He's just a little boy, for Christ's sake.' She turned aside and said something under her breath that made Barbara Prout laugh.

'What did you say to her?' shouted Ray, incensed.

Daphne smiled defiantly. 'I said he's deranged, throwing milk bottles out of windows with notes in them, creeping around the town at night when he should be home in bed, staring through people's windows.'

'He does not stare through people's windows—'

'You may not have noticed, Mr March, but your son is a little Peeping Tom. We've all seen him watching us.'

'He's imaginative, that's all,' said Ray defensively.

'Overimaginative,' corrected Ken Prout, 'and you believe his silly lies. Nobody is trying to get you to move, March. Nobody hates you. We have no opinion of you at all, in fact.'

'Well, I've had a chance to form an opinion of you lot,' said Ray furiously.

'And I proceeded to give it to them,' he told his wife when he returned home a few minutes later.

'Oh, you didn't say that,' said Angela in disbelief.

'I did.' There was a hint of pride in Ray's voice. 'Sod them all. I don't care whether Billy's right or wrong, I won't have my word doubted in public like that. My father used to say he had nothing but his pride.'

'And you think that's a good thing?' asked Angela. 'You have to learn how to get on with other people or you never get on in life, that's what *my* father used to tell us. It's just as important to be liked as to be successful.'

'You're joking,' said Ray. 'You think people like politicians? Company directors? Captains of industry? *They* don't get on by being liked.'

'Well, we're not successful,' said his wife. 'According to your theory everyone should love us.'

Ray poured himself a tumbler of Bell's and went to bed early, reasoning that it was impossible to argue sensibly with someone you had chosen to marry.

Oliver had stopped taking his calls. Whenever he rang, Mr

Price curtly answered and fobbed him off with some flimsy excuse. *Et tu, Brute*, thought Billy. Well, if Oliver couldn't be bothered to find a way around the ban, neither could he.

And then April found him one afternoon at the top of the water tower.

'I've come to say goodbye,' she said. 'I'm sorry we didn't get a chance to finish the model town.'

In the dying afternoon, her face was as pale as moonlight. She was thinner now, and her weight loss was accentuated by the narrow black overcoat she had pulled tightly around her. Thick brown stockings showed at the hem. Her hair was pushed up beneath her tam-o'-shanter. One small thin scar remained on her upper lip as a reminder of her date with an ordinary man.

'That's okay,' said Billy. 'I'm going to get rid of it soon anyway. I may burn it, or blow it up spectacularly in the garden. We're doing explosives in chemistry. Where are you moving to?'

'It's a place in Essex, just a small town. I have an aunt there. We're going to stay with her for a while, until we can find a flat.'

'That's nice for you. At least you're getting out.'

'The thought of moving to my aunt's fills me with repugnance. A house full of messy neurotic women, what an unendurable nightmare.'

'You can leave me your address if you like.'

'I could, but I'm not going to.'

'Why not?' Billy frowned, hurt.

'Because we'll write for a while, then less and less frequently, then finally we'll stop altogether, and our friendship will be dead. This way I'll leave while our friendship is still alive.'

He thought for a moment. 'I know what happened that night, you know.'

'I know you do. All the more reason for us to be apart.'

'I don't understand.'

'Between us we have enough grievances to warrant some form of revenge. Divided, we are safe.'

'You really think so?'

'Oh, I'm sure we'd be terribly dangerous together.'

'Perhaps you're right. I'm safe by myself. I take after my father. Not the revenge type, I'm afraid. Too much procrastination.'

'Well then, Prince of Denmark, I must be going.' April crossed the red brick roof of the tower and took him in her arms. 'Goodbye, Billy March, you are a very special boy and I shall miss you,' she said, lowering her face to his and slipping her warm pink tongue into his mouth.

As he watched her slim form descending from the roof chamber, Billy realised that he was happy.

She had left him with his first proper erection.

CHAPTER TWENTY-TWO

The Icarus Effect

'Neighbours in Miranshah on the North Western Frontier in Pakistan fell out over the ownership of a stray chicken, and resolved the dispute with assault rifles, grenades and rocket launchers, leaving four dead and seven wounded.'
– *Observer*

'YOU UNDERSTAND why you've been called in here, I suppose?' asked Mrs Davenport.

'Yes, ma'am, for fighting in the corridor.'

Billy stopped analysing the patterns in the carpet and raised his head. A sharp spring wind was pummelling the study windows. The playing field beyond gleamed, luminous and frozen, in the setting sun, and a few teams of blue-kneed boys were still shouting for passes in the distance.

'Is that what you call it. I'd call it something rather more serious than a fight. Gavin Diller's nose is broken, and two of his ribs are cracked. I know it means nothing to you, but he will have to be dropped from the first eleven for the remainder of the season.'

The headmistress turned her attention to the wretched child before her. He was far too thin, and there were dark rings beneath his eyes. His neck and chin were smothered in spots. The boy was staying up all hours in front of the television, she supposed, and subsisting on a diet of junk food. These families simply couldn't be trusted to bring up their offspring in a responsible manner. She expected to see such children on the estate schools, but not here. In two years' time Sherington would become a fee-paying private establishment, and those who couldn't make the grade would be out on their collective ear before the changeover.

'How may times has Mr Batley had to break up a fight in which you were involved, March? We must be approaching double figures by now. What was the reason for the disturbance this time?'

'They called my parents names, ma'am. They started hitting me first.'

How his voice jarred. Those ghastly glottal stops would hold him back unless he took some elocution lessons. She almost felt sorry for him, but Billy March simply did not learn. He'd been here for nearly seven months and his behaviour had become increasingly erratic. His marks had plunged from excellent to abysmal, his interest in class affairs was now minimal, and yet there was a keen intelligence in those sad blue eyes, if only it could be unlocked. She wanted to be lenient, but knew how quickly the parents would complain if she failed to punish pugnacious and disruptive elements.

She had all the ammunition she needed to expel the boy; in fact, two of the other teachers were insisting that she did so. But something held her back. She knew for a fact that Diller's broken nose was the result of an accident. But if March was innocent, why did he not explain himself? Why did he never seek to blame others? Why did he have to be such a natural scapegoat? It encouraged bullies like Diller to attack him. He enfuriated her, because he refused to empower her with a method of helping him. Billy March stood there covered in the cuts and bruises of a dozen vicious encounters, and she wanted to hit him almost as much as his classmates did.

'I understand that you told your form master you are unhappy in this school. Is that correct?'

'I hate it here.'

'Hate is a very strong word, March. What exactly do you hate about the place? The teachers?'

'No, ma'am.'

'The lessons, then?'

'No, ma'am.' This was accompanied by another solemn little shake of the head.

'Then what?'

'The others.'

'The pupils?'

'Yes, ma'am.'

'Ah. There, sadly, you have picked the one part of the equation about which I can do very little. Do they pick on you?'

'Yes.'

'And why do you think that is?'

'Too many hormones, not enough brain cells.'

He'd hit the nail on the head there. March was too smart to be popular in a town like this. Intelligence frightened the herd.

'You may well have a point.' She looked at her watch, knowing that she would have to wrap this up quickly. She was due to kick off a staff meeting in ten minutes and was dying for a cigarette.

'I've threatened you with expulsion before, haven't I?'

'Yes, ma'am.'

'I don't want to know the reasons behind this latest skirmish. What I need to wring from you this time, Mr March, is a promise that it will never happen again.'

There was a brief silence. The boy had a look of utter defiance in his eyes. For the first time, he frightened her.

'I can't give you that, ma'am.'

She felt her temper flaring despite her determination to handle the matter calmly. 'And why not?'

'Because they treat me like an inferior.'

'Why does it matter what they think of you?'

'It would matter to you, wouldn't it?'

Something about his reply rattled her. For an awful moment she remembered the Roman Catholic refectory in Aylesbury where she grew up. 'Go back to your class,' she snapped. 'You're on detention for the next two weeks.' His eyes never left hers, never flickered or betrayed the slightest emotion. 'And the next time anything like this happens,' she said, controlling the tremble in her voice, 'you are out of this school for good, do you understand?'

Billy understood. In the solitude of his bedroom, above the scale model of the town, he now kept a large graph-paper chart on which he plotted each new indignity. A complex series of coloured symbols indicated the nature of the offence and the perpetrator. Clearly, like Dickensian villains, they would not stop until they had succeeded in driving his family into madness and penury.

After the Vauxhall had broken down and Barbara Prout had refused to drive his mother to the hospital to have her cartilage X-rayed, Billy had longed to throw a brick through next door's window, but did not dare. Instead he had stored away the grudge and helped his grimacing mother down to the bus shelter while Barbara drove off on an extended shopping trip.

Angela's bandages had come off, but the ligament had refused to knit properly, and the pain continued. She did not complain; it was not long now until the operation, just over a month. She didn't want to be a burden.

While his parents plodded through the usual weary arguments downstairs, Billy sat on his bed and updated his red notebook. He had taken to looking for signs and portents in the neighbourhood, indicators of shifting fortune. Then he correlated the changes on his wallchart, aware that it would only take one more coloured square to make his father throw in the towel.

That square was finally marked the following Monday, when Ray entered his bedroom in a state of confusion and said simply, 'I can't wake your mother.'

'What do you mean?' he asked dully, following his father from the room.

'She's normally awake before me, but she's not moving.'

They walked along the landing to the main bedroom, but Ray hesitated before the door, and Billy had to push it open, going ahead of him. The room was unnaturally still. It smelled of wintergreen and roses. The curtains were unopened, and sunlight was inappropriately attempting to force its way into the room. Angela was curled up in a foetal position, with her head tucked down below the pillow, too still to be asleep. Billy wanted to run from the room, but his father was blocking the door.

'How could she be dead?' said Ray softly. 'There was nothing wrong with her last night.'

On the bedroom table stood an empty wineglass and a mug, and her usual bottle of sleeping tablets. He wanted to pull back the duvet and touch his mother, but he knew without doing so that she was dead. The scene before him was as lifeless as a waxwork tableau. He tried to think what this meant, but his mind fuzzed up with panic. Behind him, Ray was muttering on about her always 'sleeping heavily'. Billy looked back at his mother, forcing himself to reach over and touch her exposed arm. His fingers recoiled instantly. Her skin was as slick and cold as vinyl. Her hopes for her own life were over. Her dreams were now beyond the reach of the living. Somewhere she swam alone in the darkness.

Billy pushed out of the room past his moaning father and went downstairs to the telephone. He felt light-headed and slow, as if he were floating far above his own body and controlling it from a great, cool height. He calmly pulled the directory from beneath the telephone and looked up Dr McMann's number. After he had dialled it and explained what had happened, everything else took care of itself.

The doctor arrived twenty minutes later and suggested that, as no immediate cause of death was apparent, an inquest would be called for. He was sorry for the additional distress this would cause but offered to attend as the family's representative, a move that Ray was too dazed to oppose.

The intervening hours passed like clouds. Father and son barely spoke. Ray handled the calls to his wife's family, and always managed to make it sound as if he was apologising for having married her in the first place.

The inquest findings produced no real surprises. It had been an easy enough mistake to make. Lately, his father had been giving Angela a late-night toddy to help her sleep, hot milk and Scotch. She had been taking painkillers and sleeping tablets, and when these had ceased to be effective, the warmed whisky had provided a welcome substitute. But it made her forgetful, and she lost track of the tablets she took. She had slipped into a deeper slumber than usual that night, and her heartbeat had softened until it became the faintest murmur, and then even that had gone.

The coroner refused to allow a verdict of misadventure after Dr McMann successfully argued that the medicines he had prescribed were 'open label', meaning that they were clearly marked with their contents, and instead, much to Ray's great distress, recorded a verdict of suicide.

Ray refused to allow any of their neighbours to attend the simple funeral, held in a small nondenominational church to the north of the town, and spent the day crying noisily on the arm of his sister-in-law. Carol-Lynn organised everything with alarming efficiency, as though she had been through the process many times before, and Billy stayed by her side, preferring her no-nonsense company to the maudlin recollections of his father.

There was no discussion about what to do. The following week, they packed up the contents of the little house and hired a van to transport their belongings back to the city. The ever-helpful Jason Brickett reminded them of his capabilities as an estate agent and put in an offer to the council for the remainder of the property's lease. Billy wasn't sure of the outcome and didn't care.

Ray sat at the table with a full tumbler of whisky and stared about the emptied kitchen, exhausted. He looked ten years older than he had two weeks ago, started as the front door slammed, surprised to see his son.

'I thought you were going to say goodbye to your friends.'

'I haven't got any friends.'

'Don't talk stupid. There's that boy—' He thought hard, but the name would not come.

Billy had not seen Oliver in weeks. 'When are we going?'

'The van's due back in half an hour.' His father was puzzled. 'Isn't there anyone you want to say goodbye to?'

'No.'

'Me neither. I just don't like to leave your mother.' He gave a bitter snort. 'She'll hate being stuck here.'

Billy decided to get out of the house before things got even more depressing. 'Did you pack my bike?'

'Not yet.'

He went around to the shed and collected his bicycle. The scale model of the town lay broken backed in the garden, where it had landed after he had angrily shoved it out of the bedroom window, along with his red diary.

He left his father and cycled across town to the water tower. It was risky climbing the redbrick turret in broad daylight, but he no longer cared.

As he reached the top the sun broke through the clouds, swathing the streets below in light. From up here the place looked quite attractive. It was a town on the edge of boom times; to the east, scaffolding and steel shorings staked out an area of future development. To the west, a slip road to the motorway was being constructed. No doubt in time the golf course would appear, providing Invicta Cross with the luxurious amenities it required to maintain its maturing status. There was nothing for him or his father here.

Billy felt a great sense of relief flooding through him,

knowing that he would never set eyes upon the town or its people again. Greenwich was now filled with fashionable media folk, a borough too smart and expensive to return to, so they were moving to his uncle Reg's old flat in Tufnell Park, one of the last areas of central London to refuse gentrification. Reg had moved to Spain and left them his flat only because he considered it uninhabitable.

A new school would be found for him; perhaps even a new job for Ray. They would get by somehow. He stood among the warbling pigeons, gripping the crumbling brick surround of the tower that was such a central element of the town below but entirely separated from it, and the strange lightness he had sensed just after his mother's death once more filled his body. He felt as though he would be able to fly if he could catch just the right updraught. It was tempting to try. Perhaps Ray, like Daedalus, could manufacture the apparatus his son needed to become lighter than air. Perhaps this urban Icarus would simply sprout pale golden wings and climb to the spiralling flame-bursts of the sun . . .

He began to pull himself up onto the wall, but a sudden gust at his back nearly tipped him over the edge and he snapped back to his senses. It was the wrong thing to do. It was not what his mother had done. She would have quietly seen things through if only she hadn't made such a stupid mistake.

With a heavy heart he descended the spiral staircase and climbed back out over the wall, knowing that there was nothing for him here, wondering if there ever had been. He thought of April in her long military coat and scarf, as stern as any soldier, and of her mother, as nervous as a mouse, gnawing her knuckle at the window, of his own parents holding hands like children, smiling and hopelessly lost in the confusion of newly constructed roads, and knew that what April had told him was true; for those who were misplaced or left behind, it was the same as being dead.

As he cycled away from Invicta Cross, he bade farewell to much more than just a town.

CHAPTER TWENTY-THREE

Falling Fortune

'A two-and-a-half-year feud between respectable North Devon neighbours finished in a £50,000 court case that shattered a judge's faith in human nature. The Foxes fell out with the Swainstons over driveway rubbish and continued fighting with them about dogs, loud radios, door slamming, bird boxes, rain barrels, fences and the positioning of a caravan. Mr Fox (described by his own parents as "psychopathic") daubed his neighbours' house with offensive graffiti; Mrs Swainston hit him with a broom. The Foxes had their car attacked with paint stripper. Mr Swainston recorded over 1,000 grievances in his diary. Both sides patrolled their properties at night. The judge complained that it was the most wretched and miserable dispute he had ever heard, and enough to turn anyone into a misanthropist.' – *Daily Telegraph*

THEIR RETURN to London was less than triumphant.

They had been away for under a year, but almost as much had changed in the topography of the city in that time as it had in their own lives. A grand new vision of the future was under construction; the back-to-back slums and warehouses of the docklands were being demolished to make way for advertising agencies and public relations companies, vast glass cathedrals that appeared to have been taken from designs by Albert Speer. Between these awesome finance palaces were odd little office blocks with primary-coloured pediments and gables. Where waste ground once afforded spectacular sights of the river, steel-rimmed apartment buildings and designer restaurants stood in shuttered shadow, blocking the view. Billy and his father peered in through frosted glass panels at bored-looking security guards and failed to recognise the streets where their relatives had passed their lives.

Most shocking of all was the spot where their Greenwich house had once stood at the bottom of Westcombe Hill, for in its place was a deserted six-lane highway connecting Blackwall Tunnel Road to the start of the M3. On either side of this concrete swathe the old neighbourhood remained intact, but now the area seemed dead. The high street's original shopkeepers had sold up and fled, so that Purbrick the tobacconist was now a closed-down video outlet, Lynch's the grocers was a minicab company, and the Lyons' bakery was boarded over. On either side, blocking off the flow of people and cars that had kept the area so busy, high concrete walls stood, smothered in graffiti.

The oddest thing was the eerie silence that had fallen on the neighbourhood. The old families had been replaced by residents who were willing to make use of the divided town. Rose bushes planted by former tenants before the war still thrived in the fume-filled air of Westerdale Road's remaining section, but no one was seen tending them, and no children played in the streets. It was as if some benign watchful spirit had departed, leaving the surviving occupants to fend for themselves.

In the next road, the Victorian police station and the Sunday school hall still stood, the former with its floral beds immaculately intact, the latter now converted into a furniture factory outlet. Even the library stubbornly remained, wedged beneath the stone awning of a flyover. But if the architecture of the town survived, its community had not. Like thousands of others throughout the country, the streets had been destroyed as surely as if enemy planes had bombed them flat.

Billy and his father's apartment in Tufnell Park was cramped and gloomy, the daylight cut off by the arch of the railway bridge that crossed the road. The property's previous owner, Ray's uncle, had left the rooms decorated with ancient brown wallpaper, adding to the overall oppressiveness of the place.

The pall of Angela's death hung over them constantly, clouding their thoughts and colouring their conversations. They analysed the past until it became a litany, devoid of meaning. The apartment badly needed renovation, but Ray seemed unable to rouse himself. Billy enrolled at a local school and drifted disinterestedly through the lessons. Here in the city, the classes were large enough to become lost in.

Billy became increasingly wary of his father, who complained bitterly at the slightest provocation and seemed determined to avoid leaving the apartment for the outside world. His conversation was drawn from his view of a world seen from a grimy first-floor window. Even though she lived miles away, Ray's sister-in-law started calling by to see if he and Billy needed anything.

With so little comfort at home, Billy eventually began to take his studies more seriously and discovered some small aptitude in the fast-developing field of computers and communications. But each success was mitigated by memories of the past. Every evening he returned home after school to be confronted with the evidence of their damnation. Ray sat in his armchair watching soaps and quiz shows with a half-full glass of whisky at his elbow. He never allowed his son to see him refill it, so Billy found it impossible to judge how heavily he was drinking.

The following year, Ray was officially diagnosed as agoraphobic, and a helper started visiting to clean up the place. His father was just forty-five years old but had developed the behavioural patterns of an elderly man. He no longer combed his hair like Elvis. It was greying and falling out in handfuls. His youthful energy had dissipated in the chill air of Invicta Cross, and nothing, it seemed, could encourage its regeneration.

In 1987, on Billy's sixteenth birthday, father and son took a rare trip out to the cinema. They saw *The Untouchables* and went for a Chinese meal. Each time he ventured from the apartment Ray promised to start getting out more, but each time the promise vanished on his return to the safety of its womb-dark walls. He had vowed to seek treatment for his depression and to do something about the damp patch in Billy's bedroom, but his plans and ideas came to nothing.

After the meal, the two of them sat on an embankment bench looking out at the ebbing river, and his father asked him what he planned to do with his life. It was the first time he had broached the subject since Angela died.

'I'm not sure,' said Billy carefully. 'I'm good with figures. I like electronics. Seems like it's the right time to get into computer technology.'

'Sounds like a good idea, so long as it makes you happy,' said his father, watching one of the new commuter ferries crossing the river. 'Always knew you'd do me proud one day.'

'Well, you're not going to make me proud, are you?' said Billy. 'Not unless you stop drinking and find yourself something to do with your life.'

Ray seemed not to have heard him. 'We should never have gone to that bloody place,' he complained.

'Let's not go over that again,' said Billy. 'It wasn't the town, it was us. You can't let the past hurt you forever. Come on.' He stood up and rebuttoned his jacket. 'I don't want you getting cold.'

'I killed her, you know.'

'Please, Dad, don't start this again.'

'I should have kept count of what she took. I should have been able to warn her. She didn't take her own life, Billy.'

'I know that, Dad.'

'She would never have done such a thing.'

'Come on, let's go home.'

'I haven't got no home. Not a real one.'

Billy watched as his father rose unsteadily from the bench. He needed a haircut. He looked like one of those sad old rockers who still dreamed of having a band long after there was any chance of achieving success. Billy took him home and tucked him into bed, ignoring his teary reminiscences. He saw now that Ray had gone too far ever to recover. He would not find a women to replace his wife. He would not find a job. He would not connect with reality again. In a strange way, he had finally found himself a purpose; he had become a mourner, part of the past.

That night, for the last time in his life, Billy found a

reason to cry. He knew he had lost his father as completely as he had lost his mother.

He left school shortly after, planning to work in one of the new computer software companies that were setting up across the city. He received mildly encouraging responses to his applications and, turning away from the events of his childhood, concentrated on securing a good job.

The Old Street company that employed him paid a lowly wage, but the work was steady and there were decent prospects. His workmates found him difficult to draw into conversation and eventually left him alone, which was what he wanted most of all. He tried to dismiss the past. He scaled down his dreams. In his own fashion, he found peace.

Just over four years after they moved back into the city, one final, inevitable tragedy struck. Billy was called out of his office by an apologetic policewoman, who sat him down in a corridor and carefully informed him that his father was dead.

Ray had been cooking himself a meal, but had fallen asleep in his armchair, having consumed his usual half pint of Scotch. The smouldering chip pan had filled the apartment with dense, oily fumes and he had choked on his own vomit. Billy listened to the policewoman, but felt nothing inside. It was as though something he had long expected to happen had finally come about. When people gave up so completely, perhaps it was best to let them go.

Angela's sister, ever reliable, insisted on arranging the funeral, then asked Billy to come and live with her family. She had barely enough room for her own brood, but was happy to welcome him into her home. Billy thanked her and explained that he was old enough to take care of himself.

He sold the flat for a small profit and rented a one-bedroom first-floor apartment in Camden Town.

Billy matured. His height stopped just above six feet. His hair lengthened and his bones gained flesh. Physically, he became a different person. But inside, he sometimes felt that he was stuck with the grievances of a fourteen-year-old boy. After eighteen months the Old Street company suddenly folded without warning, stranding its startled staff, and Billy was back at the job centre. Work was not so forthcoming now. Each position had dozens of applicants, most of whom were better educated and qualified. Billy took extra evening courses and worked behind a bar in Euston to pay his way. He reached a qualified level of happiness. He wasn't expecting the breakdown when it came.

He had not even been aware that it *was* a breakdown. He remembered becoming confused and angry over the minor details of his life, rent arrears, a row with the electricity board. There was the argument at Camden Station ticket barrier where the police were called. Another fight, more serious this time, in an Islington pub. A visit to a clinic, a lady doctor who made him write out endless lists, and an eight-week stay in some kind of halfway house, a dismal building that smelled of disinfectant and boiled cabbage and was filled with pitiful-looking men clutching their belongings in old plastic Safeway's bags.

And deep in his heart, against his best intentions, he

never forgave and he never forgot. Powerless to banish the past or rectify it, he lived on in a kind of half light, passively reacting to a fast-changing world. The years settled into one another, their passing barely registered by a man who no longer felt himself to be a part of the planet.

One night in yet another cheap Camden room, he was watching a news feature on his portable about the changing face of Britain's countryside and was surprised to find that, following a nationwide poll, the town of Invicta Cross had been awarded new status as the place with the best quality of life in Britain. He considered calling from the foul-smelling pay phone on the landing to give his own opinion about the quality of life there but recognised this as being something his father would have done, and stopped himself.

Instead, he watched the screen.

There before him was the town, barely recognisable but for the old water tower, which had now become the centrepiece of Britain's newest and largest US-style shopping mall. Stupefied shoppers in pastel shell suits passed before the camera like convicts in a chain gang. Crying children were mollified with balloons presented by a horribly creepy clown.

Unable to take any more, he turned the set off. There was an article about the award in the *Daily Mail* next day. 'Wouldn't it be nice,' ran the double-page headline, 'if one day all towns were like Invicta Cross?'

After that, Billy concentrated harder than ever on finding decent employment. He landed a place as a trainee programmer in an electronics firm in Holborn and buried himself in work. He stayed late into the night and carried on through most weekends, and spent his few remaining spare hours watching television. One evening he saw a party political broadcast encouraging people to invest in the future. 'This is our chance to build a new world for our children,' it said. 'Everyone deserves a fresh start in life.'

As he sat before the phasing screen, Billy looked up at the damp wall above his narrow bed, listened to the drunken couple killing each other in the next room, and wondered if this was what the prime minister had meant by a fresh start. As the sound of shattering glass mingled with the roar of trucks on their way to King's Cross, he pulled the threadbare candlewick counterpane over his ears and burrowed deeper into his bed.

PART TWO

1995

'Democracy is the art of saying "nice doggie" until you can find a rock.'
– Will Rogers

CHAPTER TWENTY-FOUR

Haddock

'This is the part you've all been waiting for, you poor despairing readers. You've ploughed through that ghastly catalogue of woes and now you want some proactive behaviour, some positive action. You want to see heroic young Billy choke the remorse from his tormentors' throats. You want to get to the part where truths are told and good triumphs and the guilty are punished. All that will happen, I promise you. Fortune's tide starts turning now.' – *The Red Diary*, entries recommencing April 1995 after a ten-year lapse.

IT WAS years later and the most mundane of encounters, on a wet Saturday morning in April 1995, shopping in the Camden Town branch of Marks & Spencer's. He recognised her the second he saw her, which was surprising, considering how she was dressed. She had come out shopping in a yellow gingham flared skirt, a sequined purple bolero jacket and matching polka-dot stilettos, and looked like a deranged version of Doris Day. She seemed to be having some kind of altercation with the floor manager.

'April? April Barrow?'

She was wearing a pair of winged pink-tinted glasses and peered myopically over the manager's shoulder at him. Suddenly she gasped in recognition.

'Henry!'

'Billy,' he said, hurt. 'Billy March. Invicta Cross. Remember?'

'This is my husband, hello, darling,' said April, suddenly shifting the manager to one side and pointing at Billy. 'He can explain *everything*.'

'Well?' The manager turned to him and folded his arms, ready for a story.

Behind his back, April was signalling violently. In one elastic-mesh glove she was waving a boil-in-the bag haddock. Billy watched her mouthing words and slowly gleaned her purpose.

'That's right,' he said, trying to piece things together. 'I'd left my wife for a minute, to go and get my...' She was making opening and closing gestures with her hands, now pulling something out. 'My wallet,' he said, relieved, 'and my wife...'

April mimed dropping the haddock into her purse.

'Accidentally...' She shook her head violently. 'Or rather, she thought I'd already paid for her groceries. Grocery. Fish.' The manager looked sceptical, to say the least. 'And I hadn't,' he added lamely.

'And I thought he ha-ad,' she said in a ghastly singsong little-girl voice.

'So you see, it was a perfectly understandable mistake,' he finished, 'and I'll be happy to pay for the ... haddock.'

April was shaking her head again and performing an unzipping motion.

'Or the bananas,' he said.

The manager would have made more of a fuss, but a loud argument between a group of backward-baseball-cap-wearing youths near the yoghurt display distracted him, and he eventually dismissed them.

'Gosh, thanks awfully for helping a chap out,' said April in exaggerated twenties English, turning to plant a perfect bee-sting lipstick kiss on his cheek. 'I would never have guessed it was you in a hundred million – the cheek of the man, accusing me of stealing! Tell me, is the manager still looking in this direction? Say nothing, don't move, is he watching us?'

Billy checked over his shoulder. 'Erm, not really.'

'Let's get out of here. Do you have time for a cup of coffee? Can the purchase of your groceries be delayed or do you urgently require vegetables?'

'Yes, I suppose—'

But she had already grabbed him by the arm and was leading him from the store. Pushing through the harassed mothers and screaming children at the entrance, they made their way along the road to an overly fashionable coffee bar that seemed to be constructed entirely from razor-sharp wrought iron. The barman recognised April and immediately began steaming milk for a cappuccino. Billy ordered the same and settled at a rickety *faux* rusted-metal table.

'Let me take a good look at you,' said April, putting her glasses in her bag.

'You don't need those, then?' asked Billy.

'Good God, no, they're just part of the disguise. Hang on a minute.' She unfolded a plastic shopping bag, opened her legs and pulled a pair of vacuum-packed fillet steaks from beneath her skirt. 'Here's a tip,' she said with a grimace, 'never shoplift frozen food. I had an aunt who died after shoplifting a five-pound frozen duck. Stuffed it up her cardigan and of course it slowed her heart down. Or did I read it somewhere? Reality, fiction, fiction, reality; it's so easy to get confused these days.' She continued to fill the bag with an assortment of vegetables and desserts.

'You mean you just stole all that?' asked Billy, watching in amazement as she shoved the packed bag beneath her chair.

'Well I wasn't about to pay their prices, was I?' she said, incredulous that he would even consider doing so. 'It's all very well for the Prime Minister to go on about increasing freedom of choice in the marketplace, but that only works if you can afford to hit the marketplace to begin with. You look so different, I can't believe it. Are you really him?'

'Who, Billy? Well, I'm a lot older now. I'm nearly twenty-five. We left Invicta Cross ten years ago.'

'And you've never looked back, right?' April stared at him radiantly. The transformation in her was extraordinary. She was gorgeous, but in a very odd way. Her mousy hair was now a perfect shade of bleached corn-gold, cut in a fifties bob and decorated with a glittering plastic Alice band. Her lips were pursed in a flawless bow of high-gloss jungle red. A double strand of imitation pearls adorned her ivory neck. Her sapphire-blue pupils were highlighted with even bluer Brady Bunch eyeshadow. Her cantilevered breasts owed their appearance of solidity to an old-fashioned Playtex Living Bra. But there was something unsavoury about her as well, something sensual and abnormal. She looked rather like a glamorous drag queen who might just turn out to be a woman after all.

'So,' she said, 'isn't this too exciting? You must tell me what you've been *doing* all this time!'

She spoke a little too loudly, too enthusiastically. Her voice had changed, too. She had lost all trace of her Newcastle accent, adopting instead a kind of cut-glass finishing-school brogue more suited to television shows from the nineteen fifties. Doris Day on visual, Celia Johnson on sound. The people at the next table were staring at her.

He ran through the intervening years, omitting much, but she seemed to be barely listening. She nodded sympathetically, though, when he told her of his father's death.

'I just can't believe it's you, Billy,' she sighed, 'so tall and handsome! All those muscles! I would never have recognised you.'

'You've changed a lot as well.'

'Any girl can look glamorous. All you have to do is stand still and look stupid; Hedy Lamarr said that. My mother died soon after we moved, you know. I wasn't very well for a while.' She made a key-turning gesture. 'Had to be locked away for a bit, I'm afraid.'

'Why?' he asked, puzzled.

'Oh, I kept setting fire to things,' she said airily. 'And I set fire to something that had someone in. It was all a bit of a mess. The hospital helped me to regain order in my life. Sorted out my inferiority complex, took away my guilt. I managed to fool them most of the time. But I have a sister.'

'I didn't know you had a sister.'

'Not a *sister* sister, a hospital sister I have to report to in the evenings. Every night. It's the most ghastly bore, I know, but it helps to give me peace of mind.' She was trying to tell him that she was a mental patient on day release. He studied her, alarmed for the first time. She didn't seem entirely safe.

'Have you ever been back to Invicta Cross?' he asked,

215

spooning sugar into his coffee.

'Surely you jest,' said April. 'Those people helped to ruin my life.'

'And mine,' he agreed.

'But look at you now, how prosperous you appear!' She tugged at his lapel. 'Quite the man about town.'

'I've done well for myself,' he admitted. 'It's nice to have some money finally. Too bad my dad didn't live long enough to enjoy it with me.'

They sat and talked for over an hour, although he wondered if the only thing they really had in common was their demoralising history. It was obvious that April had not attempted to come to terms with her past, but then neither had he. She wanted to know why he had not married and settled down. He avoided the subject of his inability to form any permanent relationship, and it soon became clear that she was doing the same.

'Well,' she said finally, rising to her feet and dragging out the shopping bag. 'Thanks again for rescuing me.' She examined the table's cruet, then slipped it into her pocket.

'Don't forget your haddock.' He passed her the plastic packet that had dropped from beneath her jacket.

'Billy, listen to me for a minute.' She absently picked a nylon fluff ball from her fish. 'Do you think that the past ends and the future can start whenever you want it to? That you can put everything away and begin again?'

'No.'

'No, I thought not. Listen, I'm not doing anything much at the moment. Would you like to get together, maybe? To talk about old times? We could always take a day trip back to Invicta Cross and smash all their windows.'

He barely heard her. Seeing April again had brought

everything back. 'The sad thing,' he explained, his voice hardening, 'is that people don't avenge themselves in their own lifetimes. Artists die in poverty, businessmen collapse after a lifetime of loyalty, workers die in ignorance, and arrogant little government men conduct social experiments on everyone. People suffer without ever understanding why, April, and they don't do anything about it.'

'It would just be a *date*, Billy.' She tried to sound casual. The people on the next table were listening to every word. 'You know, drinks or something—'

He shook the storm clouds from his head. 'Sure, of course. We could go to dinner if you promise not to pocket the silverware.'

'Where I've been eating they give you a plastic spoon, not silverware,' said April.

That night they went to dinner at Quaglino's, in Mayfair.

The next night they dined at Belgo Centraal, in Covent Garden.

The night after that they ate at Langan's Brasserie, and he caught her trying to steal the silver tray in the foyer that held the Mint Imperials.

April never told him about her medication. She sneaked the tablets when he wasn't looking, pills to stop depression and fits, insomnia and paranoia. She didn't tell him that her instability of mind was so great she was not supposed to form liaisons with males. She had been told to check with the hospital first. But the hospital was never able to trace her again, not even to tell her that her prescriptions were running dangerously low.

Because three weeks after she met her childhood friend again, April Barrow married him.

CHAPTER TWENTY-FIVE

The Empire of Lights

'Of course I knew I shouldn't be marrying April. She clearly wasn't all there. I watched her in restaurants, washing down tablets and chattering on brightly, clutching each conversational straw and clinging to it. I loved her vulnerability. It made me want to protect her, but it also made me feel guilty – because what I planned to do might tip her over the edge for good. I decided then that I would only go through with the plan if she wholeheartedly agreed.' – *The Red Diary*

WHEN DARRYL Merrick's father left home for another woman, his mother quickly took a new lover, an alcoholic sheet-metalworker named Dave, and it wasn't long after he came to share their cramped Sheffield council flat that he began returning home drunk and making sexual advances towards Darryl's younger sister. When the boy made the mistake of standing up to the man his mother was desperately encouraging him to call 'Father', he was repeatedly punched on the neck and shoulders with the steel tyre lever Dave kept in his workbag, and the beatings continued simply because Dave felt the boy was 'too soft'.

Bruised black and blue, Darryl ran away from Sheffield at the age of sixteen and headed where he thought the money was – south. Eighteen months later he was living on the street, selling the *Big Issue* and trying to get enough money together to rent a small place of his own.

Barbara Prout knew nothing of the boy's history, of course. All she saw was an intimidating lout with a ring through his eyebrow begging for money in broad daylight, right in the middle of the town.

Naturally, she did what any right-minded citizen would do; she called the police to have him taken away. Just to make sure that the constable did a decent job, she purchased a decaffeinated cappuccino from the mall's mock-Brazilian coffee bar opposite and sat in the window to watch the arrest.

Just after the protesting boy had been dragged off, a brand spanking new convertible BMW pulled up at the kerb where the boy had been squatting, and a tall sun-tanned man stepped out. Barbara couldn't see his face properly (he was wearing reflective Italian wraparound sunglasses) but could tell he was handsome. She checked out his square shoulders, his firmly set jaw, his wavy brown hair, his seal-grey Armani suit, the discreet gold at his cuffs, and her heart skipped a beat. This was a man with style. And he had stopped here to look in the window of Brickett & Co Estate Agents. Perhaps he was thinking of buying property in Invicta Cross.

This was more like it, thought Barbara, sipping daintily at her lukewarm coffee. Just the sort of man they liked to attract to the area. She patted a curl back in place and checked herself in the mirror. Horrified by the thought of going grey, she had lately taken to darkening her hair.

Many of the women who attended her church warned her that the use of cosmetics indicated excessive vanity, but if she was economical in their use they never needed to know, did they?

She looked back at the attractive stranger to find that he had entered the estate agent's office and was lost from view.

Georgina Bovis quickly twitched the corner of the net curtain back to its rightful place. She hoped he hadn't seen her at the window. If there was one thing she hated, it was appearing obvious. Anyone would think that she had never seen a man before. But what a man – unless she was very much mistaken there were firm muscles hidden beneath the broad arms of his grey suit. His hair was the colour of burnished chestnut, as they said in the kind of novels Daphne Metcalf churned out. His smiled revealed a row of dazzling capped teeth as he held the door open for Tracy Evans, one of the trampier property agents from Brickett & Co.

Gorgeous car, all black, even black leather seats. He had wisely chosen not to travel in Tracy's beaten-up Datsun. She was digging around in her handbag, chattering incessantly, obviously flirting with him. How did she get her hair to look so dry? Finally she produced the house keys with a flourish and led the way up the overgrown garden path of number 19 Balmoral Road.

Oh my God, he had come to see the house right next door! He had to be a prospective buyer; he looked too prosperous to be a surveyor and too stylish to be a developer.

Georgina fell back against the wall and offered up a

silent prayer, that the handsome man with the black BMW would like the area, buy the house and get to know the lady next door.

Bob Metcalf was exhausted. His feet ached, his head ached, everything ached. He never felt good any more. The computer software business had really taken off, and Astrodine, the company for whom he worked, was rapidly expanding, but the new prosperity hadn't made him rich, just tired. As the treadmill picked up pace and Astrodine slipped into the fast lane of the information superhighway, Bob found himself drowning in E-mail and conference calls, working ever-longer hours to stay ahead of inflation and keep his spoiled-fat-bitch-wife in the luxury to which she had become accustomed.

He replaced the lead-free pump hose back in its holder and screwed his petrol cap back on. He longed for the days when garage attendants filled your tank for you and asked if you'd like your windscreen washed. He noticed the car as it pulled into the Esso station first because it was a brand-new Mazda Sport, secondly because the paint job was a specially customised opalescent pink, and thirdly because the woman behind the wheel was sensational.

She had bobbed blonde hair in a Barbie-Doll cut, glistening moist lipstick, matching red Lolita sunglasses and shapely legs that went on for days. She was wearing a tight black skirt and a fluffy red sweater that barely hung from her alabaster shoulders. He wanted to meet her, but he didn't have to want for long because she came over to him, tick-tacking on perilous stiletto heels.

'You look like a man who knows his way around,' she said in a soft little-girl voice, standing very close to him.

'Could you possibly direct me to the town of Invicta Cross?'

'You're already in it,' he replied, gesturing about him. 'It starts right here.'

'How wonderful!' breathed Barbie. 'Such lovely air and countryside. Crispy clean and chessboard neat. Everything that's horrid and smelly tucked away. I think I'm really going to love living here.'

Bob's pulse surged. 'This is where I live, too,' he pointed out.

Barbie lowered her gaze. He couldn't tell if she was being bashful or studying his crotch. 'I hope I get to see a little more of you,' she said with a saucy smile.

In 1987, Barbara Prout had found God. In 1988, her husband had found Golf. Now, in 1995, their twin obsessions were still the Saviour and the Sandpit. On Saturday mornings Barbara and Ken made up a foursome with Sandra and Justin Brickett on the exclusive new course that had been built at the back of Balmoral Close, and on Sunday mornings Barbara teed off against the devil, leading clap-happy sing-alongs in St Peter's Church, a newly constructed addition to the original building that looked more like part of a drive-through hamburger chain than a place of worship.

Barbara was surprised when she saw the little pink sports car with the 'Honk If You Love Jesus' sticker pull up opposite, and wondered if one of the younger members of the congregation had come visiting. But no, the wholesome-looking young lady who alighted made a beeline for the house next door to the Bovis residence. The property had been empty for nearly seven months, and according to Justin was unsaleable due to a recurring damp problem, but there she was heading up the drive with a set of labelled keys in her hand.

She remained inside for about twenty minutes, during which time she could be seen passing before the upstairs windows making notes, then re-emerged speaking rapidly into her mobile phone. The little pink car drove off, but the lady returned an hour later in a glistening black BMW with a very handsome man at her side. The two of them went into the house once more, and stayed there for the best part of an hour. When they came out again, they uprooted the For Sale sign that was staked in the front lawn, dropped it onto the rear seat of their car and drove off.

Dr McMann had just closed his practice for the day when he saw his wife, Ruth, talking to a smartly dressed couple outside Brickett & Co. He should have stopped and offered her a lift but knew that if he did so she would make a point of introducing him to her friends and, given her propensity for social climbing, the last thing he wanted to do right now was spend half an hour playing one-upmanship with total strangers.

But were they total strangers? There was something vaguely familiar about them. As he waited at the red traffic light, he studied the couple more carefully. The man was elegant, expensively attired; the woman looked like she had dressed to appear in a Broadway musical, too glitzy, too bright. What an odd pair they made, and yet so balanced. He looked again. The feeling was nothing readily identifiable, just an odd sensation he had about them, something in the way the man stood, the way the woman was speaking. Then the lights changed and he pulled away, his interest diminishing in proportion to the retreating figures in his rear-view mirror.

The town had changed. Invicta Cross was barely recognisable. It had expanded in every direction. The old Val-U-Rite supermarket had been demolished, and a DIY superstore constructed of what appeared to be blue corrugated iron stood in its place. An ersatz town square, cobble clad and pedestrian friendly, had been created beside the old community centre, which had become a fifties-themed fast-food restaurant and had sprouted ornamental concrete pillars in pastel shades. The area reeked of prosperity. The fields had all gone, so that the town was now connected to the outlying suburbs of East Grinstead.

Every childhood has its secret haunts, but Billy March's favourite spot had become unassailable. The old water tower from which he and April had sketched the town now sported an illuminated Safeway sign at its summit and formed the centre of a gigantic shopping mall, a temple of glare-free glass and tubular steel with the old redbrick structure at its core. A vaulted atrium was filled with unnaturally glossy potted ficus trees, chromium elevators were outlined in pink neon, and a shiny steel fountain piddled aquamarine water into a huge brick dish, around which sat confused pensioners and zoned-out shoppers. Anaesthetic music tinkled from speakers: 'We've Only Just Begun' by the Carpenters, rearranged for xylophone and strings, and still sounding like the Prouts' door bell. The overlit lanes contained all the usual stores: Body Shop, Mothercare, Dixons, Our Price, Boots, Top Shop, stretching away toward the stale-smelling food court. Even more elderly couples sat beneath the fig trees like lost children waiting to be collected.

As Billy reached the six sets of sliding doors at the building's west entrance, he had a shock. There in a Plexiglas case stood a model of the entire town, *the* model, the one that had been pushed from a bedroom window in a fit of misery. The glue had discoloured and the painted wood had faded a little, but it was still intact. A plastic plaque attached to the front read: INVICTA CROSS, CIRCA 1985.

It looked like an aged diorama of the kind found in neglected provincial museums commemorating forgotten battles. He later discovered that there was another model at the mall's east entrance, showing the new layout of the town. This one was labelled: BRITISH HERITAGE GOLD AWARD WINNER: BEST NEW TOWN 1995.

He made a silent promise not to leave Invicta Cross again without destroying the neatly painted balsa cubes. April was waiting for him at the car, armed with several shopping bags. The new mall appealed to her. It was symmetrical and spotless, a harmonised environment rendered disturbing and disorienting by its repetitive, regimental design and the relentless emphasis it placed on shopping.

'Just think of the happy times we'll have purchasing luxury items here,' she said, waiting for him to open her door. 'I've already made a start. Fragrance-free fruit-extract shower gel. Seriously Sensitive tissue regenerating cream with root-strengthening mousse. Porridge Padder Oatmeal Substitute. Death-by-Chocolate fudge chip ice cream. Twenty-Four Hard Jungle Dance Trance tracks on two CDs. Herpes Hide-'n'-Heal stick. Power Rangers Gum. Walt Disney's *Peter Pan*. I Can't Believe It's Not Potato. Spray-'n'-Shine Limescale Blaster. A cuddly teddy containing heart-shaped Belgian chocolates. Oh, and this.'

She slapped a large luminous cloth banana on his jacket.
'Lint Banana, Smells of Fruit, Peels Fluff Right Off. We'll
be model consumers, Billy. No telltale sores and stained
toilet bowls for us. We'll be smelling clean and smiling
brightly even in the throes of death.'

He decided that perhaps he wouldn't tell her the plan
just yet. It was better to wait until they were settled in. On
the way back to Balmoral Close he made a detour.

'Where are we going?' she asked.

'Old times' sake,' he explained. 'You'll see.'

But he turned the corner to find that half of the road he
was searching for had been torn down and replaced with a
discount sofa-bed outlet.

'Wait here – I'll only be a minute.' He left the engine
running.

The tobacconist's shop still stood at the corner but the
owners were new, and knew no one. He tried one of the
houses, then another. An elderly man came to the door and
listened to his question. He remembered that the funeral
director's son had moved up to London, and that somebody had said he was getting married. Disappointed, Billy
returned to the car.

'Nobody knows where Oliver Price is any more,' he said.
'You'd think someone around here would remember.'

'Never mind,' said April, 'we'll look up someone else we
knew.'

'I'm not interested in looking up anyone else.'

April stared listlessly from the window. More concrete.
More cars. Less trees. Less grass. The depressing drive was
conducted in silence. Twenty minutes later they arrived
back at the house and let themselves in with the estate
agent's key.

'Well, what do you think?' said Billy.

'I don't know yet. I haven't seen everything.'

'I mean, do you still want this?'

She reached up and touched his face. His skin was as cool and smooth as suede. She loved his jaw line. It hadn't been there when he was fourteen. He had changed so completely, blossomed like a butterfly, transformed into an angel.

'It's not a question of wanting,' she said honestly. 'There's nothing else left for me now.'

It was time to tell her. Billy walked to the window and looked out onto the street. The sun was setting behind the trees with a vulgar flourish of colour. There were still a few heliotrope clouds in the sky but the houses were already in darkness. The dying daylight in the close reminded him of an eerie Magritte painting he had once seen, *The Empire of Lights*.

'I'll put in the offer tomorrow. I'm sure there'll be no trouble getting it accepted.' He studied her face carefully. 'I have something I want to tell you, April.'

'You can tell me anything, Billy. We're married now.'

'You realise we came here for a purpose.'

'Of course, silly. We're going to give them a taste of their own medicine, those were the words you used.'

'I didn't tell you how.'

'Then tell me.'

It grew dark in the room as he told her. 'I don't want you to be frightened. There'll be no danger to you, I promise. I'll take all the blame. Once we move here, there can be no turning back.'

'I know. I'm not frightened.'

'Not now. But you will be.'

'That's okay. I spent enough years being scared. You don't know me, Billy, you don't know what I've been through. The nights that never used to end, the terrors in the dark that made dying seem so attractive. I'm like the Bride of Frankenstein, Billy, I belong dead. That's what my mother once told me. She nearly died giving birth to me, you see. I didn't get enough oxygen. "God made a mistake," she said, "you were never supposed to live. You'll never be normal." She was right. But now when I get upset, my mind simply ... goes somewhere else. I can't be frightened any more. And since we met again, I've stopped having bad dreams.'

Billy nodded toward the window. 'They're already watching us. Have you noticed?'

She raised an eyebrow. 'Oh, yes. I spotted some Terylene twitching the moment I stepped out of the car. I don't think Georgina has replaced her curtains since I was last here. She hasn't aged well.'

The room had disappeared in shadows.

'The electricity isn't on,' he said. 'Come to the end of the road.'

They locked up the house and walked to the rear of the close. Where the side drive to number thirteen had once stood was an ostentatious gate bearing a sign in British racing green and raised gilt that read: THE INVICTA CROSS GOLF SOCIETY. FOUNDED 1986.

Nothing was left of the house that had once stood on the site between numbers twelve and fourteen. The driveway leading to the clubhouse filled the gap.

'You can't see that it was ever there,' said Billy, amazed. 'That's the second time the Marches have lost a house.'

April gave his arm an affectionate squeeze. 'Don't worry,

darling,' she said. 'We'll make sure that it's the last one you ever lose. We'll have change of address cards printed. *Jack and Polly Prentiss.*'

He had insisted that they could not keep their old names. Even if the neighbours didn't remember them now, someone might when the trouble started. April thought the names sounded as if they had originated in an old Hollywood musical. She had left the details to him. The hardest part had been transferring their credit rating. Consequently, only the cars had been purchased in their old names. Everything else would belong to their new identities.

As the sun disappeared behind the trees, the residents of Balmoral Close peered around their curtains to study the pair who stood side by side before the gravelled golf club drive and marvelled at the way they made such a perfect couple.

CHAPTER TWENTY-SIX

Invitations to a Masque

'I made a list. It went like this: the Prout family – Ken, Barbara and Simon; the Bovis family – Alan, Georgina and Sherry; the Metcalf family – Bob, Daphne, Brad and Emma; the Brickett family – Justin and Sandra; Dr McMann and his wife; Morris Diller and his son, Gavin; Mrs Davenport, Sherington headmistress. And anyone else who got in the way, of course.' – *The Red Diary*

'ANCHOVIES CAN be attractively presented, but their pungency is undesirable, I feel, reminding one of unclean genitalia. Personally speaking, I'd be more comfortable with sun-dried tomatoes, although the glossies insist that provincial Italian finger food is no longer à la mode.'

The caterer stared at April and forgot to write anything down. April reached over and tapped her pad with a long coral-pink nail. 'Nix the anchovies, hon.' She rolled her eyes heavenward and adopted a thoughtful pose, index finger extended against the side of her face. 'Spring rolls are an acceptable snack food, aren't they? Vegetarian ones covered in sesame seeds. And a punch would be nice, orchard fruit with a hint of the exotic – mango perhaps, but nothing that would disorder the bowels or stain one's teeth.'

The caterer made a half-hearted note and continued staring at her client. In her blue gingham pinafore dress Mrs Prentiss looked like June Allyson in *Good News*. Until you arrived below waist-level, that was, where the dress divided to reveal a tiny pair of tasteless crotch-pinching purple briefs. She looked further down to the fetishistic spike-heeled PVC boots that clung to Mrs Prentiss's calves and tried to imagine what kind of party her client was planning to throw.

Daphne Metcalf turned the blue vellum envelope over in her hands, searching for clues. She examined the invitation again, but there was nothing more to be gleaned from it. These days she rarely accompanied her husband to neighbourhood parties, or to anything else for that matter. Since the success of her recent novel, *Hollywood Adulterers*, she had felt it was time to ameliorate her circle of acquaintances, and this meant denying the anti-intellectual residents of Balmoral Close access to her. Socially speaking, it was time to step up. Her book had reached number three in the *Sunday Times* bestselling paperbacks list and her home, with its spectacular new extension, was soon to be featured in *Hello!* magazine. She tried to spend more of her time in London, but Bob was looking for an excuse to fight with her, and she was damned if she'd give him one. It was bad enough that they had been forced to attend counselling since her son's brush with the law; a messy divorce, just when she was breaking into the big time, was the last thing her career needed now.

She was surprised that her husband managed to stay in the same house with her. It was odd that as their marriage had deteriorated, their in-house technology had proliferated. The Metcalfs had faxes and modems, E-mail,

Internet and call waiting, all those systems of communication and nothing to say to each other. And here they remained, locked in negative equity, unable to tolerate each other's presence and unable to leave. She felt like Salman Rushdie.

She looked back at the invitation. This one felt different, a cut above the usual spring bottle-and-barbecue bashes on offer. From her seat in the conservatory, where she perched in an enormous canary-yellow kaftan with an Apple Macintosh Powerbook on her lap, she could see the rear of the new arrivals' house. The husband was clearly prosperous; his car and clothes had been chosen with discernment. She had only managed to glimpse the wife but had already noticed that there was something slightly odd about her. She looked too perfect, like a character from an old TV commercial for kitchen cleanser.

Daphne set aside the invitation and attempted to concentrate on the chapter she had started, but the words eluded her. She raised her eyes to the window again. The warm May morning had drawn a low mist from the damp gardens, and through it she could make out a solitary dark figure, digging with a steady *chunk*, his shovel dipping and rising in even cadence. From what she had heard about the damp problems in their house, she would have imagined that gardening was her new neighbour's lowest priority. Now he had set aside the shovel and was attacking the hole he'd made with a pickaxe. His face was contorted with anger as he swung the tool above his head like a weapon and brought it down with a great crash. She forced herself to concentrate on the first draft of her latest book, and she returned her attention to the text-filled screen.

*

*You are invited to attend a house-warming evening
in the new home of
Jack and Polly Prentiss
at 19 Balmoral Close, Invicta Cross, Surrey
at 8.00 pm this Saturday.*
RSVP

Georgina Bovis could only just read the fancy script. She
was supposed to wear glasses but couldn't bring herself to
do so, fearing that they would make her look undesirable.
She checked the front of the envelope; it had been
addressed to Georgina, Alan and Sherry Bovis. Funny how
Jack and Polly Prentiss knew their names when they hadn't
yet been introduced.

She turned back to the invitation, noting the expensive
paper, then propped it on the mantelpiece behind Alan's
car-park pass, where he might actually notice it. Parties
always made her think of sex. These days, everything made
her think of sex. She was starting to regret finishing her
affair with Graham Birdsmith. An illicit shag with a
hypertense weatherman had been moderately preferable to
having Alan huff and puff on top of her for three minutes
once a fortnight.

She heard a key turn in the lock. Alan was working late
again, so Sherry had come over for dinner. Georgina's
daughter was twenty-one now and lived on the far side of
town, sharing a maisonette with another local girl. They
both sold cosmetics in a Croydon department store. If she
saw the invitation she might want to come along, and she
was still single. Georgina tucked the card further back; she
didn't need the competition. Everyone remarked how like
her mother Sherry was; as Georgina rose to freshen her

drink, she prayed it wasn't true.

Dr Ernest McMann handed the card to his wife. Ruth
peered over the top of her spectacles and grunted.

'I thought she seemed rather vulgar in that nasty little
car,' she said. 'Overdressed, or underdressed or something.
Far too young. You're not supposed to have money at that
age. She'll probably get on well with Bovis *mère et fille*.'

'When did you see them?' The doctor was carrying a
mug of tea back to his armchair and knew if he spilled any
on the carpet there would be hell to pay.

'I see everything,' said Ruth, answering a different
question. 'I watched them moving in. Beige tartan arm-
chairs and a quite indescribable sofa. Best not to respond,
I think.'

She was about to tear up the invitation when her
husband plucked it from her hand. 'Well, I'm going to stick
my head around the door, just for half an hour. The
Bricketts are going, and the golf board could use some
youthful blood.' The club had never really achieved the
smart profile they had aimed for. There was a lot of good
money in Invicta Cross, but very little good breeding.

'I suppose if the Bricketts are putting in an appearance
we'll have to do the same,' sniffed Ruth, 'but the area is going
to the dogs if you ask me.' Ruth always thought that the
neighbourhood was declining in quality. She charted each
tremor to the status quo on a mental graph that judged the
worth of a man by the state of his shoes and the state of his
wife, in that order. The thorny topics of class and morality
had been woven through her everyday conversation ever
since the McManns had left India almost thirty years ago.

'My mother always said that the trouble with this

country began when we started allowing immigration.'

The doctor looked at his wife's petulant lower lip and narrowed eyes and wondered if she realised how horribly close to parody she appeared. Her views were those of the Whitehouse brigade, decades out of date, her conversation peppered with distorted memories of how much better it had all once been. As he watched her fussing and tutting with the newspapers, he reflected that she seemed to be displaying the earliest signs of senile dementia. He hoped not, because he often found himself agreeing with her views.

'The marvellous thing about Ken Russell's filmed version is that it never dates,' said April as she rolled a red Bex Bissell back and forth across the new blue carpet. She was wearing a tucked-yoke nylon blouse with bell sleeves and matching velveteen lurex Capri pants. She looked like a TV housewife transmitted on a set with the colour turned too high.

'The costumes were designed by his wife, Shirley, and were completely faithful to the period, lending a timeless, pure quality to each scene. The "Room In Bloomsbury" number remains unsurpassed.'

April was talking about *The Boy Friend* again. It was her favourite film. Billy was half listening as he unwound pages of newspaper from cups and stacked the china on the shelf behind his head. April had come complete with her own crockery, utensils and bed linen. Sometimes he felt that he had unpacked her out of a box labelled 'Deluxe Model Wife'. Physically, she was perfect. Mentally...

He did not love her yet, but he felt sure that he would one day, in his own way. At the moment it was a marriage of convenience, but afterwards they would have time to get to know each other. They had something special in common, after all. They were both damaged and angry and prepared to take revenge. That was a good enough start to any relationship.

'It was Barbara Windsor's finest hour, of course. She was particularly fetching in her frilly satin French maid outfit. How many replies have we had so far?'

'It's early days yet,' said Billy. 'They're waiting to discuss it with each other. If one jumps, they'll all jump.' Mrs Davenport's invitation had been sent to the school and returned with a polite note. She had died of cancer in 1983.

'The caterer was most amenable.' April happily trundled the sweeper back and forth, not cleaning so much as posing for an imaginary magazine photograph. 'I just hope that the house is ready in time. I want everyone to love us.'

'They will,' said Billy, carefully setting down the last cup. 'I'll make sure of that.'

The amazing thing was that nobody had recognised him. Of course, when the residents of Invicta Cross had last seen him he had been fourteen, an awkward boy who barely spoke above a whisper and hid his face behind a lank fringe. Now he was tall and muscular, his spectacles replaced with blue contact lenses, his nose straightened by a little corrective surgery, his posture improved at the gym, his sense of style created by the city. April was hardly more recognisable. No longer the reclusive schoolgirl hidden away by a nervous housebound mother, a child whose obsessive neatness was born of a desperate need to transcend her jumbled home life, she had blossomed like some outrageous Asiatic bloom, alien and exotic. April was more fragile than he, more in need of protection from others and from herself. Her honesty was liable to give the game away, because any insights she provided to the workings of her disordered mind would be bound to provoke alarm. And it was essential that they appeared to be normal.

'Oh, a woman's place is in the home, absolutely,' explained April. 'A husband simply has no idea how to remove dust balls from behind a headboard. How do you begin to explain defroster timings to a man? Or how much soap powder you require for a hard-water heavily soiled wash? I want Tupperware, and lots of it. Matching pastel stay-fresh boxes provide a dark insight into the lives of lonely women who hoard their leftovers, don't you think?'

Daphne Metcalf looked doubtfully at her hostess, unable to tell if she was joking or mad. Polly Prentiss was immaculately dressed in a shoulderless rouched gown of midnight-blue satin that was draped around her fabulously contoured body like an art installation. She made the rest of the women in the room look faded and ill. Her breasts had a shameless perkiness Jayne Mansfield would have envied.

'My mother used to drink vodka and warm milk from a Tupperware beaker,' she continued. 'Billy's mother—' she hastily corrected herself '*Jack's* mother – preferred warm milk and Scotch every night until she overegged the recipe with nitrazepam. I had planned to make a punch for this evening, something purple and lethal in an enormous cut-crystal bowl big enough to drown kittens in but *Jack* said no, nothing too exotic.'

'I think Mrs Metcalf would like her drink freshened, darling.' Billy stepped between the two women and deftly removed Daphne's glass from her hand. 'Why don't you see how the caterers are coping?'

This party was very different from the one Angela March had nervously hosted in the same street ten years earlier. The room hummed with respect; he could feel it emanating from the well-heeled crowd. Seventeen people had been invited, sixteen had accepted and one was dead. That seemed a good batting average. What shocked him most was how only the children had really changed. Everyone was a decade older, of course, so that the median age of the street tipped more into the thirties and forties, but there seemed to be no new arrivals. Balmoral Close was jealously guarded from outsiders.

Their neighbours were tanned and lean and leathery, except Daphne Metcalf, who was as white as full-fat cheese and quite gigantic. Sherry Bovis was an attractive girl, lean and boyish, unlike her mother. The policeman and his son had not been invited. There were limits. In their places were Adolpho Garibaldi and his wife. They remained in a corner, exchanging hushed platitudes with passing guests like a pair of priests welcoming back a lapsed congregation.

It had been essential to create a plausible background for April and himself. If anyone asked, he owned property in the city and might be persuaded to invest in Invicta Cross, and his wife was a half-French aristocrat (it was all he could come up with to excuse her bizarre conversation). He planned to avoid complex explanations, knowing that April would never be able to remember what had been said to her.

Meanwhile, his wife gathered information as she moved around the room; sometime in the late eighties, Georgina Bovis had been caught in bed with the local weatherman by her husband, but he had taken her back on the promise of her future fidelity. Justin and Sandra Brickett now had a six-year-old son, Dexter. Justin was on the directors' board at the golf club, as was Ken Prout. His wife, Barbara, had become involved with the American evangelical movement. The Metcalfs' delinquent son had left home to live in London with a pregnant girlfriend following a hushed-up incident involving assault and battery. April reported the snippets to her husband when she passed him in the kitchen.

'You seem to know a lot about the area, Mr Prentiss,' said Justin Brickett, as curious as ever. Apart from sprouting grey sideburns, he had not changed. 'Do you have any family connections here?'

'My parents were once thinking of buying property nearby,' he explained. 'I did some investigating for them.' From the corner of his eye he saw Georgina Bovis refilling her glass, her fifth trip to the bar in less than an hour. He made a mental note. 'How long have you lived here?'

'This is our fourteenth year,' said Justin proudly.

'Has the close altered much in that time?'

'Oh, there's been some building, a few people who didn't suit the area upped stumps and moved on, but most of us here—' he gestured around the lounge, 'have been together for years.' He decided not to add that they were all stuck with each other now that the property market had slumped so horrendously.

'So you've had no trouble in the area, then?'

Justin appeared to think for a moment. 'Not really.'

'From the residents,' he prompted.

'Oh, that. Well, we had troublemakers in once at the end of the road, a problem family, thieves, very badly behaved,

239

but we soon saw them off. It's been quiet around here ever since.' Justin was proving a mine of information. Thieves, indeed! He decided to probe further.

'There seems to have been a lot of recent construction work.'

'Indeed, well time marches on, that's progress for you. Prime commuter belt country, the backbone of Britain, Tory heartland, no wonder people want to come here.' He raised his tumbler and examined it. 'Think I'll get myself a refill.' He laid a friendly hand on Billy's shoulder. 'Think about what I said. If you decide to take up a hobby, I don't see any problem getting you into the club. There'll be a space on Saturday mornings for the little lady as well. You make a lovely couple,' he added enviously. 'We'll soon get you on board.'

'That's very decent of you,' said Billy. 'Very decent indeed.'

'Your clothes are very – unusual,' said Daphne incredulously. 'Where on earth do you get them?'

'Frederick's,' said April, as if it was obvious. 'I do all my clothes shopping there.'

'Frederick's. I'm not familiar with that company. Is it in Croydon?'

'No, Hollywood.' She failed to add that she purchased the more fetishistic items through a notorious plain-wrapper catalogue. 'I buy my underwear here, of course, mostly from a shop called Dominatrix in Bayswater.' She wrinkled her nose in a friendly between-us-girls smile. 'For those ... special evenings when you just can't fight the smell of wet leather.'

The doctor and his wife kept to themselves. Ruth examined the furnishings with tightly pressed lips, commenting that everything looked rented. She was right, but did not know it.

The evening ended a little after eleven. As they closed the door on the last guest, April caught her husband's eye and gave a cold smile. It was the look of a woman who had met the enemy and recognised her own superiority.

Billy returned the look. It was just as he had hoped it would be. Their guests had been too preoccupied with their own petty squabbles to notice that a young man who had lived here before in very different circumstances was once more in their midst. As he had moved through the group listening to their inconsequential banter, he knew they had forgotten all about the boy whose life they had twisted apart. But he did not forget as easily. He remembered every last one of them, and he watched as they circled about him, cajoling and flattering, flirting and smiling like whores before a count. Once Billy March had not been good enough for these people. They had seemed effortlessly superior, with their easy money, their natural confidence and the *droit du seigneur* of a decent education, but from the height of another decade they could be seen more clearly for what they were. He returned to the lounge with a sigh and removed the Mozart concerto from the CD player.

That night he went to the attic and withdrew the last of the cardboard boxes yet to be unpacked. From it he pulled the battered red leather notebook, in which was contained a complete record of the indignities committed against the March family, complete with photographs and signature samples from all of the neighbours.

While his oblivious wife splashed water about in the bathroom, working her way through a medley of songs from *The Boy Friend*, he began to place check marks against several pages in the book, seeking solutions to the impossible tasks he had set himself in the days to come.

CHAPTER TWENTY-SEVEN

Tasteless Gestures

'The hardest part was getting started, I suppose, finding the right way to channel so much anger. I couldn't rely on April to help me. I tried to avoid getting her involved at all. I knew that people would one day want to know why. Why did I do it? The answer to that would have to be because if I didn't, nobody else would. Why should wrongs be allowed to go unavenged?' – *The Red Diary*

'JUST SHOW ME what it is, then there won't be a mystery, will there?' said Barbara Prout sensibly, holding out her hand. Ken hesitated, rising from the breakfast table and taking the envelope with him. 'It's nothing,' he said, scratching pensively at the odd little moustache whose appearance had coincided with the loss of his hair four years ago. 'The usual junk mail.'

'Then you can let me see,' snapped his wife. Since she'd found God she had stopped shaving her armpits. He could see fine wisps of hair sticking out of the sides of her nightdress.

'You wouldn't be remotely interested in it, I can assure you.'

'Let me be the judge of that. I have all sorts of interests you don't know about.'

The large brown envelope labelled 'Private and Confidential' was the third to come through the door in as many days. Shocked, he had hidden the other two in his side of the wardrobe.

'Come on, Dad, tell the truth and shame the devil,' said Simon Prout sarcastically. He was only thirteen but was already experienced in the mysterious ways of the Lord. He looked at the enormous pine crucifix Barbara had Araldited to the wall above the dining table and offered up a silent prayer summoning the Lord to come and lay waste to Invicta Cross with a scourge of scorpions.

'Really, I'm going to be late for work if this silliness doesn't stop,' complained Ken. 'I'll call you just before lunch to—'

Seizing the chance to expand his parents' ever-widening marital rift, Simon snatched the envelope from his hand just as he was trying to stuff it into his briefcase and dutifully passed it to his mother.

Barbara slit open the top of the packet with a lethal-looking paperknife (a gift from the grateful people of Zambia in recognition of the United Church of Utah's contribution to their wellbeing, namely a red iron bible hall and a series of visits by loud, overzealous, hectoring American students) and gingerly removed the contents.

The first thing she saw was a middle-aged lady having sexual congress with an overexcited Alsatian. She only reached page six (bored-looking woman inserting an eel) of *Animal Crackers* before hurling the magazine across the room at her husband.

Unfortunately she missed and struck Simon above the

left ear. The periodical fell open at a double-page spread featuring two schoolgirls doing something incredible with an obliging goat, much to Simon's delight and the collective horror of the rest of the family.

'This is addressed to you,' said Alan Bovis, weighing the box in his hand. The last few years had not been kind to the exhausted salesman. The remaining strands of his blonde hair had disappeared, and his sagging skin held the drinker's mottle of tropical coral. If work was his mistress, she was an unrewarding lover. There had been a time when Georgina had longed to know what made him such a loyal employee. Her respect for him had made her care. Now she knew that he worked so hard because he considered the office his home. Sharing a bed with his wife was the job.

She looked doubtfully at the parcel. 'Are you sure it's for me?' she asked. 'I've not ordered anything.'

'It's got your name on the lid.'

The sticky tape proved difficult to remove with stick-on nails, but she finally managed to raise one of the flaps. When she saw what was beneath the pink tissue paper inside her eyes widened, and she gently resealed the lid.

'Well, what is it?'

'There's been a mistake,' said Georgina hastily. 'This isn't for me.'

Before she could stop him, Alan had snatched the box from her hands. He wrenched open the lid and removed the object inside, an immense beribboned wobbling phallus carved in veined black rubber, which owed more to the fevered imagination of its sculptor than strict biological accuracy.

'Oh, but it is for you, my darling,' he said, angrily

245

rooting inside the box and producing a card, which read simply: 'Think of me while I'm away, all my love, Graham.'

'You're still seeing him, aren't you?' he said wearily. 'How fucking predictable of you.' Alan remembered how often his wife's affair with the marauding weatherman had supposedly been ended; the thought that she might still be seeing her ex-lover had frequently crossed his mind. This confirmed his suspicions.

'Don't be so bloody silly,' said Georgina, returning the plastic penis to its box. 'You know what Graham's like. He wouldn't say boo to a goose. He would never do a thing like this. He has no sense of humour.'

'He must have had to get involved with you. I'm going to go round there and stick this through his letter box. Just be honest with me for once.'

'I'm not seeing him, I swear to you,' she insisted. 'Someone's playing a stupid practical joke.' Her husband silently checked the package's postage, noting the local frank mark. Some joke. If Graham hadn't mailed this, it meant that someone else in the neighbourhood knew he had been cuckolded.

'I suppose this is your idea of a joke,' called Daphne Metcalf. She was bent over on the front doorstep examining something. Bob couldn't help noticing that her buttocks touched either side of the door frame.

'What are you talking about?' he called back, folding the sleeve of his shirt back over the ironing board. Daphne had forced him to iron his own shirts after becoming involved with a feminist writers' collective in the late eighties.

'This ... disgusting ... thing.' She rose to her feet,

holding a large beige object by its edge. 'I suppose you've been talking to your pals at work about me again?' Her voice barely withheld its hysteria.

Puzzled, Bob left the ironing board and approached her.

She was standing half in shadow, and it was hard to see the object she held. It was the size of a bowling ball, but irregularly shaped. As she closed in on him he could smell it, the bitter, cuprous tang of stale flesh and blood. The pig's eyes had rolled up in their sockets, zombie-like. A coarse pale tongue protruded from an open mouth that was surrounded by sharp brown bristles.

Daphne held the severed head by its right ear. It was leaking a black syrupy substance onto the tiles. 'You told them I'm a vegetarian, didn't you?' she hissed.

'Of course not,' said Bob. He didn't suppose anyone remembered or cared about his wife's dietary habits. Daphne was very sensitive on the subject, and had long ago made him promise not to discuss it with anyone. She'd wanted to avoid all those boring conversations with bullying meat eaters. Now it appeared that the cat – or rather, the pig – was out of the bag.

But who could be responsible for such an offensive prank?

Sandra Brickett looked out of the window and asked, 'Justin, did you order anything?'

Justin was bobbing about on his JourneyMaster Exercycle, pedalling hard and going nowhere. Sandra had insisted on him using the device every morning to reduce his love handles, but it seemed to be having no effect. 'No, what sort of thing?'

'Come and have a look.'

Panting, he climbed from his static transportation and wiped his forehead with a Nike sports towel. There below them in the middle of the driveway, a ton and a half of builder's sand lay in a vast orange heap. It looked as if a giant had dropped his ice-cream scoop onto the drive from a great height.

'What the bloody hell—' He took the stairs three at a time and threw open the front door. A delivery note was weighted with a house brick at the side of the sand pile. The consignment had been accepted by Bob Metcalf.

'So you're denying any knowledge of this, are you, Bob?'

'I certainly am,' replied Bob uncertainly. Justin Brickett stood a foot taller than him and was on his front doorstep rudely waving the paper a few inches from the tip of his nose. 'Where did you find it?'

'At the foot of that great ... heap,' shouted Brickett, pointing back at the Everest of sand obscuring his garage. 'Are you telling me you didn't sign for it?'

'Of course not,' he said indignantly. 'Why on earth would I do that? I'm not an idiot, you know.'

'Is that so?' Brickett snapped the paper taut. 'Then whose signature is this, pray tell?'

Holy shit. He was right. Bob Metcalf found himself staring at his own handwriting.

'Is this or is this not your signature?'

Bob reached up and took the page from Brickett's hand. 'It certainly looks like it.'

'So you admit—'

'I just said it looks like it. I didn't sign it, I didn't sign anything.' It was uncanny, though. The penmanship was his, even the kind of pen used was like his own. Brickett was barking at him again. Typically, he was ready to believe a piece of paper over a human being. 'Are you sure you remember everything you do, Bob?'

'You know your trouble, Justin?' Bob snapped back. 'You're an officious prick. Why do religious people always think they're so damned right about everything?' And he slammed the door in Brickett's face.

It was only once he was inside the hall that he mentally kicked himself, remembering that he would be seeing Brickett on official business tomorrow. Justin sat on the board of the golf club, and Bob Metcalf's membership was up for renewal.

The plague continued throughout the month.

An unordered washing machine arrived at the house of Dr McMann, and the doctor had to finance its return from his own pocket. An extensive valet service was performed on the Metcalfs' already clean car, setting Bob back eighty-five pounds. Two dozen anchovy and mozzarella pizzas were delivered to the golf course, and the pizza company insisted on payment. A pair of debt collectors arrived to repossess the Metcalfs' garden turf, and tore half the garden up before the misunderstanding was sorted out. The fire service, the AA and the St John's Ambulance Brigade were all called out on a variety of false alarms.

But there was a darker side to the pranks.

Authorisation for the various services and deliveries always appeared to be authentic. The Bovises had sent the washer, the Prouts had ordered the pizzas, the Metcalfs had rung the fire brigade, the Bricketts had demanded the turf. But of course, nobody admitted it.

Jack and Polly Prentiss commiserated with their

neighbours. They were even careful to include themselves when somebody arranged for Dyno-Rod to call at every house in the area. Along with the other residents of Balmoral Close they had their photographs taken for the *East Grinstead Advertiser*, where they were quoted as saying that it was a shame decent people couldn't be allowed to live their lives in peace. The pranks became a nuisance people quickly learned to live with. They were soon forgotten.

But the suspicion that was sewn between friends and neighbours grew like the weeds springing up between the golf club's fences. And a new sense of hostility began to settle across the street like a poisoned veil.

'Oy, try and keep some of it in the mug,' Sergeant Morris Diller shouted after PC Midlock, who had just set tea and biscuits down before him, and in doing so had soaked the top page of his notes. He shook the page over the bin and studied the smudged type again. It looked like someone in Invicta Cross was playing silly buggers, upsetting people with pizza orders and raising false fire-brigade alarms. There were dozens of complaints here, all demanding some form of action, but what did people expect him to do about it? There was no common purpose, although the nuisances had all occurred in two or three roads and were particularly centred on Balmoral Close. He turned to the next wrinkled sheet, checking dates and times, and one odd thing struck him. A number of the complainants appeared to be accusing each other. Usually neighbourhood feuds took place between a pair of aggrieved parties, not among six or seven separate households. Disputes involved noise and boundaries, but looking through the interview statements none of the usual grievances had been aired.

He shifted the damp file to the top of the radiator, unable to see what he could do about the situation. It was probably the work of bored kids, copying their dads' signatures, making calls in phoney adult voices. They'd slip up sooner or later. His own son used to pull the same kind of pranks. The kids around here had too much money and too much time on their hands. As the weather grew warmer they would stop trying to impress each other and would find new pursuits, like hot-wiring cars and vandalising public buildings. Now those were the kind of crimes he knew how to cope with. Meanwhile he would arrange for PC Midlock and his mates to pass the Sherington School gates at going-home time and put the fear of God into a few of the local pupils.

He took a sip of tea and congratulated himself on solving another of Invicta Cross's pressing social problems.

CHAPTER TWENTY-EIGHT

Obligatory Sex Scene

'And then, of course, there was the matter of sex.' –*The Red Diary*

'YOU DON'T like sex very much, do you?' said April, running a pink fingernail through her husband's curly dark chest hair. Two in the morning, and theirs was the only bedroom light on in Balmoral Close. 'I mean normal sex.'

He did not reply. To be truthful, the whole subject of intimacy bothered him. He had decided that their relationship was to be based on companionship, not copulation. It was essential that he should not become distracted from his purpose.

'I wonder what they all get up to in their little bedrooms,' she mused. 'I imagine they penetrate each other with the utmost hatred. Don't suppose there's much wife swapping going on. Such a sexist term, I feel. Why not husband swapping?' She looked down at the supine form beside her. 'We can do something else, if you prefer.'

He nodded uncertainly at this.

'Yes, perhaps it would be better. Okay, Billy. I'll let you up.'

She unpeeled the leather gag from his mouth and hunted

about under the duvet for the key to the rubber handcuffs that were pinning his wrists to the side bars of the bed head. The straps and ropes tightly binding his ankles were not so easy to remove. Nor was the variety of steel and rubber accoutrements she had clipped and stretched around various parts of his anatomy. The gag had left a gentle red bruise across his face, like the imprint of a boot. He tried working his jaw, but found it difficult to speak. His nipples were killing him.

'Perhaps I can think of something else,' she said, dropping a tangle of sexual equipment onto the floor and laying back against the pillow. She was a pink and yellow goddess, a painted, perfumed, pumped-up version of the young girl who had leaned into the wind at the edge of the parapet. She complained that her breasts held the translucence of inflated condoms, so she rubefied them with a light dusting of powder until they glowed like the bosoms of a neon cowgirl.

'I mean we should keep attempting this, seeing as we're a married couple. Although, of course, the sheer legality of it all takes the edge off. I'm not terribly adept at normal sex. My first experience of a man's body was no gentle touch but a hostile invasion. I had hoped for an embrace, a moment when the flesh of two people might brush and spark like electricity terminals. Instead I got an overweight, beer-breathed circus bear jabbing his stubby cock into me. since then my sexual experience has been limited to the odd spot of frenzied frottage in the grounds of the hospital after lights out. It's left its mark, I can tell you. So. Is there anything you particularly want to try?'

His eyes drifted from the technicolor perfection of her breasts to the see-through black panties that skimmed across her shaven mound. Crimson musical notes were embroidered on them in bugle beads. He reached across and ran the taut material between his fingers as his member began to uncrease.

'Ah,' murmured April, resting the tips of her fingers on her powdered nipples. 'I always felt that sexually I would prefer to drift on the ocean of the abnormal. It gladdens my heart to salute a fellow traveller. The correct night attire sharpens the senses. What waist size are you? I'm sure we can come to some sort of improvised arrangement.' She lowered herself until her knees were either side of his chest and allowed her buttocks to graze his groin. 'But let's not try anything too extreme at first.'

CHAPTER TWENTY-NINE

The Madness of Confinement

'I wanted to be Sweeney Todd to her Mrs Lovett, an empowered Hamlet to her mad Ophelia. I left nothing to caprice. I checked the list again. Sixteen names. Sixteen chances to restore a life that had been hurled triumphantly out of sight.' – *The Red Diary*

THE STREETS of Invicta Cross smelled of fresh-cut grass. Lawns and hedges had been trimmed into tight green slices, a velvet geometry of approved street decoration. Garage doors gained fresh coats of paint in committee-chosen shades, running the gamut from blue to grey to green (reds and yellows were not allowed) so that some streets looked like pastel-paint charts.

At the mall, everything was primary coloured, coated in tones that bellowed the language of selling.

'Remember, you're in a sacred place, so show some respect.'

April reached over and snatched the baseball cap from his head. 'We are entering the Holiest of Holies. Try to walk with a little more piety.'

She entwined her fingers with his as they reached the central point of the Invicta Cross Mall. Here, at the confluence of walkways, they stood before the glass case that housed Billy March's model town. April looked up at the vast glittering atrium, each level overspilling with polished ivy leaves, and watched in awe as silvery pods slid silently up and down the walls, disgorging shoppers.

'They come to worship at the Church of Limitless Credit,' she whispered. 'To reassure themselves that peace of mind can be purchased over the counter. Shopping is the one true religious experience. The mall is shaped like a crucifix – nave there,' she pointed, 'cross axes there, major transept there, and at its heart, on God's altar, your model stands as a blueprint for a better life.'

He never tried to understand her when she spoke like this. Her excitement was palpable. A distant fire filled her eyes, and her skin seemed flushed and was hot to the touch. She displayed an almost sexual zeal that he found alarming and wonderful. She would probably have become a born-again Christian if her gnosticism had not been diverted onto stranger paths.

They stopped before the broad steel fountain in one of the café areas and perched themselves around a tiny circular marble table. The sculpture's feeble micturition accompanied the Muzak rendition of 'We've only Just Begun' that tinkled from hidden wall speakers all around them.

April smoothed out the creases in her gingham skirt, then carefully checked her purchases. 'The beauty of this place,' she explained, 'is its simplicity. They don't sell anything you need. Apricot facial scrub, Belgian chocolates, bio-pulse meters, the Abdominiser, garlic crushers, ergonomic wine racks, liquid-crystal egg timers, Magic Eye books, designer underwear, none of it essential, but all of it providing inner peace. Reality's just hard work, and our fantasies are all created for us. Everything comes ready made, even dreams. Our imagination must be fully mapped out before we can truly be free, because once there is nothing more to imagine we can relax. We need to relax. Our desire to kill comes from the madness of being confined.'

She had been without medication for two days now. He saw the strain in her face and knew that it was time for him to act.

'Look,' he said, 'the Bricketts and the Metcalfs have had a serious falling out over the business with the sand. So have the Bovises and the Metcalfs, mainly because Georgina suspects Bob of spilling the beans about her daughter's lesbianism.' April had heard that Sherry's flatmate was also her girlfriend, and Billy had been able to put the information to good use. 'And of course everyone hates the Prouts.'

'Oh, so everything's going to plan, then. That's good.' She looked around vaguely, as if the mall was filled with fog. 'What pointless luxury shall we purchase next?'

He was falling in love with her, a little more each day.

Suddenly she had risen to her feet and was waving at someone. 'Cooee! Georgina, over here!'

Georgina Bovis bore two Body Shop bags, a carrier from the Gap and the defiant look of a woman who knew she was being talked about.

'Polly, how are you? I'm all shopped out.'

'This *is* a wonderful surprise,' said April happily, as if they had just bumped into each other on the far side of the earth. 'You must take some refreshment with us.'

The Shangri-la Tearoom had seventeen different varieties of tea, all in little sachets on strings, like tampons. Billy gloomily sat before his Crimson Zinger as Georgina chattered on to her new friend.

'But it's ghastly, don't you think?' she said, pulling up the string from her cup and looking for somewhere to drop the dripping crimson sac. 'I mean, we've never been particularly close, but we've always been able to rely on one another, and now I don't know who to trust. It's no secret that I've fallen out with Bob Metcalf.'

'But I thought he was your friend, Georgina.'

'Well, he seems to have been making disgusting accusations about my daughter to anyone who will listen.'

'That's awful,' said April, fighting to contain a smile. 'What sort of disgusting things has he been saying?'

'He's been telling people that she's a *lesbian*.'

'That's ridiculous,' said April indignantly. 'Sharing a flat with one doesn't make her one.'

'What do you mean?'

'Have you not met her friend, the very tough-looking girl with the shaved head? She drives a post office van.'

'I thought her flatmate worked at the store.'

'She was released from her position some weeks ago, I believe.'

Georgina looked crestfallen. 'I didn't know that.'

'Ah, well then. I hear that someone sent environmental health officers around to the Prouts yesterday, something to do with a disorderly bonfire in their back garden.'

'There was a fire all right,' said Georgina, sidetracked, 'but Ken doesn't know who set it. He was at work, and Barbara was out shopping. I got a call from the council because they'd had a report that I was running a business from home – imagine that! And Daphne Metcalf got a call about noise pollution, *another* anonymous complaint. The police won't do anything. Less than useless. I spoke to Morris Diller – he's a senior officer at our local constabulary – and he seems to think it's kids, but I imagine it's one of the builders, someone with a grudge. Who else would do such things?'

April smiled vacuously back at her companion. 'Who indeed?' she said.

'You've been spared the worst, of course, because you're new, but what must you think of us?'

'Oh, I'm sure it's just a malicious prankster,' she said, smiling as she sipped her tea. 'He's bound to be caught soon.' She caught Billy's eye. 'They always overstep the mark eventually. What do you think, darling?'

'Jack, you strike me as a sensible sort of chap. What do you think I should do?'

Justin leaned forward with his square chin resting on his fist and an earnest expression on his face. His manner had none of its usual aggressive confidence; he seemed pathetically grateful for any crumbs of guidance his neighbour could offer. Nobody suspected the new arrivals; on the contrary, Mr Prentiss exuded an aura of trust and respect that encouraged virtual strangers to unburden themselves to him, even though his wife was a little odd. Of course that was to be expected, what with her being foreign.

'Well,' said Billy, after a moment of pretending to give the matter serious thought, 'if Ken Prout really thinks you've been posting him pornography, he must have a very good reason.'

'He says he has a copy of my signature.'

'How can you be sure that he's telling the truth?' asked Billy. 'He must have known that his accusations would be upsetting. Why would he want to annoy you deliberately?'

'I don't know, I really don't.'

Justin looked out across the fresh green gardens. Summer skies had finally arrived, but the temperature was still low for the season. Behind them, April could be heard singing an old Doris Day song, 'The Deadwood Stage'. Her voice soared painfully off-key each time she got to 'Whip-crackaway'.

'Sandra says I'm giving the matter too much credence,' said Justin, turning from the sound in mild alarm, 'but I'm at the end of my tether. This used to be such a happy street. Now it seems that everybody is at one another's throats.'

It was true. Only last week Justin and Bob Metcalf had ended the bad feeling that had settled between them since the sand delivery incident two weeks ago, and Bob had lent Justin his electric lawn mower in a gesture of reconciliation. When Justin returned it the damned thing blew up in Bob's face, nearly maiming him for life. Dr McMann told Bob that he was lucky he hadn't lost an eye. Now they were at war again.

Billy was solicitous and enquired whether the lawn mower could be repaired, but Justin explained that his neighbour had thrown the lethal device away. That was lucky. He didn't want anyone finding the mercury-fulminate detonator he had superglued inside the mower tank near the ignition button. It annoyed him that he had missed the chance to blind Bob Metcalf, but there would be other opportunities.

Meanwhile, as the new voice of reason in Balmoral

Close, he dispensed wise advice. The neighbours recognised him as a successful man. They looked up to him, and he was careful to reassure them. That made it so much easier to set them against each other. All a man needed was a nice smile, inner calm and a sense of authority, and he could get away with murder.

'I wouldn't eat it, if I were you,' said Bob Metcalf, disgustedly surveying the giant chocolate layer cake that stood in the middle of the kitchen table. 'You're already the size of Belgium.'

'I'll do as I damned well please,' snapped Daphne, hunting for a knife. 'I don't need permission from you.' The accompanying typewritten note had explained that the cake was a gift from the Prouts, lovingly handcrafted by the evangelists, to make up for any past upset between the two families.

She cut herself a large slice, drizzled it with cream and pressed her spoon into the calorific morass. 'It was baked by religious fanatics,' she said sarcastically. 'They'll probably stick a burning cross on our front lawn if we don't eat it.'

'I couldn't think of anything more disgusting. No wonder you don't sleep at night.'

Daphne took a mouthful just to annoy her husband. Bob peered closer at the cake and wrinkled his nose. 'What's that terrible smell?' he asked.

Daphne swallowed a chocolatey chunk and thrust another spoonful in her mouth. She knew he was just trying to put her off. Bob was sniffing about the cake like a bloodhound. Suddenly he seized the knife and plunged it into the centre of the confectionery, tearing it in two.

There, embedded in the chocolate sponge and topped with swirls of icing, was an immense brown bolus of human excrement. The tail-end of the log-like turd had been spooned away by his eager wife. Daphne took one look and her gorge rose.

'Oh – my – God!'

She deafeningly regurgitated the contents of her stomach in a copious yellow fountain that flooded across the table and swamped Bob's open briefcase.

Later that morning, Bob Metcalf and Ken Prout actually came to blows on the front lawn of Ken's house. Across the road, Billy watched from the window.

'God's love is all encompassing, remember,' said Barbara, emptying the morning's groceries onto the kitchen counter. Simon had been dumped by his first girlfriend the week before. Barbara felt that this was a sign from the Lord and a blessing in disguise, as she considered him far too young to start dating. Simon had spent the entire weekend moping around the house in his dressing gown. 'It is far greater to be loved by Him than by a mere mortal. Do you hear me?'

'Give it a rest,' grunted Simon, who was sick of hearing about how wonderful God was to everyone. Simon hated God for stealing away his mother and turning her into a weirdo. 'If he was so great he wouldn't allow wars and sickness and famine.'

'That's His way of testing our faith.'

'That's his way of proving he doesn't exist. Except to emotional cripples.'

'You wouldn't say that if your father was here, young man,' said his mother, fishing to the bottom of a paper sack and pulling out a bottle of pills.

'Well, he's not here.'

'No, he's gone for a round of golf.'

Barbara knew where her husband was, and it wasn't on the fairway. He had gone to the police to report a letter sent to the Bovis family accusing him of conducting an incestuous relationship with his own son. The Bovises had kindly brought it to his attention, but something in their manner had suggested to Barbara that they believed there was no smoke without fire. The parting between the two families that morning had been a cool one. She went to the sink and poured herself a glass of water, then snapped the lid from the bottle of tablets. The doctor had put her on Prozac two weeks ago, but so far her endless depressions had failed to lift. Nothing came out when she shook the bottle, so she thrust her fingers in.

And screamed.

In between the pills were over a dozen broken pieces of razor blade. As the curved metal shards bit into her flesh, the tips of the index and middle fingers on her right hand were badly slashed. Several slivers of metal went deep underneath her nails as she struggled to free her hand from the bottle. She screamed and screamed, and spattered crimson droplets all across the snow-white pine-fresh counters, and when the bloody pill bottle was later retrieved from beneath the sink it was seen to have been booby-trapped, and issued by the neighbourhood physician, with a signature from Dr McMann himself.

Alan Bovis felt sick.

His face had gone numb, and he was having trouble breathing. After pushing aside a half-finished bowl of Orchard Muesli he felt the contents of his stomach roll over and headed for the bathroom, but vomited before he reached the basin, violently splashing the remains of his breakfast over the landing stairs. In a panic Georgina called Dr McMann, but he was already out on a call. She made Alan sit still and wiped his chin, and watched as he shook and began to cry. His skin was wet with perspiration and freezing cold.

'Perhaps it's something you ate,' she offered.

'Only had half a bowl of cereal,' said Alan, and then he was sick again.

'What did you have last night?' she asked, holding a plastic wash bowl between his knees. 'You were drinking; did you eat something?'

'It hurts, Georgie. Oh God, it hurts—'

'Describe the pain,' she kept saying, dropping to her knees beside him, not knowing what to do.

'Knives,' gasped Alan unhelpfully.

If Georgina had gone down to the kitchen and examined the milk bottle that stood on the counter, she would have seen a tiny pinhole in its silver lid. That was where their charming new neighbour had injected a weak solution of sodium fluoroacetate, a colourless, odourless poison used to treat seeds. It also blocked cellular metabolism if ingested. The dose was not strong enough to kill Alan Bovis.

Not this time.

CHAPTER THIRTY

The Pain Principle

'Revenge is an act that requires concentration, and I had no intention of being turned from my path. But there was April. I hadn't meant for there to be any physical involvement between us, but she handled the subject in her own inimitable way, as if it were a no-nonsense household chore like the washing up.' – *The Red Diary*

A SWISS château.

A Bali beach hut.

An Art Deco Miami hotel.

All of them under blue, blue skies.

April was idly leafing through travel brochures in the lounge. 'Where shall we go after you've finished your business here?' she called. Billy was in the breakfast nook fixing a cuckoo clock to the wall. He had promised her a holiday when it was all over, but he had been rather evasive about what 'it' was. Nor had he explained that they could never return.

'Oh, I don't mind,' he replied, 'a Greek island would be nice.'

'Their cuisine leaves much to be desired. They don't seem to have heard of sauces. The men are incapable of shaving properly and the women all wear black sacking. What about Italy? Too many Catholics, of course, but such an attractive race. The men are delightfully saturnine and largely uncircumcised. And pasta, though fattening, is a sensual foodstuff.' She carefully cut the eyes from a photograph of the pope, then snipped off the top of his head. 'Germany is a possibility. The cuisine is filling, the men literate, thoughtful and merciless in bed. We could visit the town of Ebensee, where they filmed *Where Eagles Dare*.'

Her husband set down his cuckoo clock and wandered into the lounge. Twenty minutes ago an ambulance had come to take Barbara Prout to casualty. He took an objective peek at his wife. 'What are you wearing?' he asked quietly.

Her eyes lowered with pleasure as she glanced across her sparkling silver one-piece. 'This is a teasingly taut Rayon Mylar lounge outfit, bonded to hug tight and stay shapely, as seen on the Virginia Graham show.'

Her nipples and, for that matter, the clear outline of her genitalia showed through the non-natural fibre as she crossed and uncrossed her legs on the tartan armchair.

'My footwear?' she pouted. 'A hi-style three-inch fashion wedge of crystal lucite finished in gold alligator leather and black tracey kid. Since you asked. My Cossack lounge boots with the pink mink lining are too warm for spring.'

She was teasing him. She had always known that there was no chance of them having a normal sex life. Indeed, they had not attempted full sexual intercourse since they were married. That was not what they were here for.

April could not bear to have a man touch her sexually. For the first few years she had wondered if her rape at the hands of Gavin Diller had left a damaging psychological scar, but lately she had come to believe that no man could give her the satisfactory stimulation she was capable of providing for herself. She looked up at poor Billy, understanding all too well how he felt. Now that she had discovered his penchant for certain types of clinging fabric she would be able to offer him a more fulfilling sexual experience. As a teenager she had ached for freedom and independence, but now – irony of ironies – she wanted to be the kind of unreconstructed housewife that men like Gavin Diller dreamed of finding: pliant, obedient, faithful, doting. Women like that were uncomplicated. Complication bred confusion, and April could not afford to become confused. When she became confused she stole things, and burned things, and turned upon herself.

Billy was determined not to become aroused. He had important plans to make, contingencies to allow for, outcomes to resolve. He had no time for this but could feel the blood rushing into his engorged member. He willed it away, forced detumescent images into his head: Mother Teresa, The Oklahoma City bombing, Andrew Lloyd Webber, Auschwitz, Oprah – but nothing worked.

The lights were low in the bedroom because April had thrown her nylon lace Capri pants over the lampshade. She stood at the end of the bed, balancing daintily, raising her hair like a model from a forgotten soft-core magazine, *Reveille*, perhaps, or *Tit-Bits*. Her Cat's Meow acetate baby-doll nightie was trimmed with maribou and purple rayon-satin bows, and clung to her staunch breasts through static electricity. Her high-cut, split-crotch bikini panties were hung with black and pink tassels, and it was into these that she inserted her busy fingers as she ground down hard with her right foot.

The shoes, she knew, were important. Black lace-up, knee-high leatherette conquistador boots with four-inch spiked heels. They had been advertised in the catalogue with the copy line: 'You'll need a whip to beat these off!' And luckily, that was exactly what she had. She also had a muir cap, expandable steel nipple clamps, rubber wrist restraints, her Leather Cave Bootboy mouth gag, a full-leather body harness, ankle chains and chromium-plated split testicle weights for heightened pleasure.

She had suspected that Billy liked to be hurt, but her suspicions were not confirmed until one morning at the mall, when April had conducted a confidential conversation with Georgina Bovis about pleasuring the male.

'They lose interest once they come,' her experienced neighbour had volunteered, flattered to be treated as an expert, 'so it's your job to make sure they don't come until you're ready.' She had had no idea that they were discussing very different concepts of sex.

'How do I know when he's ready?' April's eyes had been wide and innocent.

'They make a face,' Georgina had explained. 'Like the one they make when they're lifting heavy weights.'

'Like they're in pain.'

'That's it. Sex is like a fox hunt. So much of the fun is in the chase that the kill is always a disappointment. Men like it more if you make them die slowly.'

Now, as her fingers probed deeper, hotter, wetter, she pressed down with her heel once more, this time breaking the skin on Billy's bare chest. A neat bubble of blood swelled on his tanned epidermis and dribbled down into his navel as he issued a grunt of agony beneath her. He closed his eyes tight, lost in private flesh fantasy as he manipulated himself through the restraining nylon pants she had given him, his punishment becoming her pleasure.

April reached across to the bedside table for a candle and a box of matches. She had seen Madonna do this in a film once. As she lit the candle, her husband writhed beneath her, groaning, his eyes fixed on the candle.

No, not on the candle – on the pure yellow flame of the combusting match.

She smiled to herself as the tallow began to drip. Let nobody, she thought, as they approached the slow, low gradient of a mutually exclusive climax, tell her that she didn't know how to service her man.

CHAPTER THIRTY-ONE

Thirty-Seven Seconds

'It was Friday evening. I allowed myself three days in total to wrap everything up and get out of town. I was going to start with the Bricketts, only it turned out they were driving up to London for the evening to see *Sunset Boulevard*. You should never change a plan if you haven't thought through all the possibilities. Once you start having to improvise, anything can happen.' – *The Red Diary*

THE POLICE were useless. Strike that, less than useless.

On her usual seat in the conservatory, Daphne Metcalf indignantly hammered away at her laptop, sending an angry letter to – whom, she had not yet decided. What, she typed, was being done? What a reflection on the local police network this was! Hate mail, obscene calls, torture devices – where would it end? Someone had called Georgina Bovis to tell her that her daughter was a dyke. It was true, of course; Sherry had been living with another girl for nearly a year now, but her mother hadn't known, and this seemed a particularly cruel way to break it to her. And now her husband had fallen sick, and the doctor appeared to have no idea what was wrong with him. Much as she didn't like the woman, she seemed to be having a particularly rough patch of luck.

Perhaps it was time for the residents of Invicta Cross to employ a private security firm. Who in Balmoral Close – apart from the new couple – could be trusted? There was obviously some kind of vendetta taking place here, a secret feud, a long-nurtured revenge, something that went back years and stemmed from deep within the community. Or was it merely another symptom of the breakdown of modern society? *The idealised vision of an affluent suburbia is a liberating development*, she wrote, *but it brings a heavy price of its own.* Invicta Cross prided itself on being a community, but what an abstract, vague concept that was. How easy to aspire to communal living, only to scream like a stuck pig when a neighbour played his radio loud.

She read the piece back, knowing that she could probably flog it to her old boss on the *East Grinstead Advertiser*. It was a heartless thought, she knew, but in a funny way this was the most interesting thing to happen in the neighbourhood in years.

Something crashed in the hallway.

'Why don't you just walk straight through the front door,' she muttered under her breath as Brad left the house. There it was, a living example of the failure of the private housing system; her own son, raised in the comparative luxury of a brand-new town, who had advanced from shoving a broken beer glass into someone's face to selling dodgy timeshare apartments and God knows what else somewhere on the seedier outskirts of the city. She closed down the computer and lowered its lid. A few minutes earlier, Jack Prentiss had called to ask her over for a glass of chilled white wine, and she had accepted the offer. Bob was working late again, single-handedly saving the company, and she hadn't seen Emma, who at the age of twenty was more sexually active than a British Airways crew on a stopover, for several days ...

Sod it, she could wait here for her husband to return and expound her sociopathy theories to a man with the mental agility of an edible bivalve or be neighbourly and chance her hand at an intelligent conversation with a handsome semistranger. Absolutely no contest. Besides, it was Friday evening, and she always had a few glasses of wine on a Friday evening. She rose and began a search for suitable apparel.

April was thrilled to be entertaining again. She had slipped into a crêpe Paradise portrait-collared French lace bolero jacket and was arranging dainty whorls of ham and mozzarella on an oval serving plate when the door bell sounded.

Daphne Metcalf had squeezed herself into a pair of Armani jeans that were so tight her eyes were popping out, and heaven alone knew what the zip was doing to her vulva. She had run a comb through her hair, but her roots were showing in a neat black line. She was smiling expectantly, like a child waiting to be given something.

April followed in the wake of their guest's overpowering perfume through the hall to the lounge. As Billy offered Daphne a drink, his wife sniffed her scent with a barely suppressed shudder of horror and showed her to the sofa.

'It was nice of you to invite me over,' said Daphne. 'I hate to admit it, but sometimes it gets quite lonely in there with just me and the computer.'

'Is your husband away?' asked April.

'No, he's just – never there. Always taking care of business somewhere.'

'I understand you're writing a new book.'

'That's right, Polly, I've nearly finished it.'

'Do tell us what it's about. I can hear you from the kitchen.' *I could hear her from the coast*, she thought, retreating to the canapés.

'Well, it's a romance set in Ancient Greece,' came the reply. 'It's a classical setting, but hopefully my readers will find the subject timeless.'

'You mean it's like *Jupiter's Darling*?' April unpeeled the plastic from a tray of Safeway's hors d'oeuvres that looked spoiled. She checked the sell-by date: over a month ago. She threw the tray into the microwave, convinced that once they were reheated and smothered in sour cream Daphne would not notice the difference.

'I'm not familiar with that—'

'It's an Esther Williams film, a masterpiece of the musical comedy genre.'

'Oh—' a small silence – 'this is about a slave girl who falls in love with a wealthy shipbuilder.'

'Oh, I know, this is another one of those – what's the technical term for them – shipping and fucking novels, isn't it?'

Surprisingly, there was no rude reply forthcoming. April cut the mouldy crust from a slice of bread and dropped it in the toaster as she considered the silence. Daphne seemed to have adopted that same attitude of contrition that was gripping Justin Brickett. It certainly didn't take much to make them unsure of themselves. She suddenly felt sorry for Daphne, always having to shore up her confidence with mention of her writing because she received no support from her perpetually absent husband. Billy thought the people here were ogres because of the way they had treated him, but they weren't really. They were just as trapped as he had been.

Billy had put a Chris Isaak tape on in the lounge, and she sang along as she waited for the microwave to ping. 'It takes two hearts ...'

She watched vacantly as the tray rotated behind the tinted glass. '... two hearts just to hold your love ...'

There was a squeak, and an odd scuffling noise, then silence from the other room. A chair leg scraped sharply. She looked back at the microwave clock. Thirty-seven seconds to go. It had gone very quiet next door. She walked back into the hall and stuck her head around the frame.

Billy was astride Daphne Metcalf's back, holding her by the tops of her arms. Her legs were on the floor and her spine was bent back. Her head was shoved up against the side of the sofa. As her limbs gave spastic, angry twitches, Billy hammered at the handle of the broad-bladed Sabatier carving knife that protruded from the back of her neck. Grabbing her hair he hauled her over to the little fish tank, batted away the blue plastic lid and shoved her face in. Daphne attempted to scream, but found her mouth and throat filling with water. The knife handle jutting from the base of her skull made her look like some kind of overweight stick puppet. There didn't seem to be any blood. Then April saw why. It was pouring from the point of the knife, an inch of which was sticking out of her throat.

'Well, don't just stand there, darling, give me a hand.' He kept Daphne's head beneath the water level and freed one hand to beckon her over.

April felt her brain overheating in confusion. She was unsure what was expected of her. The part of her mind that made her understand what she saw was cutting out. She took a step forward and stopped.

'Please, April,' pleaded Billy. 'She's too heavy for me to manage by myself.' Daphne was thrashing about like a wild animal, punching at the backs of his legs with her right fist. He pulled her head out of the tank and rammed it into the side, but the glass was too thick to break. A wave of water sloshed onto the carpet. Two glittering fish flopped across the floor and disappeared under the sideboard like skittering gobbets of molten gold.

'Billy, you're making everything wet!'

'I'll clear it up later, I promise. Put the plastic underneath her.' He pointed to a large transparent roll beside the sofa. Where had that come from? Had he planned to do this? As April grabbed the sheeting, she saw Billy free the carving knife. He raised it before him, then stuck it into Daphne's back several times. Once he managed to bury it up to the hilt, a good eight or nine inches.

'Christ, I don't believe this,' he moaned, annoyed. She was still thrashing about, her sneakers drumming against the floor. 'Behind you, pass me that.' He was pointing past his wife's head to the kitchen counter.

April looked around and saw the iron. She picked it up and passed it to him. 'Careful,' she warned, 'it's still hot. Morphy Richards, they retain the heat very well.'

He crowned Daphne with the point of the iron four or five times, jamming it at her head until there was a large blood-filled triangular dent in her flattened hair. His last blow made the sound of a spoon cracking the shell of a soft-boiled egg. Daphne stopped moving just as the microwave pinged off.

Thirty-seven seconds to die.

There was surprisingly little blood from the knife. Most of it had been absorbed by Daphne's heavy woollen sweater. He rolled her into the plastic sheet and knotted it tightly at either end, then sealed the edges with plastic tape. Now blood began to pool rapidly along the bottom of the sealed tube.

'Shall I put the kettle on?' asked April, flustered and unsure of her role.

Billy looked up at her. 'What for?'

'A cup of tea.'

He could see that she was close to tears. 'Let's get rid of the body first, shall we?' He began to shift the plastic roll toward the doorway.

'Billy?'

A grunt. The elliptical roll flopped over. Another grunt. 'Yes?'

'Why did you do that to Daphne? She was our guest. She came over for *drinks*.'

He thought carefully for a moment. If he said the wrong thing now it was all over, and he could not allow the rest of the plan to be jeopardised. He looked back at the body. 'She was one of the people from the past, April, one of the bad ones.'

'She didn't really seem that bad.'

He wanted to put his arms around her, but his hands were covered in blood. 'Listen, April, you have to trust me about who is bad and who isn't. You haven't seen what I've seen. Trust me?'

She pouted at the plastic roll, then decided. 'I suppose I have to. You're my husband. You're the boss. I'm the little woman. The ball and chain. The trouble and strife. I'm Twiggy to your Christopher Gable.'

If that was the way she wanted to behave, he decided to let her. The puzzled tremor in her voice suggested he should change the subject altogether.

'Tell you what. You clean up in here, and I'll take care of this silly old thing, how about that?'

'Oh, yes please, Billy.' She stepped over the bulky corpse and went into the kitchen for the J-Cloths and Sparkle, scouring sponges and Fairy Liquid.

While her husband dragged Daphne Metcalf's cooling cadaver into the garden.

CHAPTER THIRTY-TWO

The Broken
Commandment

'The tabloids will turn me into a cold-hearted killer, of course. No one will think for a moment that these people did not deserve to live, that they led empty, poisoned lives, that they committed random, thoughtless acts amounting to a lifetime of cruelty. With each punch I used to hammer the knife into Daphne's neck, I struck a blow for freedom, liberation for all those quiet victims who passed their lives being endlessly trodden on. Winston Smith's tormentors told him to imagine a boot stamping on a human face forever. With Daphne's death I eased the painful weight of that boot for a moment.' – *The Red Diary*

TWIGGY WAS in a white chiffon trouser suit, her face a pale moon of innocence. She was miming to the gramophone record when the needle skipped and the song stuck, imprisoning her in the same repeated lyric. Embarrassed, she continued to mime before the audience.

'This is my favourite part, watch. DeThrill imagines how it would be if he turned the whole show into a Hollywood production; the orchestra swells, cue fantasy sequence, and

Christopher Gable comes spinning on dressed as a bellhop.'
April sat forward in her chair, her chin on her knuckles,
staring intently at the screen. The dancer appeared from the
bottom of the screen in a silver suit, spiralling around a vast
revolving turntable as the soundtrack soared. 'Of course it's
a homage to Busby Berkeley, but none the worse for that. The
leading performers exemplify the Art Deco period, so slim
and elegant. Their glamour has an unforced purity that
seems to come from within.'

She had watched the sequence five times in the past hour.
She shifted in her seat, eyes flicking from character to
character. He watched her hands drop to her lap, where
they kneaded and knotted as she allowed the film sequence
to calm her fraying nerves.

Her behaviour was unstable at the best of times, but it
was impossible to tell how badly the next forty-eight hours
would affect her. The moment his life had been leading to
for so long had finally arrived. He had planned for it alone,
allowing no room in his heart for anyone else. But there
was April, poor lost April; he could not bear to see her
hurt.

She was quickly retreating into the world of her celluloid
desires. She had grown more confused in the hours since
the killing of Daphne Metcalf, a puzzled frown periodically
clouding her face, as though she was trying to remember
something important. Perhaps this fugue was preferable to
reality and would cushion her from the excesses of his
behaviour.

'Darling, would you like another cup of tea?' he asked.

Her eyes never left the screen. 'If you're making one. And
a chocolate biscuit. I like this bit, you see, where the camera
goes through the girls' legs. Billy?'

He stopped in the doorway. 'Yes?'

'Do you think you'll go to hell for what you did?'

'I'm not religious, April. Anyway, I don't believe I can be damned for trying to restore a natural balance.'

'I think you're allowed to break some of the commandments under certain special circumstances.' The quicker she forgave him, the quicker she could forget about Daphne. She watched some more of the film. 'Billy? What did you do with her body?'

'Now I don't want you to worry yourself about that.'

'I just wondered, that's all.'

He sighed as he found a tea towel and began drying a pair of blue and white striped mugs. 'She's on her way to the sea.'

'How?'

'You don't need to know all the details, darling, really. It'll only upset you.'

'Please.'

'All right. After I sealed her body in the plastic sheeting, I left a hole in the top and steeped it in a solution of ethyl chlorocarbonate and hydrochloric acid. Later on I lowered it into the sewer tunnel at the edge of the patio. The street's main pipe passes beneath the garden. All I did was widen our drainage shaft, break into the ceramic pipe with a pickaxe and put the lid back on once I'd finished.'

'How did you know about the drain being there?'

'I still have a copy of the area's original Ordnance Survey drawings in the back of my red diary, along with my chemical tables. And I've been able to get my hands on the updated plans from Justin Brickett's office.'

'You know everything about this town,' she said admiringly.

'I wouldn't say everything. There's so much building going on, it's hard to keep track of new developments. Listen to that rain.' He went into the kitchen as she cocked her head and listened. 'That's what I was waiting for. It should have washed her far away by now. It would be better if we got a really big storm. They've been forecasting one for days.'

'You're right. Thunder would be a more appropriate response to your activities. You're a driven man, Billy March. You have a purpose, and I won't stand in your way.' She was sounding strange again. He knew he would have to keep her away from the neighbours until she could successfully simulate normal behaviour.

'You finish watching your film. I'll bring you a nice cup of tea. Then I'll tell you about a little job I have for you tonight,' said Billy.

'It's nothing like—'

'Of course not. I told you, April, I'll take care of the nasty things. The worst this will do is get a little mud on you, and I'll make sure that you're wearing your over-shoes.'

'You're so good to me, darling. We'll be so happy when we're finally home, you and I.' She settled back in her chair and studied the glittering screen. Beneath her slippers the carpet was still damp with water from the fish tank. The iron stood in its usual place beside the serving hatch, carefully scrubbed clean of any incriminating hair or skin particles. Apart from the damp patch, two dying goldfish behind the sideboard and a single perfect penny-sized drop of blood beneath the television, there were no other signs that a brutal murder had taken place in the room.

*

All through that terrible Saturday, Georgina Bovis kept taking warm milk up to her husband, thinking that it would settle his stomach, not realising that this second bottle was even more liberally laced with sodium fluoroacetate than the first. Before the overworked Dr McMann could return for another visit, Alan Bovis began to have convulsions due to the violent fibrillation of his tired heart's muscles. He started to cry continuously and complained of knives turning inside him. Then, following a brief, eerie moment of reflective calm, he suffered a spectacular coronary, dying noisily and painfully after undergoing respiratory failure due (the doctor would later tell her) to severe pulmonary oedema.

What this meant in real terms was that his face turned blue, his eyes rolled back into his head with an awful crunching sound and he thumped about in the bed, flailing and crashing and tearing his ligaments like Linda Blair in *The Exorcist* while his wife screamed in helpless horror.

At 6.30 pm on Saturday evening they took Alan's ruptured body away in a discreet white plastic Ziploc bag with a sheet over it, and Georgina Bovis was placed under heavy sedation. At the moment there was some confusion as to the cause of death because the patient's symptoms had seemed so contradictory. McMann could not rule out the possibility of a post mortem. As he left the house, he decided to wait until a more appropriate time to discuss the matter. Several sets of curtains shifted as he waved the ambulance out of the drive, but no one came out of their house to offer help, sympathy or even simply to ask what was going on. The manicured façade of Invicta Cross remained unruffled.

Sherry Bovis was summoned to take care of her mother

and, after arranging for her girlfriend to take care of the cats, arrived in Balmoral Close with an overnight bag. She wrapped her weeping mother, now nitrazepam fed and barely conscious, in a duvet and settled her on the couch for the night. When she went to make herself a sandwich, she found the letter that had been sent to her father, informing him of her sexual proclivities. Mortified, she stormed over to Bob Metcalf's house ready for a fight, but found that he was not at home.

During the very same minute, an enfuriated Bob Metcalf was leaving the Invicta Cross constabulary with his daughter for the second time in twenty-four hours. Sergeant Morris Diller had not allowed him to file a missing persons report the first time because his wife had only been missing for four and a half hours, and she was required to be absent for a full day and a night before anyone would get off their arses to look for her.

Emma Metcalf had spent the drive over staring accusingly at her father, as if she expected him to suddenly break down and admit that yes, it was his fault, he had driven his wife away. In the police station she made sarcastic remarks about him under her breath the whole time and told the sergeant that her father had probably committed murder.

'I don't know why you're pretending to be interested in where she's gone,' she said as they climbed back in the car. 'If she has any sense she'll never come home again.'

He did not know his daughter now. He did not like the sullen, arrogant young woman she had become. He could not understand what had made her so selfish and suspicious. She had wanted for nothing as a child; she had always been daddy's little girl. Indeed, she was the reason

Brad had constantly accused him of favouritism.

It occurred to Bob that Daphne might have gone to stay with her literary colleagues in London, but although he had her address book, he had absolutely no idea who any of her city friends were. A darker thought crossed his mind: that she had finally carried out her oft-repeated threat and left him. Her coat and bag were missing. If she had her credit cards on her, she could be travelling anywhere.

Bob was right in that respect. Even now, Daphne Metcalf was heading south on her cloacal passage to Brighton and the open sea.

CHAPTER THIRTY-THREE

God and Golf

'Once I started raising the boot of oppression, it was easy to continue. And it kept getting easier.' – *The Red Diary*

BALMORAL CLOSE was very quiet on Sunday morning. It always was, but now a caul of silence had been drawn across the dull redbrick houses. Curtains were drawn, lights were off. The days when parents stayed in bed reading the papers had vanished with the concept of corner-shop deliveries. The unbroken cloud base was as lugubrious as lead, a sky full of broken promises, sunlight little more than a memory.

Barbara Prout rose quietly in order to disturb her husband as little as possible, although she knew he'd be on the fairway in little more than an hour from now. She washed and dressed, donned a raincoat and headed down to the car. It was her habit on a Sunday morning to visit her church as early as possible, before the ever-swelling congregation of young mothers turned up with their children for the tambourine and electric guitar singalong at eleven. She parked her Renault behind the church and entered the low brick building for an hour of peaceful prayer.

The time was now 8.45 am.

Although her religious conversion was treated with derision by the rest of the family, supplication brought Barbara strength and inner peace. Regular attendance at the services also gave her something to do. She was bored with life in Invicta Cross. Her husband spent all of his free time on the golf course, sublimating his frustrations into improving his handicap, and her son hated her beyond and without reason. At least God was always there for her. Noting the sound of rain on the roof, she rose from her knees (she preferred the old-fashioned method of prayer – it was more of an effort), made her usual donation even though the place was empty at this hour and no one would have minded if she had left nothing, and stepped into the porch with her raincoat wrapped tightly around her. The rain was lashing across the car park, all but obscuring the cemetery beyond. Whispers of thunder sounded in the distance like a far-off sea.

As she had no umbrella she dashed to the car, beeping the alarm off as she ran, slipped into the driver's seat and gave an involuntary shiver as she inserted the keys in the ignition.

She was halfway through humming the first verse of 'Mine Eyes Have Seen The Glory Of The Coming Of The Lord' when the firestorm that blasted out of the dashboard and roasted her alive raised the temperature inside the vehicle so quickly that all of the windows blistered and shattered in seconds. There was little noise beyond a dull *whump* as Mrs Prout and her Renault were despatched in different directions. It was an oddly unspectacular end, as if the explosion had scaled itself down to show some respect. Beyond the occasional pop and hiss and crack, the fire roared dully on, the thick black smoke it caused battered flat by the heavy rain. Barbara Prout's fatty bottom fried in its own juices, and her bones cracked into ebony sticks.

The wreckage remained undiscovered for three-quarters of an hour, and by the time an inquisitive cleaner approached, it had blackened and cooled. Very little sign of Barbara Prout remained. She seemed to have melted into the seat, although the white ceramic caps of her teeth stuck out from the globuliferous headrest, the upper and lower sets far apart, as though she had been laughing hard when the ignition spark had triggered the nitrate-filled guncotton so expertly packed behind the steering column.

The burning belt of Barbara Prout's raincoat had drifted down from the sky and draped itself over a marble headstone carved in a crucifix, as though she had ascended to heaven and left behind her signature.

Ken Prout donned his favourite check trousers and a heavy plastic slicker, and arrived at the clubhouse just before ten, while the course was still empty – not that there were ever many players. It was time he and the other members faced facts; the place simply hadn't taken off. The course was undemanding and ill planned, and problems with the water table had created areas of permanent marshiness.

Ken had thrashed Justin Brickett the previous weekend, and planned to do so again today. The estate agent had caused quite a furore earlier in the week, effectively banning Bob Metcalf from the club by refusing to renew his membership. Just when they needed every green fee they could lay their hands on. The man was a congenital idiot and, he thought, adding a private smirk, a failed yuppie. Invicta Cross had pretty much failed to match up to everyone's expectations. Not so much paradise lost as paradise never quite attained.

He wheeled out his bag to the first hole just as the skies opened up. He didn't mind a spot of rain, but this looked as if it was in for the day. A hell of a wind was rising in the trees. Still, in the absence of his partner, he decided to tee off and at least get in a few practice shots. He sorted himself out a decent driver and squared up to the tee, pausing to wipe a rind of mud from his white patent-leather loafers. But when he had a proper squint at the fairway, his mouth fell open in surprise. Someone had dug dozens of pits across the green. There were flaming great mounds of earth scattered about, and ditches everywhere! The grass he and his fellow members had seen nurtured to the consistency of billiard table baize had been randomly hacked up with the blade of a shovel.

This was the final straw! Hurling down his club, he strode across the fairway for a closer look. In the distance someone was sheltering beneath a tree, lost in shadow, watching him. Too tall to be old Brickett. Who the hell was it?

'Hi, you there!'

He broke into a run, avoiding the wedges of soil that now littered the course. As he reached the cover of the cedar trees he could make out the figure more clearly. The chap was experimentally swinging a heavy old-fashioned wooden-handled club back and forth as if about to play through.

'Prentiss? Jack, is that you?'

'Hello there!' his nemesis exclaimed, stepping away from the shadowy bole. 'Just thought I'd get in a quick round before brunch. You never know, I might take it up as a full-time hobby.'

Ken struggled to get his breath back. 'Haven't you seen the green, man? Some idiotic bastard has vandalised it with a shovel!'

'That was no idiotic bastard. That was my wife.' He shifted the iron back and forth, shaking out his hips. 'She enjoys a spot of gardening, so I suggested she came over here and practise a few holes.'

'Are you insane?' spluttered Ken. 'There are enforceable laws designed to protect the private property of taxpaying citizens, and they cover the vandalising of natural assets like the green.' Typical Prout-speak, basic bollocks.

'My wife certainly covered the green,' Billy said. 'I only sent her over to bugger up a couple of the trickier traps and spoil your morning, but it looks like she went raving mad. She must have got carried away. She does sometimes, when she's enjoying herself.'

'Well, she'll go to jail for this.'

'She's been in prison all her life, Prouty-Prout, one that you people helped to build for her. Tell me, do the names Billy March and April Barrow mean anything to you?'

Just as his neighbour was about to reply, Billy swept the heavy iron through the air, around and upwards, catching Ken a resounding clip under his chin. His jaws snapped shut with a bang, chopping off a thin red crescent of tongue and cracking his dental plate in half. Surprisingly he managed to remain standing, but reached forward in shock and spat out the broken halves of pink plastic plate in a torrent of blood and saliva.

Before Ken had a chance to lose his shocked expression, Billy swung the club again. This time the slap of metal on bone had a startling effect. The businessman shot over onto his side, his feet knocked from under him on the wet grass.

He landed hard on his back, just in time to receive another smack across the other ear. Something gave with a sharp crack, and a streak of blood instantly welled across Ken Prout's face. His right eye had been damaged and was bleeding wildly. It looked like a poached egg in a bed of boiling tomato sauce. Billy placed his boot on the man's throat so that he could not cry out.

'You probably don't remember little people, do you?' He twisted around the top half of his body and stared off into the distance. 'How far do you reckon it is to the green from here? Looks like a Par 3. I could only find this club, and it's probably not appropriate. Belonged to my old dead dad. Not one of those modern lightweight jobs I'm afraid, but it can pack a hell of a punch.'

He reached down and settled a golf ball on Ken's trembling lips, gently prising open his mouth by stepping on his chin with the toe of his boot.

'Okay, I'm going to give this one all I've got. I'm after power rather than accuracy.' He swung the club as high and as hard as he could, but the wedge missed the ball by a full inch. Ken was squealing and writhing beneath his foot. 'Let me try that again. Try to keep still this time.' He pushed harder on Prout's throat with the arch of his boot, swung the club in a high arc above his head, and swept it down. The resulting smash removed the last of Ken's front teeth and shattered his nose into a fleshy fountain of blood.

The ball rolled several feet and came to a stop in a patch of long grass.

'Oh dear. I think I need a lot more practice.'

He brought the club down as hard as he could on Prout's head, feeling the powerful muscles in his arms send the shaft forward, feeling the plates of his victim's skull crack apart as the driver squashed into a slit of viscous pink that could only have been the accountant's exposed brain. Then, dropping the club beside the body, he sauntered off beneath the cover of the restless cedars, artlessly whistling a chorus of 'A Room in Bloomsbury'.

He left the course by its deserted rear entrance, pulled off his string-backed gloves and the rubber overshoes he had borrowed from April and dropped them into the rushing darkness of the storm drain at the still-unfinished end of Gaveston Crescent.

Then, after purchasing a Sunday *Independent*, he headed home for a breakfast of eggs, bacon, toast and marmalade with his lovely satin-gowned wife, and waited for all hell to break loose.

The Joy of Revenge

'I've checked the list again, and started marking my progress with a series of crosses placed in boxes, like this:

- ☒ Barbara Prout
- ☒ Ken Prout
- ☐ Simon Prout
- ☒ Alan Bovis
- ☐ Georgina Bovis
- ☐ Sherry Bovis
- ☐ Bob Metcalf
- ☒ Daphne Metcalf
- ☐ Brad Metcalf
- ☐ Emma Metcalf
- ☐ Justin Brickett
- ☐ Sandra Brickett
- ☐ Dr McMann
- ☐ Mrs McMann
- ☐ PC Morris Diller
- ☐ Gavin Diller

I've decided to include the doctor's wife because she has been instrumental, I'm sure, in keeping the Marches out of

Invicta Cross society. Her husband was an influential man, and it was said she kept him under her thumb. I have also decided not to harm Sherry Bovis or Simon Prout, even though the latter was irritating as a child. That leaves fourteen potential victims (I have plans for the rest of Invicta Cross), of which four are already despatched, leaving ten outstanding, and three of those (Gavin Diller, Justin Brickett and Brad Metcalf) requiring termination with totally extreme prejudice.' – *The Red Diary*

SERGEANT MORRIS Diller watched the rain squalls sweeping across the aquamarine glass canopy of the Invicta Cross Mall half a mile away and returned his attention to the paperwork before him. It was 2.35 on a Sunday afternoon. He was furious about having to miss his traditional Sunday lunch, especially as the wife was doing roast lamb, his favourite. Suspected homicide was beyond his field of responsibility, and even if it had been within his power to commence some kind of investigation he would still have been disallowed, because he knew the victims personally. Instead, because Invicta Cross came under the southern metropolitan police AMIP district in cases of serious crime, and because his own superintendent was off sick, he would have to wait for the East Grinstead boys to come down tomorrow morning. That left him with Police Constables Midlock and Bimsley. The former was a probationary officer and therefore theoretically not allowed out by himself, and the latter was possibly the clumsiest man he had ever met and a danger to everyone.

Meanwhile, the torrential rain was washing away any chance of finding evidence at the two sites. At the moment, he was the most senior officer available at the station (the chief inspector was on indefinite leave following a nervous breakdown, and the only other inspector was off with a throat infection), so the responsibility for taking some kind of action was his, but what could he do beyond cordoning off the areas surrounding Ken Prout's grotesquely battered body and the blackened wreckage of Mrs Prout's car? He had no authority to perform any further duties without clearance from a commanding member of staff, and anyway, there were no officers available to start door-to-door interviews. What a balls-up. But then nothing like this had ever happened in the area.

He forced himself to think. It seemed unlikely that anyone living in the neighbourhood was withholding significant information. If the Prout car fire was arson and they were looking at a pair of homicides, it was more likely to be the work of outsiders coming into the affluent area to exploit it. As yet there was no proof of accompanying robbery, but he was sure it would turn up. What if there was a gang of troublemakers turning nasty, coming over from one of the nearby council estates? The nearest ARV was stationed permanently at Croydon. Would he be able to commission the use of the vehicle?

Then there was the matter of Daphne Metcalf's disappearance. It seemed impossible that the incident was related, but suppose she had been abducted – what were they meant to do, sit around waiting for a ransom note to appear? Nothing in Morris Diller's training had prepared him for this. Most of his daily work involved burglaries, auto theft, threats from noisy neighbours, purse snatchings and lost pets. This was Invicta Cross, not New York or Croydon. He ran a hand through thinning wisps of ginger hair and released a sigh. The whole thing was beyond him;

he hadn't the faintest idea what to do, so until someone arrived to give him specific orders, he decided to do nothing.

April looked the part perfectly as she carried in the steaming Sunday roast, from her quilted oven gloves to the *She's the Boss* pinafore she had knotted over her purple scoop-neck taffeta blouse. She was fascinated by the idea of presenting the correct image of the ideal housewife. Matt Monroe was on the stereo singing 'On Days Like These'. It was a Kodak Moment. Billy was at the table with his napkin tucked into his sweater collar, and here she was presenting her husband with a flawlessly arranged Sunday lunch: roast beef, roast potatoes, Yorkshire pudding, peas, beans and aromatic Bisto gravy. April had no knowledge of cookery and had simply microwaved the precooked items she had purchased at the mall. The gravy was more of a chore, but she had managed to remove most of the lumps by straining it through a scarf. Unable to operate the Kenwood for the Yorkshire pudding batter mix, she had blended it in a Tupperware bowl with her vibrator. The important thing was that it looked right. Surface was all. If you looked beneath, who knew what you might find?

Since Daphne Metcalf's death, something had begun to happen inside her. Her vision had grown hazy and everything around her was bathed in a soft borealis of light that evoked the technicolour comedies of Doris Day and Rock Hudson. It was the oddest sensation, as if her limbs were unable to make contact with hard surfaces and she was floating very slightly above the ground. Nothing seemed real any more. She wondered if she was becoming a movie character. Perhaps the three-dimensional world would slowly collapse about her and resolve itself into a simple flat plane. It would certainly make life easier, she thought.

Billy smiled lovingly at her as he drizzled scalding gravy on his half-charred, half-frozen lumps of meat. He reminded himself to be careful in his conversations with her.

'What would you like to do this afternoon, darling?' asked April, removing a chunk of ice from her beans and tossing it onto the carpet.

'I thought I'd be neighbourly, pop over and see how the Bovoids are doing.' He couldn't visit the Prouts. They were dead, and their child had been taken away, howling and kicking, by an uncle with a distinctly paedophilic glint in his eye.

'What a nice idea.' She smiled again. 'Eat up. Apple turnover for dessert.' Behind her, the record skipped endlessly, trapping the lyric of a Tom Jones song, 'I'm Not Responsible'.

At first there was no answer from the Bovis house. Then Sherry Bovis slowly opened the door. She looked as if she resented the interruption.

'You must be Sherry,' said Billy. 'I thought I'd come over and have a chat with your mother.'

After a moment of hesitation the girl stepped back to allow him entrance. Georgina was sitting in the lounge with the blinds drawn and her head in her hands. There was a strong smell of whisky about the room. A young woman in a black baseball cap and jeans sat beside her, a plain-clothes WPC or perhaps an off-duty nurse. Sherry hung about awkwardly, kicking at the carpet with her trainers.

'What do you want?' Georgina's voice was barely above a whisper.

'I just came by to see if you were all right.'

'That depends what meaning you assign to the phrase, doesn't it? My husband was *taken away to the mortuary* last night after *vomiting himself inside out*. I'm *all right* in the sense that it's me who's alive, not him. They think it was some kind of poison. I'm not allowed to touch anything in the kitchen until someone calls to take it all away for analysis. I'm being treated like a murderess.' She started to cry quietly.

'How awful,' he said in as awed a voice as he could manage. 'Is there anything at all that I can do to help?'

'You could try finding out what's going on around here,' she snapped, clawing at her wet eyes. 'Daphne Metcalf has gone missing, and I suppose you've heard about the Prouts.'

'The Prouts? No, has something happened to them?'

'You could say that, yes. Barbara was burned to death in her car by some kind of – I don't know – *bomb*, I suppose, and the police are swarming all over the golf course after finding her husband's body in the middle of a dug-up green. He'd been battered to death. Tracy from Justin Brickett's office found him when she went over with her boyfriend for a practice round this morning.'

'Perhaps they had some kind of suicide pact,' he offered. 'Perhaps they all did, like one of those biblical sects.'

'For Christ's sake, my fucking husband is dead!'

'A sudden loss in the family doesn't excuse you from common civility,' he said, trying hard not to sound offended, trying even harder not to laugh. 'I'm sorry your husband vomited himself to death – in fact, I can still smell some of it lingering – but Barbara Prout must have suffered just as, if not more, terribly. She was such a lovely, devout

297

woman. To undergo such a violent and premature cremation; she must have thought she'd missed a prayer and gone straight to hell. Something like this makes us all aware of the ... irresponsibility ... of not keeping an extinguisher in the car.'

'I think you'd better go now, Mr Prentiss,' said the smart young woman by Georgina's side, sounding like a soap-opera nurse. He suddenly realised that this had to be Sherry's girlfriend.

'I'll call on you when you're feeling a little better,' he offered, retreating to the hall. 'You might try hanging a Glade air freshener out here.' He slammed the front door loudly behind him and headed across to the Brickett household, forcing the gleeful grin from his face.

Several rings of the doorbell *chez* Brickett produced no response, so he returned home.

As darkness fell on Balmoral Close the rain began again, and the promised storm began to break above them.

'Listen,' said April, wheeling in a TV snack trolley filled with Jaffa Cakes, almond slices and pastel sections of sickly battenburg, 'God's rearranging his furniture. Isn't this nice, snuggling up in the warm, just the two of us?'

She crouched by the video recorder and slid in a cassette of old 'I Love Lucy' episodes, then sat down on the couch, feeding cheese straws between her perfectly glossed lips, and watched as Ethel Mertz argued with her headstrong neighbour.

Billy poured himself a Scotch and gave the problem careful thought. Four families were now locked tightly inside their houses like molluscs in tidal pools. There was no point in trying to prise them out. It was better to wait until they showed themselves in the open. Meanwhile, he could use the breathing space to put another little cross on his check list. He downed the whisky in one and rose, collecting his overcoat from the back of the chair.

'I'm just popping out for a while, dear.'

A look of confusion clouded April's face. 'Billy? You won't – go far, will you?'

'Of course not,' he reassured her. 'I'll be back before you know it.'

'I'm afraid the doctor is out on a house call and won't be back for at least an hour,' explained Ruth McMann when she opened the door. 'If you want to see him, you'll have to attend his clinic at the centre tomorrow or make an appointment with his secretary.'

'Actually, I was hoping to get together with your husband for a few minutes,' said Billy, checking the rainswept street to make sure that no one had seen him arrive, 'but in his absence I can make do with you.'

'I don't let people into the house when my husband isn't here,' Ruth complained nervously. 'You read about such awful goings-on.'

'But you know me, Mrs McMann. You came to my party, remember?'

'That's not the point. There are terrible things happening in this neighbourhood. One doesn't know who to trust any more.'

'Cut the shit, you suspicious old bitch. I won't take my gloves off. I'm not staying long.' Overhead, a peal of thunder broke theatrically. Billy shouldered his way through the door and slammed it shut behind him. Before the old woman could scream he clamped his hand across her mouth and unbalanced her, hauling her backwards toward the lounge. It was like dragging a loaded refrigerator about. The old cow weighed a ton, too many overcooked dinners down the line, and her shoving nearly tipped him onto the floor, but he managed to get her as far as a high-backed wooden kitchen chair and slapped her down into it so hard that she was momentarily dazed and silent.

He looked about the cluttered room. Time to wing it, be a little creative. He snatched an antimacassar from the back of a nearby armchair and stuffed it into her mouth, then flicked a half-completed cardigan from its knitting needles and used it to bind her trembling liver-spotted hands to the chair. He was able to tie her legs with the ball of wool she had left on the floor. Her eyes were flickering imploringly at him as he turned the fire out, twisted the gas tap back on and dragged her closer until her face was level with the jets of the fire. But was modern gas toxic? Shit, he had no idea. He hated having to improvise after carefully laying so many plans. Didn't they treat it in some way? It was still explosive, but was it poisonous? For the life of him, he couldn't remember. What an irony, considering his comprehensive knowledge of physics and chemistry. After this he vowed to return to the plan and stick with it to the bitter end.

Ruth McMann's muffled screams were growing clearer as she worked the gag from her mouth with her tongue. She was as strong as a bulldog. He had to do something fast.

Presumably the doctor kept his drugs at the clinic. There was unlikely to be anything lethal here in the house. He shoved the antimacassar deeper into her throat and began to search each of the downstairs rooms in turn. There was no time to find out how much Mrs McMann knew about her husband's part in the great March conspiracy; all he could do was quickly search the place for evidence.

Incredibly, it was as he had always suspected. The evidence was right there in the mothball-reeking tie drawer of the doctor's old walnut wardrobe. He picked up the object and turned it over in his hand. This had to be the same one. It meant that the doctor had lied about its loss all along. It confirmed the events of ten years ago. It made everything real, not imagined.

With renewed energy he stormed downstairs and tore open the kitchen drawers, hurling trays of cutlery to the floor. Her knives and forks were all so fucking dainty. They looked as if they would buckle on her tough old skin. He managed to find a decent-sized carving knife but didn't want to risk covering himself with blood; she looked like a bleeder, a great sack of thick, reeking blood. Under the sink he discovered a three-litre bottle of paraffin and decided that it would have to do instead.

The old woman was still when he returned to the lounge, a motionless lump of brown woollen fabric and fawn support hose. She had managed to kick off one of her shoes but was still bound to the chair. Her venomous eyes followed him as he paced. The room stank of gas but had not been sealed tightly enough to cause an explosion. He emptied the bottle of paraffin over her head, matting her thick white hair with the pink fluid, then retreated to the doorway. What if he threw the match in and the room simply erupted? He could be killed. And a sudden fire would cause her body to be discovered too quickly. *Fuck it.* If only he had brought one of his timers with him, he could have used the electric element from her kitchen heater, a box of Swan Vestas, a strip of old rag and a saucer full of paraffin to fashion a crude but efficient incendiary device. Instead, he would now have to get his hands dirty.

He kneeled astride her and tried holding a cushion over her upturned face, but the damned thing was kapok filled, and he could still hear her breath rasping through it. By now her cheeks, nose and lips were swollen and purple, her eyes squeezed shut in agony. She wasn't going to go without a fight.

There was only one thing for it.

He brought in the sharp, thin-bladed carving knife from the kitchen and sawed through the sagging jowls of flesh that bedecked the lower part of her throat, keeping her head turned away from him so that her blood spurted out onto the hearth and not over his trousers. He'd been right; she was a bleeder. Pints of the stuff pumped from the ragged deep gash into the fireplace. She made silly little mewling noises like a fox in pain, then shut up and got down to the serious business of dying, during the process of which she noisily voided her bowels.

Billy waited until he was sure she was dead, then slipped from the stinking room, opened the front door and pulled it quietly shut behind him. As he walked briskly off along the silent street, the fabulous adrenaline of pure rage burst over him like a storm wave smashing a rock. It was the most liberating sensation he had ever experienced. He knew now that redemption could be achieved through the power of revenge. A cleansing flame burned strong in his heart.

His fingers closed around the silver money clasp in his jacket pocket, and he grew surer than ever that he was doing the right thing.

CHAPTER THIRTY-FIVE

Opportunities for Job Advancement

'The police station is small, too small for an expanding area like Invicta Cross. The council aren't prepared to let it become any bigger; it would look bad if their gold-medal town needed a full-sized crime squad on call. They want to be able to show that Invicta Cross is a model community in every way, which means they are ill equipped to handle what I am throwing at them and will probably have to get outside help. It will all take time, and that is the one thing they don't have.' – *The Red Diary*

SERGEANT MORRIS Diller was having a nightmare, the problem being that he was awake. The incident room was freezing, but he could feel a trickle of sweat in the small of his pudgy back. People kept staring at him, as if they expected him to impart privileged information, but he knew no more than anyone else. He was not the most senior officer now at hand, the inspector with the cold having turned up half an hour ago, but he was the longest-serving resident at the station and knew most of the victims by sight. Victims! A possible total of five – so far. Here –

in Invicta Cross, where no serious crimes were ever committed.

Diller was no detective. He logged complaints, did the slogging, handled interviews, managed the odd bit of footwork when they were short-staffed, but was never called upon to think for himself. Invicta Cross didn't have any detectives but Croydon did, and any minute now they'd be arriving with their mobile phones and Psion organisers ready to rip up floorboards and provide counselling for the bereaved. Then the press would descend to file their stories about the model town that had gone so wrong. He felt the case slipping through his fingers before an investigation had even commenced.

Right now, while the town was still in shock, while the station was still awaiting orders, *now* was the time to do something that would make a difference. He tried to clear his mind and think, think good and hard about the people he had known since he'd walked Balmoral Close on the beat so many years ago. If he could only get in on the ground floor of the enquiry somehow ... Then he remembered the tea-stained file of nuisance complaints he had left on the radiator to dry.

Sergeant Diller did not believe in unseemly haste. But he took the stairs back to his office two at a time.

At first, Gary Mitchell thought he'd been made the victim of another office joke. The fax listed a possible five cases of suspected homicide in the southern part of Invicta Cross over the course of a single weekend.

The assistant editor of the *East Grinstead Advertiser* was usually copied on the area's main police reports, more out of courtesy than for any practical reason, but this morning, the kind of wet, grey Monday when nothing much ever happened, he had expected nothing more than some statistical analysis of rising assault figures. The paper published on Fridays, leaving the journos' staff room eerily quiet until at least Tuesday. The *Advertiser* was a rag built on a bedrock of local advertising. It was easy reading, uncontroversial, nice and responsive to the easily offended sensibilities of its tutting readers. Occasionally it conducted crusades against obvious targets, a bookshop branded pornographic for stocking safe-sex pamphlets, a woman doctor operating beyond proscribed medical practices, an unwanted lorry route, and had covered the odd unnatural death in its time, usually the demise of a pensioner asphyxiated by his paraffin stove or an old lady who had ventured to the city only to fall prey to crack-crazed muggers. But four suspicious deaths and a fifth person missing, all in one weekend! Mitchell had never seen anything like this, and he'd been on the staff for nearly twelve years.

He tried to locate the paper's only crime reporter, but the lad hadn't turned up for work yet, and his home number was connected to a faulty answering machine. Mitchell walked back to his office, made himself a cup of tea, scratched his paunchy stomach and re-examined the fax. One woman missing since Friday night, suspected abduction; one man taken sick and suddenly dying on Saturday, suspected poisoning; one man beaten to death with a golf club on Sunday morning; one woman burned to charcoal in her car outside *a church* for Christ's sake; one elderly woman bound and stabbed in her own home. In the space of two days Invicta Cross had turned into Camp Crystal Lake.

This was too good to be true.

But wait, no, *not* good, because this was too big to stay in the area for long. The London boys would get hold of it and the contacts would quickly be lost, snapped up in the thrust and flurry of blank cheques. How could a local paper compete with national interest? But if the police had a lead and if the suspect was local, they could have another Jeffrey Dahmer, another Fred West, another Dennis Nilsen on their hands! It wasn't as big as Oklahoma City but at least it was British. He read through the details again but found nothing to suggest that the Met had anything to go on. The staff-room clock read twenty to ten. He could feel the time slipping away.

He put a call through to Sergeant Morris Diller.

Diller was arguing with his boss, trying to make himself heard above the noise of a roomful of disagreeable, territory-protecting officers when the call came through. He had to take the phone out into the corridor, which was awkward because the cord barely reached outside and he was forced to crouch near the floor. The sergeant's relationship with the editor went back a long way, to the days when he had been a constable and Mitchell had been covering dog shows, and it had evolved over the course of a decade into a symbiotic and financially beneficial system.

'I've got a real problem here,' Diller explained. 'The case won't be ours. It's fucking crazy, the one time something really big happens around here and Serious Crimes have to come down from Croydon Central, bypassing us and East Grinstead, just so they can wander all over the neighbourhood flowerbeds shouting at each other on walkie-talkies. Apparently all they're going to let us do at this stage is provide them with local information. They're going to piss all over us, Gary, unless we can come up with some inside stuff of our own. You know our boys deserve a crack at this.'

'What do you want me to do, Morris? If you haven't got any leads, how do you expect us to help you? What the hell happened over there?'

'How should I know? The residents are dropping like midsummer fucking bluebottles and even if most of it just turns out to be one great big fucking embarrassing coincidence, at least two of the victims were absolutely, definitely murdered. That means everyone down here is going to start covering themselves, because they know there'll eventually be some sort of an enquiry, and the cockups always come out. Look at the shit the local boys took during the Fred West investigation.'

'So what more do you know that you haven't told me?'

There was a small, suspicious silence. 'Nothing much beyond the fact that one of the people on that list used to work on your newspaper.'

'Which one?' Mitchell had never been a particularly observant writer and was more interested in jealously protecting his patch, which was part of the reason for his inability to progress beyond the *Advertiser*. These were qualities he shared with Diller, who had repeatedly failed to achieve the post of inspector for similar reasons.

'The missing one, Daphne Metcalf. Writes these women's novels about Americans fucking. Didn't she used to do a feature column for you?'

'I think she was just a freelancer.'

'It still gives you a headline.'

'And you want what in exchange, exactly?'

'All right. They've started a door-to-door, but knowing the residents around here, nobody will have seen a fucking thing. Someone *has* to fucking know what's been going on. We've no obvious connections so far, and I don't think the whizz kids are going to turn up a common m.o., so how about going through the files for me—'

'Shit, Morris, we're still in the process of transferring the back copies to disk—'

'You've been doing that for around two years, how long is it going to take?'

'They switched us from IBM to Apple a while back and the systems weren't compatible.'

'Look, just go through the ones you've done so far, whatever, go through the actual hard copies. Look for gangs of kids who've had past trouble with the residents. Try and find me someone resentful, a gardener who got fired, a crack-head burglar who went down, a stroppy Scouse builder, I don't know, anyone you think might have a reason to kill his neighbours.'

'People have all sorts of reasons for killing their neighbours, Morris. Don't you read the papers? People's tolerance levels aren't very high any more. Didn't you see that old couple who were done for harassment, coming out of the court house with fucking tea cosies on their heads, pretending to be terrorists? We get weird stuff from the courts coming in here all the time. People shove shit through each other's letter boxes, set dogs on each other, burn their houses down because someone left his telly on too loud. There's a lot of stress about. Anyway, why do you reckon it's someone with a grudge?'

'Nobody leaves an old dear like Mrs McMann in a state

like that without hating her pretty badly, chum. We're not talking about a quick fucking whack on the back of the head. Just see what you can turn up. You must have met a few neighbourhood nutters in your time – you've been here forever.'

Mitchell took this as a reference to his lack of advancement to superior, London-based periodicals. 'Have you been through the station complaints book?' he asked.

'That was the first thing I did.' Diller thought it through for a moment, then decided to tell him. 'Someone has been playing silly buggers with these people for about a month, sending them pizzas they didn't order, shit like that. It all went down on the reports, but nobody here did sod all about it.' He had to include himself in that category. Several residents had been to see him personally. 'We all thought they were schoolkid pranks.'

'Pretty severe for a prank, burning someone alive. Bit beyond *Candid Camera*. This is going to take a couple of days, Morris. The main files aren't kept here any more. They shifted them to Croydon when we merged with the *Gazette*. I've got a feeling they only transferred the front pages to disk.'

'So much for fucking technology. Just do it as soon as you can,' said Diller, 'and I'll make sure that you get the jump on our friends from the city. Some bloke from the *Sun* has already started calling here. He's rung three times in the last hour.'

'Fuck me, how did they hear about it so quickly?'

'Come on, those boys can smell shit from five hundred miles away. Ring me on my private line as soon as you've got anything, all right?'

Mitchell replaced the receiver and leaned back in his chair. It made a change for the police to need his help. Perhaps some good would come of this after all. He began to search for the number of the central archive at Croydon.

CHAPTER THIRTY-SIX

Suspicion

'I wonder how long it will take people to start putting two and two together. Surely someone will remember the events of ten years ago? They say people are forgetting the lessons of the past because nobody learns from them any more. Perhaps they'll learn from me.' – *The Red Diary*

'WHAT THE hell do you want?' asked Georgina Bovis, half invisible in the darkened hall.

'I came to see if you were all right, Georgina. I heard about your husband.'

'Oh, really? Is it written up somewhere or did you just listen to the neighbourhood gossip? So *now* you come around. Does it take a bloody death for you to come and visit me, or did you just fancy shagging a widow? Well, I have nothing to say to you, Graham.' But she did not shut the door.

'If I could come in for a few minutes, we could just ... talk for a while. You must be feeling awful.' Graham Birdsmith reached the top step and peered in disconsolately. Georgina had been crying again. Her hair was raised in stiff clumps and she was still in her dressing gown and slippers. He could not help guiltily noticing the tantalising glimpse of tanned breast that appeared as she rewrapped the gown about her.

'Come in for a minute, then. Bring the milk with you.' Graham scooped up the two pints on her doorstep and slipped inside. Force of habit compelled him to check the street for witnesses.

They sat in the overheated kitchen while Graham made tea and Georgina lit a fresh cigarette from the stub of her old one.

'It seems,' she said, waving the smoke away from her face, 'that nobody can actually tell me what he died of. Old McMann's been his physician for the last twelve years, but he's only useful if you've got an ingrown bloody toenail or a cold. He's never had to deal with anything like this. Besides, he's got problems of his own.'

Graham threw her a questioning look.

'There was an intruder at his house last night. Someone attacked and killed his wife. She was a miserable old bitch, true, but I wouldn't wish a murderous assault on her. I wish I knew what the hell was going on. I've asked for police protection but that apparently involves paperwork, and nobody has the power to authorise it at the moment. They don't seem to have any positive information. Alan may have died from peritonitis, or may not; we have to wait until they do an autopsy. Funny, I can't shake this feeling of being a murderess.'

'What do you mean?' Graham poured a little warm water in the teapot and rinsed it out.

'Well, he was lying upstairs in bed, shaking and throwing up, and I was trotting about behind the doctor trying to explain that he hadn't eaten anything unusual, that we'd both had the same supper, and I felt as if it was my fault, as though I'd killed him and was trying to cover my tracks. Like that Victorian woman who kept feeding her husband poisoned beef tea. So strange.' Without any warning she noisily burst into tears. 'Oh, Graham, what am I going to do?'

'There, there.' Instantly he was at her side, rubbing and patting her shoulders, but it was difficult to be genuinely caring because he'd only ever gone through such motions with her in a sexual manner. He tried to give her a big-brother hug, but the gesture of consolation was awkward coming from a man who had been her lover behind the deceased's back. She was still crying, great wet sobs shaking her ribcage as he carefully untangled himself.

'Here, some tea will help.' He stirred the bags in the pot and poured out two mugfuls. 'Which milk do you want?' He held out the two fresh bottles, one red-top, one silver-top.

She halted her tears for a moment and sniffled, looking up. 'The silver,' she replied quietly. 'The other one's revolting. It's skimmed. I always got it specially for Alan. He couldn't have fats. Bad for his heart ...' The sentence trailed off into another low wail. Even in a time of tragedy, Graham Birdsmith was mindful of his love handles and poured some of the red-top milk into his tea. He was sure Alan wouldn't have minded.

'I saw the police as I came home from work,' he said, stirring two sugars into his mug. 'Looks like they're going around asking questions. Not that anybody ever sees a thing around here. You'd have to murder half the neighbourhood before someone sat up and took notice. I wonder if they've been to Billy March's house yet.'

'Billy—?' Georgina sniffed hard and smeared the tears

from her eyes. 'God, I'd forgotten the Marches. That was years ago. What made you suddenly think of them?'

'Just the fact that he lives next door to you.'

'What?'

'I saw him in the paper shop at the weekend; don't think he recognised me, though.'

'Graham, what are you talking about?'

The weatherman sighed, explaining as if talking to a child. 'The Marches' boy, the one who used to go around accusing everyone of things, he lives next door to you. I saw him come out of there just now and get in his car.'

'No, they're the Prentisses, Jack and Polly, you're getting confused.'

'No, I'm bloody not,' said Graham indignantly. 'I recognised him the moment I saw him again. Well, not from his appearance, he's changed so much I'd defy anyone to—'

'Graham, how did you recognise him?'

'He was in that funny paper shop, the one past the junction on Windsor Terrace, down by the lower end of Gaveston Crescent—'

'I know where you mean.'

'He was trying to locate the house of a childhood friend, but the storekeeper couldn't help him. This blonde called to him from the car, "Billy March, are you going to be all day?" I nearly said something to him, but I decided not to in case he didn't remember me.'

That was it, that was where she had seen them both before. No wonder they had looked so familiar that first day when they came to look at the house. Her eyes widened in dawning realisation.

'My God, that woman he's with! It's the morose little

314

girl who used to hang around him when he lived here before! She must have changed her name ... Graham, you don't think he did this, do you? He hated everyone, accused us all of – terrible things, I forget now. And they were always in trouble with the law. But they've been gone for, must be ten years. You wouldn't still be angry ten years later, would you? Not enough to try and murder some-one?'

Graham didn't answer. He was sipping his tea, thinking.

'What should we do? Stay here a minute.' She left the kitchen and headed upstairs to her bedroom, throwing off her dressing gown, and pulled on a pair of jeans, a T-shirt and a sweater. She dug out her sneakers from beneath the bed and pushed her feet into them, then returned to the kitchen. Graham was still seated at the table.

'Wait here,' she said. 'I'll go over and have a talk with Polly, ask her what she knows.'

'Do you think that's wise?' asked Graham, rubbing his right eye with the back of his hand. 'I mean, what if the guy's a complete lunatic?'

'Graham, you saw him go out. Anyway, I *know* the man, he's completely normal, as sane as you or I – saner.'

'All right, but shouldn't we just call the police first, to be on the safe side?'

'Maybe you're right. Give them a ring.'

She searched around for her jacket, locating it beneath a pile of dirty washing.

Graham pulled the phone to him and called Directory Enquiries, then punched out the number of the Sherington Road constabulary. Incredibly, the line was engaged.

'Try them again in a few minutes,' instructed Georgina. 'Of course, you know what will happen when you get

315

through, they'll make a note of the call and we'll never hear another bloody thing. Look, I'm only going to go across the lawn to there,' she pointed at the porch next door. 'You can watch me from the window, just to make sure I'm all right.'

She opened the front door and beamed back at him, a different woman to the miserable wraith who had answered his call half an hour ago. 'I won't be long, all right? Stay and have something to eat with me?' Incredibly, there was a coquettish hint of sexuality in her request.

Graham watched as she darted out into the drifting rain and stepped gingerly across to the neighbouring lawn, then wearily began to rub his face once more.

Georgina rang the bell and stepped back, waiting. She could not see any lights on, but it was only just starting to get dark. Above her, thunder rolled ominously across the sky. She tried the bell again. She looked back at her own house and could just make out Graham's pale form at the rain-blurred window. He seemed to be leaning forward with his head resting on the glass.

When she turned back to the doorway, April was standing there. She was wearing a piercingly bright crimson acetate taffeta flamenco gown and had what appeared to be a Georgian toasting fork in her right hand. She looked quite demented.

'Georgina, darling,' she squeaked happily, 'how lovely to see you! Jack's out at the moment, but he shouldn't be long. Look at you, you're getting soaked. Come in out of the rain and I'll mix you a cocktail.'

'No, it's fine, I'll just —'

'Don't be silly, I insist. Come in right now, before you

catch your death standing there.'

Georgina threw a final helpless glance back at her own house, and was ushered into her neighbours' lair.

CHAPTER THIRTY-SEVEN

General Knowledge

' "There is no such thing as insanity, only the decision to act insanely." Whoever said that should have been locked up, because he was wrong. Sometimes we follow our impulses not because we know they are right but because failure to do so would be a betrayal of our true desires. There is a painting by Etty in the National Gallery entitled *The Destroying Angel and the Daemons of Evil Interrupting the Orgies of the Vicious and Intemperate*. The picture is of a bad society being swept away by one that is fairer but capable of infinite cruelty. Hey, nobody says avenging spirits have to be good.' – *The Red Diary*

GARY MITCHELL pulled again at the steel box, and this time it came free with a screech of metal that raised the hackles on his neck. He rose to his feet, dusting down the knees of his trousers, and dragged the container over to a poorly lit reading area. He tried to read his watch; just gone 7 pm, the latest he'd worked in years. The *Advertiser*'s back issues had not been transferred to microfiche. Single file copies of the weekly paper had been stacked in these poorly sealed tin containers and left to rot in a damp basement. Whole months were missing, and everything was out of order.

But there was something he had to find, something from the middle of the last decade about a family that had been run out of Invicta Cross under some kind of a cloud. It was the first thing he'd thought of when Diller mentioned looking for someone with a grudge.

He lowered his ample rear onto the narrow secretary-chair and began checking the date of each issue. This batch came from the early months of 1986 but had crinkled with moisture and yellowed so badly you'd have been forgiven for thinking it was a hundred years old. He really had to hand it to the *Advertiser*. The paper consistently managed to link global events to its own little corner of the world; in January, the tale of an East Grinstead war veteran paying a holiday visit to Florida's Cape Canaveral was spuriously tied to the US Challenger space shuttle disaster, and the accident at Chernobyl gained a tangential connection to a charity appeal for new radiotherapy equipment at a Croydon hospital.

At a more local level, it reported on demonstrations over one of the proposed channel tunnel rail links through East Grinstead, and the paper refused to carry the government's controversial new AIDS awareness ads, accusing them of being in poor taste. He tried another issue, and another. Dog show, multiple sclerosis charity run, mayor opens fête (a story that would not have looked out of place a century ago) – and damn it to hell but here it was, a follow-up to an earlier article by the look of it, sharing pages four and five of an issue dated 18 March 1986 with a disabled swimmers' gala and the opening of a new carpet warehouse, an article headed 'Problem Family Leave Their Dream Town'.

The incredible thing was, he had written the piece himself and completely forgotten about it. The boy had come to him with a wild story about neighbours conspiring with the police to make his family leave town. He hadn't believed the boy, a skinny, strange child who was clearly confusing his facts with his emotions, but he'd managed to squeeze a lot of mileage out of the subject matter. Arguments had raged on in the letters page long after the family had returned to the city.

Before scanning the text he searched for the original feature but failed to locate it in the last of the morgue's containers. It looked as if the first item fell beyond the ten-year barrier, in which case it would be held at yet another location in a filing system in even greater disarray. This article would have to do for now. He swivelled the ancient angle-poise to give himself as much light as possible, then folded back the page and began to read.

As he did so, he started to see just how perfectly the story he had written a decade ago fitted the bill. At this stage it wouldn't matter whether the aggrieved party – he'd be around twenty-four years old now – was guilty or not. In the morning Invicta Cross would be a madhouse, crawling with police, sightseers and gutter journos, and this issue of the *Advertiser* would give him an edge over those flash city bastards with their designer overcoats and expense accounts. While they were running about waving their chequebooks at the neighbours, he would be leading a manhunt that, even if it went in the wrong direction, would still grab a head start over the pack.

It was Tuesday tomorrow; his press deadline was late Thursday afternoon. Even allowing for the fact that the *Advertiser* was a weekly publication, his would be the first in-depth story armed with a barrage of facts, and the beauty of it was, he was the only one who had any kind of a lead. He needed to seal up these steel containers and make access to them difficult. It wouldn't take long for the London pack to come after them. No problem; only a handful of people knew where the back issues had been moved, and he would arrange for them to keep their mouths shut. Having carried out the groundwork ten years earlier, this was one story he was not prepared to lose.

He needed to come up with a name that would stick; *The Invicta Cross Massacre* was a little too bald and sounded too much like that series of random shootings in Hungerford. It needed to be bigger. What had the Jap papers called their subway gas-bomb attacks? Wait, Invicta Cross had won Most Popular Something-or-other in Britain, hadn't it? How about the *Dream Town Assassinations*? No, it needed to alliterate. *The Suburbia Slaughters*. What if the attacker was someone with a grudge? How about naming him, something along the lines of the Invicta Cross Avenger? No, it sounded too much like a TV show. Fuck the *Advertiser*; he'd sell this to the nationals, tie up exclusive rights. Hell, if he had the wrong man he could still use the research for a 'Ten Years On' article in his own paper.

But first he had to locate Billy March, preferably before tomorrow morning, and find out what had happened to his family after they'd blown town.

Morris Diller stood at the corner of Windsor Terrace and Balmoral Close with rain dripping from his brow and forced himself to think. There was virtually no time left. A full investigation was now underway. Men and women

from other divisions were appearing at the station hourly
His office had been requisitioned by a suntanned man in a
flashy suit whose first question had been to ask where the
nearest internet modem was connected. Unable to answer
Diller had been forced to direct him to someone younger
who knew. Things could only get worse from here.

He studied the houses and thought of the faces people
chose to present to the world. Neatness seemed all important; rows of trimmed hedges with surfaces so smooth and
corners so sharp that they seemed carved from blocks of
green polystyrene. Rose bushes and rhododendrons pruned
into globes, dimpled glass porch lamps, an array of
filigreed net curtains, red metal gutters sluicing the rain
into green plastic barrels. Quite a contrast to the dirty,
chaotic flat in which he and his son had lived since
Marjorie left them. It was a good job he was a policeman;
he might have been taken for a suspect otherwise.

It had to be someone who was jealous of all this stability.
An outsider, someone from a broken home, someone who
would gain satisfaction from causing so much pain and
misery, someone known to them all. But what was the
motive? Why did people do this kind of thing? He tried to
recall the outcome of the Hungerford massacre, but it
escaped him. Was it sheer frustration, a warped view of the
world, revenge for a perceived injustice?

It was no good. He had not been trained to think in this
manner. He should have trained as a detective. He'd been
given the chance long ago but had been scared off by the
training, the discipline, the departmental protocol. An
overwhelming sense of waste assailed him; a wasted career,
a wasted life.

Well, it was too late to do anything now. The awful part

322

of it was, he felt sure that the answer was close at hand. Half-formed ideas passed through his mind like ghosts. Memories threatened to surface. If only he could remove the blind façades of the buildings before him like the front panels of so many dolls' houses and just be allowed to observe the occupants . . .

Suddenly feeling old and pointless and stupid, he turned from the secretive streets and started back toward the station. The newcomers would take over now, filling the neighbourhood with statistical analysis and surveillance equipment. But they lacked the one thing older officers could bring to the investigation. They had no idea what it was like – really like – to live here. Over the years he had logged complaints about the widths of driveways and the noise of spin-dryers used after 5 pm. His own wife had frowned on any woman hanging her washing out after noon, the inference being that she was a sluttish house-keeper. To understand what was happening here, they would have to appreciate the survival of a suburban world governed by rules more recondite and capricious than those of an Egyptian court.

CHAPTER THIRTY-EIGHT

Cleansing Fires

'I wonder if the generation that comes after me will make the same mistakes, and know instinctively that they will. In which case, what point is there in taking revenge at all? And what does it make me, a hero or a villain? But even as self-doubt assails me, I am reminded of one truth. A man who fails to obey his God is nothing, and Eblis had chosen my path long ago.' – *The Red Diary*

BILLY HAD been circling the wet roads in the glistening black BMW with just his sidelights glowing, resisting the gathering dusk, but had finally been forced to switch on his main beams.

Like molluscs in a rock pool...

He drove through the car park of the mall with blood lust in his eyes, hoping to see someone he recognised leaving the climate-controlled sanctuary, but the area was too open, too overlooked. All around him, shoppers were transferring sackfuls of purchases from their trolleys to their cars.

Disappointed, he headed back into his own neighbourhood. He knew that time was of the essence. In order to catch a murderer, you usually needed to make an arrest within forty-eight hours of the crime. That was what a policeman had once told him. Fewer than eight per cent of all murders were cracked after that time had elapsed. It was important to get this over with as quickly as possible. Do what he had to do, then get April away to safety. He didn't care what happened to himself. It was only a matter of time before somebody figured the whole thing out. Too many people knew him; all those lazy, dormant minds just waiting to be asked to remember . . .

He coasted slowly past the McMann household and saw a light glowing in the lounge. As he watched, the doctor appeared briefly at the window and drew the curtains. *You'd think he would prefer to stay with friends rather than linger at the scene of his wife's grisly death*, he thought. Still, McMann's name was on the list waiting to be checked off, and while he was in the neighbourhood . . .

Pulling into the kerb, he collected a Biro from the glove compartment, then climbed out and opened the boot, removing a large square box wrapped in brown paper and protective plastic. He wrote his message on a plain white card and slid it beneath a flap of the package. Then he carefully printed out a standard mail-order form he had kept for the purpose, noting down a number from the back of the red diary.

He slipped out of the vehicle, set his delivery on McMann's doorstep, rang the bell and ran back to the driver's seat. His car had pulled away and turned the corner before the good doctor had even opened his front door.

April smiled inanely as she dropped a martini olive into an old-fashioned cocktail glass. She gave the drink a brisk stir and passed it to her guest. On the Dansette stereogram, Julie Andrews was singing 'My Favourite Things'. April smiled again and sat beside her tearful neighbour. 'Tell me,' she asked, her face a sudden picture of solicitude, 'how are you coping with the awful trauma of sudden death?'

'I don't know, April. I don't know if I am coping. Everything is falling apart around me. I can't believe he's not there any more, it all seems so unreal . . .'

'We all have the blues some days, Georgina, whether old Mr Reaper comes a-calling or not. I often become – disconnected. When the storm bites, when the bee stings, when I'm feeling sad—' She looked over at Georgina, coaxing her with her very best smile. 'I always sing when I'm feeling down, don't you? Join in with me, it will help, I promise you – when I'm feeling sad, I simply remember, come on . . .' April raised the arm of the stereogram and reset it earlier in the song.

Alarmed, Georgina demurred.

'No, really, it will make you feel so much better, come on now.' There was an edge to April's voice that suggested Georgina had no choice but to sing along with her hostess.

'I simply remember my favourite things, and then I don't feel so bad . . .'

'I simply remember—'

'My favourite things—'

'My favourite things—' Georgina was starting to cry again.

'And then I don't feel so bad. Let's try that again, shall we?' She reset the arm of the record player once more.

'When the storm bites, when the bee stings, when I'm feeling sad, come on, louder . . .'

'I simply remember my favourite things, and then I don't feel so bad.'

'There, that's brought a little colour to your face. There's nothing like Julie to cheer a girl up. Chin chin.' She raised her glass. After an uneasy moment her guest raised hers and they both drank. Whether she really was that strange spindly-legged girl or not, Polly Prentiss was clearly insane. Unnerved by the impromptu performance, Georgina decided to leave while she could still get out.

'I have to go, Polly.'

'Don't be silly, I have a whole pitcher of martinis mixed here. It'll only go to waste.'

'No, I really should be—'

'Oh dear.'

'What's the matter?'

April held up her cocktail glass and examined it. Hers was blue. Georgina's was clear. 'These are meant to be exactly the same.'

'Well what did you put in them?' she snapped a little too sharply.

'I think it's supposed to be Curaçao.' She sipped from her glass, tipping her head to one side as if listening to voices, then ran a pink tongue over her lips. 'Yes, this one is definitely Curaçao.'

Georgina wanted to ask what hers was, but found that she could not move the muscles of her mouth. Her limbs had started to tingle. Then the muscles in her left leg went dead.

'I'm so silly. I poured mine from the pitcher and yours from the bottle because I mix my cocktails rather strongly for most people's taste. Here, it's written on the label.' She picked up the bottle and examined it. From where

327

Georgina sat it looked like a regular bottle of Gordon's.

'It says right here under ingredients, gin. And mine has a vodka base. So that's a little mystery cleared up, isn't it?'

Her neighbour tried to nod, tried to move the fingers of her hands but nothing appeared to be working at the moment.

'Wait a minute, it's the glass! I remember now that I wasn't supposed to use that glass. Billy warned me about it. "Don't use the glass," he said, "it's coated with a mixture of boric acid and silver nitrate. I'm saving that for someone special." Oh well, let's hope you're someone special. Do you feel special?' She raised a forefinger as the track changed. 'Oh, listen to this, this is my absolute favouritest track.'

Georgina's mouth was on fire, a terrible burning that seared across her tongue and stabbed down into her throat. She attempted to scream but an awful gasping wheeze of fetid air came out. Her neck muscles tensed like cords that had suddenly had great weights attached. She clutched at the sides of the armchair but could not feel her hands. The conflagration descended into her chest, releasing flares of pain. The hot wetness she felt spreading at her crotch suggested that she was peeing herself. She felt a scourge of heavenly fire filling her body in a great cleansing rush of flame, purifying, scorching. Her hallucinating mind was filled with the image of a fiery angel ascending from its human shell in absolution of all her sins.

As she dropped into a severe state of toxic shock and slipped from the couch to the carpet, the last thing she heard was Julie Andrews warbling on about climbing every mountain and fording every stream.

*

Dr McMann picked up the package and shook it, but nothing rattled. It was heavy, nearly a foot square, and addressed to his dead wife. Her credit card details were printed on the receipt that had been Sellotaped to the top. She had ordered something, and now it had been delivered and the silly woman was not here to receive it. He felt tears welling in his eyes. He had only called by the house to put a few items of clothing in a bag. The rooms were dead without her presence. Her perfume lingered faintly in the hall, as if she had just stepped out for a moment.

He had decided to stay at his brother's flat in Bayswater until the funeral. His personal experience of inquests was enough to make him keep well away from the one involving the woman he had – after his fashion – loved. The police had (offensively, in his opinion) required him to leave a contact number if he left town; was he to have no peace?

And now this. He carried the box into the lounge and set it down. Bloody catalogue goods – she was always ordering things she could just as easily have bought at the mall, then forgetting all about them. Lately she had discovered the QVC shopping channel and had taken to ordering steak knives, earrings and gardening gloves. And this from a woman who passed her days complaining bitterly about the modern world. What had she quoted their joint credit card number for this time: a foot sauna, a support pillow?

It was suddenly important to know what she had bought, as if the knowledge would add to his memory of her. He pulled the top flap free and thrust in a paperknife, carelessly tearing away the brown wrapping paper. Odd thing – the sides of the box appeared to be made of some kind of metal; it felt like aluminium. What was it, a tin of biscuits?

As he unclipped the lid of the package, he was puzzled by the little clicking sound it made.

The detonator sparked with a brief fierce light, and three-quarters of a pound of crude nitroglycerin crystals exploded upwards into his face.

The incendiary device was surprisingly powerful. It removed the doctor's head from his body and buried his pocket watch deep inside his chest cavity. It blew out the entire rear wall of the lounge, instantly shattering all the ground-floor windows but curiously leaving the upper floor intact, sent a steel standard-lamp base through the television like a spear, shot a single shoe through the kitchen skylight seventy-two feet into the air to land in the next street, and propelled a complete set of fish knives and forks out of their mahogany canteen on the sideboard straight upwards, blade and tine first, to embed themselves quiveringly in the ceiling.

As Billy drifted the BMW around into Gaveston Crescent three streets away, he heard the dull boom of the explosion, then listened for the echo as it bounced among the houses, and the subsequent clamour of a hundred triggered car alarms that wailed in response to the blast like an appreciative electronic audience.

'We're going for a little walk.'

It was easy because she was so light; there was hardly anything to lift. She was not dead, just sleepy, so April was able to slip her hands beneath Georgina's armpits and pull her from the armchair. Then she walked her in a slurring gait through the kitchen and out into the garden. Georgina was very quiet and did as she was told, clutching quietly at her stomach when she tried to sit down. She could no longer feel the lower half of her body. She had seen her soul take leave on golden wings. Once the soul was gone you had no more need of your physical self, so it hardly mattered that her nerve endings had died. This way, her departure from life would be painless, like being in hospital. She felt like a little girl again, tucked in bed with a soaring temperature.

April sat her on the patio while she took the lid off the drainage chute. The back gardens were silent and still in the steadily falling rain. But what if someone was watching from one of the upstairs windows? She raised Georgina to her feet once more and shuffled her over to the rushing dark hole.

'No – no—'

'Ssh, it's all right, we're nearly there now.'

'Please – I need—'

'What, dear? What do you need?' Georgina did not reply. She was straddled across the shaft, crying lightly. 'There, you see, you simply don't know.'

April gently pushed her feet together so that she was placed squarely over the sluice. Georgina opened her mouth as if to speak, but no sound emerged. Then April released her arms. In the last moment before she fell, Georgina smiled beatifically, as though what was happening inside her was a miracle. Then she shot straight down into the flooded drain. She made no sound, although she banged her head against the wall as she went.

April peered in, trying to watch her neighbour's passage to the arterial sewage pipe, then rose and replaced the iron lid. She checked the windows of the houses on either side but saw no movement behind the net curtains. Satisfied that she had helped her husband to achieve his aims, she re-entered the house to dry her wet hair and change into a smart new lounge outfit.

CHAPTER THIRTY-NINE

A Mad, Mad World

'Anyone can see what is in the light. The true hero steps into darkness. And now I have moved deep within an eclipse of the soul.' – *The Red Diary*

BRAD METCALF was not at all happy to be returning to Invicta Cross. Now that he had seen what a big city had to offer, he loathed the town he'd left behind, hated the peace and pettiness of lives conducted behind lace curtains. It was so squeaky clean and quiet here that the police didn't even bother to patrol the streets; their observations were less efficiently recorded than those of the local Neighbourhood Watch committee. It was weird to think that on council estates just a few miles away kids were jacking up in pensioners' doorways, brothels were being run from tower blocks, gangs were sorting out their differences with swords and shooters, and worse. No wonder his mother found it difficult to write about real life. She had never experienced it.

Well, he had his own life now, and not one that his parents would approve of. He only came to see the family when Daphne absolutely insisted he be there. He made his stepfather uneasy; Bob was always asking where his money came from. What was he going to do, tell the truth and say he got it from selling coke at a wicked mark-up through the Croydon nightclubs?

The old man had called him up demanding to know if his mother was staying with him. As if! So she was officially a missing person – what could he do about it? Coming home wouldn't help. But his stepfather had insisted, and now here he was, walking across the end of Gaveston Crescent because his Porsche had been repossessed; he'd been forced to take a bus because he hadn't been able to find a cab in the rain . . .

Billy was about to turn the BMW into Windsor Terrace when he saw a hunched figure crossing the unbuilt, darkened end of the crescent. His face creased into a sly grin – what an incredible, fabulous piece of luck! A quiet street, a powerful weapon and a perfect target: the child of a sworn enemy! But now the figure had spotted him and was slowing in puzzlement.

Time to act before it was too late.

He stamped his foot down on the BMW's accelerator, calling into use its maximum torque power as he roared down the empty half-constructed road and mounted the low kerb, slamming into the side of Brad Metcalf's body, which was turning in surprise at the roar of the car's engine, and released a whoop of joy as he watched the boy cartwheel crazily into the air like a crash-test dummy before smashing headfirst into the back wall of an attractively appointed unsold two-bedroom maisonette thirty-six feet away.

As the boy's shattered frame toppled over into a pile of wet bricks with a shocked squeak and leaked life juices from every orifice (in addition to the several new ones it had just gained) he cranked up the cassette – 'This Cowboy Song' by Sting – gunned the gas and slithered the BMW around the corner, heading for home.

'What's for dinner?' Billy asked happily as he hung up his coat in the hallway. No reply came from the lounge. 'April?'

She was on her knees scrubbing at a wet patch on the floor in a pair of elbow-length canary-yellow rubber Marigolds. On her the gloves ceased to be an item of cleaning convenience and became fetish wear. 'She spilled her cocktail,' she explained, looking up in contrition. 'I didn't want it to stain the rug.'

'Who spilled her cocktail?' He started to notice small signs of disarray about the room. 'What's been going on here?'

April sat back on her knees, blew a single, perfect unruly lock of hair from her eyes, and smiled nervously. She began folding her floorcloth very neatly in her lap. She was play-acting again, a performance pitched somewhere between Marilyn Monroe in *The Seven Year Itch* and Doris Day in *More Over, Darling*, innocence personified. Something bad had happened here.

She sighed heavily, a sitcom wife about to be rebuked for inviting a celebrity home to dinner, then rose and straightened the seams of her stockings. 'Georgina Bovis came over for drinks, but I made a mistake mixing them and she got the wrong one and went to sleep, so I did what you did.'

Billy was confused. 'What I did?'

'Yes, because she went to sleep!'

'What do you mean, you did what I did?'

'I put her down the chute to the drain and sent her out to sea, like you did with Daphne. Honestly, if people realised how *easy* it was to do this, they'd be helping each other do it all the time.'

'You shouldn't have tried something like that all by yourself, April,' he said softly. He had never considered that she might have the capacity for murder, even if she chose to refer to it as 'helping someone'. He knew that in the past she had committed arson, in the process of which someone had died, but this was the conscious decision to take someone's life, no matter what you chose to call it, and he was surprised that she had decided to assist him.

'How do you feel now?' he asked carefully.

'Very tired, Billy. Why do I feel so very tired?'

'I'll run you a hot bath and let you get some sleep. I think it's going to be a busy day for us tomorrow.' He paused in the doorway. 'I'm glad about Georgina, I really am. I just hope nobody saw her come into the house.'

Across the dividing concrete strip between the carports, at the window in the lounge of the Bovis house, Graham Birdsmith lay sightlessly lolled back in his seat, his shirt glistening in a spray of poisoned sputum. He had taken his tea using milk intended for Georgina's husband Alan, the milk from the bottle with a tiny syringe-hole in its red cap.

Before his vision had clouded into a blotched and boiling crimson sea, he had registered his former lover's nervous glance toward him as she entered the house next door, and a voice beneath the furious rushing that filled his head had tried to warn him that his half-hearted and unfinished affair with Georgina Bovis was about to be concluded forever.

*

She cried very quietly, curled like a foetal child deep within the bed. She clung to Billy's hand, folding his body protectively about her. For a while her tears ceased and she lay peacefully. The street was silent, and each rustling movement she made seemed magnified into a roar. She asked if they would ever be like normal people, and he could not find it in himself to lie.

'No,' he said, 'we will never be normal now. It's too late for that.'

'When will it be over?' she asked, and he whispered, 'Very soon.'

'Are we getting rid of the pain?' she whispered back.

'Soon there will be no more pain for either of us,' he promised, and meant it, knowing that the events of tomorrow would decide their fate. 'Nobody is dying without a reason, you know that, don't you?'

'How do we know our reasons are right?'

'Inside everyone there lives a god who guides our actions. We listen to them. They tell us what is right.'

'Do I have a god inside me?'

'Of course you do. Everyone does. It's just that ours are different to most other people's. Ours are older and braver.'

'I had a lovely dream,' she said. 'We had a white house with a balcony, surrounded by waving cypress trees, and two children, a boy and a girl, both beautiful. The girl in pigtails and a white linen skirt, the boy in short trousers, navy blue. We weren't in England. We were somewhere nice, where the countryside wasn't all spoiled. France perhaps. The fields were lush and filled with summer mist, the kind that warms itself away by mid-morning. The sun was hot on my face, and everything was clean and neat – the house, the fields, us. We were alone in a perfect world.'

Outside, a police car passed the end of the close, its siren seesawing eerily through the still night air. The sound was enough to break her train of thought.

'Well,' she said softly, 'it was a nice dream. It lasted nearly five minutes.'

But even as he tenderly looped his arms through hers, he realised that she had adopted the mannerisms of another blonde actress. Her final sleepy remark was a quote, perhaps unconscious, a line of dialogue softly uttered by Dorothy Provine, dressed in a white flared dress and a yellow chiffon scarf, as she wistfully dabbed her neck at a water fountain, while her companions searched for the treasure of their dreams, buried beneath a big 'W' in a widescreen, technicolor sixties movie.

CHAPTER FORTY

Hot Leads

'Perhaps there is something to be learned from the grotesque farce of the O. J. Simpson trial. I may be able to use my brief moment in the media spotlight to draw attention to the real culprits here in Invicta Cross – although it might take more than a few prime-time soundbites to explain the involvement of Eblis, the father of all devils, and why this demon should ensure my ultimate triumph over those who would have us live in fear.' – *The Red Diary*

TUESDAY BARELY bothered to dawn. At 6 am the rain began again, and by the time the police had their first run-in with the press the drizzle had become a gloomy downpour that absorbed all light and colour from the streets. Only the yellow plastic police cordons attached to the lampposts stood out, turning the lawns and driveways of Invicta Cross into sections of film set.

Morris Diller had been up all night. The makeshift operations room in his office remained filled with arguing personnel, and he had fallen asleep on a bench in the corridor with his raincoat wadded behind his head.

Finally, with permission from the Met's AMIP Area 4 at

Croydon's divisional police station, the sergeant had been allowed to schedule a press conference – his first – for noon that day. He was already learning that the way to handle the fourth estate was to strike deals with it. In exchange for the proposed press briefing, he exacted a collective promise that there would be no attempt to question friends and neighbours of the deceased before the police had finished their own interviews. Naively, Diller thought that this gentlemen's agreement would hold until noon. It lasted for less than forty minutes.

In addition to the three forensic teams Croydon had marshalled, a full complement of detectives from its murder squad had now descended on the peaceful town and were conspicuously parading through the neighbour-hood, questioning its residents, checking tyre treads and dusting doorjambs, although in this they were hampered by the intensity of the inclement weather.

Diller ground his teeth as he watched the blue serge circus come to town. Croydon was the tenth biggest city in Britain, and its thirty-three square miles housed criminals as tough as any found on the streets of New York. Accordingly, its police force was one of the most aggressive in the country, too tough for the sergeant, who had been turned down by it on three separate, humiliating occasions and was now being grudgingly raised to the position of sergeant by way of compensation. With no clearly defined role in the developing investigation, he left the station and returned to the rain-soaked streets.

'Would you mind moving, mate?' said one of the footprint men, shifting him from the wet front garden of number 23 Gaveston Crescent and taping it off. 'You're not makin' our work any easier, y' know.'

Let them have their moment, thought Diller, as he watched a pair of photographers setting cameras on tripods beside the pile of blood-streaked builder's rubble where Brad Metcalf's crushed body had been found. His bad humour grew as he looked down and saw the toecap of his boot dipped in a gutter full of blood and rainwater. He would have the last say in this. He knew the turf better than any of these fuckers. Invicta Cross was his and would yield its secrets to him alone, no matter how many outsiders were sent to trample across its manicured lawns in search of the truth.

The man who opened the door looked as if he'd done time on more than one occasion in his life. The badly healed razor scar beneath the stubble-covered drinker's jowls, the roll-up wedged behind the ear, the beer gut straining the BHS shirt, the indiscreet tattoo on the arm; he might as well have been wearing a badge. He eyed Gary Mitchell as if expecting to be handed an eviction order.

'Help you?'

Mitchell caught a sough of sour whisky breath. It was 11.05 am on Tuesday, in the least attractive part of the North Peckham housing estate, about as far as you could get from the manicured gardens of Invicta Cross. Although at this moment the police were busy reducing the difference between the two communities by digging up the latter's rose beds, sticking patrol cars on every corner, upsetting everyone and leaving litter all over the place.

'I'm looking for an old friend of mine, wondered if you could help. His name's William March. I think he used to live here.'

The only other relative mentioned in the *Advertiser*'s

article was Billy's aunt Carol-Lynn, mother of three, then living in Hackney. Directory Enquiries had turned up nothing under her maiden name, but a knackered-sounding town hall secretary working as the local registrar of council tenants had a history for her, single and married, which she happily and quite illegally released to Gary after he fed her a load of bollocks about being her doctor and needing to contact her urgently on a matter concerning her medical history. He'd been counting on a guess that she had never officially married and that the residence had been entered under her own name. There it was, sure enough, an entry marked under the surname March. These people were so fucking predictable he could map out their miserable, mistake-filled lives from first cry to last gasp. It was hard to suppress a smirk of satisfaction when he found that her current address was also listed. It was the first bit of detection work he had done in years, and made a change from covering charity wheelchair races.

'He don't live here. He ain't never lived here.'

'Then is Carol-Lynn in?'

'Nah, she fucked off with the kids about two years ago. We're divorced, it's all legal.' *Yeah*, thought Mitchell, *right*. 'What do you want with her, she owe you money or something?'

'Quite the reverse,' explained Mitchell. 'She's got some cash coming to her if she can tell me where to find her nephew, Billy.'

The big man grinned as realisation slowly dawned. 'Billy? Well you didn't say Billy, did you? You said William. You wanna come in or what?'

Charmed, thought Mitchell, stepping over a pull-along pony in the hall. Still, anything was better than hanging about on the street in this area. Somewhere at the back of the flat a baby was crying. A skinny young hippy girl with dark-rimmed eyes, bleached yellow hair and a necklace of lovebites appeared briefly in the hall dressed only in her underpants and a white T-shirt, then ducked away in embarrassment. *Might have known he'd shack up with someone like that*, Mitchell thought, *he looks the type. Probably keeps her smacked up to her eyeballs.*

'In here.' There was nothing in the lounge except an armchair, a free-standing tubular racking system containing about five thousands pounds' worth of video equipment and several stacks of unopened blank tapes. He decided it was best not to ask about that. Carol-Lynn's ex-husband had chosen not to introduce himself. Old habits obviously died hard.

'I'm a journalist,' Mitchell explained, eyeing the single armchair and deciding not to sit when he saw the baby bull terrier pulling at a leathery slice of pizza protruding from the back of the cushion.

'Get down, Spanky.' The dog was sent flying with the broad back of a hand. 'You wanna sit down, cup of coffee or something?'

'No, thanks, I'm fine,' said Mitchell. 'This is the deal. I interviewed Billy March ten years ago, and we wrote up his story. Now my paper wants to do a follow-up, and they've authorised me to offer him – and anyone who can help me to find him – a considerable amount of money.'

'How much is considerable?' asked the nameless barbarian.

'Ten thousand pounds,' he decided. It was the first figure that came into his head. *God forgive me for I am a lying sinner*, thought Mitchell.

The Neanderthal became quite agitated at this. 'Look,' he said, 'I'll level with you, I dunno where he is right now, but I can easily find 'im.'

'How?' asked Mitchell, pleased that his victim had taken the bait. 'I need to do this very quickly. It's a limited offer.'

'After his dad died, he rented a flat from a bloke Carol-Lynn worked with at the hospital. I still see the bloke all the time.'

'But you don't keep in touch with Billy?'

'Nah, it's her side of the family, innit? You know his life got all fucked up and that.'

'I know he had a rough time. Some people have nothing but heartache.' Mitchell tried to sound sympathetic, but it wasn't very convincing.

'So I'll give 'im a call then, shall I, this bloke I know?'

'If you would be so kind,' said Mitchell, thinking, *The Cro-Magnon probably assumes I've got a wad of cash on me, thinks I'm going to start peeling off notes and flicking them at him.* 'Once I've spoken to Billy,' he explained, 'we'll talk about some sort of financial settlement.'

'Yeah, that sounds cool to me.'

I'll bet it fucking does, thought Mitchell.

He watched and waited as the primitive crashed about in a sideboard drawer full of rubbish, then pulled a dirty scrap of paper out and squinted at it. He punched the number into an obviously stolen state-of-the-art telephone and turned away as he raised the receiver, speaking softly into the mouthpiece.

When he rang off, a look of great achievement crossed his battered face.

'He says if we go round there now, he'll take you right to Billy's door.'

Mitchell considered this. 'Where does he live?'

'Camden Town.'

'Then what are we waiting for?' he shrugged. 'Let's go.'

Room 346

'It's time to complete what I began, and in order to do that I must prepare to leave Invicta Cross. I'll almost be sorry to see the place go. Eblis, my night demon, approaches – his eyes are blinding orbs of fire in a black, unforgiving sky. I feel his dark leather wings beating heat into my face and hear the roar of searing flames as they flare at his command and prepare to incinerate all my sins.' – *The Red Diary*

'THIS IS going to be tricky – but not impossible,' he said, watching from behind the net curtains in the lounge as police and journalists moved their cordons closer. They had begun conducting some kind of question-and-search manoeuvre at 8 am, working along both sides of the close from the far end. The Bovis house had a separate yellow plastic ribbon taped across its garden gate, and a bored-looking policewoman had been posted at the front door. The end of the close had been sealed off with police vehicles. It was an eventuality he had not properly con-sidered.

'Do you want another cup of tea?' asked April, smooth-ing out the flounced trims of her taffeta pinafore. She looked beautiful this morning, but vague and somnambulant, somehow shifted apart from the real world.

'I've had three in the last hour, thanks. Are you sure the drainage shaft was clear when you put the lid back on last night?'

'Positive. I heard the splash at the bottom.' She paused for a moment, the most agonising of frowns momentarily darkening her face. 'I told you. I dropped her upright, and her arms lifted out from her body as she fell. She was wearing a charm bracelet, and I heard it catching against the brickwork on the way down. It was the worst sound I ever heard.' A look of horror crossed her face, but her mood brightened with the speed of a spring cloud clearing the sun. 'Do you want a biscuit? There are vanilla cream Hob Nobs and ginger nuts.'

She could be so unnerving at times, but he knew that this constant switching to and from her dreams was the only way she could cope now. Concentrating on the commonplace kept her sane. 'No, thank you,' he replied, forcing a smile for her.

'Lunch will be a while yet. Your favourite. Roast things. Even so, let's not dawdle . . .' She raised her palms. 'Hands, wash them please and don't leave the towel unfolded.'

'Why don't you put your feet up for a while, April?'

'I've too much to do today, silly!' she said brightly. 'I know, I'll go and Hoover the twins' room.' The fact that they had no offspring, identical or otherwise, did not seem to faze her.

He shut the door gently behind his wife and returned to the window. Everything was in place, and providing the downpour hadn't damaged the fuses, the rest of the day should pass without a hitch. What worried him more was the possibility that he and April might be detained before he had a chance to complete his work. The car was their biggest liability. One look at the dented radiator told you that it had recently been hit by something. Hopefully the rain would have washed away any bloodstains, but a single forensics expert worth his salt would quickly find something to link him with the Metcalf boy. What had Brad Metcalf been doing here, anyway? He no longer lived in the area, and he hated his stepfather. Perhaps he had come at Bob's request to try and solve the mystery of his mother's whereabouts.

There was another problem to consider. He could not tell how April would stand up to questioning. Her conversation was abnormal at the best of times. What would interrogating officers make of her now? She'd be fine for the first few minutes, but would dementedly implicate herself – and him – at the first sign of pressure.

There was only one thing for it. He would have to provide himself with a safeguard. They needed to make a quick exit from the close without appearing suspicious, and that would involve enlisting the help of someone else. He ran through the list of surviving neighbours in his head.

He checked his watch and saw that there was time for the makeshift plan to work. He was starting to enjoy the challenge of thinking on his feet. It was a board game now, with the added problem of trying to guess the most recent moves of the other side's pieces.

He went to the sideboard and checked the chambers of the cold, oil-slick army gun he had stowed behind the table mats, then hefted the weapon into a side pocket of his fatigues and called upstairs to April.

'Darling,' he shouted, 'get your raincoat on, ready for

when I come back. I'm just popping out for a few minutes to make a neighbourly call.'

Morris Diller was growing angrier by the hour. At the last minute, the sergeant had been refused permission to speak before the press. The superintendent with the flashy suit had decided he was too much of a loose cannon to be presented to the public. Instead, a senior officer from Croydon took over, seating himself before a bank of microphones at a makeshift table in the Invicta Cross Community Centre's bare conference room. He confirmed that an investigation was taking place into alleged 'terrorist activities' in Invicta Cross, and fielded the loaded press questions with the dishonest charm of a dance-hall lothario.

Diller was seething. It was not enough that he was constantly denied transfer and promotion; they couldn't even trust him with a simple piece of liaison work. After all this time he was still being treated like a dimwitted constable. No one had even bothered to ask him for his assessment of the situation. He would show them.

As the senior officer reached the end of the question period he had allocated to the journalists, Diller stepped smartly into his vacated place and checked that the microphones were still switched on.

'One other thing,' he said, the timbre of his voice causing a squeal of feedback. 'As an officer with many years of experience dealing with this community, I believe we may be looking for more than one person. I think we should be searching for a highly organised military team.'

The other officers stared at him in fury and confusion.

'Why's that?' called several people at once. The room silenced with anticipation.

'Because of the manner in which these attacks were carried out,' replied Diller, savouring the limelight. 'A military manner. Explosives, poisonings, ambushings, you don't have to wait for the bloody forensic tests to come back to know that both the materials used and the methods employed are consistent with someone who's been in the army. I'm an ex-army man myself, I ought to bloody know. We have to ask ourselves why this area has become a military target for terrorists.'

A dozen arms were raised, a dozen questions were launched at him and everyone was shouting at once, but before Diller could expand on his theory he was rudely dragged to one side by two of Croydon's finest. He found himself being pulled into the corridor by his jacket sleeves.

'What the hell do you think you're doing, you moron?' hissed McIntyre, the DCI in charge of the Invicta Cross operation, a fierce-faced man with the sallow complexion of a heroin addict. 'You're giving the impression that the area's got some kind of covert military status which makes it a legitimate target.'

'What does that matter so long as we catch the bastards?' asked Diller defensively.

McIntyre rubbed his face wearily. 'If it had occurred to you to think it through, you might have asked yourself whether there really is anything of military sensitivity in the area.'

'You mean there is?' said Diller, surprised.

'The Territorial Army's Southeast England Munitions Facility is here,' the DCI explained. 'The depot that supplies our boys in Northern Ireland. Location classified – until now, that is, when, thanks to you, hacks from all over the country will be searching for it.'

'I didn't know about that, I just saw the evidence and reckoned this guy was an ex-squaddie, or someone with access to army supplies. I was just giving them an opinion.'

'Fair enough,' agreed McIntyre. 'Now I'll give you an opinion, you single-cell organism. You've just said goodbye to your career advancement once and for all. I'm going to see you have less job responsibility than a traffic warden.' He beckoned to the constables. 'Now get this idiot out of here.'

Gary Mitchell looked up at the garish red and blue building that stood behind the fruit stalls of the market. 'This is a public house,' he said. 'I thought you said we were going to your mate's place?'

'This is it,' said the Neanderthal, pushing open the door. 'He's the landlord.'

'I remember this boozer when it used to be a right dump,' said Mitchell, 'and it looks like it still is. I thought the pubs around here were all ponced up when Camden became trendy.'

'Not this one. Wotcher, Jack.'

'Harry-boy.'

The landlord of the Skinner's Arms leaned over the counter and gave the Cro-Magnon's outstretched hand a meaty pump. As if to prove himself the tougher of the two, he sported livid razor scars on both cheeks and had a bald patch in the jagged stubble above his hairline, attesting to some partially successful brain repair.

'This the geezer what's looking for Billy March?'

Mitchell could have been forgiven for thinking he'd wandered into some forgotten Sid James film; these comedy Krays with love and hate tattooed on their knuckles, the smelly public bar with its fifties flock wallpaper and moult-ing red leather seats – who did they think they were trying to kid? Then he noticed the others seated around the room, youngsters barely old enough to have heard of the sixties, wideboys with drape jackets, bootlace ties and winkle-pickers, bouffanted girls in low-cut sweaters for whom the term 'busty' was invented, all smoking and boozing and playing the game, their nice middle-class accents and politi-cally correct attitudes tucked safely away while they acted out the scenario of being hard and working class and cool enough to really annoy their parents.

'This is one of them theme pubs, isn't it?' asked Mitchell, looking for somewhere to stick his wadded chewing gum.

'It used to be a real villains' joint,' explained Jack. 'Then the kids discovered it. Makes a bleedin' fortune now. None of yer old lags sittin' in the corner with ten Woodbines and 'alf of mild between 'em all bleedin' day. All the hostel alkies and day-release patients used to come in 'ere but we cleared 'em out. I offered to have the place redecorated, but the kids preferred it like this. Your Billy used to drink in here.'

My Billy, thought Mitchell, *my ticket out of here*. 'So where can I find him now?' he asked.

'He ain't done nuffink wrong, has he?' asked Jack. ''Cause he's not a bad geezer an' I don't wanna grass 'im up.'

'He hasn't done anything wrong at all,' replied Mitchell. *What's a few murders between friends?* 'I just need to locate him as quickly as possible.'

Jack and Harry-Boy had a few quiet words together, presumably to do with the division of spoils. Finally Jack nodded, downed the dregs of his bitter, nipped out the end of his roll-up and thrust the smouldering stump behind his hairy ear, and raised the flap of the bar.

'Lemme just check summink.'

He crossed the saloon bar and sat down beside a smooth young operator with a greased Elvis quiff, skull rings and a blue Hawaiian shirt.

'Who's he talking to?' asked Mitchell.

'Bal's the singer with the resident band, the Earls of Suave. He sees who comes and goes. He'll know if Billy's been in.'

Jack returned and beckoned the other two. 'Yeah, 'e's around all right. Come frew 'ere an' we'll go aht the back.'

He led the way into a yard filled with metal beer barrels, then through a door into the street behind. Jack's natural sense of subterfuge prevented them from leaving by the front of the building. They crossed the road and arrived before the double doors of a grim redbrick Victorian institution, the Arlington Road Hostel. The steps were occupied by shabby, desolate men drinking cans of strong lager. As they entered the gloomy foyer, Mitchell held his hand over his nose and prayed that this ghastly field trip would reveal some useful purpose.

The smell of disinfectant stung his nostrils, but it was not powerful enough to hide the ingrained stench of the thousands of unwashed bodies that had passed through here over the years.

'I didn't think places like this still existed,' he gasped.

'As long as there's a need for them they'll always be 'ere,' explained Jack. 'This way.'

He led them to a broad stone staircase rising in the centre of the building. The sound of distant, desperate arguments, mad rants and coughing fits could be heard above their

ootsteps. The building grew brighter as they rose, grey
unbeams slanting through the tall dirt-caked windows.
Apart from the warning notices tacked on the walls, there
vas no way of telling the year, or indeed the century, through
vhich they were moving. If Florence Nightingale had turned
he corner ahead of them with her hand shielding a hurricane
amp, Mitchell would not have batted an eyelid.

'This is it.'

Jack pushed open a pair of modern red fire doors added
by the council, and they stepped into a long tiled corridor
vith dozens of plain wooden doors leading off on either
ide. The smell of institution lunches filled the heavy air,
cabbage and mashed potatoes. They stopped before number 346, and Jack knocked. The three men waited and
istened; a cough, the scrape of a chair, someone moving to
he door and pulling back a bolt.

Revealed in the widening gap, the room's resident at first
appeared to be about forty-five years old, though closer
examination revealed a man of less than thirty. He wore a
atty grey towelling robe over a pair of jumble-sale suit
trousers. Mitchell examined the tall stooped figure with
distaste. His unshaven jaw jutted defiantly, his lips pressed
into a thinness that suggested he was used to justifying
himself to others. Lank chestnut hair fringed his hollow
eyes, turning them to pools of shadow. 'I got someone here
to see you,' Jack said warily. 'This is Gary Mitchell. He's
from the newspapers.'

When the man finally spoke, his voice was surprisingly
scratchy and aged, as if it was being relayed through an old
gramophone.

'I've met you before, Mr Mitchell,' whispered the gaunt
apparition. 'I'm Billy March.'

353

CHAPTER FORTY-TWO

Forgiving the Past

'While I was trying to construct a method of escape from Balmoral Close, I wondered if anyone would uncover my secret, but dismissed the thought.' – *The Red Diary*

'**I HAVEN'T** been back to Invicta Cross in over a decade,' said Billy March, perched on the iron bed that constituted one of the two pieces of furniture in the narrow room. 'Why would I want to return there?'

'You were done an injustice,' replied Mitchell, seating himself in the only chair. 'You told me so yourself when you were just fourteen years old.' March hadn't changed, but he had weathered beyond his years. He looked like a forgotten child star who had aged badly.

'What's goin' on then?' asked Jack. Mitchell had forgotten the knuckle-draggers were still there. The publican and Harry-Boy were standing by the door with puzzled looks on their simian brows.

'This is a delicate matter,' Mitchell explained. 'I wonder if I could ask you gentlemen to wait downstairs in the lobby for us.'

They glanced at each other, trying to discern some form of deception.

'Please, this is difficult for Billy, having to rehash the memories of the past. I just need a few words alone with him. We'll be down to join you in no more than ten minutes, and then we can conclude our arrangement – you have my word.'

Mistaking him for a gentleman, the men reluctantly squeezed back out of the room, closing the door behind them.

Mitchell was disappointed; his only theory appeared to be false. The spirit-broken man seated on the single bed before him could not possibly be the Invicta Cross Avenger. In his eyes were the vaguest remnants of the imaginative teenager he had met ten years earlier, but nothing else had survived.

'You know what's going on in your old home town, then?' he asked, lighting a cigarette.

March seemed puzzled by the question. He clearly had no knowledge of the events that were unfolding in Invicta Cross.

'It's been on the telly.'

'There's no television here.'

'Don't you read a paper? Front page stuff, this.'

'I haven't read one in months,' March replied wearily.

'Allow me to enlighten you. Someone's been playing silly buggers in the street where you used to live. Poisonings, bombings, hit and run, you name it. Taking out all of your old neighbours.'

'I don't understand. Who's doing this?'

'Well, *you*, I thought, but apparently I was wrong. Tell me if any of these ring a bell.' Mitchell produced a fax from his pocket and read out his list of victims' names.

'Yes, I knew all of them,' replied March, who was

rummaging through a holdall beneath his bed. 'And they knew me. I have the original article you ran in the paper somewhere under here.' He carefully uncreased a much-folded page of newsprint.

'And you're sure you've never been back there since?' asked Mitchell, studying the broadsheet.

'Not once. I was too busy having a lousy time here. My father died, I lost my job. I drank a little, then I drank a lot. Now I'm no different to anyone else in this place. A little more unemployable, perhaps.'

Blimey, get the violins out, thought Mitchell. 'But you were angry with the people who did this to you,' he urged, trying to force his theory. 'The neighbourhood conspired against your family, you told me so yourself; they drove you out—'

'They didn't do any such thing,' said March, returning the clipping to its rightful place. 'I thought there was some kind of big conspiracy going on at the time, but there wasn't. I understand that now. I always did have a strong imagination, but once my father and I moved back to London and I got to thinking about it, I realised that our neighbours were just behaving the way people do. They weren't being deliberately malicious, just – I'd had no experience of the suburbs. All those petty-minded people protecting their territory. The only adults I'd ever met were Londoners, and they were different, more . . . easygoing. So many people crammed on top of each other in tiny flats and terraced houses, it wasn't surprising. But Invicta Cross people were as alien as Martians to me; I guess I read too much into their behaviour. I always overreacted as a kid. When we were still living in Greenwich I attacked the man from the council who came to tell us we had to move – I hit him with a bicycle pump. Like I said, too sensitive, too much imagination. What happened, happened. I've made my own mistakes since then. And I've learned to forgive the past.'

Mitchell was on the verge of giving up. His only lead was a dud. His meal ticket was disappearing, uncashed. This bloke was a sad burnout, and those two goons were still downstairs, waiting to be paid. They'd probably kick him to death when they discovered he had no dosh for them. He flicked his cigarette stub through the transom and rose to leave the room, then paused on his way to the door, a thought striking him.

'Since you left, nobody's been to visit you from the good old days, have they? Nobody you used to know?'

'You mean old neighbours, enemies, people like that?'

'Anyone.'

March thought for a minute. 'Somebody did come by a few times, but he wasn't an enemy.'

'Who, then?'

'His name was Oliver Price. He used to be my best friend at the school in Invicta Cross.'

'You say he *used* to be your best friend? You fall out with him or something?'

'Nothing like that. I think he got into trouble for spending too much time at our house. His father made him stay home more. We just stopped hanging around together.'

'And yet he came to see you here. What did you talk about? Old times?'

'No, not really. It was all rather depressing.'

'And you've seen no one else?'

'There *was* someone.'

Mitchell brightened. 'Yes?'

'Just a social worker. Wanted to get me a job at Blockbuster Video.'

'So you've no idea who might want to hurt the town, and you've never been back there yourself, not even for an afternoon.'

'I hate this room, Mr Mitchell. The rain comes in under the sill, but you have to have the window open because the radiators don't turn off so it's always boiling, and the smell of disinfectant stings your eyes. But I'd rather be here than there.'

It was hopeless, like getting blood from a stone. He had no other questions to ask the Avenger here, and no other leads to follow. Then he remembered the newspaper he'd stuffed in his pocket before leaving the newsroom.

'One last thing,' he said, 'I've got something to show you.' He pulled a back issue of the *Advertiser* from his overcoat and opened it to the middle pages. 'A little while ago Invicta Cross suffered a rash of malicious practical jokes. We ran a feature on the subject, published some pictures of the victims with their comments. Tell me if you recognise anyone.'

March took the newspaper from him and studied it carefully. 'I know all of them. They're all our old neighbours. Except this one.' He tapped one of the photographs. 'That's the man I was telling you about, my friend.'

'Your friend . . .'

'Oliver Price. He doesn't live in Invicta Cross now, hasn't done for years.'

Mitchell looked down at the page and studied the handsome tanned face of a man described by the caption as 'Angry resident of Balmoral Close'. The article was headed 'Pranks Turn Friendly Neighbourhood Sour'.

'Are you sure this is your old school friend?'

'He's changed a lot, but it's definitely him. Wait, I'll show you.' March dug into his holdall again, pulled out a crumpled classroom snapshot and held it up before the journalist. Mitchell found himself looking at a blurry end-of-term photograph that could have been just about anyone.

'Of course,' said March, 'you have to add on ten years.'

Mitchell checked the newspaper photograph again. There didn't seem to be much resemblance. 'Why is your old pal pretending he still lives in the neighbourhood?'

'I can't imagine. Oliver would never go back there. When he came to see me he told me he'd recently relocated to Ireland. He used to be stationed there and liked it so much that when he left the army, he decided to move back and buy a place just outside Dublin. He was just visiting London for a couple of weeks. He invited me to visit him.'

'He was in the army?'

'Bomb disposal.'

Mitchell collected the overcoat that had been draped behind his chair. 'I need you to come with me.'

'I don't want to go back there.' March remained seated on the bed, the newspaper still open in his lap. He had been away too long; he was frightened of returning now.

'People are dying, Billy. If your old friend is involved, I think maybe you can help stop him. Listen, we can't go through the front of the building. Is there a back way out of here?'

'Why should I help you?'

'Because you may have forgiven the past, but it still needs putting right. And you might just get some peace of mind after all these years,' said Mitchell, pulling him up from the bed.

CHAPTER FORTY-THREE

Identity Crisis

'At first I considered changing my name from Oliver Price to Billy March by deed poll. Then, when I married April, I grew so used to being called Billy that I didn't feel the need to change it legally. I had spent such a large part of my life thinking about my friend that it seemed entirely appropriate eventually to become him.' – *The Red Diary*

AS HE walked toward the Metcalf house with murder in his heart, he reminded himself of the past with every step. *I'm doing this all for you, Billy March, so that you can be free of your ghosts. It's all because of you.* Sadness filled Oliver's heart as he remembered the golden moments of their briefly shared childhood and how everything had turned bad so quickly after that.

On that momentous day when the two boys had first met in the fifth-year classroom of Sherington Senior School, Billy March had been a revelation; a jet stream of excitement, energy and ideas. Oliver had never met anyone like him. He brought new life into the school – the nervous, electric danger of the city. It bothered the other kids, of course, made them uneasy, showed them how they might have been in another life. Oliver had known instantly that here was someone he could look up to, someone who might be his friend forever. Billy was sensitive and funny and took care of him even though he couldn't take care of himself. Billy was his hidden face, his wild side, the sunlight of his eclipse, the boy he could never be. Billy was more than human – he was a god.

But even gods were beset by demons.

Oliver had watched his friend grow more miserable with every passing day. His parents always quarrelling, the neighbours conspiring behind his back, his school work suffering. Within weeks of his arrival in Invicta Cross, Billy March was walking around with the look of a trapped animal.

He stopped being a god. He became a mere mortal.

Oliver, who believed in gods, who read the books in the Chapel of Rest and believed in Eblis, the father of all devils, was desperate to do something that would help his friend. But there was nothing he could do. He was fourteen years old. He had no power to change their world . . .

That was then . . .

. . . This was now.

He broke off the thought and rang the doorbell beneath his finger.

Emma Metcalf answered the door and took a half-step back in surprise.

'Oh, Mr Prentiss,' she said, clearly expecting someone else. 'Are you here to see my father?'

'If he's accepting visitors.' Oliver stepped into the hall without waiting for a reply. The house was in semi-darkness, and something smelled bad, an unemptied bin bag in the kitchen. None of the downstairs curtains had been opened. Emma was wearing a black Donna Karan two-piece suit, and looked as if she'd spent the night asleep in it. For some reason she was holding an egg whisk in one hand. Her make-up was smeared; she'd been crying. Odd, thought Oliver. He didn't think she cared much for her family.

'He's in the garden,' she said. 'He told me he didn't want to talk to anyone, but I suppose he might talk to you. You can go on through.'

'The garden? It's pouring.'

'He's in the shed. He's been in there all night. He goes there whenever he's really upset.' This snippet of information was something she would never have admitted to a neighbour under normal circumstances. Oliver passed through the kitchen, past shelves full of china dogs and copper jelly moulds, and pushed open the back door. The shed. How convenient.

There were tools in the shed.

'So you went to school together,' said Mitchell, pulling away with a squeal of tyre rubber as the lights changed. 'Yeah, well. I had a lot of mates at school, but I wouldn't expect any of them to commit murder for me.'

'This was different,' said Billy. 'All the trouble I had, he shared. His father was a funeral director, divorced. Oliver had no home life to speak of. He spent his evenings over at our house. My mother usually fed him. He got very angry about what happened to us.'

'Even so.' Mitchell took a left turn into a one-way system, avoiding Croydon. Invicta Cross was still twelve miles away. 'Seems a bit fucking extreme, doesn't it? Surely you're the one who should have wanted revenge, not him.'

Mitchell was right. It didn't make sense. Why would

Oliver return to Invicta Cross and cause havoc when *he* was the one with the motive?

'When we get there I want to talk to him alone,' said Billy, remembering that the man seated beside him was, first and foremost, a journalist.

'Fine. I need to call Diller, my contact at the cop shop.'

'Morris Diller's still there?'

'Yeah, still in the same desk by the window. You know him?'

'You could say that.'

'Well, we have a deal to conclude.' He punched out Diller's direct number on his mobile phone and swore when he received an engaged signal.

Bob Metcalf was a colourless man at the best of times, but this far from a temporal optimum he was virtually transparent. His face was the same shade as the fawn woodwork behind his head. He looked like he'd died and come back as a ghost. The gently tired creases of his face had deepened into distinct lines.

'I just want to know the truth, Jack,' he wailed, knotting his hands over the end of his Black & Decker Workmate. 'I have to know if she's alive and well, or if the same thing has – has – happened to her—' He tried to catch his breath but was rapidly becoming asthmatic.

They sat opposite each other in the darkened shed, the rain pattering hard on the tar-paper roof above them. On a shelf at one end stood a half-built balsawood aircraft carrier, clearly a Metcalf hobby-as-therapy item.

'And now your poor son, as well. How awfully unfortunate.'

'It's as if we're cursed or something—'

'Well, if there's anything I can do,' said Oliver solicitously, 'help with the funeral arrangements, arrange a cremation, just let me know. Do the police have any idea who did it?'

Bob wiped his nose and looked up miserably. 'I don't know, I don't think so. They can't tell if it's the same person as the others, or if it was even an accident.'

'Such a tragedy. He was so young.' Oliver's gaze spanned the shed wall, where Bob's tools were hanging in neat descending rows. You could do a lot of damage with this stuff, he thought. Pipe wrench. Needle-nosed pliers. Claw hammer. Masonry chisel. Staple gun. Pity there wasn't a chain saw. Bit too noisy for the job, anyway. He should do it quickly, put Bob out of his misery. He hated to see a grown man suffer.

'How's Emma coping?'

'Very well. She's been a pillar of strength. She's not worried about her mother at all.'

That's because she hates her guts, he thought. *She's not too keen on you either, if I remember correctly.*

'She's convinced Daphne will come home any hour now. But I know she's dead. Probably lying under a clump of bushes, strangled in a railway siding.'

'Why do you say that?'

'Well, isn't that where they always find bodies on those *Crimewatch* programmes? *Bodies*. My *wife*. My *son*. The police want to put a watch on the house. They're saying the rest of us might be in danger. But we can't be, can we? Who would do such – who—' His clenched fist pressed against his cardigan-clad chest, gasping.

'Take it easy,' said Oliver, 'there's no rush. Catch your breath. Do you have an inhaler?'

'I – I put it down somewhere . . .'

'Don't worry, I have the same problem. Here, you can use this.'

Great Eblis was clearly on his side, he decided, removing the small black metal spray tube from his pocket. He had prepared the mixture earlier and had decanted it into an old Gold Spot mouth-freshener tube that he had repressurised. The chemicals contained within were appropriate to a garden shed, an incredibly toxic malathion/parathion/chlorthion/sarin blend. The first two were lethal insecticides, the third sometimes confused with nose drops but quite deadly, and the last, when absorbed in spray form, acted as a high-powered nerve gas that killed in minutes. The cocktail they formed was so strong it was a wonder it hadn't eaten its way through the aluminium container. He'd been trying to think of an easy way of administering the poisons. It had not occurred to him that Bob might be asthmatic.

'I don't need a mouth spray,' said Bob, trying to read the lettering on the side of the tube. It was typical of him to question the advice of a trusted friend.

'It's not a mouth spray, Bob. It's a special asthma treatment I got from the hospital, works absolute wonders. You just breathe it in.'

Bob looked doubtful as he raised the spray to his mouth and nostrils, set his forefinger over the pump button – then lowered the tube.

'What do *you* think, Jack? Do you think she's left me? Or do you think there's a chance that this madman has got hold of her?' His asthmatic breath was easing. He wouldn't need the spray if he calmed down.

'I just pray she's not tied up somewhere, unconscious

and barely alive, at the mercy of a raving nutter,' said Oliver maliciously.

The thought had Bob gasping again, and he raised the spray to his face once more. Oliver held his breath and leaned back, out of harm's way.

Bob managed two full squirts, looked surprised, then released a thin squeal of pain and a series of disgusting liquid coughs and fell over the Workmate, instantly paralysed but still alive. Sulphurous vomit began to dribble from his nose.

Oliver could not afford to leave the shed until he was quite sure that Bob was dead. To be on the safe side he would have to allow about fifteen minutes. Easily solved. He reached over his neighbour's convulsing body and took a claw hammer from the wall. Then he selected a three-inch masonry nail from a neatly labelled box on the shelf and inserted the sharp point into Bob's conveniently upturned left ear. He carefully held the nail upright, as though positioning a picture hook, then gave it three good hard slams with the hammer. Something cracked on the second blow, and the third allowed the full length of the nail's shank to bury itself inside Bob Metcalf's brain. The shiny steel head protruded like a high-tech hearing aid. Oliver wiped the narrow crust of blood from the edge of his palm and replaced the hammer.

He was just admiring his handiwork when he looked up and saw Emma Metcalf standing in the doorway of the shed, her mouth silently opening and shutting, her eyes wide with shock.

'Ah – Emma, your father's had a – a bit of an accident ...'

'You killed Brad and my mother too, didn't you?'

He took a step toward her, too weary to try and explain.

'Tell me why,' she screamed.

'I'm finishing something that began a long time ago, Emma. In a few minutes we'll go shopping and bring it all to an end, but first I need to talk to you.'

He was still several feet away when she turned and ran blindly into the rain. He tried to catch up with her but slipped on the wet grass. By the time he had righted himself and regained his footing, he could hear her crashing over the fence of the next garden. What was she doing? Surely her most logical course of action would have been to go back through the house and summon the police who were dotted all over the front lawns of the close.

No; she had been terrified by what she had just seen. How long had she been standing there in the doorway? How long would it take for her to start thinking rationally? Did he have minutes or seconds left before the finger of blame pinned him down? He still had to finish the plan, and time was running out. He loped back up the garden *chez* Metcalf and telephoned his own home.

'April.' He tried to steady his ragged breathing. 'It's time to leave. I'll meet you over at the Bricketts' house.'

'The Bricketts? But I'm in the middle of baking, or washing up, I can't remember which.'

'Just stop what you're doing and meet me there in exactly one minute.' He slammed down the receiver and checked the close from the Metcalfs' lounge window. Police vehicles blocking the end of the road, a number of constables gathered beneath umbrellas and what looked like a forensic team at work on a saturated section of lawn. Tricky. He looked back at the garden. Emma Metcalf was nowhere in sight. Taking a deep breath, he turned up the collar of his Schott jacket and headed for the front door.

CHAPTER FORTY-FOUR

Home Again

'They say that murderers exist in a moral vacuum, that they lack empathy, feel no remorse. I've become a murderer because I have too much empathy for Billy's plight, and my remorse is all for him.' – *The Red Diary*

'IT DOESN'T look as if it's changed at all,' said Billy, amazed. 'Just expanded. I'd forgotten how clean everything looks here.' He slammed the passenger door of Gary Mitchell's Ford and walked up to the yellow plastic tape of the police cordon. *Welcome home*, he thought, looking over at the Balmoral Close street sign. Ahead of him, through a grey sheet of rain, he could see a number of officers in reflective yellow jackets standing in the doorway of one of the houses. They were questioning Adolpho Garibaldi's mother. He couldn't believe the ancient Italian matriarch was still alive. She had to be nearly a hundred years old.

'Which house did Oliver say he lived in?' asked Billy.

'I don't know.'

'You must have his interview notes on file or something.'

'We're not the bloody *Guardian*, you know,' said Mitchell indignantly. 'In our paper the articles are there to fill up the spaces between the advertising.'

'Let's just tell the nearest officer, then,' said Billy, ducking under the cordon.

'Oh no you don't.' Mitchell seized his lapel. 'I'm not giving away this story so easily.'

'What do you mean? You're not giving anything away.'

'I am as soon as they take over. I want to be in at the arrest.'

'Then we have to know which house he's in,' said Billy. 'I want to talk to Oliver alone. If I think he's the one who's behind all this I'll call you in to join us, and you can decide when to inform the police.'

'How are you going to find him?' asked Mitchell, exasperated. 'There are at least twenty houses to choose from.'

'Leave that to me. Show me how your mobile phone works. What's the name of the estate agent for this area?'

'Well, there are several.'

'Who's the biggest?'

'That would be Brickett & Co.'

'Nothing to do with Justin Brickett?'

'He owns it.'

'Of course he does.'

He called Directory Enquiries, obtained the number, punched it in. Above them a deafening roll of thunder roared, making them both start. The noise was like a building collapsing.

'Hello, I'm an old friend of Justin's and I wondered if – not in today, I see. Then perhaps you can help. I need to know if you've sold or rented out any property in Balmoral Close in the last few months. I'm thinking of buying a house, but I'm not sure about the area. I'd like to talk to someone who's recently moved here and see what advice they can give me. Yes, I'll hold. Thank you.'

It felt good to be in charge of his actions again. This was the most positive thing he'd done in years. He shouldn't have left it so long. He looked about and remembered cycling these streets in the rain. The frustration and sheer helplessness he experienced then came flooding back. Childhood fears stayed with you forever – unless you found a way to banish them.

'Yes, still here. You have? A Mr and Mrs Jack Prentiss. And what number is that? Thanks. If I need any further help, who should I ask for? Tracy. I see.' He rang off, flipped the phone back at Mitchell. 'He's in number nineteen, on the left-hand side.'

'How do you know it's him?' asked Mitchell as they set off.

'Are you kidding? *Jack Prentiss?*' He released a wheezy laugh. 'First of all, according to the girl I just spoke to they're the only couple to have been placed in the street in over three years. Second, if you're going to pick yourself an undetectable alias you shouldn't use a name someone will be able to connect you with.'

'I'm not familiar with the name.'

'You wouldn't be. Only a couple of people would.'

'Uh-oh.' Mitchell slowed down as they passed a group of police officers standing behind a wall of manicured rhododendron bushes. 'The whole bloody street's crawling with cops.'

'You want to involve them?' asked Billy. 'Now's the time to do so.'

'No!'

'Then keep walking, and look like we're heading somewhere with a purpose.'

They passed the backs of the constables conducting their interview at the Garibaldi residence, on past two members of the forensic team who were standing on either side of a concrete sundial arguing about prioritised authorisation. He checked his watch; just past noon, and yet it was barely light. It felt strange to be back in the close, walking along familiar pavements. It all looked smaller somehow, less mysterious.

The porch of number nineteen was in darkness; there were no lights on in the house. He rang the bell while Mitchell kept watch, peered through the stained-glass yachting scene in the door, then rang again; no answer.

'Come on.'

'Where are you going?'

'There might be a window open at the side. If not, we'll have to open one.'

'That's breaking and entering.'

'Have you got a better idea?'

The side hall window was locked tight. He moved on past dripping rose bushes to the kitchen window and tried to raise the frame in its casement. That, too, was locked. The interior was too dark to reveal any features.

'Give me your scarf.'

'What for?' asked Mitchell. He was beginning to doubt his own wisdom in bringing this gaunt, striding man along with him. After all, there had to be a reason why Billy March was wasting his life alone in a rundown hostel. What if he turned out to be a complete nutcase? Against his better judgement he unwound the scarf from around his neck and passed it over. Billy hefted a decent-sized stone from the rockery and wrapped it, then stood still and watched the lowering clouds.

'What are we waiting for?'

'Cover.'

A flash of lightning, then four seconds later another demolition of thunder. Billy cracked the wrapped rock hard against the kitchen window and the pane split in two. One half fell in with a smash that came after the main peal of thunder had finished. They froze, waiting; nothing. Billy slipped in his arm and unlocked the catch.

As soon as they were inside, he decided to check the ground floor for signs of life. At first glance the kitchen seemed normal. Then he noticed oddities; a stack of burned frozen dinners in the sink, a crotchless rubber fetish outfit hanging from a saucepan rack, cocktail glasses on the floor. There was a lemon meringue pie in the mop bucket on the counter. What had been going on here? It was too dark to see clearly, and they didn't dare turn on a light.

The kettle was still hot. The room had not been vacated for very long. He moved on to the lounge, a cacophony of pastel-shaded fifties furniture; a kidney-shaped coffee table, poker-work pictures of clowns and bowls of lilacs, a black and red wire statue of a rickshaw boy, a TV set with sliding wooden doors – and a framed photograph on the mantelpiece.

A wedding portrait, although it looked more like a Polaroid, taken in a dismal council registry office just after the exchange of vows. The handsome groom was Oliver Price, without a doubt. But his new spouse . . .

There was something familiar about her, but what? The bobbed blonde hair looked wrong somehow, unnatural and wig-like. He held his hand over the top part of her head and found himself looking at a picture of grown-up April Barrow, no longer an awkward teenager, now a bizarrely radiant bride.

*

Emma Metcalf had no idea where she was going. She was moving through an alien landscape where nothing made sense and no one was safe. She longed to be snuggled down in the great green sofa between her parents watching a James Bond film. She wanted the reassurance of a childhood Christmas. Instead she was beset by evil; she had nothing and no one to turn to. She stumbled on, across the wet baize of the front lawns, one shoe missing, her smart designer suit covered with mud, and forced herself not to think of her father lying on the bench with bloody upturned eyes, a puke-leaking nose and a nail protruding from his ear.

She slid over as she was crossing the Prentisses's diamond-shaped flower bed and lay there sobbing, unnoticed by the police and ignored by the world, until Billy March opened the front door and scooped her from the wet soil.

CHAPTER FORTY-FIVE

Deal

'I realise I've made one small mistake, using the name Prentiss, but I honestly don't think anyone will pick up on it. Not in time to save the town, anyway.' – *The Red Diary*

THE POLICE station at Invicta Cross was a beige brick bungalow with a wheelchair ramp and geranium beds, a number of small waiting, incident and interview rooms, a cheerful staff area and three basement holding cells. It smelled too clean to have ever been busy. As constabularies went, it was a quiet, uneventful place. Radio messages were broadcast via the larger headquarters at East Grinstead. Today, though, the station had become a halfway house seemingly filled with lunatics. Cameramen and interviewers had set up in the more photogenic corners of the car park, sound men were waving microphone booms in the direction of anyone in a uniform. The teams from Croydon had expanded their makeshift operations centre all the way down to the staff room, and Morris Diller was as much use as a bollard, the main difference being that bollards didn't usually step aside with a mumbled apology when traffic tried to pass.

The grounded sergeant removed himself from the line of

fire and perched behind one of the secretarial desks, where he could at least monitor incoming radio reports. In the next room another interminable briefing session was taking place, but he had not been invited to attend. So, once again he was in the wrong place, waiting for orders while somebody else took the responsibility and the glory.

The anger knotted deep inside Morris Diller's stomach; the greatest criminal assault ever to occur in this area, and he had been forbidden to leave the station. He sat there bitterly grinding his teeth and watching as the cameramen in the car park hastily gathered their equipment and sprinted toward anyone who entered or left the building.

McIntyre, the Croydon DCI, had told him to touch nothing and go nowhere, but he could be of no use here, so what point was there in staying? He felt more comfortable on the street. Always had done, if only he'd been prepared to admit it to himself. So how come he'd ended up behind a desk that had now been commandeered by someone nearly half his age?

Nobody noticed as he crept past the briefing room and slipped into the storage facility at the end of the first-floor corridor. Diller helped himself to a set of Rover keys from the car pool drawer and headed for the rear exit. A young man balancing a Betacam on his shoulder came racing toward him as he drew level with the patrol car, but he managed to seal himself inside the vehicle and pull away without being identified. He knew that Balmoral Close would be sealed off by now, but somehow he needed to be near the source of the tragedy in order to understand what was happening.

Diller pulled the car over at the entrance to Windsor

Terrace and opened the complaints folder that lay on the passenger seat. Rain was drumming hard on the roof; the grey road ahead was a blurry miasma. In the prank file someone – PC Bimsley, probably – had scrawled out a chart of Balmoral Close, indicating who lived where. Prout, Metcalf, Bovis, Brickett, the names were all familiar. He hadn't had many dealings with the Garibaldis, but they weren't on his mental list of suspects; they were old and respected and kept to themselves. One name stubbornly refused to be placed. Prentiss, at number 19. New to the close. No separate complaint logged from this address, although there was a secondhand report of a mass prank being played on the street that had included them.

Prentiss. *Prentiss.*

Why did it ring such a bell?

As the realisation kicked in, he punched out a number on the car's mobile phone. No service. Damn. He left the vehicle and headed for the call box on the corner. Gary Mitchell answered his mobile on the second ring.

'Gary? Diller.'

'I've been trying to get hold of you, Morris. Where the fuck have you been?'

'I'm not at the station. Listen, I have something—'

'Yeah, and I've got something for you, but I need to know what you're going to do for me.'

Mitchell had presumably only just arrived back in town. He couldn't know what had been happening since he'd left.

'I don't think our deal's applicable any more, Gary,' said the sergeant.

'Why, what's happened?'

'Call yourself a fucking journalist? All hell's broken

loose here. People are running around like chickens with their heads cut off. There's so much fucking media attention on the investigation they'll probably make an arrest whether they've got a proper suspect or not.'

'You reckon they've got their eye on someone?'

'No, but I have. Listen, Morris, I think I know how this bloke came by his identity.'

'That's funny – so do we.'

'You have to tell me if you're holding anything back, Gary, you know that. It's obstructing the law if you don't.'

'Fuck off! I want exclusive rights to the story, a promise that none of your mob will talk to the other papers before you get anything from me.'

'You know I can't arrange that. Be reasonable.'

'Hang on.' The line went dead for a full minute. Who else was with him? wondered Diller. Who was *we*? He was beginning to wonder if the connection had been cut when Mitchell came back on. He sounded drunk or excited, or both.

'If we tell you something that can confirm his identity, you have to promise that you lot won't interfere until we've had a chance to talk to him.'

Diller had no authority to arrange such a thing. The investigation was out of his hands, not that it had ever been in them. But he might still be able to win back some respect if he could aim the Croydon team in the right direction. 'All right,' he lied, 'I think I can arrange that. You've got yourself a deal. What name do you have for me?'

'Get your arse over here first,' ordered Mitchell, sensing that after all these years of sparring with the sergeant he finally had the upper hand.

CHAPTER FORTY-SIX

Kidnapped

'Eighty-five per cent of all domestic murders are committed by a relative or a trusted friend, did you know that? Murder comes easy to me, vengeance feels good, but it is fear that drives me on. I know I am ending an injustice, but I can feel the flames of hell roaring at my heels.' – *The Red Diary*

SANDRA BRICKETT answered the door and smiled nervously. She was wearing no make-up. April noted with satisfaction that her eyes had all but disappeared.

'Thank God for a couple of friendly faces,' Sandra said, hurriedly welcoming them into the hall. 'Can you believe this? We're under siege! Prisoners in our own homes. What a nightmare. I thought the police had come back with more questions. Have they been to you yet?'

'No,' said Oliver, 'they're still working their way around the close. I think old Mrs Garibaldi has slowed them down a bit. Is Justin here?'

'He's in the kitchen. Come through. I'll put the kettle on.'

Justin was seated at the table in white shirtsleeves and red braces, working on a home computer. He gave the impression that it was a perfectly normal day for him. His six-year-old son was beneath the table, rolling a giant-wheeled truck back and forth across the burned-orange cushion tiles.

'Sit down,' he said, 'I've been trying to get some work done here, but my printer's playing up. The police have asked us not to leave the area. It's playing havoc with my schedule.'

'They want to take us to Croydon for a further interview,' explained Sandra, setting out four cups. 'Because we know all of the people involved. I've told them we can't leave until we get a babysitter.'

'What do you make of all this?' asked Justin. 'They just announced on the news that we might have become some kind of military target. The presenter called us "a town under a reign of terror". Why is this suddenly happening now? That's what I'd like to know.' Hunched over the computer talking to himself, he seemed to have lost the confident edge that had made him appear a natural leader. His wife was fussing with the cups as if her life depended on the beverage's correct presentation.

'Terrible,' Sandra interjected, 'all those people killed and missing, people we've known for years. Their children have grown up with ours, we've had dinner together, played golf together. Bob Metcalf's son was the victim of a hit-and-run accident, did you know that?'

'That's rather what we wanted to talk to you about,' began Oliver, his blood-crusted fingers sliding around the handle of the revolver that was pointed nose down in the pocket of his fatigues. 'You see, we know something about all this.'

April nodded happily, as if agreeing to a shared interest in gardening.

'Oh?' Sandra immediately removed her attention from the teapot to eye them suspiciously. 'What have you heard?'

'It's not what we've heard, it's what we know to be true.'

'What do you mean, exactly?'

'It's difficult finding where to begin,' he said, accepting a steaming cup from Sandra. 'It goes back a long way. Do you remember a family called March? Got themselves into a spot of trouble with the neighbours. Can you recall what that was about?'

'God, the Marches.' Justin shook his head in wonder. 'I wondered what you were going to say for a minute. I haven't thought about them in years. Ghastly people. Lunatics. They accused us of trying to run them out of town.'

'Did you never wonder what happened to them?'

'Not at all. Why on earth would we? Good riddance to bad rubbish. We all felt the same.'

'I'm glad you remember them. Do you also remember a girl called April Barrow, lived with her mother a few streets from here? Kids used to call her place the Witch's House.'

'Vaguely, why?'

'Never mind. Try and think, Justin. The golf club wasn't built then.'

'You're right. It must have been nine or ten years ago. I think we were still waiting for planning permission.'

'You needed to get the March family out of their house, didn't you? Without their agreement you couldn't build an entrance to the club that would conform to the council's specifications.'

'No, that's not true; not true at all,' said Justin indignantly. 'I asked them if they'd be willing to negotiate some kind of arrangement with their housing officer, but they weren't interested. But it wasn't a big deal.'

'Why not?'

'Because Ken and Barbara Prout had already agreed to let us relocate the drive on their property. I just checked with the Marches in case we needed to put forward a backup plan, that's all.'

Oliver was dumbfounded. 'But Dr McMann got Ray March fired from his job.' He dug in his pocket, withdrew the silver money clip and threw it onto the table. 'He accused him of stealing this.'

'Oh, that,' said Justin. 'Ernest was so embarrassed about that. He'd made such a fuss at the garage, then he found it in the lining of his overcoat pocket when he got home. It was too late to help March, but he told me he sent him some money anonymously. He felt bad about it for ages, always thought that he'd helped drive them away. But where did you get hold of it?'

'Are you telling me there was no conspiracy to get the March family out of Invicta Cross?'

'Of course not. The kid had a bee in his bonnet about that, even went to the local papers and told them a lot of rubbish about what he thought was going on. He had a wonderful imagination, that boy, a decent mind, but it was all just a little bit out of whack.'

Oliver released his hand from the gun barrel in his pocket and mopped his forehead with a squashed piece of Kleenex. He could smell the oil from the firing mechanism on his fingers. He felt himself growing angry with Justin for confusing him and undermining his motives. 'I don't understand. Who made the obscene phone calls, who kept sending the family dirty letters?'

'How should I know?' asked Justin impatiently. 'How come you know so much about them anyway? It was years ago, nobody cares now.'

Oliver squeezed his eyes shut and forced himself to remember one thing; conspiracy or not, the lives of Billy March and his family had been destroyed. He rose to his feet, leaning against the draining board beside Sandra. That was April's cue. She could sense that something was about to happen. She followed the direction of his glance and moved nearer Justin.

'Sandra,' said Oliver, 'could you pass my tea?' Puzzled, Justin's wife did as requested.

'Well?' snapped Justin. 'What's your interest in this?' He was watching him expectantly, waiting for an answer.

Oliver took a gulp of tea, spilling some, then set the cup down and examined the palms of his hands. 'I'm sorry – could you hand me that towel?'

She passed him a towel from the rail beside the sink, and he wrapped it over his hand as he raised his fist and suddenly brought it up against the left side of Sandra's chest. There was a flash of light within the checkered cotton and a sharp thud, like a lead weight being dropped on cork flooring, and Sandra fell away with a blackened crimson hole in her baby-pink cashmere sweater. She hit her head on the edge of the sink, the seat of a chair and the floor as she fell, sliding awkwardly beneath the table, her legs jackknifing open obscenely beneath her. Before Justin could cry out April had stuffed a shoulderpad in his mouth and Oliver had dropped behind him, snapping his wrists into a pair of rubber handcuffs.

The Bricketts' son screamed as the shock of his mother landing beside him took effect, and started to cry. Oliver aised the gun again, feeling Justin stiffen behind him with a muffled bellow. He watched the boy for a moment, then owered the barrel.

Justin Brickett swung at April with his right leg, but Oliver caught it at the calf and stamped hard on his ankle until he heard the bone crack.

'Now,' he said, rising breathlessly and aiming the gun at Justin's temple, 'let's get his car keys and get out. The boy can stay here.'

April peered cautiously around the front door. The WPC outside the Bovis household was still in position, but was facing away from them. The nearest officers after that were about two hundred yards on and looking vaguely in her direction, but the rain was falling torrentially again. She hoped it was enough to obscure their vision.

Holding open the front door, she waited while her husband pushed Justin Brickett ahead of him to the door of the jeep. The estate agent could put no weight on his broken ankle, and was forced to lean on Oliver's shoulder. As soon as he was loaded into the back of the vehicle, April crossed around to the front of the car and climbed into the driver's seat. Oliver kept his gun aimed at Justin's head from between the seats, pushing his hostage's body down as low as it would go.

'You're Billy March, aren't you?' croaked Justin. 'You're not going to get very far.'

At the end of the road they were stopped by a young constable in a hooded yellow slicker, who demanded to know their destination. April wound down the top two inches of the window.

'We have a hospital appointment to attend,' she said. 'My husband is a diabetic.'

The constable peered in, but could see very little in the gloomy interior. 'Do you want someone to come with you?' he asked.

'No, we'll be fine. We'll only be gone for about an hour. Someone should bring you boys a nice cup of tea. I'll make you one when I get back.'

She stared straight ahead as the young man made a note of the jeep's licence plate, then waved them on.

Then she drove to the Invicta Cross Mall as fast as the speed limit and the wet roads would allow.

CHAPTER FORTY-SEVEN

Utopia Limited

'People say murderers make deals with devils, but I made a deal with just one demon. Eblis, born of a single pure explosion. Eblis, a creature of fire and air. Eblis, who first showed me the terrible beauty of the cleansing flames.' – *The Red Diary*

JUDITH FENCHURCH was bored and frozen. The twenty-three-year-old WPC had been hoping for a more demanding role in the investigation that was unfolding around her. She wanted to help conduct the door-to-doors, to comfort, explain and advise. Instead she had been posted beneath the dripping porch outside the Bovises' silent, empty house. The husband, Alan, had died at the weekend, and his wife had not come home last night. Her daughter had gone back to her own flat for an hour only to find the place empty when she returned, and was now kicking up a fuss at the station, saying that her mother had been abducted. Georgina Bovis's handbag and purse were still on the kitchen counter, and according to the daughter she never went anywhere without them. Sherry had managed to miss the contorted corpse of her mother's lover only because Graham had slipped behind the settee. Judith's colleagues spoke of strange events occurring in other houses, too. There was a maniac loose, or perhaps they were under alien attack. Either way, WPC Fenchurch wasn't getting a look in.

She stared out across the neighbourhood, but could barely see through the rain. On the other side of the road two soaked young officers were moving from house to house conducting interviews. A few minutes ago she had seen an attractive young couple dart through the downpour from their own house to the Bricketts'. A woman she later recognized as Sandra Brickett had admitted them. Fifteen minutes after this the front door had opened again. The couple had emerged with another man and had gone to his car.

Something about the awkward way the trio had been moving alerted the WPC, who finally decided to risk a charge of dereliction in order to cross the gap between the houses and peer in through the Bricketts' kitchen window.

At first sight everything seemed normal, but Judith's eye was drawn to a chair which lay on its side by the cooker. She pressed up against the wet glass and cupped her hands around her eyes, trying to see inside the unquiet shadows. Something in the kitchen was moving.

Behind the chair she could see a whimpering child, and now the bloody body of Sandra Brickett came into focus. Her legs were protruding from beneath the kitchen table. What she had taken to be maroon linoleum was a silky lake of blood. She ran back across the garden and shouted to the nearest officer, who broke a window and entered the house.

The young constable at the top of the close had been told by the woman driving Justin Brickett's jeep that she and her husband were going to attend a hospital appointment, but she hadn't specified where. The couple in the car had not yet been identified, but the constable had noted the jeep's licence plate, and the number had been sent out to all patrol vehicles in the Greater Croydon area. The press were being prevented from entering the cordoned streets while the door-to-door interviews continued. What more could they possibly do?

Billy watched as Emma Metcalf scrubbed her head with a bath towel and stifled her tears. Mitchell was pacing about behind her, his face a mask of confusion or intestinal gas, it was hard to tell which.

'If we take her to the police they can do whatever's necessary. Just don't involve me, Billy. If old Diller finds out I've got involved in this without telling him, he'll take me in for questioning.'

Billy kneeled beside the crying girl and gently removed the towel from her face. 'Please, try to remember what he said to you, if he gave you any clue where he was going next.'

'I wasn't listening to him properly. He was going to kill me, for Christ's sake. He was walking toward me with blood dripping from his hands and I freaked, I just turned and ran.'

'But he did speak to you?'

'Yes.'

'Try to think, Emma. We're the only people who know this man's identity. We need to try and stop him.'

'The police are supposed to be doing that.'

'They can't if they don't know who he is or where he's gone.'

'Wait a minute.' She lowered the towel and pulled her hair from her eyes. 'He said something about going shopping.'

That made sense. There was only one place Oliver could be heading, one place the three of them had shared. He had seen it from the window of Mitchell's car on the way into town, still standing even though it was now part of a new complex. Shopping meant the Invicta Cross Mall, and the mall meant the old water tower. He rose to his feet and beckoned Mitchell. 'Let Emma lead the police to her father. You have to come with me,' he said. 'I don't have a car and I don't know how to drive.'

'And I thought you wanted me along for my personality,' said Mitchell. 'Where are we going?'

'Long before there was a town here, this was all woodland,' said Billy. 'But for centuries there was a village here.'

'This is no time for a fucking history lesson, March.'

'The village was called Prentice Field. Ten years ago I built a model of Invicta Cross, its houses, its roads and its surrounding land. I did some research at the library and found out about the village. Most of the local books got their information by referring to a late-eighteenth-century farmer's journal kept by one Jack Prentice. The village was presumably named after him. But the developers of Invicta Cross ignored the land's historical significance and started again from scratch. They concreted over the past.'

'I don't see how that links you to this mate of yours,' complained the journalist, holding open the front door.

'Oliver Price helped me build the model. He was always on about the fields beneath the town, and what you would find if you stripped away the modern roads. I told him you would return the land to Jack Prentice and do the world a favour. Don't you see? It's Oliver's joke.'

'If you're suggesting he's going to get rid of the entire town and make it all fields again, we'd better find him before it stops being funny,' said Mitchell as they stepped out into the downpour.

Morris Diller crunched the Rover's gears and felt the rear tyres slip on the wet road. As he passed the entrance to Balmoral Close he pulled over. He should never have agreed to come here. For all he knew the Croydon mob might have been warned to keep an eye out for him, but he doubted it. Nobody had noticed him leaving the station, and worse still, nobody cared. He killed the engine and slipped out of the car, peering over a hedge into the sealed-off close. Gary had told him that they could meet up at number nineteen, but there was no sign of his wreck of a car in the street, and no way of getting through the cordon without being recognised.

Puzzled, he returned to the Rover and punched a number into his car phone, leaving the receiver down in hands-free mode. He needed to be around the journalist if there was any chance of a rewarding revelation.

'Gary, where the fuck are you?'

'Sorry, Morris, we couldn't wait any longer. It's very important that we confront this person face to face, and we think he's gone to the shopping mall. You're going to have to meet us there. This is your big chance.'

Your big chance for a story, Diller thought, looking up. *I had my chance and I've just shafted it.* McIntyre was leaving his van and walking angrily toward him. He must have spotted the Rover from the corner of the close. He hadn't reckoned on the DCI returning to the enquiry site so quickly.

'Get out of the car, Diller,' he shouted. Several junior officers turned and watched.

Because of the hands-free system, McIntyre couldn't see that he was on the phone. An idea occurred to him. He wouldn't be able to get there now, but perhaps someone else could. 'Gary, call my son, Gavin, at home. Get him to meet you. Tell him everything you'd tell me.'

'Why should I do that?'

'He'll help you. You want your exclusive, don't you?'

'All right, but you'd better be able to—'

'Yeah, yeah.' He quickly cut the call as McIntyre drew level with the car. Fuck him, and fuck Mitchell. By the time the hack found out that he'd been double-crossed, they'd have this nutter banged up.

'Diller, get out of the fucking car!' screamed McIntyre.

Diller's son was now twenty-six, and had been out of work for the last three years. He still lived at home with his father, whom he was lately starting to resemble. He spent his time between Giro cheques, eating Mcburgers and watching TV. His application to join the Metropolitan Police had been refused on a health technicality (weight), but he was in the process of reapplying and, thought Morris, a chance for his son to show some public spirit could turn out to do them both a bit of good.

The smile slowly vanished from his face as he turned to face the wrath of his superior.

'Your father wants you to cover for him,' said Mitchell.

'Fuck off,' said Gavin Diller, 'I'm not doing his dirty work. What's all that noise in the background?'

'I'm negotiating a roundabout with my free hand and I'm on my last battery units, so listen carefully. This is important for both of you. Your dad sounds like he's been dropped in the shit and could do with a hand. It might do you some good as well. You're still trying for the met, aren't you?'

'Yeah,' conceded Gavin.

'Then this is your chance to make a bit of an impact. I've got a hell of a story breaking here, and you can be in on it.'

'What's the catch?' Gavin was in his dressing gown watching the speed-skating championships on Sky Sport with a lapful of tea and toast, and didn't fancy being dragged out into the rain without a damned good reason.

'No catch. You'll see when you get here. You'll have to trust me until then.'

'You must be bloody joking,' said Gavin, finishing his toast, 'trust a newspaperman?'

Mitchell had no more time to argue. 'We'll meet you outside the main entrance to the Invicta Cross Mall.'

'When?'

'Now, you fuckwit, now!'

'All right, but this had better be bloody good.' Gavin replaced the receiver and thumbed up the volume on the TV remote.

'We're going to have to get rid of him,' said Oliver. 'He's too much of a liability.'

They were making their way across the vast car park to the entrance of the mall, but Justin Brickett's ankle made a terrible grinding sound when Oliver forced weight onto it, and the agonised man could barely walk. He had managed to spit the cotton pad from his mouth, but his hands were still cuffed behind his back.

'You can't be one of us, so you want to destroy what we have,' he said, stumbling and spitting streaming gobbets of saliva. 'You won't get away with it.'

'It's you lot who always *get away with it*,' said his abductor. 'All Billy ever wanted was to earn some respect.'

'Well, excuse me if I don't get into an argument about the fucking class system with you. I can't walk with my hands cuffed. You have to take them off.'

'I should have parked nearer the entrance,' said April. 'What are we going to do with him?' Her hair had matted into a sodden yellow carpet beneath the rain's onslaught. She looked lost, cold and abandoned, but seemed more focused somehow, as if being on the move gave her less to worry about. 'We can't leave him behind,' she cried, barely making herself heard over the pounding downpour. 'He'll tell the police everything and they'll take you away.'

'That won't make any difference now,' he shouted back. 'They'll know it's us as soon as they find Sandra's body, and they'll have further proof once they check the BMW.'

'What are we going to do, Billy?'

Billy. Jack. Oliver. He tried to clear his head and think lucidly for a second. The mall entrance was approaching. 'Finish the plan,' he said. *Some plan*, he thought, *what a mess*. The careful calculations he had pored over for so long had been altered irrevocably the moment they had decided to invite Daphne Metcalf over for a drink. His impulsive decision to get rid of her while the chance presented itself had, in hindsight, been a foolish one. He should have stuck to the damned plan, but now it was too late to do anything but go forward. He wondered if the town itself was controlling his actions. He released Justin from one half of the rubber cuffs and held on tight to the connecting chain, pulling him forward.

'Billy, it will be all right, won't it?'

He had never told April how it would end and, loyal to the last, she had never made a point of asking. Seeing her look up at him with total trust in her rain-tic'd eyes, he could not bring himself to tell her now. 'Yes,' he said, 'everything's going to be all right.'

Another moment and they were inside the mall – at least, two of them were; Justin had snapped the wet chain through Oliver's hand and was using the motion of the swinging door to try and make a run for it. Without stopping to think, Oliver swung around and raised the gun, firing through the closing glass gap. The bullet clipped Justin on the side of the head, flicking away the top half of his ear in a crimson spray, and he slipped over on the wet tarmac, cracking his forehead on the edge of a concrete flower trough. April gave a little gasp and turned away. Behind them in the mall's main thoroughfare, people screamed and froze before assessing the situation and hastily vanishing inside shops.

Oliver grabbed April's hand and pulled her along behind him.

It took a moment for the shoppers in their path to register that the man in front of them was brandishing a gun before they melted away to the sides of the corridor; such hardware was uncommon on the streets of Invicta Cross. Oliver slid to a stop, searching left and right.

'Which way now, Billy?'

'It should be over there on the left.'

'I can't keep up,' gasped April, starting to become upset

again. But he was right; there was the decade-old scale model of the town in its scratched Perspex case. Invicta Cross, built on the site of Prentice Fields. There was even a little label among the sponge-and-balsa-wood trees, marking out Jack's original village. Well, in a few minutes the town would be back to the size of a village again, and the fields would show through once more.

'There's no point in both of us going over. Wait here.'

He released her hand and ran over to the model, dropped to his knees and felt around behind its painted chipboard stand. Then he rose and returned to her, his wet trainers squeaking on the plastic tiles.

'The tower,' he said, pointing up through the aquamarine glass canopy of the atrium. 'There's a door into it behind the escalator.'

They ran across the main hub of the mall, through an avenue of endless identical potted fig trees, around the edge of the steel fountain with its sparkling sapphire funnel of water, past wrought-iron coffee tables with leaking individual teapots and plastic tubs of fake milk, past pastel pyramids of chocolate, reeking cosmetic displays, illuminated billboards of hair-care breakthroughs and crotch-torturing designer underwear, past frightened pensioners and numb housewives and desperate teenagers and endless boarded-up unsold units, utopia limited, the end of the dream.

Behind the base of the main escalator they found one of the mall's fireproof employee-only doors. Oliver shoved on the bar and pushed it open, then searched the wall of the stairwell. He found what he was looking for: a long-handled fire axe with a bright red blade. Unclipping it and resting it against his shoulder, he beckoned to April and sent her ahead of him up the darkened staircase. The walls had been plastered smooth and painted white, and red metal safety railings had been installed. There were no pigeons warbling here now, but the dimensions of the old water tower were still the same as they had been ten years earlier. Being inside the tower brought memories flooding back.

'Billy, I want to rest soon,' April called down.

'Just a little longer, darling,' he replied, spanning the axe across his soaked shoulder blades, 'then we'll both be able to take a well-earned rest.'

He knew that the cordon of police, journalists and cameramen was tightening around them. He prayed that there was enough time left for him to finish what he had set out to do.

CHAPTER FORTY-EIGHT

Reunion

'He appeared to me in the flames, you see. I had the desire for revenge, but not the means. Billy was the one with the imagination, not me. I was just the odd kid nobody talked to. I blamed my father's profession for that. But I had him to thank for the life-giving flames. When he pushed the button there would be a terrifying hiss, and then the rows of jets would burst into spears of light. And there, spontaneously combusting into being, was the father of all devils. In those brief moments before the coffin started sliding in on silent rollers, he spoke to me from the heart of the purifying fire. Eblis embraced all sinners and hugged them into flakes of dust and crumbs of bone. He showed me courage, and through it, power.' – *The Red Diary*

THE CAR phone in the Rover was not a secure line. Croydon had monitored the call and picked up the information. Now police vehicles had begun to pour into the central car park of the Invicta Cross Mall, closely followed by outside broadcast vans.

Gavin Diller had managed to tear himself away from the television and, seized with the same infectious sense of panic that was driving the media circus, was now thudding across the tarmac toward the mall with the best of them. As he approached the entrance to the shopping centre huffing and heaving, he spotted Mitchell and another man waving him down.

The journalist grabbed his arm and propelled him through the mall doors.

'We have to hurry,' he shouted, 'the police will have this place sealed off in a few minutes.'

'That's the idea, isn't it?'

'The *idea* is to be inside before they do it.'

'Why, do you know where this bloke's heading?'

Gary looked back at his companion, then grinned over at the policeman's son.

'Oh, most definitely,' said Billy.

Oliver slammed the back of the axe against the door again, and this time the lock nearly gave. The noise echoed down the stairwell, but it couldn't be helped. 'I set the transmitter up in here just over a year ago,' he grunted, swinging the axe as hard as he could. 'I hope no one's found it. I should think it's still safe. It's only a tiny thing, not very powerful. Didn't need to be strong to be effective.'

The door bounced open with a deafening crash, and they were in. Fragments of the past filled April's tortured mind as she stared about the arched brick chamber and over the edge of the parapet at the town below. For a moment she was fourteen again. Stinging tears sprang into her eyes.

'Oh, Billy...'

'You mustn't lose faith now, my love. It's nearly over. I have to take care of the past by restoring it to the present.' He ran over to the far wall and ducked beneath the brick outcrop where young April had once sat with her box of coloured pencils.

'It's still here,' he called back. 'I disguised it so that it looks like a standard BT junction box, just in case anyone stumbled on it.' He dug into his trouser pocket and produced a small key to unlock the metal panel at the front, flicking up a pair of plastic switches. 'Won't be long now. About a minute and thirty seconds.'

'Before what, Billy?' she asked finally. 'What's going to happen?'

He reached out for her hand and brought her to the brick parapet, pointing down through the roof of the atrium. 'Beneath the scale-model of the town,' he explained as gently as he could, 'inside the wooden platform it's standing on. I packed it with trinitrotoluene. Not as powerful as nitroglycerin, but it was all I could get hold of.'

He didn't tell her that he had paid one of the security guards three hundred pounds to let him into the building at night. He'd told the guard that he was an electrician, about to get into trouble with his boss because he had incorrectly rewired part of a display system earlier in the week. If he could work on it for an hour now, no one would ever know about the botch-up and his job would be safe.

The guard, who was on the kind of salary they paid hotel receptionists at out-of-season seaside resorts, had accepted the banknotes with a grunt, watching as Oliver climbed inside the model with his electrical equipment and tool-boxes. He had wandered past from time to time, his face impassive, disinterested in the electrician's work. That was how it had been with all the people he had required to help him carry out the plan. None of them had felt that they were committing crimes. They were simply performing acts of omission, turning a blind eye at the right moment. It was one of the world's new ways, the justice of negative consensus.

He returned to the transmitter box, dropping to his knees once more. 'TNT lacks oxygen, and part of its carbon is oxidised to carbon monoxide when it explodes; you get a lot of thick black smoke. They used to call TNT shells "coal boxes" in the First World War, or Jack Johnsons, after a famous black boxer.' He smiled wearily as he worked at the box, glad to be reaching some kind of conclusion.

April was becoming frightened again. She was cold and tired. What were they doing up here? What would happen to them after this?

'I thought we were going to be together forever,' she cried. 'They hurt us and we've hurt them back, but that doesn't help *us*, does it? It doesn't make everything all right again.'

'I never said it would change what's gone before. Nothing can ever do that. You should be glad we've stopped them from harming anyone else.' He checked his watch. 'Any second now.'

The explosion was much louder than he had estimated, an eardrum-pulsing bang that shattered the centre of the atrium roof, creating a crenulated oval hole and sending shards of glass like handfuls of glittering spectral jewels into the rain-laden air. The tower shook violently, and for a moment he thought it was going to go over. Alarms were screaming all over the car park, people were running and shouting, and debris was pattering, tinkling and smashing all around the building. There was another explosion of metal and glass as the giant red neon Safeway's sign wrenched itself away from the wall of the tower with an eerie groan and crashed down into the car park, bursting across the tarmac in a satisfying smash of prismatic petals.

Oliver appeared to be satisfied. He leaned over the parapet and watched the chaos for a minute, then turned back and gave April a hug.

'You're freezing,' he said, 'look at the state of you, your hair. That's not like you at all. You're the one who's always perfect.'

Below them were more screams, more running feet, car doors slamming, something heavy and metallic falling over, and a series of small explosions, like fireworks going off. He tried to smooth a wet lock of her hair back in place and saw that her teeth were chattering. He placed a cool hand against her cheek.

'It's nearly over, April. You'll be warm again soon. I've been looking forward to this day for so long, and now it's finally here.'

He was still holding her when the tower door crashed open again, and three men barged into the roof area.

Gary Mitchell eyed the embracing couple, then stepped warily forward and introduced himself. 'I'm a journalist,' he said, not without some pride. 'I'm not here to judge you. The police aren't far behind us, although your bomb will probably confuse them for a while. This here is Mr Diller—'

'We've met,' said April, pulling away and moving back to the far parapet like a cornered cat. 'How are you, Gavin?'

'I don't know you,' said Gavin Diller, confused.

April hugged herself, staring down the policeman's son.

400

'Men. If you want one to remember you, don't have sex with him.'

A look of alarm shadowed Gavin's face as he recognised the tone in her voice. 'You're not – April?'

The man who had been standing between Gavin Diller and Gary Mitchell shifted into the light. He was of a much slighter build than the other two, with lank, thinning hair and a sickly jaundice in his face. There were dark smudges beneath his eyes. He looked disoriented and ill, like someone who had just stepped off his first roller coaster. The reporter gestured toward him, then pulled him forward by the sleeve of his sweater.

'And this gentleman is—'

April's breath caught in her throat as she stepped into the middle of the turret, raising her hand toward him.

'Hello, April.' The ailing man standing before her had a faint, dry wheeze of a voice. He looked as if the wind might blow him away across the fields.

'Hello, Billy,' she answered, not knowing whether to laugh or cry.

CHAPTER FORTY-NINE

Retribution and Forgiveness

'When the first of the explosions rip through the town, Eblis will reappear to guide my actions. With each fresh detonation he will strengthen my resolve to bring matters to a satisfactory conclusion. He will watch benignly over the conflagration and, witnessing my final confrontation, the god of the furnace will nod his approval.' – Final entry in *The Red Diary*

'I THINK this belongs to you. I rescued it from the stuff you threw out. I've been keeping it up to date.'

Billy March took in the scene. Oliver Price smiled apologetically at him as he removed the battered red book from the waistband of his jeans and handed it over. The contrast between the two men could not have been greater. Billy's old friend was tall, tanned, muscular, the perfect picture of health, and here he was, round-shouldered, as thin and tired as a cancer patient. The hazy chaos continued below. Nobody moved above.

'Oliver. You're – Oliver.' April's hand covered her mouth.

'I'm so sorry, April.'

She looked hurt and understandably upset that the man she had trusted and loved for the past few months was someone she hardly knew.

'I did it for you, Billy,' was all he said. He seemed barely surprised by their meeting.

'You loved him,' she said. 'You must have loved him to do this.'

'Of course I did,' said Oliver, looking across at Billy's asthenic figure. 'One awful day, I realised just how much. You were the other half of me. I had to force myself to stop being your friend. You always thought my father had joined the conspiracy against you, that he'd stopped us from meeting any more. It was best to let you think that, Billy, but the effort nearly killed me. I was horrified about my feelings, scared that you might find out and hate me for it. I was shattered when you left town, but I still kept an eye on you. I saved your model town from the dustmen and restored it. I campaigned to have it installed here in the mall. I wanted to heal you.'

'You can't heal people like *this*,' Billy said, finding his voice.

'When your father died you fell apart,' Oliver told him. 'I know. I was *there*. I still came up to town on day trips, just like the ones we used to take when we skipped school. I saw where you lived. I followed you to work. I wanted to apologise for not being there for you, but I couldn't. The irony was that ending our friendship made me no better than the other Invicta Cross residents, the ones who had driven you out. I wanted to help you, to take the revenge *you* should have been taking. I came to visit you in that terrible clinic. I didn't let you see me, just watched you through the window. Do you have any idea what that did to me? I wanted to be you, to take care of things you couldn't put right yourself.

'After you'd left Invicta Cross I used to attend cremations with my father, and as I stood beside the furnace in my threadbare black suit all I could think of was taking revenge for you. You weren't capable of redressing the past. I was the only one left who could do anything. You had once told me that you would never retaliate, that it wasn't in your nature, remember? The only person I had ever cared about was on day release from a nuthouse because of the people in this town. You had nothing. No family. No money. Not even your health.' Oliver was crying, but his tears were lost in the downpour falling from the remugient skies. Mitchell was about to pass comment, but his reply was checked by the sight of the gun butt protruding from Oliver's belt.

'It was while I was in the army that I decided to make amends for you, Billy. I was stuck in Northern Ireland. Got to know quite a bit about explosives. Never killed anyone, but I learned how. Read up on some other things – weaponry, booby traps, poisons. I'd always been good at chemistry and physics. I treated coming back here like a military campaign. Declared war on the neighbourhood. Reconnoitred the area. Worked out all my targets. Asked my childhood god to help me.'

The dull thud of another detonation sounded behind them.

'The other bombs are going off now. Sergeant Morris has just gone to meet his maker. I hope he was seated at his desk, the same old desk he's had for years; I planted the device in the back of his stationery drawer.' Gavin Diller gave a confused grunt but made no move. Something was burning fiercely below them. 'Getting into supposedly secure buildings and other people's houses quietly is an army trick you pick up if you hang out with the wrong sort of people,' said Oliver, 'and there were plenty of those around.

'You see, I planned everything to the last detail, then I realised I couldn't do it. The strategy had a fatal flaw. I would have to live in the area, preferably in Balmoral Close, while I was carrying it out. But the neighbours would have noticed an outsider, and I wanted to be there, right in the middle of their pain. I wanted to see them suffer for what they did to you, to us. The trouble was, I was single. An unmarried man in Invicta Cross would have stuck out like a sore thumb. Everyone would have noticed him. But a couple, a perfect couple . . .'

'Deceiver. Gigolo.' April started to cry. In the distance, another eruption echoed between the buildings.

'I didn't mean to hurt you, April, I wouldn't do that for the world. I've been very happy with you. In my own way, I really do love you.' Oliver turned back to Billy. 'I got a lot of physical training in the army, Billy. I got fit, and when my father died he left me the business. I knew I looked good, and I had some money. And then I saw you in the filthy place they put you in after the clinic—'

'The Arlington Road Hostel.'

'I didn't know what to do. I wanted to help you, not just buy you a suit or a meal. I couldn't see a way around the problems that were involved.' Oliver wiped his running nostrils on the back of his hand and looked over at April. 'Then one day, quite by accident, I ran into her, and everything fell into place. She didn't recognise me as Oliver.

Why should she? We'd only met a few times, and always with you, Billy – we were both only interested in you. So I told her that's who I was. It was perfect. With a wife I could work under cover. But April wasn't much better off than you. She'd been in and out of hospitals and clinics ever since her mother died. It was a risk I had to take. We liked each other, so we got married. That was the only way it would work. Buy a nice house, smart cars, the whole bit, give April some security, stop her acting crazy. She wasn't interested in the sexual side of things, not in the normal way...'

'Because of him,' said April, pointing at Gavin Diller. 'Because of what he did to me.'

'I hadn't thought of a way to get to you, Gavin,' explained Oliver, drawing the gun and removing the safety catch. 'You're virtually the last one to be taken care of. Looks like fate delivered you to us.'

'Not fate. My bloody dad,' muttered Gavin. He looked at the others. 'What the fuck do we do now? You've turned the whole fucking town into a fire zone. Are you happy yet?'

'That's not for me to decide,' replied Oliver. 'Billy, can you rest easy now?'

Billy March could not believe his ears. His childhood friend had killed and maimed god knows how many people and was asking him if it *made him happy*. He forced himself to stay calm. Oliver was dangerous, April looked confused and ill. He weighed up the odds as he spoke.

'I'm not like you,' he said softly. 'What has all this done except cause more pain? I forgave the past.'

'How could you?' shouted Oliver. 'Look what they did to us. There were three of us back then, not two. But you had each other. I was the one who stood by and watched. The only one who was man enough to do something about it, to take something back. Waiting for this.' He sobbed contemptuously, a sliver of saliva dropping to his chin. *'For this!'*

Before Billy could stop him, Oliver had reached forward and grabbed Gavin, shoving him halfway over the parapet. Diller shouted and fought off his attacker but could not prevent powerful hands from grabbing his shoulders and twisting them back. He was heavier, but Oliver was stronger.

'So you forgave the past, did you?' shouted Oliver. He turned to April, dragging Diller further over the ledge. 'Have *you* forgiven the past as well? Have you forgiven him for ruining your life?'

'My life isn't ruined,' said April primly, ignoring the rainwater that was running through her hair and down her face. 'I am very happy. I have a nice home, two lovely children, identical four-year-old boys called Tim and Tom—'

'You don't have any children, April.'

She looked confused. 'Don't I?'

'You don't even have your sanity because of people like this.' He dropped Diller lower on the parapet wall, scraping his blue nylon jacket up around his head, then wrenched him back up as the boy started screaming. 'Have you really forgiven him?'

'I don't know – don't keep asking me—'

'HAVE YOU FORGIVEN THIS MAN?'

'No,' she said finally, firmly. 'How can I forgive him? He raped me. He was the one who sent the letters to your family, Billy. He was the one who made all the phone calls.

Ask him what they were about. Ask him about all the notes he showed me that read "*Keep your son away from the slag.*" No,' she said bitterly, 'I could only forgive him if I could forget. And I'll never be able to do that.'

Oliver released his grip, and the policeman's son dropped over the edge. Gavin Diller plunged headlong through the shattered atrium roof, and into the dyed azure waters of the resounding steel fountain.

CHAPTER   FIFTY

Wild Justice

THEY DESCENDED to find the mall filled with dense black smoke. The emergency services were starting to arrive, but the rescue operation was hampered because parts of the flimsy roof were still collapsing. Ahead of them, an illuminated steel-framed poster depicting a slender girl in a bathing suit massaging gel into her scalp suddenly toppled forward and splintered into angry geometries of light.

Gary Mitchell pulled away from the others as they reached the foot of the stairs. 'I'm just a journalist,' he shouted above screams and crashes, 'you don't need me any more. Listen, sonny, I'll tell your story. I'll make sure that everyone gets to hear of this. You'll be famous.'

The sentiment was noble enough, but he had clearly been misinformed about the *Advertiser*'s readership profile.

Oliver raised the huge fire axe he had kept trained on Mitchell's back, and allowed him to run off into the murky pandemonium.

'Just the three of us again,' he said, pushing Billy and April towards one of the buckled metal walkways that led away from the main area of devastation. 'Head out of the west exit, that way.'

They ran through acrid fog, surrounded by screeching sirens, shouts, flashing crimson lights, passing swarms of uniformed men and women running in the opposite direction. Around them flared burning pyres of plastic, like sacrificial bonfires to the shopping gods.

Outside, at the far end of the mall's car park, they climbed through the hedge that bordered the delivery enclosure and ran into the churned brown fields beyond. Through the rain they could see two distinctly separate orange glows, fires raging in Balmoral Close and Gaveston Crescent. Their feet sank in the waterlogged earth but they stumbled on, away from the suburban conflagration.

'I've lost a shoe,' wailed April, 'my best Vinylite oriental wedges! Let's go back.'

Billy held her up just as she collapsed, dropping as suddenly and silently as if she had been waved asleep by witches. She weighed nothing. Oliver stroked the wet hair from her eyes. A false lash as thick as a caterpillar had fallen to her collarbone and was stuck there.

'She's beautiful,' Oliver said sadly. 'Damaged people so often are. Perhaps you should marry her.'

'She's already married,' said Billy.

'Not for much longer.' Oliver lowered the fire axe and unbuttoned the front of his jacket. 'I told you there would be a further three explosions. I've only counted two, haven't you?'

Around his waist were half a dozen bright yellow plastic-coated sticks of gelignite, strapped into place with duct tape. Above these were as many hand grenades. A steel ignition pin was held in position by a short chain that looped through the pins on all six grenades.

'I'd better be going now,' said Oliver. 'It was fun being

you for a while. I made you look good, Billy. People liked you. They looked up to you.' He pointed to the girl in Billy's arms. 'Say goodbye to April for me. Ask her to try and forgive me.'

'Listen,' called Billy, 'don't do this. There has to be some other way.'

Oliver blinked away the rain and looked up at the racing sky, his hands raised heavenward. 'Is he *kidding?*' He laid a hand on Billy's shoulder. 'You two could still have a chance with each other. Think about it. If the truth ever comes out, which is unlikely, she'll get away with a plea of diminished responsibility and *you*, you've done nothing wrong. Me? I deserve to die. I'm an agent of misery and destruction. Even if I wasn't, I wouldn't want to hang around. I always loved you, and you never loved me. That's the worst pain in the world, a wound that can never heal. Love is crueller than death. I was happy to take your revenge for you. Francis Bacon was right, Billy, it is a kind of wild justice, and it feels pretty sweet to me – even if it really belongs to someone else. If you want to know more about how I felt, take a look in the red diary. Oh, and you might want to keep this as a souvenir.'

Oliver pulled Dr McMann's silver money clip from his shirt pocket and tossed it across to him. 'Maybe you were right. Maybe there never was a conspiracy after all. All our enemies come from within. Well, *adios, amigo.*'

Billy watched as Oliver turned and picked his way back across the fields in the direction of town, the fire axe slung between his broad shoulders, his body silhouetted by a wall of searing flame that extended all the way across the horizon.

April, soaked through, stirred in Billy's arms.

'I had a wonderful dream, Billy,' she said, wiping the rain from her eyes. She had no difficulty using his name. It seemed the natural thing for her to do, as if he had really been there all along. 'It was summer, and we were having a picnic in the field that used to stand at the end of Gaveston Crescent. My mother was here, and your parents, and Oliver and his father. We were all talking at once. Everyone was laughing, and slightly drunk, and happy.'

'It was just a dream,' said Billy.

'I thought so. It was too good to be real.'

'Go back to sleep, April,' he said softly. 'Dream some more.'

He looked toward the spot where he had last seen Oliver, but the figure was lost inside the apocalyptic fires of Invicta Cross. A few moments later the air momentarily stilled, then a single great explosion bellowed through the atmosphere, flinging clods of earth into the rainswept sky, and Billy knew that the devastation wrought by their shared past had been brought to an end.

Invicta Cross burned.

The houses filled with flumes of fire.

Shelves dripped varnish, and mock-leather volumes of the Reader's Digest combusted.

Pale pink statues of prancing horses crackled and shattered.

Video recorders buckled and CD players softened like Dali clocks.

A hundred thousand photographs ignited, pictures of loved ones cracking and blistering in their frames.

Home computers and faxes and modems sank into a useless gluey morass, no longer part of the global network.

Lightbulbs popped like champagne corks.

Thick oily smoke blackened bedroom walls, obliterating rock stars and football heroes.

Pressurised kitchen cans sufflated, coffee beans roasted, water boiled in the pipes, flavid boxes of breakfast cereal noisily caught alight.

Dishwashers, tumble dryers, microwave ovens were destroyed in an electronic meltdown.

Cupboards that had been carefully installed with set squares and spirit levels collapsed.

Ceiling tiles dropped like pale pancakes.

Sofas lived up to their safety requirements before blustering into flame.

A million masterpieces of home improvement were vaporised in moments. People clutched cushions and teddy bears and toasters, anything but each other, and stood in the gardens screaming, desperate to save their record collections.

Invicta Cross died.

With April asleep in his arms once more, Billy stepped over pools of water filled with heavenly firestorms, and walked towards the more subdued and welcoming city lights.

EPILOGUE

Learning from the Past

EMMA METCALF lay on her side in a freshly disinfected corridor of the South Croydon A & E Unit, waiting to see a doctor about her burned left arm and leg. An hour ago she had been swabbed and issued with a temporary bandage which she had eventually applied herself. Nurses ran back and forth, efficiently ferrying the injured from one waiting point to another, and even the porters had been drafted to help keep orderly lines in the hospital's small waiting area.

Emma had been standing in a corridor of the Invicta Cross police station when the ceiling above her had been blown in by the force of the bomb planted in Sergeant Diller's desk. Her skin was raw and blistered from the flames that had belched through the collapsing metalwork, but she felt little pain. As she sat listening to the frightened questions being shouted all around her, she doubted she would ever feel pain again.

Sherry Bovis had been seated with her girlfriend on the opposite bench for the past half-hour. She was still cradling the head of an unconscious woman who had been given a sedative but not a bed. There were no more beds to be had here, and they were waiting to be ferried to another hospital. Sherry had a cut across her forehead that was still dripping blood into her right eye and badly needed stitches. She and Emma had known each other for years but had hardly ever spoken. By now the full story of what had happened in Invicta Cross was emerging, and she longed to talk about it with someone.

'Hey,' Sherry called, 'are you all right?'

Emma remained lying across the seat clutching her burned arm, suffering in silence.

'We should be friends,' said Sherry. 'These are bad times for both of us.'

Emma appeared not to have heard. Her gaze never left the spot on the wall above Sherry's head.

'It's been on the news all day. Terrible, just – terrible.' She shifted the position of the woman's head in her lap. Still no reply from across the corridor.

Emma raised her head from the bench and squinted at her. 'You think this means we have to be friends now?'

'I think – I don't know – maybe we should talk about it.'

'You mean we're supposed to learn something from this? Like it was our fault some fucking nutcase decided to blow up the town? You think we should join hands in sisterhood and be pals in the face of tragedy, and rebuild our lives like they do in those American made-for-TV movies?'

Sherry looked sheepish. 'Well – in a different way – but yes.'

'If you want to help us, I'll tell you what you can do,' said Emma, her face ugly with anger, 'you and your dyke friend can fuck off out of town.'

Seven and a half weeks later, Sherry Bovis packed up and moved to London, and a little after that Invicta Cross reopened as good as new, having changed its name to New

Invicta, to prevent harmful connotations from deterring first-time buyers. Everyone remarked that the town had been restored so perfectly, you couldn't tell that anything bad had ever happened there.

FLESH WOUNDS

Christopher Fowler

A popular businessman awakes one morning to discover that everyone hates him . . . A young woman must surrender her virginity to a grotesque enemy to fulfil her family's destiny . . . An extraordinary chain of events is set in motion when a cocktail cabinet falls out of the sky and kills a farmer . . . A depressed man decides to make his suicide the most exciting thing that's ever happened to him . . .

Oozing paranoia, black humour and a certain amount of old-fashioned gore, Christopher Fowler's collection of short stories tells a chilling tale of desperate individuals learning the hard way . . . that flesh wounds.

'Fowler takes on Stephen King and comes away with the prize between his teeth'
Time Out

'Fowler at his best – deft observations combined with convincing set pieces'
SFX

'collection of short stories that shouldn't be read late at night'
Daily Mail

WARNER BOOKS
0 7515 1431 4

☐	Flesh Wounds	Christopher Fowler	£5.99
☐	Sharper Knives	Christopher Fowler	£4.99
☐	Red Bride	Christopher Fowler	£4.99
☐	Darkest Day	Christopher Fowler	£5.99
☐	Spanky	Christopher Fowler	£5.99

Warner Books now offers an exciting range of quality titles by both established and new authors which can be ordered from the following address:

Little, Brown and Company (UK),
P.O. Box 11,
Falmouth,
Cornwall TR10 9EN.

Fax No: 01326 317444.
Telephone No: 01326 317200
E-mail: books@barni.avel.co.uk

Payments can be made as follows: cheque, postal order (payable to Little, Brown and Company) or by credit cards, Visa/Access. Do not send cash or currency. UK customers and B.F.P.O. please allow £1.00 for postage and packing for the first book, plus 50p for the second book, plus 30p for each additional book up to a maximum charge of £3.00 (7 books plus).

Overseas customers including Ireland, please allow £2.00 for the first book plus £1.00 for the second book, plus 50p for each additional book.

NAME (Block Letters) ....

....

ADDRESS ....

....

....

☐ I enclose my remittance for ....

☐ I wish to pay by Access/Visa Card

Number ☐☐☐☐☐☐☐☐☐☐☐☐☐☐☐☐

Card Expiry Date ☐☐☐☐